THE RICH
AND
THE MIGHTY

THE RICH AND THE MIGHTY

Vera Cowie

"With the rich and the mighty . . . always a little patience."
(Spanish Proverb)

Doubleday & Company, Inc., Garden City, New York

First published in Great Britain in 1981 by Futura Publications, a Division of Macdonald & Co. (Publishers), Ltd.

Copyright © 1981 V. R. Cowie

To Jenne and Marjory
with thanks for their faith, hope, and charity

THE RICH
AND
THE MIGHTY

PROLOGUE

When Elizabeth Sheridan awoke it was to see, with satisfaction, that the hands of her little traveling clock pointed to four forty-five a.m. Once again, in spite of jet lag, her internal programming had produced the right answer. Before she had gone to sleep she had repeated this time to herself; the clock in her head did the rest.

She stretched, yawned, kicked off the thin sheet—which was all she had slept under apart from a mosquito net, because on this particular Bahamian out island there were insects which bit and left marks that to a model were the kiss of death. Yellow fingers of light were probing the slats of the jalousies, and they laid themselves across her naked body. The little room was golden with early morning glow, peacefully quiet but for the morning chatter of birds and the constant but soothing shush of the surf. This particular bungalow sat squarely on the beach, like Canute, which was why she had chosen it. That and its lovely pink color; an ancient but beautifully faded rose. Springing out of bed she padded to the windows, flung the jalousies back. Sunlight bounced off the sea like a laser, of such a clarity and brilliance she screwed up her eyes, which were large, deep and green, with tiny yellow flecks, like those of a cat, and equally sensitive to light. She could feel the already powerful warmth of the sun as it bathed her naked body, and she lifted her face to its benediction, closing her eyes, because the sea dazzled like shifting sequins. It was going to be another beautiful day.

Turning to the faded and chipped tallboy she examined her face in her magnifying mirror. Flawless. Not a blemish to be seen. Picking up the pins she had carefully laid down the night before, she piled up her heavy blond hair, skewering it securely before pouring water from the large china ewer, decorated with roses, into its matching bowl. There was no running water. This island was so small, so remote, lived on by only a few families who kept goats and tilled small market gardens, that it had remained untouched by the tourism which was beginning to affect other out islands. Water came from a well, pure and coldly fresh; standing on a towel she sluiced her body with great spongefuls of it. Then for two full minutes she scrubbed her teeth.

Finally, she cleaned her face, using baby oil, removing the residue with rose-water, before applying a nonallergenic moisturizer.

She was just settling the straps of her swimsuit when there was a knock on her door and a voice caroled: "It's your friendly makeup man. Are you decent?" Without waiting for an answer, he came in.

"Morning, ducks! Ready to have your face put on?"

Harry Parkes was her *visagiste;* had been ever since she became the Flawless Finish Girl. Harry Parkes, they said, could turn Dracula's daughter into the girl of your dreams. He laid down the carpenter's toolbox in which he carried the tools of his trade, saying brightly: "What a fabulous morning—in more ways than one. Guess who just died?"

"Not the cameraman?"

"God forbid, ducks—but come to that, you might say God himself . . ."

"The director!"

Harry pursed his lips. This one didn't half have a funny sense of humor. "No . . . it's 'King' Tempest himself! Heard it on the radio." Harry never went anywhere without his transistor. "Broke into the program to announce it, they did. Seems they've been doing it on the hour every hour since it happened. He was the King of the Bahamas, you know . . . apart from his own island—that's it over there . . . Tempest Cay . . ."

Harry went to the window, where he gazed avidly at the bulk of a larger, greener island about half a mile away. "What I wouldn't give to set foot on *that* island . . . but you only do by invitation. That's his house there, on top of the hill . . . you can just glimpse it through the trees . . . a palace, by all accounts. Far bigger and more splendid than our own dear Queenie's."

Elizabeth—who topped him by six inches—looked out over his head across a stretch of turquoise sea shot with gold to where, through heavy old trees, she caught glimpses of the faded pink brick of an enormous house, its windows glittering in the sunlight, its white paint gleaming.

"Nobody knows how much he was worth . . . only that he is supposed to have more money than anybody. Billions, so they say . . . billions and billions. He owns this island, you know, and that one to the north, as well as Tempest Cay." Harry's sigh was deeply envious. "Fancy being *that* rich."

He was an avid reader of social columns and gossip magazines. He devoured *Queen* and *Harper's Bazaar* and every word William Hickey wrote. He knew who was divorcing whom and why, who was sleeping with whom, and when; who was two-timing whom, and how. He followed the doings of the jet set with a consuming interest.

As they stared out a plane passed overhead, coming into view as it banked toward Tempest Cay, losing height, wheels down. It was a Lear jet.

"I'll bet that's one of the family," Harry said excitedly. "They all have private planes." His prominent blue eyes were shining and his face was alight. He, Harry Parkes, was actually seeing what he would later read about. "Oh, how I wish I could be there to see it all!"

"Right now, there is a film crew waiting to see me," Elizabeth reminded, turning away.

Harry made a face. "All right, all right."

Elizabeth had placed a chair facing the window so that the brilliant light fell full on her. Opening up his toolbox Harry set out his equipment; pots and brushes and tubes and sticks. Once he got to work, he would turn even Elizabeth Sheridan's God-given beauty into something inhuman. Which went, he thought, eyeing her sourly, with the rest of her. But a pro. No messing about. She was all ready for him, even to her body makeup—all but her back which Bess, her hairdresser, would do later. The swimsuit was necessary because the commercial would be shot in the water, the object of the exercise being to extol the virtues of the latest extension to the Flawless Finish range—waterproof cosmetics. She would be in the water all the time. Shooting was due to start at six a.m. so as to catch the peculiar clarity of light which would vanish once the sun was fully up.

He set to work. And as he worked, he talked.

"I wonder who'll get all his money now? His stepchildren, I suppose. That stepdaughter of his always has her hand out—when it's not in somebody's pants! Randy bitch! They say she's insatiable! The things I've heard about her—but I wouldn't sully your ears, love." This was a sly dig because it was known that Elizabeth Sheridan did not care for "that sort of thing." "I saw her once, you know . . . in the flesh, as they say—and God knows she was showing enough of it! Dress cut down to her navel and no knickers . . . dripping with diamonds and positively reeking of sex! Then there's the youngest stepson—the oldest one's a drunk—now there's a playboy for you! A friend of mine works for Gieves and Hawkes and he told me that Dan Godfrey pays a thousand pounds for a suit! A thousand pounds!" Another, deeply envious sigh. Harry liked clothes. "With what he'll inherit he'll be able to afford cloth of gold . . . tilt your head, there's a love . . . and that house! Filled with treasures . . . They're English, you know, by descent. The main branch—the one with the title that is—still live in England but they say they haven't a feather to fly with . . . lost it all years ago, death duties you know . . . I'll bet they're down on their knees praying for a mention in the will . . ."

Elizabeth let his voice run over her like water. Had she so cared, she could have told Harry all about the English Tempests. As a child, she had been an inmate of the Henrietta Fielding Home for Foundlings, which stood just outside the gates of Tempest Park. Every summer she had gone with the rest of the children to the annual prizegiving which was always held in the grounds, where, after races and a display of country dancing and a tea consisting of ham sandwiches, cream cakes, and ices, they would all line up to allow Countess Tempest, who was Chairman of the Trustees of the Home, to inspect them, bestowing a smile here, a pat there, before distributing the school prizes to the curtsying girls. There were no boys. Miss Henrietta Fielding, a former governess to the Tempest family, had been an ardent feminist with little use for the male sex. On her bookshelves at home, Elizabeth still had the books she had received as prizes—usually for the highest average mark. *Little Women, What Katy Did, The Wide, Wide World, Robinson Crusoe*, and the like, except for the last, given just before she left the Home at sixteen: that had been a beautifully illustrated edition of a book on Tempest Towers. Elizabeth had pored over it, seeing in pictures what the children had never been allowed to see in reality. It had given her a taste for more, made of her a country house buff.

Years later she had gone back to Tempest Towers as a visitor; paid her half crown and followed a guide round those rooms open to the public. It was then she had remarked the difference between the pictures and the actuality. It was painfully obvious that times were now hard. There were dark patches on silk-clad walls where pictures had once hung; pieces of furniture she had gloated over were missing; there was a general air of shabbiness and seediness. The roles had been reversed. She, who had been a foundling, was now a famous model and earning a small fortune; the Tempests had been forced to open their house to visitors. She had found it very satisfying.

Henrietta Fielding had also been a shock. She had remembered the house as forbidding. Now, she saw it was only a gloomy old Victorian villa that had once been a vicarage, and it too had seen better days. It had become offices, the Welfare Department of the local Council. The old, bottle-green paint was gone; now it was blue with a white trim. The windows were open and she could hear the sound of typewriters, a telephone ringing. A different kind of bell from those she remembered.

Her first memory of the Home was a bell. The one that rang to wake her that first day . . . . she could still remember the strangeness, the fright, the bewilderment. But she soon learned that at Henrietta Fielding, everything was done to bells. You rose, washed, ate, learned, to bells. And all in silence. Miss Henrietta had been a product of her times, which were Victorian—she had founded the Home in 1890, and Victorian precepts were what she had insisted be taught her foundlings. She had even had them embroidered—by her girls, because she insisted they be taught to sew a very fine seam—framed, and hung on the serviceable but biliously green walls of every room. *Silence Is Golden* hung in the dormitories. *A Stitch in Time Saves Nine* had hung in the sewing room; *Cleanliness Is Next to Godliness* had exhorted them from the bare tiles of the Victorian bathrooms. Her girls were taught to obey them, and woe betide those who did not.

Elizabeth had learned a lot at Henrietta Fielding, dispensing with much of it once she was what she later thought of as "free." Like communal living, for instance. She had never shared anything with anybody since. Solitude's price was above sapphires, while privacy was perfection. And no bells. Her door had a knocker, but no bell. She hated bells . . .

Suddenly she realized she was hearing one. Harry paused, brush in hand, head cocked. "Hear that? That's from Tempest Cay. They always toll the bell when somebody in the Family dies . . . never stop it until the funeral's over and done with."

He bent to his work again only to exclaim: "You all right, love?" Elizabeth had gone green, a color which normally suited her but not this bile tint.

He saw her shudder. "I hate bells . . . especially death knells. They give me the shivers."

He was astonished. He had long since come to believe she had no feelings. Far too remotely controlled. But she did look queer . . .

"Well," he said sympathetically but prosaically, "you'll have to get used to this one. The Big Man is dead . . . his people are mourning him. They call him 'King,' you know . . . they're not likely to stop that bell tolling for the likes of you."

He bent to his work again. "Lose somebody you loved, did you?" Which was another surprise. He would have said she didn't give a damn for anybody.

Silence, then: "I have nobody to lose," she said.

"What! None at all?"

"None at all."

"I'm one of eight myself," he responded cheerfully, "and there are times I wish I wasn't!" He stood back. "There . . . I've given you three coats of the mascara. I know it's supposed to be a one-coat wonder but we know better, don't we, ducks? And you know Pete the perfectionist. He'll have you in and out of the water like a yo-yo."

He picked up her magnifying mirror, held it up to allow her to inspect herself. She did so dispassionately. He had done his usual flawless job. She was burnished, golden, gleaming. The mascara made fronds of her already

long lashes from out of which her amazing eyes, deep and green as sea
depths, glowed mysteriously. Her features, sculpted by hands in love with
their work, had been emphasized by skillful blending and shading, and her
wide, yet exquisitely chiseled mouth was glossily tempting.

She nodded briskly. "Fine."

She was an odd one, he thought. Never yet had he seen any admiration in
her eyes when she gazed at her own beauty. It was as though it was a piece of
machinery; to be tended and cared for but only to make sure it did its job
well.

"And here's Bess to do your hair . . ."

She came in grumbling as usual. "God, how I hate these crack of dawn
calls."

"Be thankful for small mercies," admonished Harry. "Better here than
some freezing Muswell Hill studio . . ."

Elizabeth had washed her hair the night before. It hung almost to her
waist when she took out its pins, and Bess brushed its heavy, shining mass
before gathering it into one silken length which she proceeded to divide into
three before weaving into a single, heavy plait, which she then adorned with
one enormous, vividly scarlet hibiscus bloom, placed just behind one ear.

"Right," she said briskly, that done, "let's finish off the body makeup,
then."

Harry knew it was time to go. Other models had no compunction about
standing naked in front of him or any man. Not Elizabeth Sheridan.

"See you on the beach, then . . . ta-ta."

Elizabeth stood up to peel her swimsuit down to her waist, stood while
Bess applied a shimmering, deeply golden liquid that dried to give the natural
appearance of an expensively acquired tan.

"Okay . . . that's it, then."

Bess went to wash her hands. "Trust Pete," she grumbled, "no running
water, no electricity, no nothing. Why *will* he pick these desert islands?"

"Because the commercial is supposedly set on one . . ."

"Deserted island, more like! Nobody but a few shiftless natives and that
bloody bell! It's driving me nuts already and they tell me it won't stop till he's
buried."

Elizabeth shuddered, then controlled it as Bess lifted the straps of the
swimsuit, settling them carefully so as not to disturb her handiwork. It was a
Wedgwood blue maillot; cut straight across the tops of her 38B-cup breasts
and pared away behind to the crack of her buttocks. Bess subjected her to a
final, critical examination. "Yes . . . even Pete can't complain about this
. . . Come on, then, let's get it over and done with."

Three hours later Elizabeth left the water for the last time, to flop face down on the hot sand. It did not matter now if it clung to her. Pete had finally pronounced himself satisfied. She had been in and out of the water constantly; clambering into a boat, surfacing from the depths with a whoosh!, water streaming from her, always in the eye of the camera so it could show potential customers that the makeup was unimpaired; no streaky mascara, no patches in the foundation, no washed-away lipstick.

For some reason she felt drained of energy. It was that damned bell . . . it had not stopped its sonorous, doleful tolling for one minute. Somebody stopped beside her. It was Pete, the director.

"We're going across to Nassau, do some sightseeing. Want to come?"

"No, thank you."

"There's damn little to do here."

"That's all I want to do."

"You can shop in Nassau . . . Bay Street has some good ones."

"Nothing I need."

But still he tried. God knows why he did, he thought, because it never got him anywhere, but something about her made him.

"We thought we might try Paradise Island too . . . drop a few at the tables. Maybe even win some . . ."

"I wish you luck."

Angrily, shortly: "Suit yourself. But be ready for nine o'clock, okay? We've still the night shots to do."

"I'm always ready."

Yes, he thought as he strode away angrily. But only for work . . . Harry sidled up. He had been watching. "You're wasting your time there," he advised. "She's frozen stiff . . . It's been tried by God knows how many and I've never seen her give any of them a tumble. You know her reputation . . . Frigid Liz. Lives in a world of her own, she does—and it's out of bounds to men."

Elizabeth lay on the beach until she was quite dry, trying to close her mind to the sound of the bell and failing utterly. It seemed to seep through every pore.

Even the little pink bungalow quivered to it. Someone had been in to tidy up. The bed was made, fresh water left, as well as a tall pitcher of something that tasted of pineapple and other, indefinable flavors. She drank two glassfuls straight off. Then she stripped off her swimsuit, toweled away dry sand, took the hibiscus from her hair and dropped it into a glass of water, before putting on her own navy blue Speedo. The other swimsuit she rinsed and draped over the window ledge to dry. Finally she cleaned off all Harry's carefully applied makeup before smoothing in a moisturizer followed by a coating of suntan oil.

She did everything with her usual methodical precision, yet she found she was not feeling her usual controlled self. She felt irritable, uptight, could not think what about. It was that damned bell . . . Picking up her towel and sunglasses she left the bungalow once more. She would go to the farthest point of the island, on its other side. Perhaps there, the sound of the bell would be muted, not get on her nerves so much.

The island was no more than a square mile of pink sand and palm trees. The population was about two dozen, living in small thatched cottages painted pink or blue or yellow, and only the women were about. The men were out fishing, for that was how they made their living, selling their catches in Nassau.

Elizabeth made for the beach that lay farthest away. She had picked up a book—she always had a book—and she would sunbathe and laze and perhaps sleep. She slept a great deal. Even after eight hours at night she could always go another two or three in the afternoon. But that bell was getting on her nerves . . .

Funny about bells. And it was not really because of her rigorously timed childhood that she hated them. That had been a handbell; tinny, clanging. No, it was church bells . . . tolling bells . . . Even when they were cheerful she still did not like them. She had once been driven out of the cathedral in Seville because, while she had been enjoying its thankfully cool, interior beauty, its bell had begun to toll . . .

Thankfully, the farther she walked the more muted this one sounded. She found herself relaxing, feeling better. Really, she thought, what is the matter with me? Letting something as simple as a tolling bell get to me.

She had made it her practice never to let anything get to her. She had worked long and hard on gaining an almost numbing calmness about everything. She did not have a sweet tooth, but sweet reason was a staple in her diet. That, and logic and rationality. All you had to do was view everything through their twin lenses and it was all reduced to manageability. She would reduce this bell. It was a nuisance, that was all. An irritation. She would not allow it to ruffle her equanimity. She would find a nice shady spot, read a while, then sunbathe—being careful not to overdo it because it was the whiteness of her skin, along with her flawless complexion, that was her *raison d'être*. She found just the spot she had in mind. It was quiet, shaded by a huge palm. She spread her towel, put on her sunglasses, lay down on her stomach and opened her book. Only to find that she was waiting, tensed, for each, mournful peal of that infuriating bell! It was an unwanted presence, needling her, unnerving her . . .

She found she was not reading, only staring at the page, that her thoughts were being pushed, by that bell, into forbidden channels. Death, funerals, cemeteries . . .

She absolutely hated cemeteries. Was terrified of them. Could not so much as walk past one.

It had all come to light when, at the age of twelve, the Home had been swept by an epidemic of measles. One girl had been so ill it had affected her already-weak heart and she had died. It had been while walking behind the hearse in an orderly double line, eyes downcast, that she had lifted her lashes and peeped ahead, seen to her horror a set of imposing iron gates, iron railings—and beyond them, gravestones, graves, flowers and tombs . . . And suddenly been in the grip of an uncontrollable panic. The nearer they came the worse it got. She had found her breathing changing, becoming difficult, her heart pounding, her legs trembling, finally becoming almost impossible to lift, to put one foot in front of the other. She had had to clench her teeth, suppress wild, unsubduable sobs that jolted her chest. She knew she was going to make a spectacle of herself, and the dread of that, combined with her terror of having to enter that—*cemetery*—reduced her to blank-faced terror. By the time they got to the gates she was rooted. She could only cling to the gates, eyes wide, breath choking. And when they tried to prise her fingers loose the screams broke from her throat, pealing, pealing, like the bell that had begun to toll . . .

She sat up abruptly, whipping off her glasses, breathing deeply to control her trembling, turning her face up to the warmth of the life-giving sun. Never seek to know for whom the bell tolls, she thought . . . Then, out loud: "But it is *not* tolling for me . . . and I *am* an island entire of itself . . . myself . . ."

She had striven for that ever since she left Henrietta Fielding. On her own at last, and determined never, ever again, to be a part of that particular kind of maine.

She had been sixteen, already six feet tall and weighing eleven stone. But her hefty strength had not been put to work in the kitchens of Tempest Towers, where so many of the girls ended up. Henrietta Fielding had always provided a source of cheap labor to the family who subsidized it, but Miss Keller had set Elizabeth's feet on a different road. It had been due to her efforts that Elizabeth had been allowed to take up the scholarship to the Grammar School, the Trustees being of the opinion that such an education would be a waste of time. Miss Henrietta's girls were taught to sew and cook and clean; reading was necessary to follow a recipe, writing to itemize a grocery bill. French and Latin and the higher reaches of education were unsuitable. But Elizabeth was clever. Her name had been top of the list of those who had sat for the scholarship and Miss Keller had planted the thought in the minds of the Trustees that it would be an accolade for the Home . . . As a sop, she had pledged that Elizabeth would, in her senior year, take a course in shorthand and typing; an office as against a household drudge.

And to Elizabeth, as she prepared to become a pupil at the King Henry Grammar School, Miss Keller had said, "Learn all you can, wherever you can. Knowledge is power."

She had encouraged Elizabeth in her reading, anything and everything, leaving her to find her own level. Even now, she read a book a day. Reading soon became a form of escape into the world of the imagination. And when she discovered music, it added a dimension to that world.

She left Henrietta Fielding widely read and narrowly inhibited. Armed with a certificate that said she could do 120 words a minute shorthand and sixty typing. It got her a job, at the age of seventeen, as what the agency called a "Girl Friday," actually a general drudge in a studio used by aspiring fashion photographers. Miss Keller arranged for her to rent a room in the house of two maiden ladies, ardent feminists both, who at first kept a strict eye on her until they saw she was as independent as they were—and never went out with boys. She left the house at eight-fifteen each morning, returning at six-fifteen each night, when she would go up to her room and stay there. She never played music too loud and she left the bathroom spotless. Her rent was always paid on the dot and she was unfailingly polite. They were vastly relieved.

She had become a model by chance. After four years with the studio, the manager left the running to her. She made the bookings, paid the bills, saw to it bookings did not clash, and all with such indifferently unobtrusive skill that nobody ever noticed—it or her. Until one day, carrying an armload of filters, she tripped over a loose cable and sprawled her length, banging her head on a tripod. She was helped to her feet, dusted off, her aching head rubbed, which wreaked havoc on her tightly coiled chignon. It lost its pins so that her hair came tumbling down her neck, cascading over her shoulders, removing ten years and also the covers off a beauty that made the photographer who helped her up do a double take. As she began to bundle up her hair, dragging it back into its prison wardress bun, he had stopped her with a hand. "Hang about . . . come over here . . . let's have a good look at you." He was in a bind. The model he had booked to do a four-page color spread of luxury furs had, while spooning a little sugar with her daddy, broken a leg on the ski slopes at St. Moritz, which left him in agony. The sight of Elizabeth Sheridan not in disguise was the perfect painkiller. He had dragged her under the lights, tilted her chin, which she had resented, giving him a quelling, insolently haughty look which was her first line of defense.

"Oh, yes! Which bushel have you been hiding your light under, love? Stand there a minute, will you . . . let me get you under the lens."

It revealed a marble skin, glowing green eyes, and a mass of glorious, gilt-blond hair with an odd greenish glint to it. My God, he had thought, awed by his luck. She's incredible . . .

"What's your name, love?"

Curtly: "Elizabeth Sheridan."

He had come back to her, fluffed out her hair only to have her jerk away instantly. "Do you mind!"

"Oh, yes . . . that's just right! *Very* frozen mit! Just what I'm looking for . . . absolutely *noli me tangere* . . ."

She was far too big, of course. Built like a brick shithouse, but that face . . . Not a scrap of makeup but those bones, those eyes . . . With the right makeup she would be unbelievable! What luck! He had seen her about the place, now he came to think of it. Always thought what a sullen, hulking creature she was . . . especially when you compared her to the gorgeous models she booked, always less than half her size but really, now that he had seen her *au naturel,* nowhere near as beautiful. That bloody awful hairstyle, he thought. He had always thought she was an over-the-hill spinster; now he saw she was young . . . couldn't be more than about twenty, twenty-one.

He began to get excited. Put her on a diet, get her to lose—what? Twenty pounds? She'd still be too big to model clothes, but it would help the face on top of that Amazonian body, and it was the face he could use. The cosmetic houses were always after faces . . . hair products too, and she had the most remarkable hair. By God, he thought. Why not? It's a gamble . . . but if it comes off I'm made . . . made!

"Let me take a few shots," he suggested. "See if the camera likes you."

It had loved her. She was a natural.

But her reaction was not. Derision, contempt, and downright disbelief all firmly based on the suspicion that he was having her on.

"I'm not," he said, "honest . . . don't you ever look in a mirror? Don't you realize what you are carrying on those broad shoulders of yours? I can make it—and you—famous. More important, I can make you rich. You'll get

model rates for this session even if it doesn't turn out . . . promise." He
knew, even as he made it, he would not be called upon to tell her so.

The mention of money made the necessary difference. *That* she believed.
When she had been made up, her hair done, a fortune in Russian sable
falling casually from one bare shoulder, he could see she was still suspicious;
convinced he *was* having her on; only willing to go along just so long as she
was getting paid for it. Even when, even more excited, he showed her the
proofs she was not convinced. "If that's what you want," was all she said,
much more interested in looking at his check.

"It's not what only I want . . . They'll all be after you when these come
out . . . I told you . . . the camera positively drools over you."

It turned a face, sculpted from Pharian marble and expertly made-up, into
something unbelievable. She was perfect for the sort of high-fashion, ultra-
sophistication he wanted. He learned she was twenty-one, but in the eye of
the camera she was ageless: the female personified.

He was sick of the waifs and strays who, in swinging London, dominated
the world of fashion. He was tired of geometric haircuts and faces painted to
look like clowns and skinny, white-stockinged legs in flat pumps with bows.
He wanted another Barbara Goalen; groomed to the nth degree and beyond
any man's attaining. In Elizabeth Sheridan he found her.

Afterward, when he was famous enough to be known only by his last
name, he used to boast about how he had discovered Elizabeth Sheridan.
And it was a cover he shot for the American edition of *Harper's*—Elizabeth's
face in giant close-up under a big black hat, mysteriously shadowed by a fine
mist of veiling, from under which the skin gleamed like porcelain, the eyes
like matched emeralds—that found its way onto the desk of the man who
handled the advertising for the Flawless Finish cosmetics house. The range
cost an arm and a leg and was primarily intended for the older, sophisticated
woman. On the face of Elizabeth Sheridan its sales rocketed through every
age. And when a perfume was created to complement the range, so identified
with it had she become that they named it *Sherida*. She could command a
thousand pounds an hour, while her retainer from Flawless Finish was in six
figures.

She bought herself a new flat in an old building; Edwardian rooms that
had been tarted up in the thirties but their original size unchanged. Vast,
high-ceilinged expanses, with parquet flooring and huge windows. She had a
new rather than second-hand car, could afford the best seats at concerts and
the opera. The rest of her earnings she salted away in savings accounts. All
models eventually arrived at the day when theirs was over, and hers had been
an unexpected dawning anyway. A fluke. After seven years in the business she

was still convinced that it was her height, her size, that made her different. In no way did she believe in her own beauty. Her face was her fortune, but it was the fortune that mattered. Nor did the jet-set world into which it gave her entrée impress her. If she went to the best parties, the really great restaurants, the most fashionable openings, it was in the course of her work with an escort provided by the agency. She herself, the woman as against the model, never went out with men. She was thought to be an oddball. But a worker. Very professional. Always turned up fully prepared and invariably gave you what you wanted. Once the session was over, makeup cleaned off, hired clothes gone back, she also went back into her own private world. Men—those who had the nerve to knock—never gained admittance. They spitefully spread the word she was lesbian. When that turned out to be patently untrue they said she was neuter. And left her alone. Which was all she wanted.

Elizabeth Sheridan had never lacked for company. She had herself. Every time she entered her flat, as tidy and neat and perfectly ordered as she had left it, she sighed contentedly. She could sleep in her king-sized bed in the deep silence she loved, knowing she would not have to wake up to either bells or company.

Bells . . . She came back from her thoughts to find the one from Tempest Cay was still tolling. It snapped the last, frayed strand of her nerves. "Shut up! Will you shut up?" She leapt to her feet and screamed across the water, scattering seabirds and hearing the wind toss her voice to the empty sky.

It took no notice. Went on tolling, tolling.

In a burst of fury she hurled herself down the beach and into the water, head buried in it, striking out with her powerful, fast crawl until her lungs were laboring and her leg muscles fluttering. Treading water she raised her head. She was within fifty yards of Tempest Cay and its tolling bell. It was louder here, relentlessly, metronomically keeping time. It beat in her head like blows, making her quiver with each strike. It was as though she had been drawn to it . . .

She could smell heavy perfume; flowers. The island must be thick with them. The beaches were clean, empty, large notices fixed at regular intervals along the shoreline. Too far away to read but she got their message: PRIVATE PROPERTY. Set back against the overhanging cliff was a small cottage, white with navy trim, closed shutters, and a captain's walk. Not far away was a small jetty. No boat. No people. Only that damned, sonorous, desolate bell . . .

Duck-diving, she streaked back to *her* island. Breathing hard she staggered up the beach before collapsing on the sand. After a while, she put her hands over her ears. No use. In desperation she hunted for the handful of tissues she had brought, tore one into strips, wadded them into small balls with which she plugged her ears. Better; the bell was muffled, like mourning drums . . .

Exhausted, she closed her eyes, more overwrought by her nerves than her swim, which had left her physically depleted. Please stop, she thought desperately. Please, *please*, stop . . .

With her hands over her ears as well as the plugs in them, her face buried in her towel, eyes closed, she drifted off, eventually, into a sleep that was uneasy, dream-filled. The old, menacing nightmare. She was in a dark place, no light anywhere, shut up and—she knew it with sickening terror—buried. Yet she could hear a bell tolling . . . She tried to move, found she could not. She was restricted, hemmed in, suffocating, and straining. Then she knew. The tolling bell was for her. She began to scream but no sound came from her wide-open mouth. She found she could make no sound.

"Let me out!" she mouthed. "Please . . . let me out . . . I don't want to be buried in the earth . . . I don't want to be like my mother . . . please, please . . ." She knew she was screaming; she could hear it inside her head, but from her mouth there was no sound. That was why they could not hear her. She strained and strained, feeling the cords on her neck swelling to ropes, yet the sound was still only in her head.

She woke to the sound of her own moans and to the fact that she had thrashed herself halfway down the beach. Still the bell tolled dolefully, remorselessly.

It was a long time since she had had that nightmare but it still had the power to leave her sick and trembling. As a child she had dreamed it so regularly that Miss Keller had moved her to the isolation room, leaving the door ajar so that the lamp in the hall gave her light instead of the darkness which terrified her. Which was no doubt why, even now, she could not sleep in a room with the curtains drawn . . .

She used to wake screaming as a child, making so much noise it brought the other children upright and wailing, the staff running. The first time it had happened Miss Keller had not been on duty and her deputy had been very angry, slapped her hard and told her to behave and not make a spectacle of herself, putting her in the isolation room and shutting the door so that she was imprisoned in darkness. She had screamed herself into a state of hysteria.

The next time, Miss Keller had left the door open, and through it Elizabeth had heard the angry voices.

"I am aware of the way you favor Elizabeth Sheridan," she had heard the deputy declare aggrievedly, "but it really is too much to allow her to ruin the sleep of all the other children."

"I have no favorites," she had heard Miss Keller answer icily. "If I allow Elizabeth some latitude it is because she needs it—and because of what you did. You should never have taken her without my permission."

"I had to do *something*. All she did was whine for her mother . . . it was getting on everyone's nerves."

"And also hers. What we are seeing—and hearing—now is the effect it had on her. In future, if she has a nightmare she will be brought here to the isolation room but the door is to be left open—open, you understand. That is an order!"

The angry voices faded away down the corridor, leaving Elizabeth aware that she was the cause of them. It was all her fault. She had made a spectacle of herself. Her sense of guilt was compounded with a thousand percent interest by the deputy superintendent, who never ceased to remind Elizabeth of her disgrace. She always referred to her as "the uncontrollable Elizabeth," and taunted her in front of the other children, extolling their control in contrast to Elizabeth's abandoned behavior. "You had better learn to control yourself, my girl," she had warned. "Making such scenes will land you nowhere but in Queer Street . . ."

And the terrified five-year-old, not knowing where Queer Street was but terrified of another change, had enforced on her naturally emotional personality a harshly repressive control that soon became second nature. No one ever saw the adult Elizabeth Sheridan make a scene. No matter how she felt inside, outwardly she was always totally controlled, unto automation. Never again did she cry in public. Never again did she make any display of her emotions. They were battened down and left to starve.

Now, on this beautiful little island, that carefully maintained calm was frazzled. She felt she was crumbling, falling into a heap of rubble. And it was all the fault of that damned bell . . . All because a man called Richard Tempest had died. Yes, Tempest. After so many years that name had returned to haunt her. After a childhood dominated by it, for the foundlings were ceaselessly reminded that it was on Tempest bounty that they lived and the Family was always remembered in a special prayer at church each Sunday. She had thought she had left them behind, along with that childhood. Her going back to Tempest Towers as a tourist had been an act of exorcism, she now realized; one that had not worked.

This won't do! she told herself. She forced herself to take deep breaths, hoping the oxygen would soothe her churning.

But it was no use. Her mood was friable, restless. There was no use staying here. Maybe she should have gone to Nassau after all . . .

Thank God there remained only the night shots to do. If she could only regain her normal tranquillity. She knew she would never be able to produce what was wanted if she did not . . .

Suddenly she longed for the whole thing to be over. To pack her bag and take the boat back to Nassau and the plane back to London. Away from this sense of doom, the relentlessly tolling reminder of death. She longed for the safety of her own hideaway, her own oasis of peace and calm and rest. Nothing like this had ever happened to her since that awful funeral and she couldn't understand it. She had thought there was nothing she could not take in her stride, yet she was shaken up over that horrible, hideous bell . . .

With frantic haste she grabbed her towel and beat a hasty retreat, running, running as if pursued by the ghosts of her own past. She would go to Nassau. She would get one of the boatmen to take her. Not come back until she had to. Perhaps by then she would have regained her equilibrium. She hoped so. She prayed so. If she failed she did not know what she would do . . .

ONE

Dan Godfrey was the first to arrive.

Cass had just sat down to a very early and solitary breakfast (she always turned to food when she was disturbed) when she heard the whine of a low-flying jet as it lost height over the house, heading out to sea before turning for the final approach to the strip. She checked her watch. Five-thirty a.m. Somebody was in a hurry.

This early, the sun was not yet at full power, and the breeze, already sweet-smelling as it drifted through the open windows of the South Parlor, still cool and fresh; a compound of the sea and a heady mixture of island opulence: frangipani, hibiscus, bougainvillea, the night jasmine Helen had planted in stone sarcophagi along the house walls. It also carried sound. She could hear the whisk of a broom as the terraces were swept clean for the day, the distant barking of a dog, the faint sound of voices. It carried the sound of the car from way off, its distant drone rising to a roar as it took the hill, spattering gravel as it drew to a pig-squeal stop. She heard its door slam with a heavily expensive "thunk" followed by rapid feet taking the steps at a run. Voices, nearer this time, murmured, then the footsteps came quickly along the terrace in her direction, heralding his final entrance through the French windows. Cass raised her eyes just as he stepped through them and, in a voice that would have split hairs, drawled: "Tennis, anyone?"

He ignored that. He was still in his dinner jacket, a lightweight cashmere coat slung casually—it took years to learn how—across his straight shoulders. "I came as soon as I got your cable," he said without preamble. "What happened?"

Cass was buttering a morning-made croissant, spreading thickly. "He had a stroke. Coming down to dinner last night. Felled like a log. Rolled all the way to the bottom. By the time Moses reached him he was dead. That was at seven forty-eight last night." She bit into the croissant.

The glittering, water-colored eyes hit her like a cold shower but she clenched her teeth on her shiver, holding them inimically and thinking that, really, all those pictures in *Town and Country* never managed to do him justice. They never could quite reproduce all his slender height and elegance, the shine of the fresh-water eyes, the best-butter gloss of the thick yellow hair, the Apollonian good looks, the legendary charm and smoothness (he killed at a thousand yards), or the reputation which preceded him like an advance man. The only time she ever felt safe with him was at high speed in a good car on a bad road.

Dan recognized the tone of the voice, the stare, the look in the cornflower blue eyes. Cass was not herself this morning. Normally a cross between Bella Abzug and Dutch Schultz, her A's were, this morning, very Beacon Hill. Well, he thought charitably, under the circumstances one must make allowances . . . Especially as he would be able to afford them now.

"Poor Cass . . ." His voice was honeyed, and she tensed for the sting. "Out of a job now, are we? And what will our poor Cassie do then, poor thing?"

Picking up her coffee cup, eyeing him reflectively over it: "Oh, I don't know . . . write my memoirs, maybe? I know some killer-diller stories. You know, 'Secrets of a Secretary' or 'My Thirty Years with Richard Tempest.' I mean, I may as well profit from my elephantine memory."

Dan's eyes measured her in a way that made her acutely and furiously conscious of her excess thirty pounds. "Elephantine indeed . . ." Shrugging the coat from his shoulders onto one chair, he drew another from the table, sat down opposite her. "So tell me then," he encouraged, "what has been happening? Where is everybody?"

"Helen is prostrate upstairs. Hervey—upright as ever—is with her. David is communing with his good friend Jack Daniel's while I, as usual, am left to dispose of the body."

Dan's smile carved her to the bone. "Ah, well . . . if you will spend your time whitening sepulchers. And the others?"

"Not back yet. Margery is in Venice, Mattie in Sydney, Nieves at school, and Harry at home in Tuscany. I've sent cables."

"I thought your right arm was invented specifically for the telephone?"

"You could *tell* Mattie?"

Dan's shudder was fastidious. "I see what you mean. And Helen? How did she take it?"

"Lying down, as usual."

"She folded?"

Cass's mouth turned down. "Permanent creases."

Dan held out a cup for coffee. "And Richard? How was he? I mean—was he ill or anything?"

"No. He was his usual self." Cass lifted the coffeepot.

"Which one would that be?"

Ignoring the jibe: "We flew down from New York yesterday morning. In the afternoon he played nine holes with Hervey. Before dinner we went over some very fine print. There was absolutely *no* indication. It was all terribly sudden." Cass snapped her fingers, making Dan jump and the coffee in his cup slop over his hand. "Just like that!" She smiled innocently as Dan mopped his hand, then, leaning back in her chair, reached for the first of her day's sixty cigarettes. Her nails were bitten to the quick, the fingers stained with the deep yellow of the chain-smoker. Dan leaned across with a lighter. Putting a hand on his to hold it still, she raised eyebrows to match her voice as she said, "Mmm, nice. Present?"

"From an admirer."

"Aren't they all?"

His smile was not one whit perturbed as he restored it to his pocket, and his voice was kind when he said: "You look tired, Cass." This meant she looked old. Which she did, he thought callously. One never thought of Cass in terms of age, but this morning she was looking every one of her—what—fifty-two, fifty-three?—years, plus a six handicap. Her normally ruddy cheeks were flaccid and pale, and the always fresh-snow-white shock of hair, cut like a shaggy crysanthemum, was limp as a wilted lettuce. There were shadows under the cornflower blue eyes and little red marks where her glasses had rested. And she'd been at her nails again. Home, he thought, a-sparkle with anticipatory relish. Sweet home.

"And where is he now?" he inquired.

"Upstairs. You want to view the remains? I can assure you that is all they are . . ."

Dan shuddered. "Thank you, no. I prefer to remember him as he was."

Cass's blue eyes met his innocently. "Well, God knows you've got good cause . . ." She held the ice-water eyes.

"How come you knew where I was?" he asked casually.

Cass blew smoke at him. "Oh, come on, now . . . you know damn fine that Richard always knew where you were . . . and what you were doing—especially in that house of yours in the Virgins—and don't think I don't appreciate the irony of *that,* by the way. Keeping tabs on you—on everybody—was part of my job."

His smile stripped skin. "So that is why you are so devoted to it." He laughed at the look on her face, sang in a pleasing light baritone, "Oh, the times, they are a-changing . . ."

"That's what worries me," Cass said sourly.

Not me, Dan thought, sipping appreciatively at Marlborough's perfect coffee. When the cable had been handed to him he thought it was a cancellation, stuffed it in his pocket under the press of other, more important things, like the old, grainy, black-and-white silent pornographic movie being shown in the main living room, depicting the deflowering of a terrified ten-year-old boy by a monstrously huge man. It was not until the movie was over, to a scattering of laughter and applause from the lounging group of naked people, that he remembered it. His partner, sitting next to him, had seen his face. "Bad news?"

"My stepfather just died."

A look of blazing envy changed to one of sympathy as Dan glanced at him. " 'King' Tempest? Gee, that's too bad . . . he was some guy . . . the last of the living legends."

And now a dead one, Dan thought viciously. Dead! He'd crumpled the cable in a surge of exultation—and exaltation. Dead!

"I'll have to leave."

"Jesus, Dan!" His partner's voice rose in a panic. "You can't leave me holding everyone's balls!"

People had turned heads curiously. Dan had stiff-armed him across to the wall of windows overlooking a magnificent view of silver beach, silver lamé sea, cloudless, silvered sky. No need for curtains. His was the only house on the island, which was why he had bought it.

"This is a three-day thrash!" moaned his partner frantically.

"So—let them thrash. Just so long as you keep the gag in their mouths. You know how; you've seen me do it often enough."

"But from you they'll take it! You're their kind . . . I'm not in their class."

"Without clothes they have no class. Only sex. Nakedness exposes all. Which is what they come for."

"But I've never handled one of these on my own."

"There's nothing to it. It's *your* ball. You run with it. Anyone who won't play our rules leaves the game: they all know them. *And* what happens if they break them . . ."

"But, Dan—"

"A firm hand, that's all, and never out of its pure silk velvet glove."

But in his usual fashion he made quite sure that everything was just so. This would be the first time the house had swung without him—its Master of the Revels. It was his name and reputation which filled the house and had a waiting list years long because he operated on a tightly restricted guest list. Eager swingers had to be rich swingers, and beautiful ones; the body had to match up too. That way, people knew what to expect and were never disappointed. It was his position as Richard Tempest's stepson, with his Marlborough background and access (they thought, and he encouraged them to believe) to unlimited money which gave him his power.

He knew simply everyone, and what they were worth. He had been everywhere; he was bilingual in French, had fluent Italian and a good command of Spanish and German, so he was able to attract an international clientèle. This weekend there were, among others, a French film director, an Italian movie star, a German novelist, and one of England's theatrical knights. If anything went wrong it could be Armageddon. It was because things had gone wrong once before that he was in hock now . . . Until he remembered Richard was dead. And he was rich. Nobody could own him now . . . nobody. But he could own them. Besides, the island was private; nobody came except by invitation; the beach was patrolled by guard dogs.

The guests came to shed their clothes and their inhibitions. Once they set foot inside the two-foot-thick, solid mahogany hurricane-proof door, they removed their clothes and all outward identity; names—real names—were known only to Dan. Then for three days they would indulge in naked, unbridled, and unceasing sex. Of every shape, size, and perversion. All of it—every position, every group, every daisy chain, every trio, anything and everything that happened in any one of the beds of the dozen luxurious bedrooms captured on tape and film. When the carefully chosen ones were faced with them later, they always paid up. And kept their mouths shut. It had provided a lucrative addition to what he had always considered Richard's niggardly allowance, but it was as nothing compared to what he was about to collect now. That was Fort Knox cut four—maybe five—ways. This place would be very small beer. Still, one did not knock a nice little sideline out of the way merely because a whole flock had settled on one's shoulders.

So he methodically checked the hidden cameras, the voice-operated tape recorders, the stocks of liquor and food; that there was a plentiful hoard of pornographic films. He already had a generous supply of gorgeous women, including an exquisite Japanese girl on her first swing, a pair of nubile seventeen-year-old twins who were reputed to do anything with anyone, male or female, a majestic mulatto of prodigious sexual voracity and virtuosity, and a much married pair of Hollywood stars—he a stud of heroic proportions, she a bisexual nympho. All in all, a very interesting weekend. Still, the pickings were so much better elsewhere . . .

He finally found Toby Estes in one of the Jacuzzis with the twins; glazed, gloating, sated, and replete, he at once agreed that Dan could borrow the Lear jet . . . just so long as he had it back for Monday morning . . .

Now, Dan suddenly shoved his chair back from the table.

"I think after all I will go upstairs and pay my respects," he said.

Cass smiled up at him, teeth bared. "Well, you can afford to now, can't you."

Hervey left the window, where he had gone when he heard the car, to bend solicitously over Helen, motionless on her chaise lounge, her frail body wrapped in a poem of a négligé the color of sea drift, much frilled with lace and bound with satin.

"Dan is back," he said gently.

Her ravaged eyes looked at him without seeing him, unfocused, blurred. Her mouth moved vaguely in what he took to be a smile, as always, hovering on the brink of tears. "That's nice . . ."

He drew up his chair again. "Don't you think you ought to try and sleep. You haven't done so all night."

"I can't," she said simply.

She withdrew her gaze and herself from him, fell to staring at nothing as she had done ever since her brother had fallen dead, almost at her feet. Yet she had been so calm, then, when he had expected her to go to pieces. It was only afterward that she had retreated into one of what he called her "states," where she saw nothing, heard nothing, and communed only with herself. Hervey had sat with her all night, holding her hand, offering wordless comfort but not really getting through. As she always did when life rolled over her, she had retreated from it. Dr. Bastedo had warned him not to try and

force her out of it. "Let her come to terms with her shock in her own way
. . . and in her own time."

All very well, thought Hervey now, but when will that be? He knew these
retreats; they could last for days. Her withdrawal was a shrinking from a
confrontation too brutal to be borne. If she did not seem to be aware of
things, it was because for her they did not exist. She had shut them out. But
how could you shut Richard Tempest's death out? Hervey thought. Sooner or
later she had to accept that fact, brutal or not. She was going to have to live
with it for the rest of her life.

He gazed at her longingly but with baffled despair. Her still-beautiful face
was wiped clean of all expression, the fine but still remarkably unlined skin
luminously pale and stretched tightly over her exquisite bones as though it
had retreated from something too hideous to face. Yet she still lived up to
every gushing word of *Vogue*'s eulogy of her as "Miss Helen Tempest of
Marlborough, as finely carved as Chinese ivory, as gentle as summer rain, as
distinguished as her name . . ." She was possessed of that particularly fragile
form of femininity; the kind that had men rushing to open doors and pull out
chairs, to be rewarded by a burning glance from the fine eyes—a true turquoise, large and deep and fringed with lashes as a lagoon is fringed by palm
trees. She had her brother's height—all the Tempests were tall—but her
bones were long and delicate, the flesh covering them meager. Even as a girl
she had been excessively slender, narrow-hipped and tiny-breasted. Now, at
fifty-four, the greenish blond hair was pewter gray, cut short and crisp, curling deliciously at her nape above the long, slender neck, and her carriage was
as upright as it had ever been, as it had been all those years ago when the
young Hervey Grahame, back from five years in the United States, had fallen
instantly and irrevocably in love with her.

She had been Miss Tempest of Marlborough; he, the son of the estate
factor, spotted by her brother as being promising material and plucked from
the island to be sent to Harvard Law. He had adored her from afar, silently,
worshipfully, but always mindful of his place, which had been drummed into
him by his Scots Calvinist father. It was not until Helen, meaning only to be
kind to the shy young lawyer who seemed to haunt the house, had discovered
in him a friend, that he gradually became her *cavaliere servente*, laughed at by
the servants—but always behind his back. He had a sharp tongue and an
eagle eye, and as he rose not only in the world but also in the eyes of Miss
Tempest and her brother, Master of the Island, so he rose in power and
authority, becoming Richard Tempest's lawyer and confidant and admitted
not only into the Inner Council but into the Family as well.

It was only then, finally feeling confident enough to approach her, that he asked her, for the first of many times, to marry him.

She had looked at him out of those great eyes, that sad smile on her lips, but with a luminous look that wrenched his heart, and answered: "Marriage is not for me, Hervey . . ."

"But I love you; love you with all my heart and soul. I want to look after you, care for you . . ."

A gentle but bitter sigh, a brooding look. "Love . . ." It was a gentle ghost. "Ah, for all my money I never could afford love, Hervey."

"But you love Marlborough!" It was envious, accusing.

"Marlborough will always be here. Unfailing, undemanding, always beautiful, always tranquil . . . and all I am fit for."

He had recognized the oblique reference to her nervous breakdown. Her years away from the Island in a private nursing home. Years lost to the world, and him. Years about which she never spoke. About which no one ever spoke. But the truth of her words was self-evident. In Marlborough she had created a house that was a thing of beauty which would be the world's joy forever. A glorious house filled with a perfection of the world's art; furniture, carpets, hangings, porcelain, crystal, sumptuous fabrics and fabulous colors; an Aladdin's cave of treasures which had earned it the title of "The World's Most Beautiful House," to which invitations were sought after, schemed for, and worn afterward as a decoration to be flaunted.

As a hostess she was legendary, no detail too small to escape her careful attention, so that the breathtaking whole was compounded from parts so finely and intricately worked that they fitted together seamlessly. Before she gave a dinner party everything was planned, down to the length of the tablecloth from the floor and the distance between the chairs; the china she chose to use from the six storerooms crammed with fabulous two-hundred-piece sets of Meissen and Rockingham and Sèvres, which would in turn match the porcelain handles of the solid gold cutlery, which would in turn be echoed in the flower arrangements. These she always did herself; she could take a handful of daisies and in the right alabaster urn or crystal vase they took on the qualities of a still life. And each and every detail would be recorded in the pages of her Household Books specially bound in tooled Morocco leather in her favorite green, year by year, so that she could at any time turn up the name of a guest to check on his preferences; his favorite brand of coffee and cigarettes, the toothpaste he preferred, his favorite color, his taste in food. A weekend at Marlborough meant the kind of sybaritic luxury reminiscent of the Court of Versailles or Imperial Russia.

Where else could one eat off plates decorated in gold leaf and fine enamels, using knives and forks used by Marie Antoinette, all set on a table-cloth of lace so fine, so exquisite, it could have been drawn through the eye of a needle; where you only had to stretch out a hand to an embroidered bellpull —the work of Helen herself, who was famous for it—to have your every whim gratified. People never ceased to be amazed that all this smooth-running luxury was the work of a woman who always looked exhausted, as if the effort had drained her, yet, when she walked, always gave the impression of wearing a train. Of course, people said, she had the staff to do it. The ratio of servants to guests at Marlborough must be at least six to one. But there was never any doubt in anyone's mind as to who was really responsible. Marlborough was Richard Tempest's property, but it was Helen Tempest's house.

Gazing at her hopelessly, Hervey had the glimmerings of an idea. Picking up her bird-frail hand he enfolded it in his own comfortingly. "You realize why Dan is back, don't you? Why they will all be back? Richard's funeral . . . it has to be arranged, Helen . . . and only you can do it."

Her head turned. "Funeral?"

"Yes . . . and of a famous and much-loved man. The world will be watching, but even more important, the Island will expect it."

He saw the finely arched brows knit a stitch and pressed his advantage. "Richard was a famous—and fabulous—man. He gave the public his life, and they will not willingly forgo their share in his death."

Almost involuntarily her hand strayed to the gallery-edged table by her side where her glasses lay. She wore them only when she was working; hopelessly myopic, she was oddly vain about them, never donning them in public, which had, he thought, a great deal to do with the all-encompassing quality of her smile; half the time she simply had no idea whom she was talking to.

"Only you can do it, Helen," he urged. "With taste and the pageantry the Island will expect. He was an Island man, Helen, as you are an Island woman."

"Island style . . ." Her voice trailed off, but there was a thoughtful echo to it.

Hervey reached over to pick up her notebook; supple, silky leather binding, thick, linen-weave pages, a small gold pencil slotted into its side. "Why don't you make some notes . . . begin to plan things. It will take a deal of arranging . . . an Island funeral, Helen, as only you can arrange it . . . After all, now that Richard is gone you are the Lady."

"The Lady," she repeated, but her voice was stronger. "Yes . . . I am . . ."

She sat for a moment, gazing thoughtfully into space, but he could see her attention had been caught, that her mind had seized on the idea as on to a handhold. Then she opened her notebook and he saw her write in her delicate copperplate—she had had an English governess—"Funeral of Richard Tempest VI," at the top of a clean page. He heaved an inner sigh of thankful relief. That would take her mind off death. In some strange way, she could plan and arrange the funeral down to the last tiny detail, from the hymns to be sung to the decoration of the church and the names of those people she thought should be asked to attend the obsequies. And all this plethora of intricately arranged detail would coalesce into a mass that would block out the hideous reality of her brother's death.

He left her to it; she did not notice his departure. Seraphine was sitting on her usual stool outside Helen's door. Her body servant since Helen was a baby, no one knew how old she was, only that she had always been on the Island. At Marlborough, Seraphine was a power. Moses, the butler, was ostensibly senior servant, but even he, with his thirty years' service, man and boy, deferred to Seraphine. The servants said she was a witch, because Seraphine was African. Her ancestors had come to the Island with the Tempests in the eighteenth century, and there was about her the air of a carved wooden idol. She was tall and spare, with fathomless, unwinking black eyes which could reduce to silence with a look. She never wore anything but a crisp cotton dress of palest green cotton, its skirts sweeping the floor, under a plain, white, well-starched bib-and-tucker-type apron, a snowy white headcloth hiding her hair. She did not move so much as glide, appearing before you as if she had simply materialized. Now she rose silently, hands folded, and looked at Hervey impassively from under her heavy-lidded eyes.

"I've left her preparing the funeral," Hervey said respectfully. "In some strange way I think it will help take her mind off things . . . Perhaps one of your tisanes would also help . . ."

Seraphine inclined her head. "I will see to it." She had a voice like a brass gong. Hervey knew that she would. Where Helen Tempest was concerned Seraphine saw to—and knew about—everything. She was single-minded. But nobody ever knew what went on inside that mind.

Margery had her mouth full when someone knocked on the bedroom door. She ignored it, her mouth full of her favorite food, the only one of which she allowed herself an unrestricted intake: no calories.

"*Signora la Contessa* . . ." She ignored that too. "*Signora, mi dispiace
. . .*"

Impatiently she freed her mouth to shout: "*Che c'è?*"

"*Un telegramme per Lei dagli Stati Uniti, Signora Contessa.*"

Andrea, moaning and writhing under Margery's mouth and tongue, opened his eyes briefly, only to close them again with a gasp as Margery reapplied herself with a will, his eyes rolling up and back, pelvis heaving, his hands on her breasts kneading and gripping, head twisting, body straining. Margery's wide-lipped mouth and darting tongue were past masters at the art of fellatio; she was known far and wide for her prowess. As he felt himself thrusting into her mouth, his whole body at the base of his spine gathering itself into a monstrously pleasurable orgasm, Margery, sensing it, reached out a blind hand to grasp the heavy crystal ashtray from the nightstand to hurl it, roaches of best Acapulco gold and all, at the bedroom door, where it struck heavily, shattered, scattering shards everywhere even as Andrea, with a muffled shriek, spasmed himself into her avid mouth.

It was only later, lying back in sated satisfaction, admiring Andrea's tight, firm ass as he moved, combing back with careful deliberation his water-slicked hair, lost in admiration of himself in the mirror, that she remembered the cable.

"See what that was, will you, darling?" she purred, stretching her naked body like a cream-fed cat. "He's probably dumped it outside the door."

Andrea came back with a blue-edged envelope in his hand.

"Oh, God . . . now what? Open it, will you, darling?"

Andrea's silence was so profound that Margery opened her eyes again. At the shock on his face she shot upright, snatched the cable from him and scanned it rapidly:

RICHARD DIED TONIGHT. COME AND GET IT! CASS.

Margery let out a shriek. "Eureka! Hallelujah and praise the lawd! At last, at long, suffering last!"

Her face ablaze with exultant greed, she rose to her knees on the bed, arms upstretched in quivering triumph, brandishing the cable. "I'm rich! Rich! Richard's dead and I am rich!"

Practically, like the good Venetian he was: "How rich?" asked Andrea.

"Oh, God . . . who knows? Far too rich for it to be counted . . . billions of it . . . billions and billions and billions . . . he had more money than anybody."

Thoughtfully: "And it is now yours?"

"Who else! He had no blood relatives except his sister, poor bitch, but I'm his stepdaughter . . . his *only* stepdaughter . . ."

Accidenti! thought Andrea. How fortunate he had decided to let her come this time—ostensibly to tell her it would be the last time. This changed everything. Now that her disgustingly rich stepfather was dead. He almost crossed himself piously, so profoundly grateful was he that his luck still held. He would go to Mass just to express his gratitude. Margery had leapt off the bed and was whooping and prancing around the silk-hung, carved and gilded room, reeking of sex and her own, sultry, Arpège. "I'm rich! I'm rich! I'm rich! Stinking, filthy, obscenely rich!"

Andrea went into his act. "But now you will leave me . . . to return to the Island." He sounded desolated.

Margery stopped in mid-prance before running to him, flinging her arms around his naked body passionately, rubbing herself against his now flaccid penis and nibbling on his nipples, burrowing in the mat of black hair on his chest.

"Ah . . . not for long, darling, I promise you . . . only to see him put away—and I wouldn't miss *that* for the world! And I have to see how much he's left me, don't I? But I'll be back just as soon as I can. I'd take you with me but I don't think it would look good and we must observe at least an outward show of mourning, mustn't we? But once I'm rid of Harry . . ." Her adoring expression convulsed into one of vicious hatred. "That's another bastard I'll be glad to see the back of! Such a boring, dull, *dull* little man . . . and his bloody awful hag of a mother and those two long-faced bitch sisters of his . . . he can go back to his god-awful Tuscan vineyards and rot on the vine for all I care."

Then her joy, uncontainable, broke through again. She fastened her open mouth to his and ground her pelvis against him, tongue flicking, hands sliding down his body to grasp his buttocks, fingers probing insistently between. "Let's celebrate, darling, as only we know how . . ." Margery only knew one way.

Margery Boscombe, currently—and for the fifth time of asking—the Contessa di Primacelli, was a forty-four-year-old clothes horse. She had once been sugar-fondant pretty, but too many husbands, even more lovers, too many late nights, too much to drink and too much heroin and/or cocaine, plus the long, hard slog of working her way through the Almanach de Gotha had killed it. The candy floss had turned into the brittle hardness of rock candy. Now, all she had was a daggers-drawn elegance. The once golden-brown hair was skillfully streaked to a sun-kissed blondness, carefully disordered into a mane that was supplemented by discreetly placed hairpieces, and her face, carefully plumped out by silicone injections and hiked by two face-lifts, was always tanned to give an impression of youthfulness. She was a perfect size six, ruthlessly and devotedly maintained, but her authority lay in her instinct (it could not be called intelligence, because that, to Margery, was an organization which employed spies) for clothes; an infallible rightness that made other, more beautiful women green with envy.

Margery Boscombe could wear a flour sack and still knock every other woman dead. But she always wore the clothes of those couturiers whose rock-bottom prices were sufficient to induce her to agree to wear them. The Contessa di Primacelli in a certain dress from a certain House meant a lemming-like descent of every fashion-conscious woman to its salon demanding to be made to look just like that. And invariably failing. But it enabled Margery to indulge in her other passion: gambling. Sex, money, men, and clothes were the four corners of her world, and she roamed it incessantly in search of satisfaction from one or the other—preferably all. She was a founder member of the jet set, currently, and for the sixth time, the World's Best-Dressed Woman; once rid of Harry, Conte di Primacelli, she would take on her sixth husband, Andrea, and title, Principessa Farese. But it was another title, one she had not expected to assume so suddenly, which thrilled her core-deep. That of The World's Richest Woman.

She hugged herself with delight. It could not have come at a better moment. She had detected that Andrea's battery was running low. As a lover he was the best. But one. With Andrea it was like it used to be with only one other man. And she had never been able to get enough of him either. But Andrea needed regular topping up. He ran on money. But once she dropped sufficient coins in his slot . . . He had been costing her more than she could afford. She had been forced to resort to means she knew were highly dangerous, but Andrea had become so necessary, of late. The more she had of him the more she wanted. He satisfied her completely. Only with and after him could she sleep; not feel the constant rabbit-teeth of frustration gnawing at her peace of mind. He could fill her to a point where she fragmented in one great and glorious explosion which shattered the tight pressure within, leaving her floating on that mindless sea of peace she had never thought to find again. She could not let that go.

The thought that it was slipping from her had made her cling to him frantically, sure that it was only a matter of weeks, perhaps days, before that Dillon bitch, with her cosmetic millions, picked him up and added him to her charm bracelet, suitably dipped in gold. Now, Dillon could go whistle. Now she, Margery di Primacelli, had enough money to tell the bitch to go shove hers up her ass. Andrea could spend a thousand dollars every minute of every hour for the rest of his life and there would still be no noticeable diminishment of her piles of gold. He would be hers. And she would never have to go unsatisfied again. Sighing blissfully, her hand wrapped tightly around that part of him which was worth every cent she would have, she slipped contentedly into sleep.

When Andrea awoke, his mind instantly returned to his good fortune. He lifted Margery's head from his chest. "You must send a cable," he prompted. "And see about a plane home . . ."

Margery yawned; she felt boneless with repletion. "Oh, charter one . . ." Then she rolled off him, sat up. "And to go via Paris . . . I want something for this funeral that will take all the limelight from the corpse."

Looking determined, she slid from the bed to run into the room next door —there was always one like it wherever she went—which was devoted to her clothes. Walls of closets crammed with specially made covers shrouding hundreds of dresses, skirts, shirts, suits, coats. She had a maid whose job it was to look after them. She had another for her personal needs. She also toted along her personal masseuse, her own hairdresser, and a woman who did nothing but her nails. Margery di Primacelli had been known to throw a tantrum just because a plane crash, killing all on board, had put her schedule out of whack, but a broken nail was a disaster. She had been known to hire a jet just to fly out a technician from New York. When it came to her appearance Margery was an obsessive perfectionist. She would send a dress back to the workrooms a dozen times until the sleeve fitted perfectly. Hems were measured to the millimeter and waists had to set exactly. Her furs would have clothed the world's entire population of Eskimos and she had at least a half dozen pairs of shoes for each outfit. Even her lingerie was fitted, before being hand-sewn by the nuns of a convent in Siena.

Now, she slid back mirrored doors and scanned rapidly. No . . . nothing would do . . . not the Balmain, too much the cocktail hour; nor the Yves St. Laurent, too casual, nor the Halston, and not the Karl Lagerfeld. No, it would have to be something special. She fretted about fittings. For once she really just did not have the time . . . Well, they had her forme, and woe betide if it was sloppily done . . . not that she would have any rivals. Cass would look like a sack stuffed with garbage as usual, Nieves was far too young, and Mattie would be overripe and overdone as always. While Helen . . . Helen *loathed* black.

"Darling!" she called imperiously to Andrea. "When you've fixed the plane I want you to call Dior . . . get Marc himself, I won't speak to anyone else . . . tell him it's me and I want something for a very, very important funeral . . ."

Andrea was speaking to Alitalia. "Yes . . . Tempest Cay, it's in the Bahamas . . . of course it has an airstrip . . . six thousand feet of it . . . . yes, a cay . . . that means island . . . Tempest Cay . . . Richard Tempest's island . . . yes, *that* Richard Tempest . . . 'King' Tempest . . . fine . . . the Contessa is his stepdaughter . . . no, first to Paris . . . hang on . . ."

"When do you want to go?" he yelled through to Margery.

"Tonight!" she yelled back.

"This evening . . . about eight o'clock? Fine . . . yes, the bill to the Contessa at Tempest Cay . . ."

He also sent a cable, which made Margery chortle when she read it: TERRI-BLY SHOCKED AND GRIEVED. FLYING HOME SOONEST. MARGERY.

"You should have added: MAKE SURE IT'S AN OPEN COFFIN. I WANT TO BE QUITE SURE HE'S DEAD!" She laughed.

The houselights, once dimmed, had risen again, and the glitteringly fashionable audience at the Sydney Opera House, poised like a great bird about to swoop over the harbour, was abuzz with restless speculation. Society had turned out in force to hear the Divine Diva in her greatest role, the Marschallin in *Der Rosenkavalier*. But the curtain was already twelve minutes late. Suddenly the heavy curtains parted and the manager stepped forward, hands raised.

"Ladies and gentlemen . . ." He raised the microphone a little and the buzz subsided. "I regret to announce that Miss Mattie Arden is indisposed and will not, alas, be able to sing tonight."

There were cries of "Oh no!" and "Shame!" and people began to rise, preparatory to leaving. "Her place will be taken by her understudy, Miss Marta Renson. However, those who—understandably—wish to leave will have their ticket money refunded . . ."

He withdrew to boos and catcalls.

Mattie's dresser unlocked the door, peered round it.

"I'm a doctor," the man said authoritatively. She opened the door just wide enough to let him in, keeping out the peering, curious faces milling around outside, then she shut and locked it again. She was a Polish woman of unguessable age who had been with Mattie for years. The spiteful said she was Mattie's mother, but in truth she was a second cousin—Mattie had been born Mathilda Krojlakowska in Kraków forty years before. She had removed Mattie's wig, untied the laces of her extravagant costume, managed to heave her onto the chaise longue, where she lay like a rag doll, face empty of color and expression, slack in shock, flaming hair cramped under the tight nylon cap she wore under her wig.

"What happened?" The doctor bent over her, raised an eyelid, took hold of a limp wrist.

"She get cable."

"Bad news?"

The dresser clutched at the cable, crumpled in her hand, thrust deep into the pocket of her apron. "Very bad . . ."

"What did she do?"

"She stare at it long time . . . not make sound . . . then she scream . . . such a scream." The old woman bent forward, hands over her ears. "Never I hear such scream . . . like fiend in hell . . . then she fall . . . like dead."

"Well, she's not dead but she's badly shocked . . . When did all this happen?"

The dresser pondered. "Fifteen minute . . . she all ready go on stage."

"She's not going anywhere . . . Where's the telephone?"

When Harry got back to the house his mother was waiting for him. So was the cable.

"Well?" she demanded, eyes sharp as her voice.

He handed it to her. Her English was good enough to understand its import: RICHARD DIED TONIGHT. A WAKE AND BE GLAD. CASS.

"What is this wake?" His mother was frowning.

Harry switched his smile into a grimace under her eyes. "A certain kind of —celebration—of death".

His mother crossed herself. *"Barbaros!* It is to be expected of *that* one . . . a hypocrite to the last! But you will go to the funeral. As family you must be there."

"Hardly family, Mama. Bought and paid for."

"And we know who got the best of *that* bargain! But you will go. It is your duty—and your right!" she added threateningly.

"Mama . . . he will not have left *me* anything."

"Did I say such a thing?" Her black eyes glared in affront. "But you are the husband of his stepdaughter."

"Her current husband—and that is about to change."

"Even so, you are still married to her. You will be there. It would not look right if you were not."

Harry shrugged. "It would not even be noticed."

"I would know. My friends would know. You will attend." It was an order. "You will be seen together . . ."

"For the last time."

Shrewdly: "But the most important time . . ."

"Now that he's dead there is nothing to prevent Margery from seeking— and obtaining—her divorce. She has wanted it long enough, God knows."

"On what grounds? Did she not desert you? Has she not cuckolded you through the bedrooms of Europe?"

"She needs no grounds, Mama," Harry said patiently. "Her money can buy acres and acres of them. She will be enormously rich now."

"Then you must make her pay!" his mother spat viciously. "As you have paid . . . If she wishes a divorce then she must buy that too!" She shuddered, crossed herself again. "Why, I myself know of things . . . That woman! Have I not had to suffer the shame of my own friends coming to me with such gossip . . . the things that go on in that house of hers in Venice . . . and that Venetian upstart she has in keeping—half her age!" His mother was scandalized. "But what else could one expect from a Venetian!" All her Tuscan scorn was in the last word. "And a nobody whose mother happened to be fortunate enough to marry a *billionario*. God rest his soul," she tacked on hastily.

"Even He could not do that: Richard Tempest did not have one," Harry muttered, low enough for his mother not to hear.

"I will send flowers. I remember, when he came here, how he loved those yellow roses . . . I will see to it. You will see to it that you leave as soon as possible." She rose from her chair, small, stout, tightly corseted. "Your wife is in Venice; it would be right and proper for you to fly back together—and it would save the airfare. I will call Laura di Vecchio; she too is in Venice and she always knows *everything.*"

"Mama!"

But she was away, trotting on her sturdy legs to set wheels in motion. Harry sighed. Women! Even when he was finally rid of his wife he would still have—looked like he would *always* have—his mother, not to mention his two elder, widowed sisters. Still, he thought, who could say what Richard Tempest had done with his money? With that one anything was possible. Except even he could not buy off death. Harry smiled. Then, disobeying his mother's instructions, he left the house to return to his vineyards. They, at least, would bear fruit.

Helen's suite was cool and dim; every blind of heaviest, creamiest Irish linen, lace-encrusted, bobbled and tasseled, drawn against the relentless sun, the air-conditioning purring softly.

Seraphine navigated Dan across the shadowy cavern of the sitting room, an archipelago of sea green dotted with golden islands of furniture, as though he needed a pilot, before tapping on the massive, gorgeously carved and gilded double doors of the bedroom, opening them to announce, in the island patois she affected with those who knew no better: "Mist' Dan . . ." Her obsidian eyes fixed him with a voodoo stare and her lower lip thrust itself out contemptuously. "Don' you upset her none . . . She done up enough."

Black bitch! Dan thought angrily. She took far too much upon herself, that one.

Helen was in bed, and since she spent so much of her time there it was designed so as to be lived in. Raised on a dais, it was of carved and gilded beechwood in a pattern of acanthus leaves and vines; French, eighteenth-century, but with a twentieth-century orthopedic mattress. It always reminded Dan of a camellia; thickly cream outside, delicate pink inside; a Fortuny pleating of pure silk chiffon lined with velvet to cut noise. Under its drapery, falling from the clutching hands of four plump cherubs, Helen reclined against a bank of fat, lace-encrusted silken pillows, wearing another of her fabulous négligés; this time of deeply cream slipper satin and blond Michelin lace. Her portable writing desk was on her knees, the radio—built into the bedhead along with a television set which could swing out on a specially constructed crane—playing softly. The spotlight concealed by the cherubs bathed her in a rosy glow that was immensely flattering, and as he approached she took off her glasses before raising her face, blind-eyed but expectant, for his ritual kiss; first her hand, then both cheeks, like royalty. Her smile was benign but tremulous.

"Dear Helen . . . how are you?" He was tenderly sympathetic.

"Bearing up . . ."

As only you can do it, he thought. By lying down. Only Helen Tempest could take her mind off death by planning a funeral.

"Hervey tells me you are planning Richard's funeral," he murmured. "What have you in mind? Something befitting his station in life, of course."

"An Island funeral," Helen said simply.

Dan stared. By God, he thought. A stroke of genius! Of course! "A master touch," he said, impressed. "That will go down a treat! An Island funeral! The very thing!"

"He was an Island man," Helen said.

"You mean he was born here . . ."

"Of course," Helen said simply. "You cannot be an Island man unless you were born on it."

Dan gave no sign of having felt the unthinking dig. Because he had been born in Paris, France. An Outsider.

"But what about the world outside the Island? He was not only famous, he was wildly popular . . . You will have to invite it in, you know."

Helen frowned. "No circuses . . ." It was the princess feeling the pea.

"Of course not!" Dan looked shocked. "How can it be if it is an Island funeral?" A circus in itself, he thought. Mardi Gras crossed with All Saints. "But certain people will have to be invited . . . the people from the Organization, for a start . . . and those who cannot come will want to see it on television."

He saw Helen recoil.

"Haven't they made any approaches yet?"

"Well, Cass . . ." murmured Helen. Yes, thought Dan, left to deal with the crud, as always.

"Leave it to me," he soothed. "I will see that it is all done in the very best of taste . . . otherwise Cass will use it as a free commercial for Organization products."

He saw Helen's gaunt frame quiver with distaste.

"But we really cannot put away Richard Tempest—"King" Tempest—as though he was an ordinary man, now, can we? He was too famous, too popular, too much . . ."

He saw her writhing on those pins and stuck in another. "And what about the English branch? All those titled relatives of yours . . . the Earl, at least, as titular head of the *whole* Family must, by right alone, attend." And would look good at the head of a guest list in the press; there were still a lot of people impressed by a title who would never be impressed by money. But that was what made the Tempests so fascinating to the outside world. Not only rich but aristocratic. Living on an island of their very own and reigning like feudal princes. Oh, yes, thought Dan, on prime-time television . . . I should be able to carve myself a lovely fat slice of percentage for that.

"Leave it to me," he said again, thinking: Like everything else has been, I hope.

"If you are sure . . ." Helen sounded both distressed and reluctant.

"I'm positive! They will never forgive you if you do not allow them some share in saying good-bye to Richard Tempest." Jesus, he thought, I sound like Louisa May Alcott.

"But I wanted a simple Island funeral . . ."

"And a simple Island funeral you shall have," assured Dan. Only more so, he thought. The population of the Island was about three hundred; add to that the cream of the Organization—say another two hundred—invited guests—say another hundred or so . . . then camera crews and reporters and the press . . . About a thousand in all, he guessed. A simple funeral!

"Anything else I can do to help?" he inquired solicitously.

Helen frowned, picked at her pen. "Well . . . David . . ."

"Ah, you want him sober, of course. At least sober enough to stand, anyway."

"For Nieves's sake . . ."

Not that she'll notice, Dan thought callously. That's not a gulf between those two, it's the Grand Canyon.

"I will see to it that he is sober as—as Hervey!" he said, inspired.

He saw Helen's sad smile appear, accompanied by a small dimple. "So kind . . ." she murmured vaguely, though she had always been frightened of Dan. Too quick, too clever, too smooth. Too dangerous. Her hand went to her glasses and he took the hint. He was dismissed.

It was only as Seraphine closed the door behind him that he realized he had not done what he had come for: paid his condolences. Which was when he realized she had not expected any.

Nieves smoothed her hair, straightened the pleated skirt of her uniform, took a deep breath and tapped on the door.

"Entrez!"

French was the language of the school, set on the shores of Lake Lucerne and occupied by not more than two dozen, at any one time, of the children of the very rich; young girls sent to be finished; polished and the edges rubbed off; told how to walk, talk, eat, smile, sit, stand—and spend their family money. Which shops to patronize, which hotels to stay at, which people to nod to, which to smile at, which to offer a hand to. How to give a dinner for six or a reception for sixty; how to eat artichokes and asparagus, how to talk to waiters, how to quell a menial. It was assumed, when they came, that they could already read and write, not that they would have much use for either except to study a menu and sign the bill. But they were instructed as to which was the right pen to use.

As Nieves entered the large, sunny room, furnished like a sitting room, Madame Laurent, the founder—and owner—rose and came round from behind her desk.

"Ah, Nieves, *ma petite*, come and sit down."

Nieves's heart sank. The fact that Madame Laurent came out from behind her desk, the endearment, the invitation to sit, all meant bad news. But at least she hadn't done anything wrong. That would have meant standing. She allowed herself to be drawn down onto an elegant sofa, upholstered in Wedgwood blue and white, and Madame Laurent kept hold of her hand. Nieves's heart began to pound.

"I am afraid I have to tell you some very bad news . . ." Madame Laurent's voice was hushed, tender, but she did not waste words. "It is your grandfather. I am sorry to have to tell you he died last night, quite suddenly. He did not suffer, I am told . . . it was very quick."

She felt Nieves buck under her hand, saw the already pale skin drain to chalk and the huge, melted-chocolate eyes reveal their very soft center, the fondant-pink mouth tremble.

"You are to return home at once . . . a plane is on its way for you . . . but this is a journey which should not be undertaken alone, so I have arranged for Mademoiselle de Lucy to accompany you." She leaned forward to kiss Nieves's cheek tenderly. So young, she thought, so docile, and so rich . . . oh, so rich . . . A pity, she sighed. He had been a rare one, her grandfather. So handsome, so virile, and such inconceivable wealth. This child stood to become the heiress of heiresses; they would all be after her. Already, at almost eighteen, she was unfurling her budded beauty. A Murillo Madonna, thought Madame Laurent tenderly. It was the long, thickly waving, rich dark-brown hair, the clotted cream skin, the thickly lashed, melting brown eyes. And the body was burgeoning too, though she still retained a coltish slenderness. Not for Nieves María de la Paz Boscombe y de Barranca the burden of puppy fat or spots. Money, sighed Madame Laurent to herself happily, could do *anything*.

"I am so sorry," she said, with tender sincerity. Especially for herself. There had been that unmistakable look in the eyes of M. Tempest that last time he had come to see his granddaughter . . . Ah, well, she sighed. "You are excused lessons, of course, and your things are being packed for you, but if there is anything I can do for you, *ma petite* . . ."

Nieves shook her head stupidly.

"Perhaps you would like to go and lie down." She patted Nieves's cold, stiff hand. "You were devoted to your *grandpère, non?*"

"He was all I had," Nieves answered in a thin, breathy whisper.

Madame Laurent nodded. She had heard the child's father was a drunkard. And only her grandfather had ever come to visit her, setting everyone a-flutter before his golden magnificence. "We shall not see his like again," Madame Laurent mourned, vexed. She drew Nieves gently but firmly to her feet. "I am very sad for you," she commiserated.

Nieves nodded, swayed slightly. "Th-thank you," came the breathy whisper. She turned to go, took one step, then drifted, like a petal falling, down to the sapphire-blue carpet.

Four thousand miles away, in his specially constructed studio in the great house, which had been so built as to allow the continually changing and shifting light to flood it through one wall of windows, Nieves's father, David Boscombe, lay in a drunken stupor, sprawled full-length on the old leather chesterfield Helen had discarded and he had rescued. It was the only furniture; the rest of the room was bare but for a marvelous sixteenth-century Flemish wall press, which he used to store his paints. There were no canvases, the easel was dismantled; what paint there was lay scattered about the floor in half-squeezed tubes that had dried rock-hard.

He was snoring, mouth open; spade beard, the color of an aging lion, rising and falling with his chest, his heavy-duty-sized "spare tire" oozing over the leather belt of his stained and grubby jeans, his shirt open to reveal a chest matted with the same leonine hair. But his savagely cropped head lay wedged in the corner of the massive couch, his feet propped on the other arm, arms hanging loosely. An empty bottle of Jack Daniel's lay by his hand, the last of its contents having dribbled onto the piles of newspapers that had also been dropped there, soaking into the pictures of the handsome, laughing man on their front pages, all saying, in many languages and varying sizes of type: "KING" TEMPEST DIES.

TWO

Cass was dealing with cables, but only the ones considered to be V.I.P., either politically or commercially or just plain important. (She had set up a Funeral Operations Room staffed by what were known as her "girls" to handle the sacks of mail, the satchels of telegrams, the deluge of flowers—"to an island that sits on the damned things," she had snorted.) Ditto telephone calls. Speaking to those who should be spoken to, making it quite clear without actually saying so that Miss Tempest, prostrate with grief, was unable to do so. But most of her time had been spent on calls to the Organization; setting the pigeons streaking, she thought grimly. If she knew her men —and she did, which was why she had not much time for them—there would be huddles taking place and conjectures being offered and speculations running wild as to who would occupy *that* chair, *that* Grand Central-sized room with the door marked Office of the President. All questions on that subject she answered with a cheerful "Your guess is as good as mine!"— which was a downright lie because, in this particular instance, guesses were no-nos.

Long-established custom had long since led to Roger Kendricks, the Executive Vice President, being considered heir apparent, which belief Cass had done nothing to topple. Especially Roger's. Let him think what he liked. She *knew* different. What she did not know, but did not let on, was who *would* be the next President of the Tempest Organization. Richard had said many things but never that.

But she saw to it that the balance was kept steady, that nobody panicked, that the giant cogs of the Organization continued to turn smoothly. On the telephone Cass was in her element; it was her third hand, her other ear, her chosen instrument. She could dial a number and within five minutes have her listener reduced to jelly. Which she loved. As Executive Secretary to Richard Tempest she had in actual fact been very much more than that; she had been his shadow, his repository of facts and figures, his hatchet man, his emissary, his ambassador, his girl Friday. Nobody—even Richard himself, who had created it—knew more about the Tempest Organization than she did. It was her pride and joy. What worried her now, as she sat in her office, right outside the one that had been Richard's, wreathed in smoke and surrounded by telephones and the glorious feeling of being right smack at the center of the web—where she'd always considered she rightfully belonged—was what was going to happen to it.

Thirty years Cass had labored in this most fertile of vineyards, watching— helping—Richard Tempest create a mammoth that grew and grew until it blotted out the sun; so rich, so powerful, so almighty *colossal,* that even she, who took such pride in its stature, shivered. But with joy, of course. She had liked being, as *Time* called her, "The Tempest Organization's Iron Maiden; spinster of this or any other parish but married to her job; one of the *great* unions . . ." She had cut that out and sent it home to Boston. Naturally, there had been no reply.

Where Cass came from, one conducted one's business with quiet dignity from a Victorian office downtown; never, but *never*, as Richard Tempest did, from a miniature Versailles on a tropical island in the Bahamas. Flying off in the jumbo or the Convair or the Lear jet to this or that part of the world to a Tempest plant, sales office, storage depot, or even representative. And always with Cass at his side. She sat in on everything. "Cass is my eyes and ears," Richard would say blandly, as if everyone did not know—and fear—the way he saw and the way he heard—everything. Cass could name you the man who ran a rubber plantation in Borneo or made the Organization letterhead; she knew how much everybody earned, who was sleeping with whom, who was plotting what, who was going up, who was already on their way down. She was courted, flattered, bowed to, crawled to. Nobody ever got to Richard Tempest except through her, and those who tried soon found out it was Just Not Done. Cass was Family. She had wiped noses and dried tears, lent money and kept secrets. Scolded and soothed, helped and hindered. Whenever anybody wanted anything, they always went to Cass. She grumbled, she scowled, she blew smoke in their faces. And she loved it.

Now, as Hervey went into the smoke-filled room, fanning it away distastefully with his hand and striding purposefully to throw a window wide, he could see Cass was in her element. In charge. She sat back in her chair, shoved her glasses up into the untidy white hair, and demanded: "Well? Do I get an audience?"

"Helen is not right up to seeing anyone just now, Cass. But she asked me to give you these . . ."

He laid a sheaf of Helen's thick, creamy writing paper on the piled desk in front of her. After settling her glasses, Cass picked them up, leafed through them, and her face took on an outraged expression.

"Jesus Christ! I'm only the Executive Secretary around here, but as soon as it comes time to shovel the shit, suddenly I'm Chairman of the Board!" She brandished the sheets at him. "Television! Reporters! A film crew! What is this, Macy's Parade?"

"You know very well that is the last thing Helen wants. These are only . . . probables."

"Come off it, Hervey! We all know Helen's lists! Holy writ! What in God's name gave her the idea of having the funeral televised?"

"I believe it was Dan," Hervey said noncommittally.

"Trust him! And I'll bet he'll get a cut from his friends on the networks!"

"Well, an *Island* funeral . . ." Hervey said meaningfully.

"Yeah . . . torchlight and a mixture of Catholicism and Voodoo and everybody got up like trick-or-treat!"

"You have lived long enough on the Island to know and respect our customs."

Hervey's voice was cold. Cass sighed, rubbed her nose. "Sorry . . . I always forget you are Island too . . . but you have to admit you've left a lot of it behind!"

"One *never* leaves the Island behind."

No, but you can stop its getting to you in the first place, Cass thought. Come to that—it *was* a screwy place from which to run a multinational, multibillion-dollar conglomerate, but then, Richard Tempest was known for doing screwy things—and making a thumping success out of them and causing a great grinding of teeth.

But Hervey was right . . . The Island was special to the Tempests; they had made of it their kingdom. It was a place out of the world, insulated from it, somehow, in spite of the telex communications, the radio telephone, the specially laid private lines, the airstrip, the fantastic house-cum-palace which dominated it. Hence Richard's funeral. Not back in England, from whence the family had come more than three hundred and fifty years ago; not in the United States, of which country he shared dual nationality and wherein bloomed the Organization's choicest blossoms; no, on this tiny island, twelve by five, population three hundred and some, an hour from Miami and ten minutes from Nassau by air . . . but in constant and direct communication with every single plant, office, and depot across the world which would watch it all on television. What else? thought Cass sardonically. Richard Tempest never intended he should be put away quietly. God knows, he didn't live that way . . .

"So," she shrugged, "an Island funeral it is."

"My dear Cass, if you and Helen Tempest cannot, between you, make of it a spectacle which no one who sees it will ever forget, then my name is not Hervey Wynston Grahame."

"Sure. Helen will 'suggest' but I'll do the work!"

"Don't play the martyr." Hervey was unmoved. "You are perfectly well aware you only have to lift any of those phones to have all the help you need."

His button-black eyes met her cornflower-blue ones head on. They were old and good friends, but in their jostling for precedence sometimes corners got knocked off. They were both "Outsiders," but Hervey had an advantage. He had been born on the Island. His family had worked for the Tempests since they had first come to the Bahamas after the American Revolution. Cass—a very *Im*proper Bostonian, as Dan called her, was still, in spite of thirty years' residence, not an Islander. You had to be born on it to be that.

"And now I must leave you," Hervey said.

"Where to?" Cass fired on all cylinders at once. All this work and he was swanning off somewhere . . .

"London," Hervey said. "The Bank called me. They have Richard's will . . ."

The silence echoed, but Cass caught the words that mattered. Will. Bank. London. "You didn't make it, then?" She sounded very, very surprised.

"No." He answered her unspoken question. "Richard did. And left it with Howard Watts until such time as it would be—needed."

Cass lit another cigarette with the stub of one she squashed out, grinding it to shreds, mind in top gear.

"Now why would he do that," she wondered. "Make his own will and not tell anyone—and put it out of the way in the Bank."

"Under seal," Hervey said expressionlessly.

Eyes met and held again.

"I don't know as I like that," Cass said finally.

Hervey shrugged. "Ours not to reason why . . ."

"That's as may be . . . you can bet your bottom dollar he'd have one. He always did."

"Precisely why I am going. To find out."

Cass shook her head. "Trouble . . . I can feel it . . ."

"You usually do." Hervey was very dry.

"*And* I'm usually right! I don't know where I get these premonitions from, I only know I get them—and I trust them! And, boy, have I got one right now. Something wicked this way comes, Hervey . . . you mark my words."

Tartly: "You were not misnamed at your christening," Hervey observed. "And *hers* all came true too . . ."

A knock on the door heralded more cables. "Oh, Jesus," Cass groaned. Then her eye fell on the top one. "Oh, no . . . that's all we need!" She handed it to Hervey:

MADAM IN HOSPITAL YOUR CABLE TERRIBLE SHOCK WHAT DO? JANNA.

"Sydney . . ." Hervey pursed his lips. "That's Robert Arnold's territory. He's a good man . . . get on to him and ask him to hold a watching brief; it could be anything or nothing with Mattie . . . but better play safe and do it now; if we put Richard away without Mattie she'll never forgive us."

Cass was already reaching for the telephone. Graphically she described the circumstances and gave her orders. "Keep one eye on her and the other on me . . . I want to know how she is and what she does, which in her state is liable to be anything. If she can travel she can come on the Organization plane with the rest of the Australian division; if she's not up to that, then we'll send the Lear jet—but whatever, wherever, I want to be kept informed at all times, understood? Good . . . I'll be hearing from you, then."

Hervey listened with a half-smile on his lips. Cass at her best and in her element; bossing people around. He had no qualms about leaving her in charge. She always was, anyway.

When he'd gone, Cass went back to her cables, but not for long. She heard voices, one of which she recognized. "Here we go," she thought, even as her office door was flung open and Margery, in deepest and most devastating black, made a grand entrance. A starkly simple black dress under a dramatic cloak lined with sable, a big brimmed hat shadowing a face which, try as it might, could not hide its triumph. She also reeked of Joy. Subtlety was never her strong point.

Cass leaned back in her chair, shoved her glasses up again, and raised her eyebrows. "Jesus!" she exclaimed. "You in mourning or something?"

Richard Tempest was buried at night, in accordance with Island custom; a hangover from an epidemic of yellow fever that had almost depopulated it some hundred and sixty years before, when those who died like flies had to be buried that same night. Necessity had become custom and a long-established procedure.

That of the Tempests held all the trappings of a solemn pageant. First of all, the Family of the deceased was conducted by torchlight procession to the estate-and-Family private chapel of St. John the Divine, five hundred yards from the house, built by Jonathan Tempest in 1820. There, a short service of thanksgiving was held because, on the Island, death was celebrated rather than mourned, and thanks were given for a fully lived life. Then the coffin was borne on a flower-bedecked island cart, again in procession, to the Family Burial Ground, on the slopes of the Hill, where there was much singing and readings from the Bible, after which the Family was conducted back to the house by the light of the torches and more singing.

So it was with Richard Tempest. At the stroke of nine o'clock, the great doors of Marlborough opened and Helen Tempest came out, followed by the Family and specially invited mourners. As Woman of the Island, she wore Island dress, a long skirt of vividly colored cotton and a pure white, pie-frill-necked blouse; so did every other woman. Under the light of the torches the throng was a blaze of color; scarlet and gold and green and purple, all dominated by the snowy white of headcloths. The men wore white trousers and multicolored shirts. There was no black.

Margery had thrown a conniption fit when she found that Richard was going to be buried according to Island custom. Her carefully chosen black would go unseen. But on reflection she had decided to make a stand-out impression; her Island dress was pure silk and Paris-made; the skirt an irides-cent blend of all the colors in a pool of petrol, and her blouse, exquisitely pin-tucked, was embellished with Valenciennes lace. Cass looked like an untied bundle but Nieves was sweetly virginal in pure, ice-cream white, her blouse of finely pin-tucked lawn. Mattie, who had arrived the night before, walking like a zombie and sedated unto stupefaction, had been got into her dress by Janna, but its barbaric colors gave her the look of a corpse dressed for disposal at Forest Lawn. Her flaming hair drained her face, and her enormous pansy-purple eyes were great bruises, panda circles of pain and exhaustion. David, whom Dan had sobered by forcibly holding him under a freezing needle spray, lurched on one side of Helen; Dan, superbly elegant in a masterpiece from Gieves and Hawkes, walked on her other side. Hervey hovered. Harry held the arm of his wife.

The procession parted like the Red Sea to allow the Family and their guests to take up position at its center. Then, at an unseen signal, it broke into spontaneous, full-throated singing as it moved off, lit by flaming torches as it wound its way slowly down the hill, weaving through the fabulous gardens of Marlborough toward the small church, its barbaric, torch-lit splendor followed every step of the way by the greedy eyes of the television cameras.

The coffin had been taken to the chapel earlier in the day; now, as the procession entered, the watching television audience drew a collectively amazed breath. The interior of the church was a dazzle of light and color; much white and silver, the altar ablaze with gold plate and tall white candles in silver holders under a glorious Caravaggio of the Annunciation. And, at the foot of the chancel steps, the coffin, draped in the Island flag, which was of the colors and bore the arms of the House of Tempest; scarlet and blue and gold. At its base were masses of flowers, great bursts of Island blooms; hibiscus and frangipani, oleander and jasmine; together with roses, lilies, orchids, and honeysuckle.

The moment Helen set foot over the threshold, the congregation swelled into Richard Tempest's favorite hymn: "Now Thank We All Our God."

The service was brief; simple but beautiful, a thanksgiving for a life. There was a lot of singing. The candles burned without a flicker in the heavy warmth of massed bodies—those who could not file into a pew stood in the aisles and around the walls; the gold of the altar plate blinded and the colors glowed.

Then the coffin was reverently carried by Island men out to the waiting Island cart, from which the oxen had been unharnessed to be replaced by several strong young men. The procession reformed as before, the coffin now at its center followed by Helen and the Family, to go farther down the winding road to the Old Burial Ground where more prayers were said, more readings from the Bible, the beautiful words of the King James Version. There was more singing.

But it was the final gesture, when all had been said, that caused a *frisson* in the watching millions and their eyes to blur. Helen Tempest stepped forward alone to take her place at the foot of the coffin, and there she stood, head erect, shoulders back, face a mask of calm serenity (a strong dose of Valium) while the people of the island filed slowly past her and the coffin she presided over, each one making obeisance; a curtsy from the women, a bow from the men, before laying their flowers on the coffin, from which the flag had been reverently removed. It made an unforgettable sight, and it was all done in total silence. At its end, Helen was hidden by the mountain of heavily perfumed, gloriously colored flowers.

And it was then, as the procession re-formed preparatory to departing, that Mattie broke. With a hoarse, despairing scream she tore herself from the supporting hands of David and Dan to hurl herself at the mountain of blooms, scrabbling desperately through them to get to the coffin, all the time screaming his name, sobbing wildly and hysterically and pleading with him not to leave her. The cameras were rooted to her. But even as David and Dan, after a moment's sudden shock, leapt forward to wrestle her away, the crowd had milled protectively, so that Mattie was obscured, and no one saw her picked up bodily and hustled away, only that when the procession finally reassembled, there was no sign of her.

Once more, the torchlit double line wound its way back up the Hill to the House. There Helen ascended the steps, turning on the topmost one, the Family grouped behind her, the invited mourners behind them, while the Island song was sung. Then, as if a giant hand had moistened finger and thumb, every torch was quenched, and there was only darkness and starlight. Richard Tempest's funeral was over.

THREE

Cass heard the music as she descended the stairs. Loud, brassy, with a driving beat. Herb Alpert at his best. She winced. Her head felt like a pulped melon and somebody had scraped down her throat with a wire brush. Too many cigarettes, too much to drink, and nonstop talking, but the funeral gathering had been an opportunity too good to miss. The cream of the Organization all floating under one roof; all ready to be stirred—it had already been shaken by Richard Tempest's death and his fantastic funeral—into just the right sort of mixture. So she had wielded a judicious spoon; circulating constantly, going into huddles, sounding opinions, prodding numbed brains.

At Cass's urging, Helen had given a splendid last-night dinner, and, already knocked out by the funeral, the Island, the incredible House, they were ripe for picking and laying in Cass's carefully woven basket. She had gone up to bed at four in the morning, dead tired but satisfied. She had been up bright and early to see the Organization jets depart after breakfast. Then she had gone back to bed. Ten minutes under a cold shower had brought her back to a fragile kind of life, which Hervey had proceeded to quicken by announcing that he intended to make known the provisions of Richard's will that night after dinner. Which was no doubt, she thought, feeling her way carefully down the stairs, the reason for the music.

It was. At the far end of the blue drawing room—so-called because there was nothing in the room that was not blue, from ceiling to carpet, all dominated by the Gainsborough of Serena Tempest, wearing ice-blue satin and a calculating expression—the Aubusson had been rolled back to allow Margery and Dan to dance on the polished wood-block parquet underneath. Margery had dressed for the occasion. Tight as a bandage and red as freshly spilled blood. Thousands of hand-sewn paillettes forming a glittering snakeskin, slit at the neck to the waist, allowing tantalizing glimpses of her unsupported but silicone-assisted breasts, and at the leg to the thigh, revealing her Dietrich-like legs, bare and deeply tanned, shod in stilt-heeled strappy sandals of scarlet satin. She was moving on ball bearings freshly greased with the oily slick of anticipated money, and she was high on martinis, Acapulco gold, and jubilation. Dan, not a hair out of place, was faultless in black (the only color a gentleman would wear) dinner jacket; matched her all the way. Any other time Cass would have been happy to watch them; they were both superb dancers. But not tonight. There was something positively indecent about their unholy glee. God knows, Marlborough should really have been named The No Holds Barred, but Richard had been in the ground only two days, for God's sake!

She stumped noisily over to the Buhl cabinet which concealed the stereo and made a sharp point of toning down the volume.

"Hey . . . what do you think you are doing?" Margery turned to scowl.

"We all know you are the Scarlet Woman," Cass said icily, "but isn't this ridiculous?"

"Just a little celebration," Dan drawled placatingly.

"Celebration! Am I to take it, then, that you know something I don't?"

Dan looked horrified. "Cass! You're not actually telling me there is something you don't know?"

"That will be the day!" Margery giggled.

"Every dog has one," Cass said, sweetly. Then, succinctly: "Even the bitches . . ."

Dan's mouth twitched but Margery only tossed her mane of hair. "Sticks and stones . . ."

"Come now, Cass," Dan said smoothly. "You know we've all waited for this glorious day . . . Don't tell me you're not expecting a little something?"

"What for? She doesn't need it." Margery said callously. "Where did you get your dress, Cass? Filene's basement?"

Dan's smothered laugh made Cass bridle. "Oh, but Cass is such a Very Proper Bostonian. And we all know how very careful they all are with money. The last thing they ever do with it is spend it!"

"If you had been a little more careful with yours, your tongue would not be hanging out so far for Richard's!"

"I am careful with everything!" he rebuked, hurt.

"Then stop counting your chickens! You might just turn out to have been sitting on golf balls!"

She took herself off to the lacquered Chinese cabinet that contained the bar. Martinis had already been made, she discovered. And drunk. Greedy sods! She set about making a fresh supply. With one inside her and another in her hand she retreated to the far end of the room, where distance lent disenchantment, sat herself down, and reached for the cigarettes. There was nothing wrong with her dress! So what if it was fifteen years old! She had had the sanctity of capital drilled into her from birth. Margery only believed in spending money. Dan only believed in money. But she still rubbed ineffectually at a dark spot on the port-wine velvet of her skirt, flicked at the neck ruffles. Good material lasted forever, she thought self-justifyingly.

When David came in his jaw dropped at the sight of Margery. "Jesus Christ! All she needs is a beard, then she'd be Father Christmas!"

"Ah, well, for them tonight is goodies time," Cass observed.

He went to pour himself his usual tumbler full of Jack Daniel's, brought it back and sat down beside her. He looked sober, but Cass knew how deceiving his looks could be. Still, she thought, if I know him, he'll get drunk *after* he knows how rich he is . . . Then he'll shower in Jack Daniel's . . .

Abruptly: "What do you know about this will of Richard's?" he asked.

"Nothing."

"I thought you always knew *everything!*"

"Not this time."

"Ah . . . that's why you're so crabby. Been left out, have you?"

"It's what's been left elsewhere that worries me."

"Don't you *ever* think of anything but the Organization?"

"*Is* there anything else?"

Outclassed as always by Cass's superior brain and word power, David could only retreat as usual, to vent his frustration on the dancers. "*They* obviously think so."

"*They* should know better where Richard Tempest is concerned."

David opened his mouth to ask what, for instance, closed it again as his daughter came in and retreated once more, this time physically, to a big chair by the fire, where he hid himself behind his bullfight papers.

Cass was scowling into her glass. All her alarm bells had rung when Hervey had revealed that Richard had made his own will. Wrong . . . they pealed warningly, wrong! With Hervey living on the premises! All right, so Richard Tempest had never trusted anyone, but Hervey was his lawyer, for God's sake, of thirty years' standing, privy to the most sensitive of business dealings. Yes, business, Cass thought. But this is personal. She felt the sofa give beside her, looked up to see Nieves, in a sweetly pretty white dress, buttoned to the throat and long at the sleeve, gazing with pursed-lip disapproval at the gyrating dancers.

"Hello, sweetie . . . Where have you been hiding yourself?"

"I've been to Mass . . ." And obviously thought Dan and Margery quite beyond redemption.

Nieves was a devout Catholic who never missed her daily devotions. The Tempests were a Protestant family, but her mother, Inés de Barranca, had been Spanish, of a family which had provided the Church with priests and nuns for centuries. It had been at their insistence that Nieves had been handed, at the age of nine, to the nuns of a convent which was part of the great basilica at El Escorial, where she had remained until she left it to go to Switzerland to be finished.

Except that, in Cass's opinion, it was the convent which had finished her before she started. She had been appalled when Helen had showed her the list of clothing required by the convent because, among the vests and knickers and plain navy serge dresses and thick stockings and flat-heeled shoes, there had been two "sacks." "Two what?" Cass had asked. "These . . ." Helen had said, showing them to her. They literally were sacks, with a drawstring neck. "They use them in the showers," Helen had said uneasily.

"What for?"

"They wash under them."

"They *what!*" Cass had fingered the material, thin enough to soak up water but heavy enough to conceal a wet, naked body.

"This is the first year they have been required," Helen had said. "Now that Nieves is twelve and has started her periods . . ."

"Jesus Christ! You mean from now on she is supposed to hide the fact that she's a woman?"

"It would appear so."

"For God's sake! What sort of a place is this? I know it is an enclosed convent but are their minds closed too?"

"It's what the Barrancas wanted . . . all the women of the family are sent there . . ."

"Does Richard know about this?"

"Yes. I told him."

"And what did he say?"

"He said Nieves was half Spanish and it was best to go along with the Barrancas for now. He fears they might start proceedings to acquire Nieves legally if he balked . . . He says she won't always be in the convent."

"But by that time the damage will have been done!"

And it had been, Cass thought now. Nieves was a sexual innocent and a moral prude. Not for her a brief bikini when sunbathing. The first time Cass had seen her in the plain, high-necked and high-backed navy wool swimsuit, she had gone and bought a brief polka-dot bikini and presented it to Nieves, who had looked horrified and protested: "Oh, but I could not wear that . . . it is sinful!"

"It is what?"

"It is wrong for women to flaunt their bodies . . ."

"Says who?"

"The nuns. Women should always be modest and discreet."

Which was why it had been a struggle to get her to wear shorts, or a strapless halter. In the six months Nieves had been in Switzerland, Cass had noticed a slight easing in moral strictures, but Nieves still dressed like a sixteenth-century infanta surrounded by guardian duennas. And when Cass had teasingly dubbed her "The Little Nun" she had been appalled when Nieves took her seriously and confided that she was thinking of becoming a novice. There was far too much of spiritual leavening about Nieves and far too little *joie de vivre.*

She had been brought up to regard the world as a sinful place, and was carefully shielded from the knowledge that she had an aunt known in the world as The Great Whore. The child was too young and too romantic. She spent far too much time on her knees in front of pretty statues of the Virgin. Well, one to another, Cass had thought. Not the slightest idea what life was really all about. Overprotected, hedged about by her grandfather's money and hemmed in by her mother's family's Catholicism. They lived in pious splendor in Madrid, the women dressed always in black and spending hours in church saying novenas for the men of the family seen off by the Civil War. Thank God, Richard had stood out against them when they had wanted Nieves permanently. It was bad enough when she came back from her summers with them. She tended to talk Spanish and was more dreamy-eyed than ever at the thought of becoming a bride of Christ. When she did not dream of becoming the bride of Dev Loughlin.

And that would not do either. Absolutely no way. Apart from the fact that he was old enough to be her father, he was a man of such all-pervading sexuality and powerful sensuality—of which Nieves, in her innocence, was totally unaware—that she would have fled screaming from the marriage bed. Not that Dev thought of her that way for a moment. To him, Nieves was the daughter of his best friend, whom he had dandled on his knee and carried on his shoulders. And being half Spanish himself—Nieves's mother had been his cousin—he understood her better than the rest of them. Her and everybody else, Cass thought now. I think it's time he paid us a visit. There is nothing to stop him now that Richard is gone . . .

Eyeing Nieves carefully, she could see from the outraged expression on her face that she was mentally crossing herself. No doubt she would spend an hour on her knees by her bed praying for two lost souls. All wrong! Cass thought exasperatedly. She should be meeting boys and going to parties. Between Nieves and the average teenager, who was on the pill and smoked pot, there was about as much resemblance as a baby lamb to a black panther. She should be having crushes on pop stars and slopping about in stained jeans and a T-shirt instead of high-necked shirts and skirts, though they had at last managed to get her into slacks, and she'd looked like she expected a bolt of hellfire for that! She spent far too much time alone or in church.

The only time Nieves showed signs of real life was when Dev was around, and that was a crush; heartbreakingly innocent and one-hundred-percent, triple-distilled romanticism. She could never cope with a powerhouse like Dev Loughlin unless she was wearing her rose-colored glasses, and by now whenever he appeared he was surrounded by a pink halo.

All your fault! Cass fumed, glaring across to where David was hiding behind his papers. If you took even a little interest in your daughter instead of leaving her to others, which he had done ever since he and Dev had returned from Cuba, David with a shattered jaw and beliefs to match, carrying a squalling baby and having left Inés six feet under. Even now, Cass did not know that whole story. All Dev would say was that it had been bad; that Castro had been holding them both, and that it had been Richard's money and Dev's persuasive powers that had set them free. After which, while David was having his jaw wired and Helen was preoccupied with the feeding and care of an eighteen-month-old baby, there had occurred the Great Schism, which had resulted in Dev's being placed at the top of Richard's shit list and his position as Golden Wonder Boy discontinued.

Cass had heard the row but not been able to pinpoint its reason. She had also known better, when she saw the look on Dev's face as he strode out of the house, which matched that of Richard when she went in to him, than to ask for it. It had to do with Inés and David and why Inés had taken Nieves and fled to that branch of the de Barranca family who lived in Cuba, only to be caught up in Castro's revolution and vanish in the holocaust. It was not until word was got to them that the de Barrancas, being aristocrats and Batista supporters, were being disposed of piecemeal that David made his first attempt to find them, backed by Richard's long and powerful arm and as much money as it took, Dev ostensibly going along as backup, though Cass had no doubt that anything accomplished would be due to him rather than David. It always was.

And now look where it had ended! David ignoring his daughter unless she was shoved under his nose, Nieves turning to the Church for supportive consolation when Dev was not around, and clothing him in shining armour when he was. It was high time something was done. *Had* to be done. Now that Richard was dead . . . God knows what *that* is going to mean, she thought. Because I don't . . .

She came out of her abstraction to see Hervey shepherding Helen into the room. But he does, she thought. She eyed him narrowly. Oh, yes, he knew all right. If he was a cat he'd be purring . . . Margery obviously thought so too, because she was across the room instantly, her eyes darting greedily here there and everywhere but Hervey's pockets for the magic briefcase. Which he was not carrying.

"I thought after dinner . . ." he said with uncharacteristic vagueness. Patience, to Margery, was a card game, and when she saw she had drawn the joker she fell back sulkily, had to sit and simmer while Hervey enjoyed his single glass of amontillado before dinner, chewed every mouthful of his food the statutory thirty-six times during it, then sat and drank his two cups of black coffee, his inch of Armagnac, savoring slowly, and smoked his one cigar of the day, chatting of this and that and anything but what he knew Margery was boiling to know.

Will you look at him, thought Cass. If I didn't know him better I'd say he's actually enjoying this. Any minute now he's going to pull a nasty surprise out of that briefcase and leave us all dying—and not with laughter. But she felt a jolt as Hervey, still showing mischief, turned to Margery to ask blandly: "If you would just ring for Moses . . ." She heaved on the bell rope so hard she could have swung from it, and when Moses came in, solemnly toting the briefcase like Pandora's box, her lips parted and her eyes took the shine from her diamonds.

But still Hervey took his time. With a nod to Moses and a gracious "Thank you," he proceeded to take out his half-frames and polish them assiduously, holding them to the light to ensure they were windowpane clear. Finally he set them on his rather long nose, after which he punctiliously restored his handkerchief to its pocket. Then and only then did he reach for the briefcase.

His performance—for that was what it was—had succeeded in convincing them all that they had front seats for a spectacle. Cass was convinced, more than ever, that it was going to be a circus. With them thrown to the lions. Look at them, she thought, scanning their rapt faces. Lit up like Christmas trees ready to light—and burn—their candles at both ends. There would be no Richard to curb their extravagance now; there had always been a chain on the silver spoon he had handed each of them before standing back to watch indulgently while they each dug a grave of debt.

But the dread which had laid skeletal fingers on her since learning how the will was made now enclosed her in a cold, damp fog. She did not know where she got her premonitions from; she was in no way psychic. She only knew that she got them and they were usually right.

"If we are all ready?" Hervey peered at them over his half-frames. Oh, yes, he is up to something. Something which will bring us down.

"Come now, Hervey," Dan drawled, smooth as best-butter icing. "We have been ready for this a good many years now . . ."

"Then I will begin."

He lifted the briefcase, opened it, took from it a long, legal-looking document which crackled like new money as he opened it out. Margery craned her neck from where she sat, saw it comprised several sheets of parchment. Damn, she thought. She had expected it to be short and sweet. All he had to his nearest if not dearest. But it looked as if he had made provision for the five thousand. Oh, well, she supposed he had to make some sort of gesture to long-serving employees and such like. There would still be lots left for her.

Hervey cleared his throat and she sat up straight, her face solemn, hands folded to conceal their greedy tension.

"This is the last Will and Testament of me Richard Dysart-Innes-Tempest of Marlborough Tempest Cay and by it I revoke all former and other testamentary dispositions heretofore made by me.

"Item: Whereby being sound of mind and body I do hereby make provision for the disposition of my estate both real and personal whatsoever and wheresoever after the due payment thereout of all due debts taxes and funeral expenses which may be outstanding at the date of my death in manner following.

"Item: All of which I die possessed both in the way of property real and personal whatsoever and wheresoever and all monies belonging to or forming part of my estate I do devise and bequeath in outright gift to my only child and natural daughter Elizabeth Sheridan whose history and particulars I attach in the form of an Appendix numbered One to this my will.

"Item: To enable my executors to carry out this my will I attach hereto a second Appendix numbered Two wherein they will find set out in detail all of which I die possessed and I do direct that any property both real and personal acquired since the execution of this my will be added by my executors to the said Appendix numbered Two and the whole made known to my aforesaid daughter Elizabeth Sheridan in that she may be apprised of the scope and nature of her inheritance.

"Item: I do hereby instruct and desire that should all or any of the members of my family by which I mean my sister Helen Victoria Tempest my stepson David Anson Boscombe my stepdaughter Margery Grace Boscombe de Sazerac Galitzin du Marigny-Lignes da Souza di Primacelli my stepson Danvers Adrian Godfrey and my stepgranddaughter Nieves María de la Paz Boscombe y de Barranca attempt to overset or countermand the provisions and explicit instructions of this my will then the information contained in the Appendix attached hereto and marked Three I do direct shall be produced to the Probate Court and used as evidence of my decision that they are in my considered opinion unfit to benefit in any way whatsoever from all or any part of my estate.

"Item: I do hereby appoint my lawyer Hervey Wynston Grahame of the firm of Harcourt, Grahame, Spenser and my Executive Secretary Cassandra Mary van Dooren to be joint executors of this my will and in the confidence that they will obey my instructions and wishes do direct that Probate having been granted in favor of my said daughter Elizabeth Sheridan they each receive from my estate the sum of One Million Dollars in recognition of their services on my and her behalf.

"Signed by the said Richard Dysart-Innes-Tempest as his last will and testament in the presence of those who in my presence and in the presence of each other have hereunto subscribed their names as witnesses this twenty-first day of February in the year One thousand nine hundred and seventy-one."

Hervey's legal drone came to an end and he lowered the will to survey them with some interest. The silence was thick enough to stand a spoon in. Nobody moved. They all sat as if newly turned out of their molds but still chilled to freezing point.

Margery broke it. She frowned, shifted irritably, then said in a long-suffering voice: "All right . . . I suppose it was too much to expect him not to have his little joke even on an occasion like this—but he's had it, okay? Now let's get on with the reading of the real will."

"This *is* the real will," Hervey said, very gently. "In fact, it is Richard's only will."

Her impatience gave way to incredulity which moved aside for shock. Dan, however, sounded smooth as ever: "In which case, I think we had better hear it all again, don't you? I mean—if this really is his last word . . ." His smile was all surface and no depth. "Once more, if you please, Hervey. This time with feeling."

But though Hervey did his best to color his words in the way an artist fills in a preliminary sketch, the picture remained the same: a nightmare.

It was David who brought it to life. He began to laugh. Wildly, almost hysterically, racked with disbelief and a precariously contained agony. He heaved and wheezed in his chair until Margery leapt from hers to deal him an openhanded crack across the cheek.

"It's no laughing matter! And as for you!" She whirled on Hervey, her scarlet talons plucking the will from his fingers and tearing it across, the halves into quarters, the quarters into eight pieces which she flung at him like confetti. *"That's* what I think of his last word! Lies! All of it—lies! *I* am Richard Tempest's daughter, do you hear? Me! Margery Boscombe—me! Me!" Spittle sprayed his face as she leaned forward, and her clenched fist struck her breast in time with the pronoun, making the paved bands of diamonds at her wrists splinter shards of dazzle. David sat with his hand to his face, looking dazed.

"That was only a copy," Hervey said imperturbably. "And allow me to correct your misapprehension. You are Richard Tempest's stepdaughter; a legal connection, no more. He has left his all to his own flesh and blood, my dear Margery. *Flesh and blood.* His own seed. His *real, true,* daughter."

"And bastard." That was Dan, down but not out.

"Even so . . ."

Riveted in place by facts, Hervey's confidence was unshakable.

Margery raised her arms in triumph like a boxer. "And everyone knows illegitimates can't inherit!"

"Only property that is entailed. This is not. Moreover, it has been specifically devised and bequeathed to her by name. Deliberately and with avowed intent—"

"—and malice aforethought!" Dan put in swiftly.

"I'll contest it!" howled Margery. "No no-name bastard is going to do me out of money I've sweated for, done handsprings through hoops of fire for, lied for, cheated for—even *fucked* for!" The word ricocheted round the room, making Helen wince and close fixedly wide eyes. "I'll take this to every court there is if I have to because it is my money—*mine,* do you hear?"

"One could hardly fail to," Hervey returned, nostrils flaring with distaste at her coarseness.

Dan held out a beautifully manicured hand. "That first Appendix . . . may I see it?"

Hervey went back into his briefcase, came out with a handful of copies. "I took the precaution of having copies made for each of you . . ." He distributed them like favors.

Cass held hers to her eyes but could not read. Everything was blurred, swinging crazily. She felt sick, dizzy, as if she had been clipped on the jaw.

"I think you will find," Hervey continued pleasantly, "that, as dossiers go, this one is almost inordinately comprehensive . . ."

Cass wiped her eyes on the hem of her dress, took a deep breath, shook her head and, blinking several times, began to read, could not control the jolting intake of disbelieving breath at what she did read.

"Jesus Christ! He must have had her gone over by the CIA!" And without my knowledge, she moaned silently. For the life of her she could not decide which was the more distasteful.

"I have to admit he has obviously gone to some pains," Hervey agreed.

"Yes, ours," Dan drawled. He shrugged, laid his down on his lap. "All right, so she exists. But in what shape or form?"

"This one . . ." Hervey had them all ready and waiting. Copies of a glossy, full-color ten-by-eight. Again they all stared and again it was Cass who moaned: "Jesus Christ . . ."

"What I think we may describe as a dead ringer," Hervey said helpfully.

Cass's hands were shaking so badly the picture blurred. Helen, after groping for her glasses, had congealed with the shock, while Dan sighed, regretfully. "Yes . . . that's his face, all right. It's hanging all the way up the stairs . . ." He glanced across at Helen, who was staring at it as though at a ghost. "It is also yours . . ."

But Helen did not hear. It was taking her all her time to see.

"Hair, eyes, features . . . yes, she's a Tempest all right." Dan sounded chagrined, but his face when he raised his eyes to Hervey was as calm as ever. "So . . . we know what she looks like. Now, may we also know what she has inherited?"

Helpful as ever, Hervey distributed copies of the Second Appendix. The stricken silence changed its quality, turned to a throbbing, not-to-be-borne agony. Margery moaned softly, while Dan's eyes narrowed slightly as they skimmed rapidly down pages littered with zeros. He had known Richard to be rich, but this was positively indecent! There could not *be* that much money . . . nobody had a right to own so much money—except me, he thought, feeling that knife twist as his mind registered the vast amounts of gold in Zürich and Hong Kong banks; the thousands of acres of prime real estate in every major city in the world; ditto thousands and thousands of acres of land; endless miles of railway; mortgages running into billions, armies of trucks, fleets of ships, endless forests, countless mines, and on and on and on and on . . . until the sheer quantity dulled the senses. Only one thing was not his to give away entirely: the Marlborough Trust, which funded the house. Helen still retained the ten percent left her by her mother. But *she* got the other ninety. And one hundred percent of everything else. Including us, he thought. "Really, there is absolutely nothing to your earning your million dollars, is there?" he asked Hervey bitingly.

"The hell with his million dollars!" It was Cass, rocking back and forth like a horse. "It's what he's done with the Organization! Given it away—that's what he's done . . . given it away! To a woman who makes her living as a photographer's model!" She turned a ravaged face to them. "Do you *realize* what he has done?"

"Oh, I realize everything," Dan assured her, "but, unfortunately, not in real terms."

"None of this is real," Margery moaned. "It can't be! How can it be? I don't believe it."

Dan laughed. "You had better believe it, my dear. We have been gypped—double-, even triple-crossed—not for the first time, of course—but for the last!"

"Well, I'm not going to stand for it!"

Dan shrugged again. "So sit! It makes no difference."

"There must be *something* we can do . . . there has to be . . . there just *has* to be."

"Like what?"

"We sue, of course! He was crazy when he made this will . . . we all know he was twisted as a corkscrew . . . so we sue on the grounds of insanity!"

Dan threw back his head and laughed. It was pure enjoyment but it made Margery shrivel.

"Oh, my dear Margery . . . that is indeed a pumpkin you carry between your shoulders. Richard Tempest insane! It would be like defaming God!" His laughter subsided and his face changed, became intent, calculating. "No . . . we don't sue. If you had any capability for sustained thought you would realize why. The will disarms and defangs us because it labels us as unfit. That, my dear stepsister, is the whole crux of this particular antimatter . . ."

Hervey had anticipated him, laid in the outstretched hand a sealed brown envelope. There was one for David too, and a third for Margery.

"Only three?" Dan's voice was dangerously soft.

"Richard knew that Helen would never engage in a public brawl over money, besides which she has her own. Nieves"—here for the first time Hervey glanced in her direction and they followed his eyes to see her, stiff and white and shocked in her chair—"is a minor and therefore unable to do so, while Cass is only an employee."

Cass went gobbler red, but she said nothing.

"And Harry is a stepson-in-law. Richard knew with whom he would have to contend . . ." And could do it with his hands tied behind his back, his expression said. But he was frowning as his eyes returned to Nieves, who looked as if a ton of bricks had not only hit but buried her.

Margery had ripped open her envelope, only to exclaim: "But these are copies!"

"The Bank has the originals. And instructions to release them only to the Probate Court in the event of their being needed as evidence."

Dan slit his neatly, read swiftly but inscrutably. It was worse, far worse than he could ever have planned for. In fact, he thought, it was disastrous.

David read his, then crumpled the paper before throwing it into the fire with a vicious jerk of the arm. "Nothing I didn't already know . . ." But he looked sick at being reminded.

"This is privileged information, of course?" Dan asked Hervey.

Hervey looked down his nose at such an asinine question. "And as such not to be used except in the event of contestation."

"Bastard!" moaned Margery.

"Only metaphorically speaking," Dan said absently. "It is the real one we have to deal with."

But how? It would have to be in some way that would circumvent this information's being released at all, never mind to a Probate Court. It would inevitably lead to his being indicted in another, much higher one . . .

Margery was a-shiver with panic. He had known all the time! Let her go on, sink deeper and deeper . . . knowing that. Feeling faint, she bent her head over her knees.

David watched his copy shrivel to black ash. I wish it was him, he thought. I hope he is in hell and burning, where he has had me all these years. As if I would ever allow . . . Never! Never! Not while I live. And that is something to be thought about . . .

Cass was seething with resentment. Only an employee, was she? Bloody cheek! She was as much a part of this family as any of them—more, even.

Where the hell did they think Richard got all his information from? Except for the most vital information of all. Cass felt betrayed. And hurt. Monstrously, mortally hurt. A sop in the form of co-executor. But she had no illusions about that either. That was to keep an eye on Hervey. Who always had both eyes on Helen. Helen, scythed like the rest of them, and who looked like it, had caught her right in the heart. But Cass had her own wounds to bind.

Margery had begun to snuffle and whine. "What are we going to do?" Her husband, who sat quietly in his corner, the only of them who had not expected to be invited from his corner to pick out his plum, now handed her his handkerchief, which she took without so much as a glance. "What can we do?" she moaned.

"What the hell can we do?" David demanded angrily. "It's all come apart at the seams, stupid!"

Dan laughed. "The family that holds together folds together . . ." But it was his papers he folded, carefully and neatly, before stowing them away in an inside pocket. "This has to be thought about. Carefully—oh, yes, very carefully indeed. Whatever we do, we must not rush into hasty and improvident action. Nor is there any point in holding a wake." He rose to his feet, surveyed them all. "But I give you fair warning"—pause—"I intend to hold an autopsy!"

The door slammed behind him, rousing Helen from her trance with a start. The movement jerked her upright, driving her hand against the needle protruding from her gros point so that it sank effortlessly into it. Stupidly she sat and stared at the bright blood which welled. With an exclamation Hervey had his handkerchief out and was dabbing tenderly. She just sat and let him. She looked dazed, concussed. When Hervey wrapped the handkerchief round her palm she just let it lie there. But the blood had dripped from it onto the photograph on her lap, smearing the beautiful face, dominated by eyes as large and green as her own, which stared out with a cold, hard, arrogant stare.

Hervey chewed his lip. Helen looked as if she had shattered internally. It was not one of her withdrawn stares; her eyes told him that. They knew what was going on and suffered because of it. It was not a retreat this time. Probably because, he thought—racked by pity—there was no place to retreat to.

Margery scrabbled her own papers together, clutching them haphazardly to her breast as though terrified anyone would see the awful things they contained. "Don't think you've heard the last of this!" she shrilled venomously. "I'm not standing by while some unknown bastard takes what's rightfully mine! Mine, do you hear! Mine! I don't give a damn what you say! It's mine!"

The door slammed so hard behind her that the Waterford chandelier swayed and tinkled, but for once Helen did not look up anxiously. She did not even hear it.

"Ring for Seraphine," Hervey said worriedly. "I don't like the look of Helen at all."

Cass turned her head, saw Helen's state of shock, heaved herself up from her chair and went to the bellpull.

Guilt was racking Hervey. He had been so intent on his own pleasure, on his delight in seeing their comeuppance delivered to those who had thought to lord it over everything and everyone else. He ought to have realized . . . this was something he should have communicated to her by degrees, or at least alone. It was too savage a blow for a woman of her sensibility and susceptibility. When Seraphine materialized silently, she took one look and Hervey quailed under her basilisk stare but said nothing, only picked up his briefcase and scuttled out.

Harry got up quietly, spoke for the first time, spreading his hands in a wholly Italianate gesture. "One never does expect the obvious thing," he said, in English that bore only the faintest trace of accent. Then to Cass, sincerely: "I am sorry."

Stonily: "You and me both," Cass answered. Then, in a voice that issued from behind clenched teeth: "Not the Organization, Harry . . . not the Organization." She sounded pitiful, ready to weep. Then, helplessly, hopelessly: "Why? In God's name, why?"

"I have been sitting trying to think of a reason, but there is only one, surely. She is his *daughter* . . . blood is thicker than proximity." His smile was twisted.

"Richard Tempest never gave a fuck for anything or anyone in his life!" Cass swore coarsely. "Spare me the hearts and flowers; he lacked the one and it is his sister who is so good with the other!"

"She is his *daughter*," Harry reminded, gently but inexorably.

"You mean he says she is!"

Harry picked up Cass's copy of the photograph. "No, her face says she is."

Cass looked at it. "And who the hell *is* she?" she asked bitterly. "Why did he let her be brought up in a Home? Why produce her now, like the ace of spades? Why keep her hidden all these years? And above all, why leave her the Tempest Organization? The *Organization*, Harry!" Her anguish, her distress, were palpable.

"All the better to surprise you with?" Harry asked, shrugging.

"Dan is right, as usual. This has to be gone over with a very fine-tooth comb. We do have to hold an autopsy. There is always an autopsy when there has been a murder . . ." Only the killer is already sentenced . . .

David had been staring into the fire, as though seeing pictures there. "Poor bitch . . ." he said suddenly. "At that, look what she is getting, apart from far too much money." He held up a hand, counted on its fingers with the other. "One house-worshiper, one jet-set groupie, one high-priced gigolo, one badly worn drunken failure, one Secretary of this or any other Year . . ."

"One Italian count, bought and paid for," Harry added expressionlessly.

David laughed, slapped his knee. "What more could any girl ask for?"

"Rescue?" asked Cass.

FOUR

Helen Tempest had always been a bad sleeper, and pills had early become part of her bedtime ritual. But this night even they could not draw a mercifully black veil over its monstrous events, relieve her spirit of its throbbing, merciless ache, soothe the fluttering sense of panic which kept her lying in wakeful darkness. After looking at her little Lalique crystal clock for the umpteenth time, seen it was almost three a.m., she knew there was only one way to gain peace. Perhaps for the last time.

She made no noise as she slid from her bed, reached for her négligé, slipped her feet into her high-heeled and befeathered mules. She had done it so many times before that it was all performed instinctively, unthinkingly, and in total silence. Seraphine slept within hearing distance, and always lightly.

The corridor was silent, its double doors closed on the occupants of the suites behind. She floated noiselessly past them, right down to the end, where she turned left into a cul-de-sac which ended in a magnificent pair of carved and gilded doors, white and gold, with handles in the shape of sea horses. She put both hands on them, turned slightly and leaned her weight; they swung open soundlessly. She closed her eyes and breathed, inhaling deeply the smell that was Marlborough: a compound of beeswax, pot-pourri, and flowers. She stepped through and closed the doors behind her. It was like an analgesic; she could feel all her knots loosen and fall away. Then she began her progress.

She switched on no lights; she did not need them. She knew every inch of every room, could have found her way blindfold if need be. Slowly she drifted through the rooms, fingertips touching and trailing as she passed, feeling the texture of brocade and satin, the richness of silk, the intricate filigree of carving and ormolu, the cold glitter of crystal and the polished surface of silver, her reflection gliding by vast mirrors in the manner of some sad ghost. She straightened a picture here, the position of a figurine there, bent her head to inhale the bouquet of the flowers massed in glorious profusion in superb porcelain vases or silver urns or crystal bowls, lifted the tops from brilliant, glowing Chinese jars to sniff at the fragrance of the rose petals within. Slowly she filtered through the glorious progression of rooms, saying a last good-bye to what she loved above all else. Since she had nothing else. Her lifework. A thing of beauty she had known, even as she created it, was never, would never be wholly and entirely hers. Oh, she had fought against it; concentrated fiercely on the present, when what she craved, ceaselessly, was positive assurance of the future. She felt now that she stood on a precipice, teetering, striving not to fall . . . She had lost it. It had been taken away from her and given elsewhere. To someone who had never seen it, did not know it, could never love it as she did.

So, lovingly, tenderly, she patted and caressed, smoothed and touched, feeling the serenity of its beauty soothe her sorely chafed spirit. The only sound was the faint ticking of clocks, the soft chimes as they struck the quarter hour. Moonlight fell pallidly onto polished floors, made sumptuous carpets glow, lit the deep pools that were great mirrors, pointed up the shine of highly polished furniture. The shadows were deep and the light clear. Without a sound she made her pilgrimage, finally ended up where her world had also ended, only hours before, ashes now, like those of the fire.

She stood there, and was swept by a wave of pain so fierce, so deep, that she had to bite her lips on a cry. Despair overwhelmed her, knocking her off her feet and into a chair—a favorite fruitwood bergère, upholstered in sapphire-blue Spitalfields silk. She clenched its arms tightly, gripping *something* until the wave of sick despair had passed. Then she sat, dejectedly, shoulders slumped. Automatically her fingers smoothed the silken weave, as she thought: I can't leave it . . . I can't . . . it is my life! How can I leave my life? Oh, Richard, Richard . . . what did I ever do to you that you should do this to me . . . You knew what Marlborough meant to me . . . it was you who encouraged me to immerse myself in it after . . . Her mind shied away like a terrified horse. No. Mustn't think of that. *Never*, think of that. That was dangerous . . . led to madness . . . it was all imaginary . . . none of it had happened anyway. Richard had told her that over and over and over again.

It was just that the face of the photographs . . . so like Richard and yet, not only astonishing but terrifying, even more like her own. It had been like looking at herself when young . . . Except *that* face was stronger. Uncompromising. You would not be able to fool *that* face. Its expression said: "I dare you to!" But it had been so strange, and for some reason it had sent her mind back to those days. No, she must *not* think of that. She had put it all behind her years ago; made an accommodation with her life. She would not remember a past—so real to her, so obviously imaginary to others—if she could have a future. But now she had no future. Perhaps that was why she was having to struggle against a resurgence of those dangerous, terrifying memories . . . her dreams, as she had come to term them. Better to concentrate on this reality, monstrous though it might be. On the hurt that was an open wound inside her.

You have destroyed it all, Richard, she thought, in one fell signature. The Family. The name of Tempest. When people want to know about us in the future they will go not to the history books but to the histrionics of the press. We will go down in history not as a family whose history was its pride and whose pride was its history but as the family who produced a notorious bastard. Three hundred years of honorable and noble tradition defaced by Richard's bastard . . . So he had surmounted his disability after all, and in doing so had created hers. But it was what he always wanted . . . *she* was his heir . . . a Tempest. Closing her eyes, Helen visualized the face of the picture. So like her own, young face but colder, harder. Arrogant. Controlled. Unapproachable. No hope there, no hope at all . . .

Suddenly she could bear it no longer. Without caring for noise, she fled, running into the hall, the chiffon of her négligé flying behind her as she made for the sanctuary of her bedroom, where her fingers went to the small cloisonné box which contained the little red capsules which could give her oblivion. She poured ice water, put two on her tongue—twice the normal amount —and washed them down. Then she dropped her négligé on the floor and crawled back into bed, drawing the silk sheets up and over her head, crouching in the darkness and praying for her own.

Across the corridor, Cass sat up in bed smoking. She had given up the attempt to sleep. There was far too much to think about anyway, and she was so frenetically disturbed, too churned up by a sick sense of hurt and dread that she knew it would be useless anyway. She was weighed down by a gloomy foreboding. And its name was Elizabeth Sheridan.

The copies Hervey had given her lay strewn all over the silk coverlet; she had gone through them word by word, weighing for emphasis, scanning for allusion, searching for clues, some insight as to how, where—and, most important of all—why. There had to be a reason. Richard Tempest always had one. He'd made this all so watertight, laid such careful plans; made it as clear as bright sunlight that he was determined on Elizabeth Sheridan taking up her inheritance unhindered by anything or anyone. Like Dan had said: with malice aforethought. And she, Cass, had known nothing, had been kept in ignorance. She, who had always known everything. It belittled her, reduced her standing and authority, lumped her in with the rest of the misfits. Left her standing impotently on the sidelines while the power was handed, intact, to a twenty-seven-year-old woman who made a living as a photographer's model! She writhed in her tumbled bed. The Organization given away! To a nobody. What had he been *thinking* of? Cass could not stand not knowing. She always had to know. She felt threatened when she didn't, worried and bit her nails to the quick, when she was not stuffing herself with food. Right now she was starving. But Dan's dig about her thirty pounds (and then some, she thought guiltily) of excess weight had stuck like a bur, so she resolutely forced her mind away from a couple of six-inch-thick cold-turkey sandwiches with coleslaw dressing . . .

Who the hell was this girl—well, woman. At twenty-seven she was no girl. Who *was* she? Who had been her mother? Why had she been brought up in a Home? Why had Richard not revealed her until now? And why the hell had he left her everything?

Once again she picked up the photograph, stared hard at the goddess-like face. Beautiful, she thought grudgingly, no doubt about that. She must make men slobber. Cold, though, snotty-nose disdainful, but that could be her stock-in-trade as a model—the type that stared at you insolently from the pages of glossy magazines, wearing a fortune in diamonds and dragging an equal fortune in sables along the floor with one careless, bejeweled hand . . . Yes, she looked that type, all right. But what the hell was Richard thinking about to leave her his *all!* More money than Croesus *and* Midas put together. He was thinking of hell let loose, that's what. If he was going there he was damned if he was going to travel alone. He never had liked being alone . . . And I don't like being left out on a limb, she thought. What I have to do is pry that saw from Miss Elizabeth Sheridan's tight little hand . . . Own the Tempest Organization indeed! How the hell can she do that? What does she know? I'm the one who knows it all. Me, Cass van Dooren, thirty years man and boy, the right and left hand of God. I know where all the bodies are buried. Christ, I helped bury most of them! I even dug the graves . . . Well, she thought, staring hard at the coldly beautiful face, you are not burying me! I've got too many years invested in this family and its fortune

. . . Besides, I've nothing else. Where else can I go? Back to Boston? She shuddered. No way! Teas at the Ritz and the Friday concerts and those boring weekends in Chestnut Hill. Never!

She lit a fresh cigarette from a stub and thought hard. What you have got to do, Cass, is see that she becomes aware of just how indispensable you are, that she needs you. It's one thing to own the Tempest Organization, it's something else to run it. She wouldn't know where to start. I know every inch of the way, and where it ends. If it comes to that, I'm running the damn thing now . . . have been ever since Richard died. I'm the one who has kept wheels turning and noses to the grindstone.

She leveled a hard look at the photograph. You don't know it yet, baby, but mine is the one nose that is not going to be pushed out of this joint! But what did he know about you that we are going to find out? What are you? Stupid? Crafty? Calculating? Greedy? Frightened? No, never. Not that face. *She* frightened *you*. Still, she was *in* for a frightener all right. To find out your father was "King" Tempest and had made you the richest human being who ever lived . . . let's see how you handle *that,* she thought. And while you are doing that I'll see how to handle you. I've survived thirty years by always making it my business to *know* . . . Richard always did. And look where it got him! No, she thought, I'm not giving up being Executive Secretary to God. I like the job. Even if Marlborough is full of fallen angels. I left Katherine Gibbs as the Best of my Year and I've never looked back since. The view is too good this high up; I intend to keep it. What you have got to do, Cass, my girl, is get her to ask you to . . .

Margery was not in bed. She was pacing restlessly, pausing now and then to flick through the papers spread out on her bed, as if in the interim they might have changed. She had ripped up the photographs and burned them, along with the list of names. All right, so the bank held the negatives; they were still too dangerous to leave lying around. And it was all *his* fault; *his* damned, spiteful, deliberate fault. *He* had started it all off.

Lying back on the bed, she stared up at the painted ceiling and thought back to that summer of her mother's marriage to Richard Tempest, the handsomest, most virile, most exciting man Margery had ever set eyes on. He set her mouth to dribble and her loins to itch. She had been sixteen that summer, just coming into her own, voracious sexuality and looking for ways to satisfy it. Like that gorgeous young footman seen bathing nude. Margery's mouth had watered at the sight of his café-au-lait body, the broad chest, tight, firm ass, and the goodies he carried between his legs. She had waited till he threw himself down on the beach, a-glitter with drops of seawater her tongue had ached to lick away from the thick, pendulous penis and tight, firm balls.

He had been easy meat; given her an appetite for more which she had satisfied as and where she could. Until Richard found her stuffing herself in the little beach cottage he had later given to Dev Loughlin. The boy had fled, but Margery had lain back insolently, exposing her sweat-streaked body to Richard's openly frank gaze. He had laughed, put his naked foot right between her legs and stirred deliciously, making her squirm with delight. "You're a greedy one, aren't you? Always ready and willing . . . what's the matter? Can't they satisfy you once and for all? You don't seem able to get enough of this." He had taken her hand, pressed it into his naked and bulging crotch, having shucked off his shorts, and Margery had it in her mouth before he could move. But he had put her away. "Greedy, greedy . . . I can see I shall have to teach you how."

And he had. Everything. He had been the most marvelous lover. Ever. Never had she fallen through so many wrenching, tumultuous orgasms as with him. All that summer they had been lovers, the whole thing spiced by the fact that he was her stepfather; her mother's husband . . . And nobody, not even busybody Cass, so much as suspecting . . . Oh, how they had laughed. Until she told him that she was pregnant.

"By whom?" he had asked coolly.

"You, of course!"

He had smiled. "Not I, my dear Margery. You have had a dozen other men apart from me . . . oh, yes, I know about them all. That lifeguard over at Miami . . . that great hulking fisherman over on Mango Cay, the croupier in the Casino in Havana, every member of the orchestra at the Everglades Club. God knows whose child it is. I only know it is certainly not mine."

And she had shivered, frightened for the first time, seeing what sort of a man this really was. Really terrified when he had gone on: "And don't try anything, or I'll cut you off from not only all that money you love so much but all that sex too . . . oh, I'll be full of such moral disapproval. My stepdaughter a whore! And you are hooked on them both, aren't you, because one buys the other. Is that why you forged those checks?" He had laughed, then, at the consternation on her face. "You are sloppy, Margery. If you're going to steal do it with style . . . piddling little amounts here and there will always be found out, as I have found you out. Now then, the question is, what are we going to do about it . . ."

The question had been resolved by his making her enter into the first of her five marriages. Each one to a man who had something Richard wanted and hid some guilty secret which she found out and he used as blackmail. And then their property had passed into his hands.

Her own perks were titles; becoming by turn a Duchesse, a Princess, a Marquise, and a Contessa, and, best of all, the World's Best-Dressed Woman. All on the money Richard allowed her to spend with wild, unbridled extravagance. She paid the bill by letting the men he chose use her body.

Her fifth husband had been her own choice. She had been at a low ebb, recovering from an abortion that had not been as easy as the others—probably because she had been introduced to drugs. Harry had not been like the others. He had been kind. And she could not stand kindness. She was not used to it. She had married him on impulse and regretted it as soon as she took him to bed; even more when he took her back to Tuscany to that godawful palazzo of his stuck out in the wilds, where she had been expected to live with his harridan mother and gorgon sisters.

She had bolted at once, taking with her the (entailed) di Primacelli jewels, which she had sold. And there had been hell to pay. Because the jeweler, recognizing her, had contacted Richard, who had bought them back, much to the consternation of the family. In doing so, he had discovered they were fakes. Harry had sold the real ones immediately after the war when he was desperate for money and had reproductions made, in the manner of Italy's other religion: *bella figura*.

Her mother-in-law and sisters-in-law were beside themselves with rage. How could they ever hold up their heads again, etc., etc. Margery paid no heed to them: she had enough to contend with. Like the fact that, as a punishment for marrying Harry, she was to remain married to him. Richard had bought back the jewels and given Harry, outright, their real value, in return for his promise never to divorce Margery. He had punished them both: Harry, by giving him the money he so desperately craved for his estates; Margery, by tying her forever to a man she despised. And he had the di Primacelli family forever on hooks too, because he knew they were living on face.

He always had you tied, Margery thought dully. The more you squirmed inside your bonds the more tightly you tied yourself. He was dead and she should be free, *feel* free. Yet here she was, still bound hand and foot; unable to reach out now, for Andrea. Oh, God! A sob burst from her. She would never have Andrea now . . . now, when she needed him so. She could feel the crab inside her, gnawing away; the burning, maddening itchy heat between her legs that only Andrea could ease. But she could not afford him now. She would never be able to afford him. He would go to that hard-faced cosmetics queen instead. She turned her face into the bed and wept until her face was a blotchy mass, but even when the tears stopped she still gripped the coverlet with her talon-like fingers, feeling the gnawing growing steadily worse. There was only one way she could subdue it.

Dragging herself up, Margery reached toward the little gilt table by her bed, opened the drawer, took out a small box and a tiny silver spoon. With shaking hands she poured a tiny pile of fine white powder into the spoon and placed it against one nostril while closing the other with a finger before breathing deeply. Then she repeated the process with the other nostril. At once, she felt a clean, white blast of excitement, as though a rocket was carrying her upward, then a brilliant explosion inside her head, then a delicious, tingling, soothing languor. Falling back on the bed, she closed her eyes, went totally limp, and drifted away.

Dan was in bed but he was not sleeping either. He was lying with his hands behind his head thinking, thinking, his cool, subtle mind weighing and evaluating. And the only thing he could find in his favor was that Richard's heir was a woman. His own, dear stock-in-trade. Which made it even more imperative that he knock her down from her perch. Which, if he knew anything at all about women, would already be shaky, because from the top of her pile of money it was a long way up and she had probably never been so high before. He had to get to her while she was still swaying. But how? How? His hands were tied because of Richard's flat condemnation of him as unfit, and his tongue because of that damned dossier.

You made a bad mistake there, dear boy, he reflected. You ought to have allowed for the fact that when it came to keeping tabs, Richard Tempest's breath coated you in luminous paint.

The trouble was, he decided, that she was an unknown quantity. But so was uranium until they split the atom. Somehow, he had to find a way to split *her*. Right down the middle if possible. Well, he would have to wait and see, then decide. He sat up, thumped his pillows, throwing one away because he never slept on more than one, then lay down again, composing himself for sleep. After all, he reflected, as he closed his eyes, there is no possible use in crying over spilt milk that has already soaked into the carpet . . .

High at the top of the house, David Boscombe was sketching, for the first time in years. He had set up his easel, managed to scrape up some odds and ends of crayon, and, with the photograph propped up against the Jack Daniels bottle, was attempting a sketch of Elizabeth Sheridan's face. He was working carefully, painstakingly, but the result was lifeless.

With an oath he seized the paper and ripped it apart, the old anguished frustration flooding through him. It was no use. What the hell was he doing wasting his time? It was gone. Not that there had been much in the first place . . .

Grabbing the bourbon, he upended the bottle and drained it off before hurling it at the wall.

"Damn him! Damn him to bloody hell!" It was a bellow of brute pain. "If there is any justice, that is where he is right now!"

Two floors below, his daughter lay in tear-stained and exhausted sleep under a candle-lit statue of the Virgin. In her sleep she sobbed dryly and deeply, and her hands were clenched around the rosary twined through her fingers as she murmured brokenly: "Dev . . . oh, Dev . . . Dev . . ."

FIVE

Hervey paid off the taxi on the corner by Lord's Cricket Ground. In spite of the pouring rain, innate caution bade him walk the remaining few hundred yards to his destination. That way, anyone seeing him—highly unlikely at this time and on such a night, but it paid to be careful—would not be able to say for certain where he was going, or that the briefcase he carried contained the information about which there had been so much endless newspaper speculation of late.

Hoisting his umbrella and hefting his briefcase, he paused while the taxi drove off, only to leap back with an imprecation as it sprayed him with the water from an overflowing drain. Shaking his soaked trouser legs he looked both ways before crossing the road, shoes squelching. Oh, not to be in England now that April's here, he thought gloomily. His mood was morose. He had had an irritating day, constantly punctuated by phone calls from the press asking for interviews, comments, and/or statements. Even the BBC had wanted him to appear on a chat show to expound on the legend of the late, great Richard Tempest. He had turned them all down. His official reason for being in London was the valuation for Probate of the European Division of the Organization. His frustration arose from the fact that his real reason never answered her phone.

He had been calling her at almost hourly intervals for the past three days. Only tonight, finally, had he obtained an answer. It had all made him out of reason annoyed; at the delay, at her indifference to it, at the weather, at the fact that it was eleven-thirty at night, that he had been on tenterhooks for the past three days. They had all combined to leave him feeling rather more than badly done by.

He paused to check the name of the road which ran off to the right. About halfway down he could see two white globes lighting an entrance forecourt. That must be where she lived. The name on the brass plates affixed to the pillars supporting the lamps confirmed it. Waverley Court. Shades of Sir Walter Scott, he thought sourly, skirting a large puddle. Holding his dripping umbrella carefully away from him, he entered the brightly lit lobby. A uniformed porter rose from behind a desk, put down his paper.

"Good evening, sir?" He eyed Hervey pleasantly but probingly.

Damn! thought Hervey. He had hoped to slip in and out unnoticed. But a porter . . .

"Good evening," he replied, in his Supreme Court manner. "Miss Elizabeth Sheridan, if you please. My name is Grahame. I am expected."

"Right you are, sir." The porter turned away to a small switchboard, inserted a plug. "Miss Sheridan? Gentleman by the name of Grahame to see you—yes, right away."

"You are to go straight up, sir. Fifth Floor. Number eighteen. Lift's right behind you . . ."

"Thank you."

The lift was lined with pink Art Deco glass and decorated with a large brass urn filled with artificial flowers. Hervey sniffed, contrasting Marlborough's fresh-daily blooms. The whole building had a prewar, Astaire-Rogers musical setting, as though it was lived in by men with patent leather hair and women with marcel waves.

Number eighteen was a plain white door with a card in a brass holder bearing the name SHERIDAN. No indication as to the sex of the occupant. It annoyed Hervey for no good reason. This whole damned business was like those Russian dolls Richard had brought back from Moscow for Nieves. Every time you took one apart there was another one inside. And Cass's ceaseless jeremiad since the reading of the will now came back to haunt him. He had the hollow feeling that, once again, she was going to be proved right.

"What and how and why and when, Hervey," she had finger-wagged him. "I am black and blue from stumbling around in the dark. Let in some light as soon as you can—and whether we are to be truly thankful for what we are about to receive . . . which I doubt. I know you will do your best, but, quite frankly, I am expecting the worst."

Which Dan Godfrey made it plain he was expecting him to do. "After all," he had said smoothly, "you are getting first go, Hervey. Virgin territory and all that sort of thing." A snide smile. "I am speaking metaphorically, of course, and while we all know you are as square as a city block," he went on virtuously, "we are also well aware of your positive Pisa-like leaning toward the—shall we say?—distaff side of this family. Please remember we are all having to lean over backward to accept all this."

"I know my duty," Hervey had returned acidly.

"And will do it!" Dan looked shocked. "Just so long as you don't stitch away at that bias of yours."

His smooth needling had pricked Hervey's conscience. "You are the one who is the expert at stitching up!"

"But I don't wear Miss Helen Tempest's favor . . . You will leave it off, won't you, when you go calling on Miss Bastard?"

Thunderously: "I deal in facts, not fiction!"

A sunny smile. "Fine. That leaves me free to tell my own story."

Even Margery had wanted him to pretty up hers. "It won't hurt to put in a good word or two, Hervey," she had wheedled. "God knows, we need them . . ."

But it had been Helen who had really dismayed him, made him uncomfortably aware of the truth of Dan's creamy words.

"I know you will do your best for us all," she had murmured, but her magnificent eyes had burned into his, branding him with their meaning.

Everyone queuing to grind their axes, he fulminated, stabbing his finger at the bell. Well, I am damned if I am going to wield any of them . . . The door opened and he felt every single one of them smash into his skull.

He had been prepared for the model; he had not expected to be confronted by the finished statue. He stared. She held it. His hat was in his hand instantly.

"Miss Elizabeth Sheridan?"

She eyed him up and down at her leisure. "Mr. Hervey Grahame?"

His bow was courteous, old-fashioned, and a strictly reflex action since his mind was wandering around in a daze, having run smack into a wrong premise.

"Come in." She stepped back to allow him into the small square hall, which she dominated, even as she dominated him. Truth to tell, he thought dazedly, she was magnificent! Nothing in her dossier, not even her photograph, had prepared him for the immensity of her reality. He groped around in his disordered mind for the factual description it had contained. Height: 6 ft. Weight: 150 lbs. Hair: Blond. Eyes: Green. Complexion: Fair. The understatement of this or any century, he thought. If her measurements were

unfashionably large for this thin-is-beautiful obsessed age, there was no doubt
that her face was her fortune. Yet you were not conscious of size, only of
grandeur. She was queenly. Statuesque. Or was it Junoesque? There was more
than a hint of the goddess about her, from the long fall of green silk that was
the caftan she wore, to the way her heavy blond hair was piled, à la grecque,
atop her exquisite head. She was possessed of an awesome regality and a
stunning physical splendor. Right out of Mount Olympus, Hervey thought
bemusedly. He could not take his eyes from her, only came to, with a start,
when she took his dripping umbrella from his nerveless hand and dropped it
into a stand.

"I am sorry . . ." he made the apology hastily. "Most inclement weather.
It always seems to rain when I come to London."

He fumbled with buttons, nervously straightened an already mathemati-
cally precise tie while she hung away his hat and coat, then trailed her down a
short corridor into a warehouse-sized living room, all deep shadows and stark
white light, but warmed by the fire he craved. Everything seemed to be
either unadorned white or various shades of green: walls, ceiling, white; carpet, furniture, and myriad plants in tubs, all green; white rugs scattered on a
wood-block floor the color of honey, and velvet curtains only slightly deeper
than the color of her eyes: true emerald. Arched alcoves on either side of the
fireplace were crammed with paperbacks, one corner held a stereo music
center, the other a color TV. Above the fireplace hung a Bruegel print—all
scarlets and golds and browns—and in front of it stood twin, two-seater sofas
upholstered in a green velvet so dark as to be almost black. She disposed
herself in one of them; only then did he sit gingerly on the edge of the other,
after hitching up trousers on the crease of which she could have sliced bread.
Then he frantically scrabbled for his scattered wits.

"I apologize for the lateness of the hour," he began, was appalled to find
himself out-Uriah-ing Mr. Heep—"and for the necessary . . . ambiguity of
my call, but all will be explained, I do assure you . . ." It was her effect. It
sent him scuttling for the only cover he could find: his calling.

"Before we begin"—his fingers quested a pocket of his vest, across which
was draped a gold watch-chain from which depended a small, pink pig—"I
think we should first of all establish identities. This is mine." His card was
best-quality three-sheet board, deeply and expensively engraved, matching his
upmarket appearance. Bespoke tailoring, the face of a presiding judge, a
narrow greyhound skull over which boot-polish black hair had been combed
so scrupulously it looked as if it had been painted on, button-black eyes, still
bearing the glaze of shock, a closed-purse mouth.

He saw her run a thumb over the fine calligraphy: *Hervey W. Grahame*

Harcourt, Grahame, Spenser, Attorneys at Law, with a Bay Street, Nassau, address.

She raised her eyes to him. They felt like ice cubes rubbed over his flesh. "And what does a Bahamian lawyer want with me?" Her voice was as cool as she was; crisp as newly minted notes.

"I will come to that in a moment, if I may. First of all"—Hervey cleared his clogging throat—"if I might ask you some personal questions? Merely to corroborate certain information already in my possession."

Her regard was inscrutable. She had eyes that could have been placed in claw settings. He forced himself to meet their gaze head-on, not to be intimidated. He had the impression of a shrug, although she did not move. "Ask away."

No nervousness, he noted. Not much interest, either. Only a total composure. That it was late at night, that he was a stranger, was of no matter. He had the feeling that she felt she could handle anything. He groped in his pocket for his glasses. Through them she was even more magnificent. What a presence! A goddess indeed. But had not her father been a Greek god? He cleared his throat once more. She must think him a fool, fumbling around like a callow youth instead of a man approaching sixty. He rose to cross-examine.

"Your full name?"

"Elizabeth Sheridan."

"Where and when were you born?"

"Here, in London. New Year's Day, 1947."

"Are your parents living?"

"My mother is dead. I cannot tell you about my father. I am illegitimate."

And didn't give a damn. Hervey was left in no doubt as to the unimportance of that detail. All that mattered was what she was, not who her parents had been.

"You have no idea who he might have been?"

"None."

Hervey lit the blue touch paper and retired: "That is what I have come to tell you."

Silence. Then she said: "Indeed," with absolutely no reaction.

"It is indeed so," Hervey replied warmly, his sleek primness ruffling its feathers. Upending his briefcase—softest leather in whose gleaming surface she could have made up her face—he spun its combination locks, lowered it to raise the lid, extracted from it a folded newspaper, which he leaned across to hand to her. It was a two-week-old copy of the New York *Times*, banner-headlined above a picture of a handsome, laughing man: "KING" TEMPEST

DIES. She examined it in a silence which Hervey sensed had changed. He had an impression, which gave him goose bumps, that her every hackle had risen.

But: "Him?" was all she asked, and for a moment he could have sworn her voice trembled with laughter.

"Him." Now he trembled, and with anger.

Another silence. She used them like weapons. They skewered you, hoisted you, left you dangling.

"Says who?" she asked calmly.

"He does."

"Since when—and where? He is dead."

"Exactly!"

He met her eyes meaningfully. Again he felt the ice cubes being rubbed over his body. Then a very faint, sardonically unholy smile flickered over the chiseled lips, and she said: "I see . . . You are his lawyer, of course, and what you have come to tell me is that he has acknowledged me as his long-lost daughter and has left me his all."

"That," agreed Hervey, neatly avoiding the blade, "is exactly what I have come to tell you."

This time the silence stretched.

"So tell me," she commanded.

He went back into his briefcase. His hands were trembling. She had that effect. Her father had had it too. The ability to dominate any gathering, mesmerize you with the force of a brilliantly compelling gaze, but whereas he warmed, so that you melted, she chilled, left you shivering.

"This will explain everything," he said.

She read with the speed of light. His eyes went involuntarily to the tightly packed paperbacks, a motley collection of everything. Then his eyes went back to her. It was not possible to leave her for long. The spot which lit the Bruegel caught her in the gauzy edge of its light, where it was softened to a glow, and it turned an already-white skin translucent. Her neck was long, so were her arms and legs, but in spite of her size she was graceful, though she did not so much as move as make progress. Normally, he classified women as girls under thirty, women over. This one did not fit either classification. She was young in years, yet agelessly old. That was it, he thought. There was nothing "young" about her.

Finally she looked up. "This is legal?"

"I beg your pardon!" Thirty years of unblemished reputation loaded the words with outrage, but they weighed nothing with her.

"I am illegitimate."

Hervey's face cleared. "Ah . . . you are thinking of the question of entail, but there is no bar against illegitimate issue as named beneficiaries—as you are. Furthermore, there is no question of entail involved. What your father has left you was his, only his and entirely his, to leave. And he has chosen to leave it to you."

"Why?" It was flat, unimpressed.

"I have no idea. I deal in facts, not speculation."

This time her smile was approving. "So do I."

"And these facts are true."

"Whose truth?"

"Yours, of course."

"Prove it."

"You *are* the proof."

"A resemblance proves nothing. Isn't everyone supposed to have a double somewhere?"

"In your case it is more than resemblance; it is duplication. You have your father's height, his hair, his eyes—his face. However, if it is the absolute proof you require, I would refer you to your left foot."

Holding his eyes she slowly uncoiled her left leg from under her body, holding it out so that her foot protruded from her caftan. It was bare; long, narrow, high-arched. And webbed at the toes.

"The Tempest foot," Hervey pronounced from the bench. "Your father had it, his sister has it, they had it from their mother who had it from her father and so on back for generations. It is the unmistakable sign of the true Tempest . . ." His closed-purse mouth opened to disgorge one true-coin smile. "Now do you believe me?"

Not yet, she didn't. "You said my father got it from his mother . . . how come, if it is the mark of a true Tempest?"

Hervey tipped her another, larger smile. "Because she too was a Tempest. Of the English and senior branch . . . Lady Eleanor Tempest, the only daughter of the twentieth Earl Tempest. You are, therefore, a double Tempest, so to speak . . ."

She tucked her foot under her again and he watched it go with regret. Her caftan was high at the neck and covered her completely, but he had been aware from the start that underneath it she was naked. He averted his eyes from the nipples outlined by the green silk as it was pulled against her body by the way she sat. She was sublimely indifferent. But her smile was mysterious.

"Curiouser and curiouser," she commented. Then she stood up in such a way as to make him blink. "I think a drink," she said, telling not asking. "Whiskey?"

"Please . . . no ice. My Montrose ancestors," he explained.

"You are not American, are you? There is a trace of accent."

"I was at university there, but I was born on the Island."

She brought him a liberal libation of what turned out to be a superb single malt which he sipped gratefully, feeling it warm and encouraging. She had the same.

"So . . ." She resumed her chair. "Having acquainted me with your true facts, suppose you now read me the fiction."

"I beg your pardon!"

"Reasons, Mr. Grahame. There are always reasons. Or was Richard Tempest a man with no use for them?"

"By no means! He would have them. He always did."

"Then what were they? Why me? Why now? Why everything?"

"I have no idea. He did not take me that far into his confidence."

"But you were his lawyer?"

"I was. For thirty years. But in this matter he divulged no secrets."

She leaned forward to pick up the will from the glass-topped coffee table which stood between them. "It says here," her eyes scanned rapidly, " 'to my . . . daughter Elizabeth Sheridan whose history and particulars I attach in the form of an Appendix . . .' Where is that?"

He had it ready. Again, she went through every word, but all she commented was an unemotional "Very comprehensive." She eyed him reflectively. "He went to some pains."

"Indeed."

"But I still don't know why."

"And I cannot tell you. I had no hand in obtaining any of that information. The only hand in all of this is your father's. He was a lawyer too, though he never practiced. He kept up his membership in the Law Society and was amply qualified to make his own will. Many lawyers do. And this one is a model. Very clear, quite precise. I shall have no hesitation in presenting it for probate."

"When?"

"Impossible to say. The estate is very large, very diversified . . . valuation will take months rather than weeks."

"Just how rich was he?"

This time Hervey's smile glittered. "Would you believe Croesus?"

"If you say so . . ." Totally unimpressed. Hervey felt himself becoming angry. It was like trying to penetrate a plate-glass window with a needle.

"He seems to have played his cards very close to his chest," she observed.

"Well, you were his ace in the hole . . ."

For the first time she laughed. It changed her face. "But I've won the pot!"

Not surprising, thought Hervey looking at her. But all he said, noncommittally, was: "Sometimes life is a game . . ."

"So what was he playing at here?"

"I have no idea."

She mulled silently once again, then, quite suddenly: "I suppose he was quite sane?"

Hervey hissed: "Miss Sheridan, if genius is as they say, an endless capacity for taking pains, then your father was indeed a genius. At the time he made his will he was engaged in the acquisition of some fiercely contested trade concessions. The competition was cutthroat and the stakes enormous. He scooped the pot and left the table without a mark on him. No man capable of bringing that off could be said to be any other than in his right—and exceedingly bright—mind!"

Unruffled: "I see," she said.

"Why are you objecting?" he asked bluntly. "Why are you so obdurately hard to convince? Don't you wish to accept Richard Tempest as your father? Don't you wish to accept the truth I am telling you?"

"Would you?"

He attacked directly. "Is it perhaps that he abandoned you as a child? Surely he has more than made up for that now. He has acknowledged you publicly, and in the most generous of ways. It is possible, you know, that he did not know about you until late in your life, but having discovered you set out to find out about you, and having done that took steps to make up to you for all that had been lost . . ." Richard, he thought, you should hear me now. "Do you want to be rich?" he pursued. "Do you want to be acknowledged to the world as the only child of Richard 'King' Tempest?"

"I know who I am," she said. And don't want to be anyone else, was the implication. "But I would like to know who *he* was . . ."

"A most remarkable man. But before I tell you, how much do you know already?"

She rose to her feet again, held out a hand for his glass, which he drained before handing it over.

"Only that he was very rich, very powerful, a legend in his own time. That he owned half the world but lived on a tiny island in the Bahamas. That he lived a very public life while maintaining the island as a very private domain. That he had a fabulous house on it; that he was sole owner of the world's largest multinational conglomerate; that he was married twice—each time to widows—and had stepchildren, but not one of his own . . . Gossip column fringe benefits, no more . . ."

Than enough, thought Hervey, but: "All true," he agreed, "though only the fringe, as you say. To understand your father you must first understand his family." He sipped at the fresh malt she handed him. "They are English by descent, both remote and immediate. Your father's mother was a cousin many times removed of her husband, the only daughter of the twentieth Earl who was descended—as was your grandfather on your father's side—from the tenth Earl, who was a personal friend of James I and received from him the grant of a large tract of land which is now the State of Virginia. His name was also Richard Tempest and he had two sons; it was the younger son, Richard, who settled in Virginia and founded the dynasty. He is known in the Family as the Founder. He became a great colonial lord, built himself a fine house which legend attributes to Sir Christopher Wren, and the Tempests became the greatest of colonial families, aristocrats who were appalled by the American revolution. They were Tories—loyalists. They had no sympathy with what they saw as a motley rabble of discontented tradesmen and hothead lawyers. To the Tempests, George Washington was no more than a surveyor they had once employed. Their loyalty was to England. Thomas Jefferson was their archenemy. He abhorred—and abolished—all they stood for. And when the then head of the House, Jonathan Tempest, raised a regiment of Light Horse to fight alongside Lord Cornwallis, he compounded his own end in the Americas. When the British lost, it was the end of the Tempests in that country. With the rest of the loyalists they packed up and headed for the Bahamas, where the grateful Crown made them another land grant, several of what are known today as the Out Islands. One of the islands, named by the Spaniards who first settled it La Isla de los Flamencos, they renamed Tempest Cay and set about rebuilding the dynasty. And a new great house. Jonathan Tempest had set torch to the other one as he left. Legend has it that as he saw it burn he raised a fist and swore: 'I will survive!' That is now the family motto."

Hervey moistened his dry throat with malt.

"They prospered in the Bahamas, reestablishing plantation life, having brought with them their slaves, their livestock, seeds and plants. And by one of life's little ironies, it was America which led to their becoming even more rich and powerful than they had ever been. During the Civil War, the South needed to sell its cotton to England. This the Tempests delivered, at the same time tipping off the North about other blockade-runners, so successfully that when the war ended a grateful President Grant restored their American citizenship."

Hervey smiled dryly. "A nice twist . . . And as the Bahamas were confirmed as a British possession in 1875, it meant they had dual nationality, which they still hold."

He took another swig.

"The Civil War made the Tempests very rich, and they used that as a base from which to acquire even more wealth. The Island is plentifully stocked with wood—mahogany, madeira, lignum vitae—so they built ships and used them to trade. They imported thoroughbred livestock from which to breed, they cultivated every inch of land that would bear a crop, and they invested shrewdly, until they held interests—more often than not controlling ones—in companies all over the world.

"It was these far-flung interests your father took and welded into the Tempest Organization; which is how it comes to own mines in Venezuela and South Africa; forests in Oregon and Wisconsin, coal mines in West Virginia—and in England until they were nationalized; shipyards in England and Scandinavia, uranium mines in Australia. It is incorporated in the Bahamas, of course, which means that apart from a modest property tax there are no direct income taxes, death duties, or inheritance taxes, nor do we have corporation tax, capital gains tax, profits tax, real estate tax . . . which is why the Organization built and owns large industrial estates on New Providence and Grand Bahamas islands as well as elsewhere.

"The Island is entirely self-supporting. It has its own electricity-generating plant, its own telephone exchange, water supply, hospital, school, cinema, church. What we do not have is mugging, rape, vandalism, and violence. It is safe to walk anywhere—though we do have one island policeman—an ex-London bobby. Some three hundred people live and work there, every one of them for the Family. They are the descendants of the slaves Jonathan Tempest brought with him, though all slaves were freed in the Bahamas in 1838. Our people live and work on the Island from choice. Indeed, we could populate it ten times over because people from other islands are constantly applying for permission to come and live there.

"Tempest Cay is one place everyone would like to live. It is very beautiful, a natural paradise. Miles and miles of sugar-fine beaches, tropical vegetation, a perfect climate . . . It is some twelve miles long and five miles wide at its widest point. We are some fifty-five nautical miles from Nassau and just under an hour by air from Miami. The Island has its own airstrip, which your father built with the soil from the harbor when he enlarged it." Hervey paused to moisten his dry throat again.

"We even have our own golf course, and there is tennis, riding, water-skiing, sailing, and skin diving . . ."

"Paradise?" she interrupted, with a steel-tipped smile.

"I do not think I exaggerate when I say that is exactly what it is."

Another silence. Once more she withdrew into her thoughts. "All right," she said finally, "I know what's what. We can't do anything about the why—as yet. What about the who? Why has he disinherited his family?"

She was methodically going through a list, he thought, checking every last thing. She was not prepared to take anything at its face value. On the one hand, his own innate caution approved; on the other, he did not like having to prove. But he answered her question truthfully: "That is privileged information."

"Even if they are not—anymore, I mean."

"Even so." He leveled her a look. "In any case, it is of no concern to you unless the will is contested."

"And will it be?"

"I have no such information."

Their eyes met, held, locked on. She was a great one for eyeball-to-eyeball confrontations. All part of the way she intimidated. This time he saw a total, most terrifying comprehension. She was not fooled, not for one minute. But all she said was: "So where do we go from here?"

"Tempest Cay. It is where your inheritance lies."

"But I haven't got it yet."

"That is only a matter of time, during which it is better—and safer—that you be in the center of things."

"Safer?"

"The press," Hervey said succinctly. "This piece of sensationalism is going to cause a nine days' wonder when it is revealed. Until then I cannot emphasize too strongly the need for absolute discretion and silence. The Organization is without a hand at the helm—speculation is already running rife. Nothing must go wrong. It is for this reason I called you from a pay-phone; why I called on you at so late an hour; took the precaution of walking the last few hundred yards to this flat even in pouring rain . . ." Thinly: "I have been trying for three days to get in touch with you."

"I was out of town." No explanations, no apology. She said: "It's all very cloak-and-dagger . . ."

"Needs must," he said firmly, "and what I need to know right now is how soon you will be able to leave for the Island?"

She thought. He waited. "Ten days?" she asked, no doubts, no hesitation. He had expected the usual feminine vagaries.

"But—what about your work?"

"Done. That's where I was these past three days—finishing off the photo call for the new campaign. Since I was under exclusive contract to them I am now free to go where I please. A new contract is being negotiated."

Curiously: "What is it like—being the 'Flawless Finish' girl?"

A shrug. "It pays well . . ."

Hervey smiled wintrily. "Not as well as being Richard Tempest's daughter." Then, decisively: "Allow the negotiations to proceed as normal. Anything else would give rise to comment. Say you are taking a holiday . . . Miami, perhaps." He pursed his lips. He reached into his briefcase, came out with a bulging manila envelope, which he laid on the coffee table in front of her. "One thousand pounds in cash. Use it to buy a ticket to Miami. I would suggest British Airways Flight 294 which leaves Heathrow at one o'clock and arrives at Miami International at five minutes past five their time. Do not leave the arrivals lounge. You will be met. A car will bring you to another part of the airport where I shall be waiting. We shall then fly to the Island. You have a current passport, of course?"

"Yes." Again, he caught the barest hint of a secret smile. Something was amusing her. It disgruntled him.

"I suggest you travel tourist," he went on doggedly. "Photographers hang around Miami International looking for celebrities and your face is well known. If you are approached say nothing beyond the fact that you are on holiday, but, please, shake them off before you join me.

"Don't close up this flat. Leave as though you intend to return. Leave nothing in the way of personal papers; any small, even insignificant detail which could be used by the press. When this gets out you will find your life held up to public scrutiny. Curiosity about you will be obsessive and greedy. Do not make it easy for them, is all I ask." He groped in an inside pocket, brought out a pocket diary. "Ten days' time . . . that brings us to the twenty-seventh. Yes, that will do very nicely. I am going on to Paris, Berlin, and Rome, so that date will fit well into my schedule." He made the necessary notation, put the diary away again, well satisfied. "Now . . . I am sure you have many questions to ask me."

"Indeed. Like what can I expect when I get to the Island."

He knew better than to evade. "By way of a reception?"

"They have been disinherited . . ."

Hervey sipped at his malt as a delaying tactic while marshaling his thoughts.

"Well . . . strictly speaking, although they are referred to as the Tempest Family, only your father's sister is of the blood . . . the others are his stepchildren and a stepgranddaughter."

"But all supported by him."

With judicious caution: "During his lifetime your father made more than ample provision for them . . . in the way of very generous allowances, the unrestricted use of his houses, his cars, his planes, his boats . . . his name, which was a passport they used all over the world. Over the years they have all received astronomical amounts of money—apart from Miss Tempest, of course, who is independently wealthy by reason of the Trust Fund established by her late mother. Having spent prodigiously during his lifetime and not seen fit to buy an umbrella for the proverbial rainy day, there is no reason why they should have expected your father to build them an ark." He rather liked that. "You, on the other hand, *are* of the blood. It is not unnatural for a father to provide for his natural child before his stepchildren . . ."

"In this case it is before *and* after the fact."

He ignored that.

"They know about me, of course."

"They do."

"And?"

"They were somewhat . . . surprised." And that, he thought, was somewhat of an understatement, remembering the screaming, the shouting, the weeping and wailing.

"They had expected to inherit, then?"

"They had—expectations, naturally."

"But I'm the natural one . . ." Her grin became a derisive laugh. "But I had never expected to inherit the earth. I thought that had been earmarked for the meek . . ."

Now she was laughing, but somehow he knew it was at herself, not him. "So tell me about them," she invited. "After all they already know about me."

That's what they think, Hervey thought.

"His sister, for instance."

Hervey's face lit. "Miss Helen Tempest," he announced, "a very great lady. I have the honor to be a friend of hers." He made it sound like a decoration. Hervey Grahame, F.H.T. Friend of Helen Tempest. "She resides permanently at Marlborough. Her health is delicate, therefore she does not go about much. People are only too happy to come to her."

"And the others? They live there too?"

"Only David Boscombe. Your father's eldest stepson from his first marriage. His sister, the Contessa di Primacelli, and your father's stepson from his second marriage, Danvers Godfrey, are founder members of the jet set. David has a daughter, Nieves, at present finishing in Switzerland. Then there is Cass . . ."

"That would be Cassandra Mary van Dooren?"

"Yes. Your father's Executive Secretary for thirty years and my co-executor. Very much part of the Family." And how, he thought.

Another silence as she ran that through the computer. "And Miss Mattie Arden, the Divine Diva. Where does she fit in?"

Richard Tempest's bed, thought Hervey, answering: "As an ex-officio member of the Family. She was devoted to your father and his death has distressed her deeply. So deeply she is at present in the Island hospital suffering from shock." He sighed. "We fear for her voice. These emotionally traumatic shocks can do untold damage . . ."

"Yes, she certainly can sing . . . I heard her do *Tosca* last year at the Garden."

So she liked opera. He had already noted the stack of LP's under the music center.

"So . . . there are eight of them, then."

Hervey had to do a mental count. She was right—if you included Harry, who never got included in anything.

"And left not so much as a fare-thee-well . . . and prevented from trying for one by what you call 'privileged information.'"

"Which it is."

She regarded him contemplatively. "Who do you believe, Mr. Grahame? Scott Fitzgerald or Ernest Hemingway."

He knew to what she was referring. The rich did it all the time. "They are different," he acknowledged. "Their money makes them so. It is a great insulator, tends to shut you off from reality. You will find that when you reach the Island. It can also desensitize, like all drugs, and like them it is habit-forming. The withdrawal symptoms can be extremely painful."

Their eyes met and again she smiled that smile of complicity and understanding.

"I shall remember that," she said.

"I hope so. Great wealth carries great responsibility. You have been left much more than money."

Once more they made a silent acknowledgement of shared understanding. She was very quick, thought Hervey. For such a forbidding personality, highly intuitive—or was it shrewdness? Well, time would tell. She certainly wouldn't.

He complimented her: "You have taken all this very calmly."

Indifferently: "Yes, I now know about my father."

"Ah . . . yes. Your mother. You know nothing of her?"

"Only her name."

"But you did not enter the Home until you were five. What of your life before then? Surely it must have been with her."

"I don't know. Where she is concerned, my memory is a blank. I was told, when I was older, that I was very—ill—for some time after my arrival at Henrietta Fielding. I do not remember that either."

"But—did she have no family? Did no one come forward on her death to claim you?"

"Not that I know of."

Hervey sighed. He was disappointed. He had hoped that perhaps something would have—could have—been told.

"Well, at least you know now who your father was."

"Obviously there must have been some involvement—but that is the one thing about which my father has said nothing."

Hervey fidgeted. "Your father was a man women found very attractive. There were many in his life. But it is to your mother's daughter he has left everything. I think we must therefore assume that she was—important—to him."

"Or that none of his other women had children."

Her rationality he found chilling. But it went with the rest of her. He had yet to see her show a single deeply felt emotion. Shock, astonishment, disbelief, even. Some sign of nerves; that her nullifying, controlled calm had been cracked. All he had seen was amusement. She had the classical perfection of a statue. And its lack of life.

She was watching him watching her. He gathered his wits. "It has been a most interesting and enlightening meeting," he told her truthfully.

"Indeed," she said, exactly the way he had said it. "I see now what you mean when you said you had something to tell me which would be to my advantage."

Stiffly: "I sincerely hope it will be."

Once more they regarded each other. Then Hervey rose to his feet. "If you are sure there is nothing more I can tell you . . ." He was strangely reluctant to go. She fascinated him.

"You have given me more than enough to ponder on. No doubt when I get to Marlborough it will be a different story."

Won't it just! Hervey thought, keeping his face impassive. She got his coat and hat, waited while he shrugged into them. Then she went with him to the door. There, he held out a hand. "It has been a pleasure to meet you, Miss Sheridan." And to look at you, he thought. She compelled the eyes. Any man would be fascinated. And frightened to death. Formidable, he thought. Very formidable indeed.

At the door he turned once more. "You are quite sure, now, what you have to do?"

She repeated his instructions verbatim.

"Until the twenty-seventh, then . . ." Then, in uncharacteristically impulsive fashion: "You'll do, Miss Sheridan. I must confess I had grave doubts . . . but you will do."

Her smile glittered at the edges; tipped with steel again. "Yes, I know . . ." she agreed tranquilly. Then with a look he felt through to his backbone. "But what?"

The door closed on her.

Hervey felt as though a powerful suction had been released. He heaved a sigh, then settled his homburg, hefted his briefcase in one hand, umbrella in the other, but before he made for the lift, he turned slowly to stare at the plain wooden door. Behind it, she was laughing.

SIX

"Gin!" Dan spread his cards triumphantly.

"Damn!" Margery flung hers down in disgust. "Even the cards don't run my way!"

Dan was counting rapidly. "Let me see, now . . . you owe me . . . the princely sum of three thousand eight hundred and seventeen dollars—and things being what they are, I'll take cash, if you please. No checks, no credit cards . . ."

"Is that what you tell them?" Cass asked interestedly.

"It depends on who I'm with." He flashed her a dazzle-toothed smile. "And I would advise you to start saving your own nickels and dimes, my dear Cass. It's going to be a long, hard winter."

Margery's chair went over with a crash, which caused Helen to wince, seeing it was one of a set of twelve lyre-backed Louis XVI masterpieces. "Do you have to remind us?" Her exquisitely maquillaged face, courtesy of Erno Laszlo, had curdled like sour cream. But she had valiantly shored up the ruins. Her black Halston dress, slashed across the collarbones and pasted to her body, was chopped off short at the ankles, revealing feet in plain, black satin pumps, and it was embellished with an opera-length strand of what looked like blue beads but were in fact marble-sized sapphires interspersed with smaller, but flawless pearls. As always, her eyes went straight to the nearest mirror. "I'm sick of all this waiting," she said, flicking at her hair. "Why doesn't Hervey call?"

"He did," reminded Cass.

"A whole week ago! Since then, nothing but silence. What the hell is he doing over there?"

"You mean who," corrected Dan. "Wouldn't you? He's got her all to himself; putty in his hands after the shock he's handed her. He is no doubt remaking her to his own specifications."

"Speak for yourself!" Everybody looked openmouthed at Helen, who had raised her head from her endless stitching to regard Dan with heated disapproval. "Hervey would never do such a thing—and I will not have you saying so!"

"Then I apologize," Dan said disarmingly. "We all know Hervey is as square as a city block, but even you, my dear Helen, must admit that they can be demolished by money in the amounts Richard has left."

"And not to you!" David jeered.

Dan turned his head slowly, eyed David up and down in such a way as to make him turn a thick, inarticulate red. "Ah, David . . . sober tonight? Forgive me if I did not recognize you . . ."

David turned his back.

"I still wish something would happen," complained Margery. "All this waiting around is getting me down!"

Dan smothered a laugh and she rounded on him, her face ugly. "And as for you—aging gigolos are at a premium, you know! What will you do when *your* looks have gone to seed?"

"Ah well," Cass said helpfully, "if you will scatter it around." She met Dan's eyes with a creamy smile.

"Margery does have a point," he conceded. "It really is most reprehensible of Hervey to keep her so long under wraps like this."

"But I thought that was where you spent most of your time." Cass said innocently.

He regarded her thoughtfully. "One of these days, my dear Cass, you are going to be found hanging from that tongue." His smile stripped skin. "But, then, yours are not the usual hang-ups, are they?"

Cass's face took on the color of freshly boiled lobster and he laughed softly, while Margery giggled, glad to see somebody else suffer for a change, but she sidled over to Dan. "Don't tell me *you* haven't got something up your sleeve?" she said archly.

"That's not where he keeps it," Cass muttered, still smarting.

"I do have my plans . . ." Dan was tranquil.

"I knew it!" Margery dragged up her chair. "Come on . . . out with it."

"But I shan't know which one to put into action until I have met her, will I? Everything depends, don't you see, on what *she* is like."

Cass snorted. "Richard's daughter!"

"Even so. I know one must remember at all times the opposing schools of thought on environment versus heredity, but while we know of the one, we know very little of the other . . . only that a Home is a far cry from this particular home from home which, if I am any judge, will knock her for a loop!" He crossed his legs comfortably. "Try to imagine, if you can, what all this must be like for her . . . To find out that you are not just a nameless bastard but a Tempest—albeit an illegal one—and that your father was Richard 'King' Tempest, superstar and billionaire. Why, I should think that alone would put her down for a long count. By the time she gets here, sees all this magnificence, she should be ripe for the picking." His mind dwelt lovingly on the prospect.

"How?" demanded Margery greedily.

"We ram it home—the point I mean," he went on, ignoring Cass's muffled snort, "catch her while she is off balance and knock her over—and out! See to it that she is treated as what she has become: the richest woman in the world. In other words—do a Marlborough on her."

Margery's jaw dropped. With awe and respect she gazed at Dan's sunny smile. "Of course! Why didn't I think of that? It's the very thing!"

"The State Suite to begin with, I think." Dan looked at Helen. "You agree?"

Helen's head was bent over her gros point, face hidden. "It is her house now. She may do as she wishes." Her voice was devoid of expression.

"Not right away, surely! She will be far too nervous. Everyone knows— even her—that Marlborough is *your* house, Helen . . . what *you* have made. She will be terrified to turn over in bed in case she disturbs all that green and gold magnificence!"

Margery clapped her hands. "She'll be completely cowed!"

"And when she looks around—what will she find?"

"A knife in her back?" It was Cass.

He ignored that too. "The Family. The dispossessed, the castoffs, bloody but unbowed, carrying on manfully with a full complement of stiff upper lips . . . nobly tragic, sadly resigned but valiantly carrying right on to the end of the road. Why, she will be lucky if her conscience doesn't beat her to death!"

"We all saw *Rebecca!*" Cass volunteered helpfully.

But Margery, in whom irony met rust, took her seriously. "Of course! The

average person is terrified of money in the quantities she has come into. They
have no idea how to handle it. Look at the people you read about; found
hanging or spending a fortune on shrinks or joining some weird religious cult
or even ending up bankrupt! Enormous wealth means enormous responsibility," she added virtuously, never having carried one in her life. "If we play
our cards right, as Dan says, she should be only too pleased to let us help her
shoulder the burden."

"We must play our parts, of course," Dan warned. "Which means being
polite, courteous—in a tragically noble way, I suggest. A sad sigh here, a
reproachful glance there . . . but never so much as an actual word of protest. And no airs and graces, either. That means you, Countess. No coming
the old acid, as the English say. Just be your own sweet self. Little Margery
Boscombe from One Horse, Nebraska, whose mother married the King and
was swept away to his castle. She is going to be on shaky pins. Little Miss
Nobody elevated into Big Miss Everybody; so softened up by the shock of it
all we should have no trouble planting our suggestions; that way *we* end up
reaping *her* harvest! But you leave first go to me. That's my price."

"Ha!" Cass sat bolt upright, eyes gleaming. "I knew it! What will you do?"
she purred. "Seduce her?"

She collided with the cracked-ice eyes. "Do you think I couldn't?" he
asked softly.

She shook her head. "Not for one minute. You'll have her picked clean
before she can reach for her toothbrush."

"The means justify the end—just so long as it is not *our* end," Dan said. "I
am not prepared to go *that* far."

"But she might," David said slyly. "How do you know she isn't an old
hand at your sort of fun and games?"

Dan smiled, eyes hooded. "Her fun, my games."

A subdued knock heralded the stately entrance of Moses, the butler. His
black face was impassive but his eyes were snapping with excitement. "The
strip just called, ma'am," he said to Helen. "Mr. Grahame's plane is due to
land in five minutes. I've sent a car."

Helen looked up, her hands automatically stilling, then folding away her
work. "Thank you, Moses . . ." She glanced at the clock. "I think dinner a
little later tonight . . . say, eight-thirty."

"Very good, ma'am." Moses withdrew.

Margery had jumped to her feet, hands clutching nervously at her jeweled
beads. "Sit down!" Dan commanded curtly, with a savage note in his voice.
"Let us observe the civilities by all means, but let us also not forget who and
what we are! No arrogance, I said, but let us show no humility either! In spite

of her newly acquired money she is *au fond* a no-name bastard with good cause to be nervous. She has come to us; not the other way around. She is going to have to get used to things; things long part of our life-style. Hang on to them and don't let go! No matter what she is now, we are still what we have always been—and, if you follow my lead, always will be! Remember that! As far as she is concerned, *we* are the rich and the mighty."

"She is very tall," wrote David, "gilt-blond and stunningly splendid. You remember the Tennyson bit about Maud? Our Elizabeth to the life! No malleable, shy, and uncertain girl this. We've got a hard-nosed bitch on our hands, sharp as a needle and, boy, is she good at shoving it where it hurts!

"Oh, Dev, if only you could have been here to see it! Talk about a sketch!! If you could have seen their *faces*. We knew what hers was like, you see, but now I *know* the camera lies. Because in the flesh—well, she makes yours creep. Talk about arrogant! She comes across like *she's* the one with all sixteen quarterings—only you don't get any! But she's a Tempest all right . . . funny, isn't it? About *this* one there can be absolutely no doubt . . . wouldn't you know it? Richard not taking any chances again.

"But to get back to her . . . I can't begin to tell you, though I must. I have to tell somebody. You know how he had the ultimate in that overworked word 'charisma'? Well, she has the finite in self-possession. So help me, Dev, it will take much, much more than finding out you have inherited the earth to faze this one. What we have here is no pushover to melt before the flamethrower of Dan's charm or buckle beneath the weight of the Tempest billions.

"Her history is straight Dickens. Mother a mystery (and who the hell was *she*, I wonder?) Brought up in a Home; turned out of it at sixteen to fend for herself, and, boy, has she fended! Nobody's fool and not fooled for one minute by us or anything else. And doesn't give a damn. She seeks neither approval nor approbation. Makes no overtures, has no idea how to ingratiate. Just stands there. *You* have to go to *her*. All the way. But, boy, is she worth going to! What a face! You will know what I mean when I say I have the itch to capture it on canvas . . . don't laugh, but I do! She is fascinating—and absolutely unfathomable. You know how they cover furniture in stores with protective plastic? Well, that's how it is with her, except it isn't plastic—it's plate glass. A fascinating set of contradictions. A nameless (until now, any-way) bastard who looks like a thousand years of breeding and refining have gone into her manufacture. And all giving out the warmth of a brilliant cut diamond. All you get from this one when you move in close is a cold nose. Needless to say, Dan is already suffering from frostbite.

"One thing is for certain sure. Richard knew what he was doing. What we cannot work out is why? Cass, of course, has been going around giving her usual word-perfect impression of her namesake.

"Gong's just gone . . . Time to go and change for dinner. We are giving her the Marlborough Treatment. You know—State Suite, regal grandeur, the Louis XVI Sèvres, et al. . . . Don't go away. I'll get back to you as soon as I can."

Dan was dressing for dinner, intent on tying a perfect bow, when the door of his dressing room burst open and Margery erupted through the door, incandescent with rage but dressed for the kill in a liquefaction of black satin and triple rows of pearls.

"What price your fine schemes now?" she hissed.

The Contessa's voice carried. A jerk of Dan's head dismissed his valet, who melted silently away.

"I guess I'll have to change my plans," he sang gaily, not one whit put out or disturbed.

"Bastard!" shrieked Margery, beside herself.

"Bitch!"

"What price this one, then?" she spat.

"High . . . much higher than I had counted on—or planned for." He laughed. "Do you know what she said when I showed her into the State Suite? 'How nice. Green is my favorite color . . .'" Dan found that extremely funny. "Oh, yes, we have got a right one here, as her countrymen would say." He picked up his watch—wafer thin, solid gold, Jaeger—Le Coultre.

"She'll not part with a penny," moaned Margery. "You'll never get this one under your thumb—or anywhere else!"

"If I thought you would ever pay up, I'd be prepared to lay you odds . . ."

"And how would you pay when I won? Your dossier has as many holes as mine, you know!"

Dan's soft voice turned to silk as he purred: "But my reputation is not in shreds . . . Now then, temper, temper." He had caught her upraised hand by the wrist, bending it back cruelly, so that she gasped with the pain. He sniffed as she sagged toward him to ease it. "Do I detect a layer of brandy beneath the air of Joy?" His laugh was callous. "Got to you already, has she?"

Margery wrenched her arm away so violently she stumbled back on the skirt of her dress and thwacked her spine on a knob of the tallboy. "Ow!" Her eyes filled with tears of pain. "Bastard! I hope she doesn't part with a cent!"

"Oh, I am after much more than *that!*" He smoothed his sleek hair in the mirror, picked up a silver-backed brush to quell a few ruffled strands. "You forget she is a woman." He lowered the brush to look thoughtful. "At least, I think she is . . ." Wielding the brush again: "And don't I know women?" He smiled at her through the mirror. "And don't *you* know I do."

Margery scowled. That affair was *very* old hat. And had gone very wrong.

Dan laughed, reading her easily, as usual. All Margery's words were of four letters. "A word to the stupid," he said kindly. "A soft smile works wonders . . . A man is a pushover for a woman's smile."

Margery's mouth took a turn for the worse. "That one's smile would freeze the Caribbean!"

Dan frowned slightly. "True . . . she is no cosy armful, for sure. But *you* may be sure, my sweet, that, whatever she is, I am about to find out."

"Do let me know, won't you?" Margery snapped.

Dan stuffed a clean handkerchief in his pocket, picked up lighter, keys.

"Leave this one to me," he advised confidently. "*I* know what I'm doing."

The magnificent doors to the State Suite opened to his knock and one of the maids—Lynetta, he recognized—admitted him to the sitting room. Elizabeth Sheridan was just coming out of her bedroom, screwing the final pearl into her ear.

"Oh, very nice!" Dan approved warmly, instantly. "You have risen beautifully to the occasion. I was so afraid you might sink once the oven door was opened . . ."

"You mean it hasn't already?"

His laugh was delighted. "Oh, I do like you!" he exclaimed. "Such a refreshing change."

"You mean fresh."

"As paint! And *so* like Richard."

"So people keep on telling me."

"But you are. Believe me, I should know. Take my word for it—and mine is usually the last one around here."

"Well, I seem to have taken everything else . . ."

Her eyes were knowing. Bitch! he thought, but his smile was sunny. "I am on your side, you know."

"Why?"

"I think it is the winning one."

Her eyes swept him, reduced him to something under a microscope. "Yes . . . I think you would always be on the winning one."

Lynetta came out of the bedroom to hand Elizabeth an evening bag of the same dark, almost black green of her dress, of which Dan remarked knowingly: "St. Laurent?"

"A copy. I am not model-girl size . . . but I do sew a fine seam."

"You *made* it!" he was impressed. He doubted if even Margery would have realized.

"We were taught how to sew at an early age at Henrietta Fielding. It was assumed we would need to know how."

He ignored the point of that. "Well, you can afford to buy originals now—by the gross. It is obvious you already have the taste; now you also have the money."

The dress was fine silk jersey, molded to the body, drawn tight across the breasts and into the waist, where a satin-lined sash of palest pink went right round the body to tie in front in a soft bow. It had long tight sleeves and the neckline was a deep vee, at the apex of which was pinned one perfect deep-red rose.

"You match your surroundings," he complimented, gesturing at the green and gold opulence all around them. "You are quite comfortable here, I hope?" He sounded anxious, like a hotel manager with a VIP guest.

"Quite comfortable, thank you."

"Shall we go down, then?"

"By all means . . . but to whose level?"

Oh, sharp, he thought viciously, feeling his fists curl into balls, ready to smash that flawless control. She made him want to grind his teeth. On her bones.

The drawing room he ushered her into was all yellow picked out in white; carpet, hangings, furniture, a-glitter with mirrors and two-tiered chandeliers, hung with paintings and massed with flowers, again all white. Against the silk-hung walls, the heavy brocade of the curtains, beswagged and betasseled, Elizabeth Sheridan's dress stood out like an insult.

"Now then," Dan said, "I think the time is right for one of my martinis."

"May I watch you make them? I am always willing to learn."

"And I am always willing to teach . . . anything."

He led her over to a magnificent portrait of an eighteenth-century Tempest—Francis Tempest IV, according to the little gold nameplate—which he opened like a door. Behind it was a fully kitted bar, including a small fridge. He took from it a large pitcher and a bowl of cracked ice, emptying the latter into the former. Picking up a bottle of Noilly Prat, he poured enough to just cover the ice. This he swirled round and round until the sides of the pitcher were covered in an oily film. He poured the rest away. Then he covered the ice with Tanqueray gin. With a long-handled silver spoon he stirred, three times. Taking down two traditional long-stemmed martini glasses, he filled them. The final touch was a sliver of lemon twisted briefly before being dropped in. Handing her one: "That," he said, "is a martini. Don't let anyone tell you different—or make it, either!"

She eyed it critically. "It looks lethal."

"It is! But unless you learn to carry yours while all about you are losing theirs . . ." He demonstrated by sipping deeply.

Her own sip was experimental. "All I taste is ice."

"All you'll feel is warmth."

He led her over to a marble fireplace, above which hung another magnificent portrait: Henrietta Tempest, circa 1817, wearing diaphanous silk and a fortune in emeralds. "The idea is to finish it off before the chill goes."

"Whose?" She limned the rim with her tongue, eyeing him over it. Once again he felt the urge to smash.

"Elizabeth—I may call you Elizabeth?—you are a girl after my own heart."

"Well, you are after my money." The hand raising his glass did not falter. What the hell did she use? Radar?

"I live on hopes," he answered modestly. Adding ruefully, sadly: "Now . . ."

"Well, that's all he left you."

She seated herself in one corner of an exquisite Louis XVI sofa, all gilt and Lyon silk in a singing, sunshine yellow.

Very casually he sat down next to her. "Come to that," he said, "do you have any idea just what he *has* left you?"

"A very great deal."

"That's putting it mildly. What he has left you is *everything!* In terms of what you can actually *buy*, think of your Crown Jewels, a country or two, perhaps? The Rockefellers, the Rothschilds . . ." He eyed her glass. "Drink up!" he urged. "Now that you know how to make them you must learn how to take them."

"So you can take me?"

Once again his nose hit glass.

"What do you plan to do with it, anyway?"

"What would you suggest?"

"Spend it, of course!"

"As you do?"

"I—appreciate—it."

She sipped at her martini. "What made you turn to money?"

"What else is there?" And how did we get so far so soon, he was thinking. "I mean, in this world, what are you without it?"

"Poor," she said.

"But with it, you are everything . . ."

"Am I to take it you are describing my present situation?"

Oh, she was a bitch, all right. As cold and hard as her eyes. This one he just *had* to topple.

"You would do well to consider it," he said seriously. "Normally, people in your position are very—vulnerable. Eager for advice. But I don't suppose you ever ask for *that.*"

"No," she said.

"Yes . . . you look like a woman who knows her own mind." And mine too, he thought. "Most unusual in a woman, that. But then"—his eyes smiled as the forked tongue struck—"you are not very feminine, are you?"

He was thunderstruck to find she took him seriously. "No," she said. "I'm not."

"You certainly do not conform to specifications," he murmured, his eyes moving over her in such a way as to make a very physical scan of her measurements. "Still, I must say, from where I sit, I cannot see a single flaw in yours."

"Like your technique," she said, draining her glass.

"I know my own capabilities," he admitted modestly, taking her glass from her.

"Good. So do I."

And how! he raged, going to refill their glasses. This was not going right. She was always there ahead of him. Worse. She knew exactly what she was doing and still didn't care. He was not used to indifference. Nervousness, eagerness, anticipation, doubt—but indifference! It made him burn with frustration. He could not understand it. Never in his life had he never had *any* effect.

"How do you see all this, anyway?" he asked confidentially, as he handed her the refill.

"Without prejudice."

"Of course! That is all on our side—with justification, you must agree."

"Oh, I do . . . I am sure you can justify anything."

He gulped martini. He could feel himself losing his cool. "It must seem quite—unreal—to you," he persisted doggedly. "But take it from me, it is all quite terrifyingly real."

He knew, when he saw the smile, that he had once more said the wrong thing. "But I already have taken it from you . . ."

He knew then that he hated her. If he all but died in the attempt he would destroy this one. And not only for the money. But for now, he raised his glass. "Drink up . . . The first lights the fire, the second gives the glow . . . Burn the candle at both ends. You can afford to, after all."

"You keep coming back to the money." She sounded bored.

"No, it cannot be got away from."

"You are trying to get it away from me!"

"As if that were possible," he countered silkily.

Her eyes regarded him over her glass. They were set in her face like gemstones. "What did he promise you?" It was flat, no frills.

"Equal shares."

"Then why didn't he keep it?"

"That's another story. Let's finish yours first."

"But mine is the sequel, surely."

"One should never speak ill of the dead."

"Why not? They cannot hear you."

Ruthlessly logical again. No, definitely *not* feminine. She was superbly skilled with words. Even in this house, where they were often your only weapon and therefore practice was mandatory, she would have no trouble holding her own. Damn!

"You feel cheated, then?" she was asking.

"I *have* been cheated. We all have. You have inherited everything," he reminded. "That includes his debts." Seductively: "Think of me as a deductible expense."

A faint smile. "I doubt if I could afford to."

"You cannot afford *not* to." It was a warning. Short and sour. Then he continued, wonderingly: "Were you *really* brought up in a Home?"

"Yes."

"But you have not always been like—this?"

She knew what he meant. "No."

"You—learned?"

"Knowledge is power."

"No. Money is."

He sat back, so that he looked at her in profile. It was pure as perfection. Against the flame of the applewood fire—for which there was no need but upon which Helen always insisted, the air-conditioning being turned up to compensate—it looked like the head on a coin. Not a bad angle, he thought.

"You must look like Rapunzel when you let down that hair," he said of the heavy coil at the nape of her neck. "Do you ever?"

"When the occasion calls for it."

"Then we must make one! Marlborough, as you have seen, is the perfect place for occasions . . ."

"It is a very beautiful house."

"You are a very beautiful woman."

No answer.

"You have been told that before, of course."

With absolutely no inflection in her voice: "My face was my fortune before I inherited this one."

Bitch! But there were ways to skin them . . .

The door opened and in tripped Cass, wearing a dress she must have rummaged for. "Oh . . . you have started the party without me," she protested, and the voice, the eyes, labeled it as a hunting one.

"Heaven forfend!" Dan rose with alacrity and, to his chagrin, relief. "And you always the life and soul . . ." He went to pour her a martini, which she drained in one satisfying gulp, afterward handing her glass back for more. Refill in hand, she appropriated the sofa directly opposite theirs, reached for the cigarettes, steadied Dan's hand holding the lighter. "So . . . what's new?" she asked, blowing smoke. "Apart from Miss Sheridan, that is."

"Do I bother you?" Elizabeth asked politely.

Cass snorted. "You are a cool one," she conceded.

"Overheated emotions are like cold tea and warm beer—distasteful."

Cass stared then: "At that you are right." Another concession. Come on, Cass, thought Dan. Cut her down to size . . .

"I may be wrong," Elizabeth quoted, "but that is my opinion . . ."

"Of which you are obviously plentifully supplied," Cass said sweetly. "You live up to your own reputation."

The two women eyed each other. Eyes sparkling, Dan watched from the sidelines. This ought to be entertaining, to say the least, but he frowned as he caught sight of Elizabeth's face; it was showing the first real interest he had seen. His eyes went from one to the other. Could it be? He eyed Elizabeth again, his own interest warming. Now *this* was more like it . . .

Elizabeth opened. "Mr. Grahame tells me you have worked for my father for thirty years."

"Indeed," Cass answered from a great height.

"And that you know more about the Tempest Organization than anyone."

"Cass *is* the Organization," Dan offered helpfully.

"Is that why you disapprove of its being left to me?"

"Disapprove! It is like my six-year-old nephew being nominated for President of the United States!"

Dan smothered a grin. Go it, Cass, he urged silently.

"At that, he might do better than some of the recent incumbents," Elizabeth answered.

Dan's head was swiveling as the rally proceeded. "Cass is dramatizing, as usual," he put in, stirring madly.

"Dramatizing! Clyde Fitch never dreamed up anything like this!"

"Which is still no reason for assuming the worst," Elizabeth said reasonably.

"What do you mean—assume?"

Oh, lovely, thought Dan gleefully.

"You are thinking along the wrong lines," Elizabeth told her calmly.

"The hell I am! These tracks head straight for the precipice and me—I'm for jumping!" She glared at Elizabeth. "Give me one good reason why I shouldn't."

Elizabeth did so. "Me."

Cass's expression made Dan bite his lips and control his face.

"Jesus, but you are a monumental piece of self-possession!"

A shrug. "I have never had anyone else."

"That's not my fault!"

"I was not laying blame, but don't condemn me without a hearing."

"What's your plea?" Cass asked instantly. "Self-defense?"

"No. Self-interest. I have to look out for myself."

"And aren't you a doozy at that!"

The two women were mentally circling each other, hackles raised, teeth bared. From the sidelines, Dan was enjoying himself hugely. Trust Cass to give her a run for what he still regarded as his money.

"Why don't we talk about it?" Elizabeth asked coolly. "Lay our cards on the table . . ."

"Don't do that!" Dan exclaimed in mock alarm. "Cass plays a wicked game of poker."

"There is nothing more to lose," Elizabeth went on. "It has already been lost." Her smile was cold steel. From where he sat Dan could feel the blade sink to the hilt. "With me, the buck really *does* stop here . . ."

Once more Cass was thunderstruck, then her unfailing sense of humor got the best of her temper. "My God," she said, "it has a sense of humor!"

Unruffled: "This whole thing is laughable . . . as you yourself just pointed out."

Flailing madly at the top of her own petard: "Who is laughing?" Cass demanded bitterly.

"You have been extolled to me as a lady of great common sense," Elizabeth went on patiently. "Why won't you use it?"

"Common sense is of no use in an uncommon situation!"

"No. That is when it is of *most* use, surely."

Baffled, Cass stared across at her. This was indeed an adversary.

"What are you after?" she asked bluntly.

"Information . . . There is a lot I want—need—to know. I also want the benefit of your experience."

Cass's stare had changed to one of fearful speculation. "To do what?" she asked in the voice of dread.

"Why, run the Organization, of course."

". . . just had our latest session of fun and games," wrote David, continuing his letter. "The atmosphere was somewhat strained, as you can imagine. Cass wearing her 'woe, woe' expression, Dan looking like he'd already dined on pints of double cream, and Helen under remote control. Thank God for Hervey! But I am concerned for Helen. She looks at Elizabeth like a rabbit at a stoat. Fascinated but terrified . . . Never takes her eyes off her face. Mind you, neither do I . . . God knows, it is worth looking at. But as it was, it was the only one not leaking blood. I got it from Cass that Dan had taken a nasty fall, but the worst—again according to Cass—is that our dear stepsister intends to run the Organization. Cass has blown all her fuses. Talk about fun and games. This one is an Olympic champion, Dev. Oh, yes, Olympus is where she comes from. There is something inhuman about her beauty . . . about *her*. Not subject to human frailty; no doubts, no fears. Yes, our song is ended but the maladie lingers on."

When Hervey entered the South Parlor next morning, only Cass was sitting at the table, wreathed in cigarette smoke and gloom.

"Where is everyone?" he asked, surprised.

"Hiding!"

"Come now, Cass . . ." But he could see that it was Cassandra he had to deal with this morning.

He went to inspect the silver dishes on the sideboard. Humming to himself, he heaped a plate with bacon strips, scrambled eggs, mushrooms, tomatoes, and tiny sausages. Cass eyed his plate as he brought it back to the table. "The condemned ate a hearty breakfast?"

Hervey paused in the act of picking up knife and fork. "Really, Cass! It's not the end of the world!"

Cass snorted.

"You are determined on expecting the worst, aren't you?"

"What do you mean—expect?"

He held out his cup for coffee, and chuckled. "Dan certainly didn't get what he expected."

"That was his own fault for expecting anything in the first place! This one takes a positive delight in doing what you don't expect; like acting as if nothing had happened, for instance."

"Nothing did happen," Hervey said innocently, willfully misunderstanding.

"I'm not talking about Dan and you know it!"

"I am! It gives me a glow just to *think* of his coming off worst!"

"Which won't stop him from trying again—and again!"

Hervey looked at her. "Well, we both know he is capable of anything—from blackmail to barratry—but where Elizabeth Sheridan is concerned . . ."

Cass glowered. "I'm well aware that it is not Little Red Riding Hood you've brought back!"

"Don't tell me she frightens *you?*"

"She scares the hell out of me. She's not human to start with. Who winds her up at night? And it's not blood in her veins—it's oil!"

"Would you rather a mouse? Some timid creature terrified out of her wits and awed to silence? An easy mark for Dan, snubbed into the ground by Margery, milked by David for Dev Loughlin? Would you rather have seen your precious Organization delivered into the hands of a naïve innocent? I would have thought you preferred the iconoclast to the idiot!"

"The what?"

"One who doesn't believe in graven images."

"What do you mean—believe? She *is* one!"

Hervey sighed, placed his knife and fork neatly together like a well-brought-up boy. "Cass, whatever she is we must all get used to her. She's here to stay."

"Not when the what's-in-it-for-me boys get to work on her! Let's see how she survives in *that* jungle!"

"I am surprised you don't recognize an inhabitant in Miss Sheridan."

Cass glowered. "I don't get you! I would have bet *you'd* be the one to stand around and wring your hands at the irresponsibility of it all! Why aren't you?"

Hervey gave her a long look. "In all this—business—I regret but one thing. Helen should have had the house."

Cass reared like a bee-stung horse. "The hell she should! No separating the sheep from the goats, Hervey. We all have horns! Helen is as flawed as the rest of us, which is why Richard threw her out too!"

Hervey rose, like Jove, in all his righteous wrath. "How dare you!" he thundered, white about the mouth, nostrils pinched with rage. "I will not allow you to class Helen Tempest with the misbegotten misfits in this so-called Family!"

"The hell with what *you* will allow! She stood by and let it all happen, didn't she? She slapped paint on the sepulcher along with the rest of us!"

"Helen took the larger view. She did her duty!"

"Crap! I had a dog once did its duty! No whitewash on her, if you please. She went along with the parade—even if she did have her hands over her ears!"

Cass was well away venting the frustrated rage which had been building ever since Hervey had brought Elizabeth Sheridan into the blue drawing room. "Who else stood by and watched Margery sold into high-class white slavery? Who watched Dan dutifully learn all his nasty little lessons? Who stood by and wrung her hands while David's talent was thwarted and suborned? Helen Tempest, that's who! You are a nasty little snob, Hervey. You think being born a Tempest bestows divine rights—even the bastardized form! Richard had his sister dead to rights, which is why he buried her with the rest of them!"

"I will not sit and listen to this!" Hervey rose to his feet with a roar of rage.

"Then stand—but, by God, you'll hear it!"

Cass rose to her own feet and they faced each other across the breakfast table, both at white heat.

"Just because Helen is the only other Tempest in this house is no reason to play favorites, and I'm damned if I'll allow you to!"

"It is precisely because Helen *is* a Tempest!" thundered Hervey. "Do you think I give a damn for those other hangers-on? Leeches, all of them, and not worth the checks their names are written on! I would remind you that what Elizabeth Sheridan has inherited is due just as much to Helen Tempest's dedication as Richard Tempest's whim!"

"Then why didn't he leave it to her?"

"Because he knew it was the one thing she wanted!"

"Just as he knew money was all the others wanted—but he still cut them off at the jugular! No exceptions, Hervey—I'm your co-executor, remember —and that is probably because Richard knew damn well that you would break bars and bend rules to get Helen what you think she wants!"

"What she deserves!"

"She deserves nothing—which is exactly what Richard left her! And she, as you keep on pointing out, was his own sister! The fact remains that she knew what was going on and did nothing!"

"Do you think she is not tormented by that fact?"

"I'm tormented by indigestion at times but I do something about it! She did nothing! She was too damned scared she'd be tossed out on her aristocratic ear. I know she starved under Richard's shadow, as we all did; but she went along with the brass bands and the banners, the cheering and adulation of the masses! It's a champagne potent enough to make anyone's head spin, and once you've become used to drinking it you find it hard to go back to plain, everyday water. But the fact remains that Helen's duty was to people—not a name and a tradition; lives, not lineage!"

"Helen is proud to be a Tempest! It is the only thing apart from Marlborough that she has to be proud of!"

"Tradition and honor, my ass! Just you point out to me one instance where her brother showed he gave a damn about either!"

"Helen was—is—conscious of her history; who she is and what she is!"

"I know what she is! A coward! It's time she came out from behind her past and looked at the present! Maybe then she'd see her brother just dynamited it!"

Hervey's breath blew Cass's cigarette smoke flying. "How dare you! Helen Tempest has never run away! She has been held by the circumstances of her birth, her obligations—and her state of health!"

"Crap! The only obligations she ever fulfilled were to this house! Bricks and mortar, Hervey! She hid herself away in it because she preferred them to people—to you! And to stay hidden she murdered any emotional life she might have—again with you!"

Hervey's face was white and waxy; Cass had set foot on sacred ground. "I will not engage in a verbal brawl with you any longer! You have gone too far! This is not what we should be doing; we should be sticking together, not falling apart!"

"Too late! The glue's gone and it's every dog for himself!"

"Which still does not give you the right to savage a woman who has never shown you anything but kindness and friendship. I am shocked, Cass, that you, of all people, should turn on a defenseless woman . . ."

"You didn't spare me, did you? You said I was only an employee . . . how about that for a put-down?"

Too late, Hervey saw how his remark had hit home. "If I have offended, then I ask your forgiveness. It was not intentional; I was just being factual . . ."

"What the hell do you think I'm being?"

They glared at each other.

"Let us, then, agree to differ," Hervey said icily.

As quickly as it had blown its valve, Cass's head of steam blew itself out. Her tempers were always scalding but short-lived.

"I know what Helen means to you," she said placatingly, "but Richard has also shown what she meant to him by classifying her as unfit as the rest of us."

"Which is the unkindest cut of all!"

Cass sighed. "Hervey, we are all bleeding."

"Then why do you seek to open Helen's wounds even more?"

He was hurt, recriminatory. Helen Tempest was Hervey's blind spot. In his eyes, she was always the one who was done to; it never occurred to him to think of her as ever doing anything to other people, even if it was by never doing anything at all.

"Okay . . ." Cass sighed. "Let's agree to differ, like you said, but without arguing."

"That was never *my* intention!" Hervey said pointedly. "In any case, what should be occupying our minds right now is what hers might be . . ."

Cass was on the phone, her back to the door, when she heard it open. She swung her chair round. It was Elizabeth Sheridan. Cass waved her to the chair in front of the desk.

". . . I don't care what the hell you think, Max, I'm telling you! So get off your ass and do it . . . Oh, yes I can. I'm co-executor of the old man's will, for your information . . . No, I'm not—that information is still under wraps; you'll have to wait your turn like everybody else . . . But just so as you know for the time being I'm running things—okay?"

She reached out for a cigarette while she listened to the voice-squawk on the other end of the line.

"Never mind about Roger!" she interrupted. "I want to hear from you by four o'clock this afternoon that the deal is done and I want signatures, you hear? All right, so fly out there! Do what you have to, Max, but do it!"

She slammed down the phone. "See?" she complained. "Already they're trying it on. The sooner I get back to work the better . . ."

"That's what I wanted to talk to you about."

"Oh?" said Cass.

"I want you to teach me about the Organization."

Cass leaned back in her swivel chair. "What for?"

"I'm going to run it."

"You don't say."

"I just have."

They locked eyes.

"And you want me to show you how, is that it?" asked Cass.

"You are the only one who can." It was not flattery, it was truth. But Cass was not to be persuaded so easily.

"And you think that's all there is to it? A few lectures, a few tutorials, several lessons well-learned, a written exposition or two and I give you straight A's?"

"I don't see why not. I always got them at school."

"The Tempest Organization is *not* the Halls of Academe," Cass remarked witheringly.

"I am aware of that. I know it will take time, and a great deal of hard work. But I have plenty of one and I am not afraid of the other, so why not?"

"*Why*, indeed?"

"Because it was left to me."

"That's what I mean."

"And what you can't stand?"

"Too right, I can't!"

"But you have been running it, haven't you? If you can, why can't I?"

That left Cass flat on her back, but not out. "*I* know how!"

"So teach me! Wouldn't you like to be the power behind my throne? Madame de Pompadour ran France from there, you know. According to Mr. Grahame, you know to the last microdot how the Organization runs. All I want from you is access to that information."

Cass stared. "My God, you really mean it, don't you?"

"I never say things I don't mean."

Cass believed her. That inflexibility had the hardness of truth. She drummed her badly bitten fingers on the desk top, thinking hard and fast. "At that," she allowed, "you wouldn't have a prayer without me. I sat at the foot of the Master for thirty years. Dammit, I helped him build the Organization . . . Now that he is dead I *am* the Organization."

"No," Elizabeth corrected, "I am."

Eyes held.

"It would seem that my father has thrown down his gauntlet . . ."

"Custom-made," Cass returned swiftly. "Far too big for you!"

"So I'll have it altered."

She was pure sponge rubber; came back at you every time. Cass felt excitement growing, dominating her better judgment. At that, she thought what a team we would make . . . My knowledge and experience, her drive. But there would be all those upset applecarts to contend with, and everybody scurrying around to pick up the rotten fruit to use as missiles. And there *was* so damned much to learn . . . She scratched her ear distractedly.

"I learn fast," Elizabeth volunteered. "As Mr. Grahame tells me I am here for weeks certainly, probably months, before probate is obtained, I might as well use my time profitably."

Cass squirmed. On the one hand she was flattered; her ego needed reinflating, once she had mended the holes Richard had ripped in it. And from the despondent depths in which she had wandered of late, she could see, when she gazed upward, a lightening of her darkness.

And wasn't that what she had wanted? Well . . . yes . . . though it certainly was not the *way* she had wanted it. But who had said you could have everything? And hadn't she been left with nothing? Even the thought still hurt. She had known better than to expect a miracle, but even a kind word would have been something . . . Don't be a fool, Cass, she told herself. This is carte blanche, dummy! Until such time as she is able, *you* will be running things . . . Even better, you can steer the boat in the direction *you* think it should go . . . God, she thought, the prospect growing rosier by the minute, what could I not *do!* All right, so she knew her own mind—but Cass knew the Organization . . .

"You wouldn't be making me an offer I can't refuse?" she asked bluntly.

"Yes. Because I know you won't refuse it. You can't. You haven't anything else, have you?"

Cass gagged. Christ! she thought, as a wave of pounding blood threatened to burst every vein. She stared into green eyes that were so like her father's and yet not so. There was no naked cruelty there, only a matter-of-fact truth. But she was still mortified to the point of rout. You and your fast mouth! she raged at herself. Those aren't eyes, they are X-ray machines. She could feel her temples pounding, bit hard on her ever-ready tongue. Put away the tender susceptibilities, Cass, she counseled herself, else you'll be walking with a limp.

"Well?" asked Elizabeth patiently. "Even if we started with no more than a general outline of things . . . an idea of size and scope . . ."

Like you've just given me yours, Cass thought, discomfited. Jesus, but she's a smart cookie . . . her instinctive admiration for skill bobbed to the surface among all the other debris. She had seen, all right. More important, she had understood. And this was only the beginning. No doubt about it, Cass thought, there's a computer behind the elegant storefront, and she gets her kicks from using it. Any normal—yes, *normal*—woman would be counting the shekels, surveying her property, and making an inspection of the silver. Not this one. Not here forty-eight hours and wanting to know, not how much, but where and how and why. Well, she sighed inwardly. Like Hervey told you, better an iconoclast than an idiot . . .

"Yes or no?" Elizabeth prodded.

Cass smiled. "You are right. It *is* an offer I can't refuse."

"Good." No smile, no congratulations. "Can we start now?"

Cass knew when she was beaten. "Okay . . . let's go to the fountain-head." On the wall behind her desk hung a framed map of the world, occu-pying almost all of it. She pressed the little red button that marked Tempest Cay and the map slid back, revealing a vast, sunny room whose far wall and ceiling were of glass, giving a glorious view of the gardens, dropping away to the azure sea. "Used to be a conservatory," Cass explained briefly. "Now it's a world-communications complex plus office . . ." She flung out a hand at the array of electronic equipment. Word processors, electric typewriters, telex machines, radiotelephone link, filing cabinets; only one big desk, and it was all but bare. "Richard wrote few letters . . . but he used the phone a lot. And his head was his filing cabinet."

The desk top held blotter, pen and pencil tray, a digital clock, a big desk diary, a perpetual calendar. Not a paper in sight.

"Office of the President?" quizzed Elizabeth.

"You could call it that . . . except his office was wherever he was: usually a loose-leaf notebook in his inside left pocket."

Behind the desk was a map similar to that in Cass's office but covered with tiny glass buttons.

"What are they?" Elizabeth asked, going over to peer at them.

Cass leaned forward, pressed a cribbage board of buttons on the right-hand side of the desk. Instantly, the glass buttons lit up. "Red for manufacturing, blue for distribution, yellow for storage, green for sales. It gives you a picture of the spread of the Organization."

"Fascinating," murmured Elizabeth. She went behind the desk, pulled out the chair, which looked like sacking draped over matchsticks, and sat down. "Surprisingly comfortable," she observed.

"Specially designed to support the body . . ." Cass's voice trailed off. The sight of Richard's daughter in Richard's chair had managed, as not even her gloomy forebodings had done, to bring home to her all that had happened. It was real and it was earnest and if she was not careful the grave *would* be her goal. It shook her. Everything was indeed changed. The mixture was not as before; its texture, its taste, were very different. She would just have to get used to it.

Swallowing hard on its bitterness, she drew up her own chair. That at least was the same, gave an illusion of permanence, like the facts she proceeded to hurl at Elizabeth in a barrage of self-defense.

"One thing you have to understand first and foremost is the Organization's size. Gigantic. More than three hundred separate companies welded into a multinational conglomerate. Net income last year five billion dollars . . ." She watched intently for any sign of reaction to the figure. "Last year profit was 5.5 billion on sales of 79 billion. We have fifty divisions, each one a self-operating, independent unit connected to its center; we make our own steel to build our own ships from ore we take from our own mines; we grow the cotton we spin in our own mills; grow the trees to produce our paper; use the coal from our own mines to fuel our furnaces. We are involved not only in manufacturing but in supply; in insurance, banking, travel, property, hotels, but as a purely private business. Your father was a very public man but the Organization is not a public company. Profits are plowed back; we have no shareholders to consider, no interlocking directorates, no dividends to declare. The Organization belonged to your father. All of it. Now it belongs to you. It is run by a trust, the Tempest Trust. Richard foresaw the way governments would grow greedy and plunder big business to run their countries. Which is why the Organization was incorporated here in the Bahamas. It is totally independent—"

"—and a law unto itself?"

"Most certainly not! We pay our taxes—which here in the Bahamas don't amount to much—and in case you don't know, Hervey was not only Richard's lawyer, he heads the Legal Department!"

As Cass sat back, Elizabeth took off in a different direction: "How did you get into it?"

Surprised, for she had not expected Elizabeth Sheridan to be interested in people, Cass answered: "It was the war. I was a Wac. Your father was in the British Army. I was assigned to him as his secretary when he was running a displaced persons' camp in the Russian zone. And, boy, did he run it! A born organizer." Cass's eyes sparkled. "The way he ran that camp was one sweet piece of total control. When the war ended, he asked me if I would like to work for him in civilian life—told me the plans he had for forming the Organization. He was offering me a ringside seat at a piece of history-making, and I've occupied the same chair ever since."

"What was he like?"

Cass was unhesitating. "A genius. He had a talent for making money the likes of which I've never seen before or since. Well . . . maybe Howard Hughes, until he went weirdo toward the end. He and your father were alike in that each took a sizable inheritance and parleyed it into something colossal. In Howard's case, with Hughes Tool and Bit; with your father, the hundreds of companies in which his family had an interest—usually the controlling one. Those he didn't, he soon did. Howard founded—then sold—

TWA, but your father never let go of the Organization. Howard went into movies, bought RKO—Of course!" Cass jerked up straight. "Why didn't I think of it before? The documentary is the very thing!"

"Which documentary?"

"The one Dev made . . . You'll learn more from that in an hour and a half than I can tell you in weeks. You must have heard of it. It took first prize at the Venice Festival in the documentary section in 1960."

"No, I don't know it. But I've seen all his other films . . . You *are* talking about Dev Loughlin?"

"Who else? The no longer *enfant* but still *terrible* of movies!"

"You know him?"

"Know him?" Cass threw back her head and laughed. "I love him! He's gorgeous! And he's David's Jonathan . . . as well as Nieves's idol. His documentary is part of the course at Harvard Business School. It's a classic!"

"Aren't they all?"

"Artistically, yes. Commercially, no. They never make any money. Only critical acclaim . . . But let me get a showing set up." She reached for the house phone.

"Here?"

Cass again looked surprised, then smiled indulgently. Of course. How could she know . . . Oh, yes, she did have a lot to learn.

"We have a private cinema right here in the house. Seats fifty. You a movie fan?"

"Very much."

"Then you'll love this! It's a doozy . . ." Cass spoke rapidly into the phone, arranging a showing of the film for later on that morning. "In about an hour?" she asked, cradling the receiver.

"All right. Tell me more about the Organization—and the Tempests. They lived like kings, didn't they? Even to numbering the reigning Head of the House . . ."

"Well, this island *is* their kingdom. But you should ask Helen about the family. She's a walking history of its genealogy."

"And the people who live here?"

"They're mostly the descendants of the slaves the family brought with them from Virginia; except nobody is a slave here. They live and work on Tempest Cay from choice because they know when they are well off."

Something like a gleam appeared in Elizabeth's eyes. "I wonder how they will take me?"

"Three times a day with water!"

Elizabeth Sheridan laughed. "I am much better taken straight."

"Which is how you come across," parried Cass.

"You know the old cliché . . . honesty is the best policy."

"Sure . . . if you can afford the premiums!"

They both laughed. Cass found herself warming. You could say what you liked to this one and she still caught the ball. Cass admired verbal dexterity. In a house like Marlborough, in a family like this one, words had acquired the status of weapons. Against a man like Richard Tempest they were the only ones you had. Even David, slower of wit and more sensitive than his hulking exterior proclaimed, had acquired a swift turn of speech and knew when to run with a syntax. At times they came at you like a shower of hailstones, and if you didn't duck or retaliate with your own volley, you were likely to find yourself badly battered. This one had obviously learned how to defend herself a long time ago. As Dan had found to his lacerated cost last night.

As if she could read Cass's thoughts, Elizabeth asked: "And this present family. What about them?"

Cass stalled, surprised. "What about them? I thought it was the Organization you wanted to know about."

"The Organization keeps them, doesn't it? Their allowances come out of its profits."

"Well, yes . . ."

"And from the hints dropped by Mr. Grahame, I am supposed to continue those allowances?"

Cass shrugged. "That is entirely up to you."

"And them, surely. They have been given plenty of information about me. If I am to dole out money, I should know why."

Cass hid behind a cloud of smoke. Snitching was not what she had counted on, but Elizabeth had a point.

"What do you want to know?"

"How they come to be part of the Family; who their mothers were . . ."

Cass felt relieved. There was no harm in speaking of the dead.

"Amy Boscombe was the widow of an American officer Richard knew in the war who was killed in the Ardennes. She was a nice little thing, totally out of her depth at Marlborough, but she would have lived in ten thousand fathoms for Richard. She had a bad heart, and succumbed to it in 1951. Then, in 1957, Angela Danvers became the second Mrs. Tempest. She was an 'actress' . . . stunningly beautiful and shockingly promiscuous. Dan has inherited her looks. She was killed in an air crash in 1964 . . ." Cass paused to light a fresh cigarette. "How do you get on with Dan?" she asked casually.

"At arm's length."

"Best way. *Never* let him get you horizontal. Does his best—and worst—

work that way. Makes you and a financial assessment at the same time before presenting you with the bill. Mind you"—her grin was wicked—"by all accounts you get full value for money. Watch him," she advised bluntly. "He's a cardsharp. Carries them everywhere but between his teeth."

"He sets himself out to be charming."

"Oh, he can cast a spell. Usually a nasty one. Under the sugar icing is a very hard center, but I suppose the childhood he had would harden anyone. His father—he was Wentworth Godfrey, the racing driver—was killed when Dan was six, leaving Angela with a pile of debts. The only means she had of supporting them were her looks and very minimal skills as an actress. It was her looks which kept them by means of the money owned by the men taken by them . . . She was literally passed from hand to hand until she met Richard."

"And the Boscombes?"

"Army. Middle America, middle-class. Not used to money either. It went straight to their hang-ups. Margery's are sex and gambling; David's is drink."

She made it short and succinct. There were far too many shades of gray to paint now. Besides, she had the feeling Elizabeth Sheridan tended to see everything in only the strong, primary colors.

"And Miss Arden?"

"Sick. Very sick. I called the hospital this morning but Louis Bastedo says no visitors. She's still deep in some kind of traumatic shock." Cass shook her head. "Mattie is a highly emotional lady. Richard was—well . . ." Cass spread her hands. "And losing him has hit her right where it hurts."

"She is a great singer."

"Oh, yes . . . and a real prima donna in every sense . . ." Cass paused. "What do you intend doing about them all?" So far she had only felt Elizabeth's blunt instrument. Time to wield her own.

"What would you suggest?"

"Keep them—literally, I mean. That way is the easiest. If you are going to run the Organization you will have quite enough on your plate; you won't miss a few crumbs."

"How many crumbs?"

"Half a million dollars a year—each."

Elizabeth Sheridan's eyebrows moved.

Now Cass's smile was sardonic. "Margery has been known to drop that in one session at the tables; to Dan it is just another penny in the piggy bank; to David another reel in the can of Dev's latest movie . . ."

"And Miss Tempest?"

"Money is the least of her worries. Her mother left her very well fixed."

"And Marlborough, what runs that?"

"The Marlborough Trust—which she runs."

"Obviously superbly well."

"It's her life," Cass answered simply.

"And the Count?"

"Makes his own way."

"Nieves?"

"Again down to you."

"I see . . ." Again Elizabeth swung gently to and fro. "How are the allowances paid?"

"Quarterly, by transfer to their accounts, not that you can sign *anything* until probate is granted." Cass relished that. "Until then, you are on probate too."

"Who can sign, then?"

"I can. And Hervey." Cass's smile was acidulously sweet. "Come to that, until probate you can't do a damned thing . . . Everything depends on that official piece of paper."

"But if *I* wanted money?"

"Then you could have it—but not from the Estate. Helen always has a few thousand dollars floating around . . . But what would you need money for? Everything around here is free."

Elizabeth sat up abruptly. "Right. Now, could we see Dev Loughlin's documentary?"

"Right—you keep watch while I search," Dan ordered Margery.

Margery shrugged. "It's all right. She's closeted with Cass; they won't stir until lunch. What are we looking for, anyway?"

"Whatever we can find. Remember what Richard used to tell us—know thine enemy? Well, she's ours." He looked round the vast bedroom. "All right . . . you take the closet, I'll do the drawers."

They contained underwear. Color: nude, brand: Marks and Spencer. Bra size, 38B; tights, size 10 1/2, extra long. Various sweaters—also Marks and Spencer; gloves, scarves, no nightgowns. Obviously she slept raw. In one drawer was a small red-leather box which he opened. Jewelry, and not much of it. The pearl earrings she had worn—real, he found, when he bit into them; another pair that were real diamonds, small but good. A gold watch, from Le Must de Cartier. And an odd-looking ring—a hoop of multicolored stones. It looked old-fashioned, Victorian, probably, and the stones were set into the gold, not raised. They were a diamond, an emerald, an amethyst, a ruby, another emerald, a sapphire, and a topaz. Probably picked up in some antique shop. And in spite of being the Flawless Finish girl, she used another brand of makeup. For sensitive skins. In the bathroom, the Guerlain soap was hardly touched, so obviously she did not wash her face. Well, it worked. She had a fabulous skin. Toothpaste a common brand, a hard-bristle brush. No bottles containing pills.

"Found anything?" Margery peered in.

"Nothing of any use. You?"

"She makes her own clothes, takes a size-seven shoe, AA fitting. Got a gorgeous croc handbag, though—Hermès, yet. What was in the drawers?"

"Underwear, some jewelry, nothing really valuable."

"No diary, letters, photographs?"

"Nothing . . . Let's take a look at her luggage."

It was stacked on the shelves in the closet. Empty.

"Damn!"

"What did you expect?" Margery asked irritably.

"There has to be something. There always is. The trick is to find it. It's not here, obviously. We'll just have to dig into her past."

"London?"

"Wherever . . . and the sooner the better. Hervey has already got the valuation under way. He's in a hurry."

"You think I'm not?" grated Margery.

"Leave her to me."

"Oh no you don't! I've just as much at stake as you!" More, in fact, she thought, thinking of Andrea, wanting him instantly, ravenously. "What exactly are you looking for?" she went on.

"Something we can use as a lever to pry her loose from a sizable chunk of her inheritance."

"Blackmail?" Margery brightened. That was Dan's specialty.

"Of course!" Dan swept the room with his eyes. "I think we ought to concentrate on the mystery as yet unsolved. Her mother."

"But she's dead."

"Exactly . . . How? And where? And why? And just exactly what was she to Richard? Why *her* daughter? There's a whole shoal of things to be discovered about her. Like just exactly who she was. I am hoping that what we open will be a nasty little can of worms . . ." Dan was thinking rapidly. "Here's what we do. I've got a long-standing date for polo in Hamilton next week. I'll leave ostensibly on my way there. You make up your own story . . . No . . . tell the truth. Say you are just plain bored and now that our allowances are safe there is no reason to stay, is there? Say you are going back to Italy— but meet me in London at the house. You've still got your key?"

"Of course."

"Good . . . Then use it. Until probate is finally granted we are still the rich and mighty, so act that way . . . that's what she'll expect anyway."

"And just how long will all this take?"

"As long as necessary. The deadline is Hervey's submission for probate. Once that's granted we haven't a hope in hell. According to Hervey that, thank God, is still weeks and weeks away, so time is on our side, if nothing else."

He fixed her with a hate-filled, uncompromising glance. "We *have* to find something on her. It's our only hope. She's not going to cut the cake, so we just have to cook up a little something of our own, something that will lead to a very nasty case of indigestion. I've got a feeling about all this, and it tells me that the key lies with her mother. Richard never so much as mentioned her. Stuffed us to the gills with information about everything else, but not her. Why? He would have a reason; he always did. Could be she was already another man's wife; that was always his style. And he never went for nobodies. So, if Elizabeth Sheridan's mother was a somebody, it could be that there is a moldering pile of old bones just waiting to be dug up. And our price will be for reburying them . . ."

"But Hervey told us he already looked."

"Hervey!" Dan dismissed him scathingly. "All *he* would do would be to cast an eye over the surface. I'm the one who can detect an unmarked grave from a mile away. Didn't Richard teach me how?" Dan's smile was evil.

"But it was all such a long time ago . . ." Margery looked doubtful.

"And there are probably people who want it left there."

Margery's eyes shone, and she licked her lips greedily. "You think maybe some juicy scandal?"

"I *hope* some juicy scandal—all ready-made and waiting!"

"Like her clothes!" Margery said spitefully.

They were huddled in one corner of the enormous, mirror-lined closet as though for protection, but in spite of herself Margery had been impressed. They were exquisitely made. Elizabeth Sheridan could have got a job in any of the great Paris houses on the strength of her prowess with a needle. Copies, of course—but with her size they would have to be. Big, fat cow! Margery preened in the carved and gilded mirrors set into the wall of the bedroom, narrow as an arrow and killingly elegant in Calvin Klein pants and shirt. Elegant though she might be, Miss Moneybags would have to go a long way before she could outclass Margery di Primacelli in the fashion stakes— *and* lose a lot of weight!

She sparkled at herself in the mirror. In spite of Dan's orders about London, she was going to Italy. At the thought of Andrea's naked body her own started to twitch greedily. She could always keep him to heel by a casual reference here, an indifferently dropped figure there, to the indecent amount of money Richard had left. She would have to show him a token proof, of course, but make his mouth water at the thought of its being a tiny payment on account. Nobody outside the Island knew the contents of Richard's will, and nobody would. But there was absolutely no harm in keeping them guessing, tantalizing them . . . She had learned from Richard how to steal big. The bigger the lie the more people were eager to believe it. As Richard had proved time and time again. And if Dan said something was off, she did not doubt for one minute that he would find the remains of a very big pile of stinking fish. Dan was clever and Richard had taught him well. As she had learned her own lessons. Dan was right. Now was the time to put them into operation. He was taking a quick scan of the room, eyes raking everything to make sure there was no evidence of their search. He was a past master in the art of spying—another of Richard's well-learned lessons. She smirked. Richard had taught them dirty work for his own purposes. What a lovely turnabout that they should now have the opportunity to shovel the dirt onto him. *And* that hard-hearted, icy-eyed bastard of his.

"Right," she said eagerly. "Let's get started, then . . ."

Nieves tied her horse to a post of the veranda, leaving him to graze on the sand grass growing at its foot, then, taking the key from its place on the ledge of the post supporting the captain's walk, opened the front door of the beach house and slipped inside, leaning back against its closed solidity with a sigh.

Everything was neat and tidy. She kept it that way. Nobody else ever came here. Dev only ever came to the beach house when Richard had not been on the island, ever since they'd had that row . . . Nieves sighed. Then she went into the kitchen and laid the flowers she had brought on the drainboard. After fetching the vases from the sitting room, she threw the old blooms away and rearranged the fresh ones—glowing roses, clumps of hibiscus, bougainvillea, and oleander—in the big blue and white Delft vases, placed one on the mantel to one side of the painting David had done of Dev's sloop, the *Pinta,* another on the sofa table, the third on his desk by the window.

Then she got a duster and the can of spray polish from the cupboard and lovingly dusted and polished everything: the big, old desk, on which stood his portable typewriter, a stack of feint-ruled yellow pads and an old, handleless china mug filled with freshly sharpened pencils, the high-backed Jacobean chairs Helen had given him, the window ledges behind the sheer voile cur-

tains, the big table against the wall. When she had done, she made herself a
cup of coffee in the blue and white kitchen and took it back into the living
room, curling herself up in one corner of the old cretonne-covered sofa,
wishing Dev were there, in his usual place in the other corner.

Oh, Dev, Dev . . . if only you were here! We could go sailing . . . Her
eyes went to the painting of the *Pinta*, cutting through the blue of the sea,
white and blue sails billowing, scarlet paintwork glowing, brass gleaming.

Oh, if only you *were* here . . . you would not let her dominate *you*. She
couldn't . . . Nobody can. Oh, Dev . . . it's all so awful . . . everything
has been spoiled. She's like a disease and we've all caught it . . . she's pol-
luted even the air we breathe. You never know when you are going to come
across her. I found her in my garden temple yesterday . . . *my* place, where
I have always gone, only she was there with a book . . . she never does
anything else but read . . . and when I came up the steps she raised her
head and she just looked at me . . . I just turned my back and stalked away
. . . but I wanted to run!

She scares me, Dev . . . everything scares me now . . . I don't want to
stay here but I don't want to go back to school either, like Aunt Helen says I
must . . . I'm afraid to go and leave *her* here . . . and I can't stand the
way Daddy moons around after her, the way he looks at her, like she's some
precious icon, or something . . . while she does not even know he is there!
She's cold, Dev, hard and arrogant . . . callous as they come. How can *she*
be Gramp's daughter? He was so warm, so vital . . . she's so cold, so dead
. . . Oh, Dev, how could he do this to me? I thought he loved me . . . I
believed he loved me.

If you were here I could talk to you, tell you, because there is no one else.
Aunt Helen is worse than ever these days, so vague and distant from everything. Cass spends all her time with *her*. All Margery ever thinks of is her
appearance, and I don't trust Dan . . . Only Harry is kind . . . but not
like you, Dev, no one understands like you do . . . Oh, if only I could tell
you . . .

She sat up suddenly. "Why not?" she said aloud, in sudden excitement. "I
have to talk to someone or I'll just *die*. If he can't come to me then I must go
to him—oh, why didn't I think of it before?" She scrambled along the sofa to
where the telephone rested on the table. No time to be lost. Do it, and do it
now.

Elizabeth Sheridan stood for a moment adjusting her sunglasses before stepping from the air-conditioned cool of the house into the baking heat of the
afternoon. The house walls trapped the heat so that the first six feet of shade

was airless, but as she walked over to the terrace balustrade, the trade winds blew a cooling breeze. She put her hands on the sun-bleached white stone and lifted them quickly: it was red-hot. She moved away slightly while she stood and admired the view.

Marlborough had been built on a man-made plateau atop the highest point of the island; one hundred and fifty feet of hill now landscaped into a series of dazzling gardens, cooled by fountains and decorated by statuary, ablaze with cultivated flowers and the natural wild blooms of the island; scarlet hibiscus, purple bougainvillea, golden allamanda, blood-red poinsettia, creamy white and fragile pink frangipani, the cloudy blue jacaranda and coral and orange flame vines. In between Helen had created a rustic English garden, massed with roses and neat herbaceous borders, a formal Italian garden with rectangular pools and rococo fountains, a Japanese garden filled with miniature shrubs and trees, and expanses of carefully watered and lovingly tendered lawns with the occasional marble temple built in Greek classical style.

From the top terrace surrounding the house on all sides the view was panoramic and took in the whole of the island, a dense green mat of vegetation, curving sinuously away in front of her, but splotched, as if by a careless paintbrush, with bright daubs of brilliant color; the sugar-almond pastels of the houses in the village that ornamented the smaller hill which overlooked the harbor; the vivid sails of the boats which massed it; the bone-white buildings that were hospital, school, electricity generating plant, and packing station. Just outside the village lay the farms, the fields colored according to crop: melons, avocados, corn, and tomatoes. Just beyond was the lush pasture where the pure-bred herd of Charolais cattle grazed, and that ended in the deep sapphire of the lake, dead center of the island, clotted with the pink of its flamingos. Edging it was the forest, darkly verdant with pine and iron-wood, mahogany and lignum vitae, and that in turn gave way to the smooth undulations of the golf course, where sprinklers played endlessly. They ended at the foot of the hill, where the gardens began.

Skirting the gardens and separating them ran the well-tended gravel path which led down from the house to join the macadamed road which ran the length of the island, circling the golf course, slicing through the forest, around the lake and pastures, cutting the farms in two and disappearing into the village.

And all around was the sea; every shade of blue and green according to depth, with other islands set like emeralds in its blueness. The heavy warmth of the air was perfumed by the opulence of the tropical flowers; in the distance the horizon shimmered with heat.

Turning from that view, Elizabeth slowly walked the length of the now-faded pink tessellated marble of the terrace to its other end, which over-looked the airstrip, bleached bone-white, and the private harbor, dominated by Richard Tempest's yacht, *Tempestuous*, a lovingly restored San Francisco Flying Clipper, gleaming white and gold, surrounded by the smaller fry of Chris-Craft, sailboats, rowboats, and dinghies.

Nothing moved except the tide, causing the boats to rise and fall, but from the hangar at the near end of the strip came the sound of metal being hammered and the faint throb of an engine.

Turning to survey the view, Elizabeth's eye was caught by a sudden gleam of sun on water, but coming from what looked like a mass of leaves. Curi-ously, she walked by the side of the house to the flight of steps leading into the gardens, and saw the reason why. What she had thought was leaves were in fact vines, and it was from beneath them that she caught the blue gleam of water and the dazzle of something like gold. Descending the steps she found they disappeared beneath the roof of vines and ended on the marble floor of a man-made grotto, hewn out of the living rock and cooled by a series of waterfalls constructed of huge clam shells, the last of which trickled endlessly into a huge, circular swimming pool, its bottom lined with a mosaic repre-senting Neptune being drawn in his chariot by dolphins. It was this which glittered, gold and lapis lazuli and scarlet and green, under the clear water. One side of the pool was lined with changing cabins, the other held diving and spring boards. After the heat outside it was deliciously cool; the light, filtered through the vines, muted and kind to the eyes after the glare of the sun. The constant flow of water was soothing, and the cool shimmer of the pool inviting. In an instant, shucking off her clothes as she went and leaving them where they lay, Elizabeth took the half dozen steps to the poolside where she did a perfect dive to plunge naked into the still waters, and swim round and round the pool and under the water, until she surfaced for air before duck diving again.

She was floating on her back, hair streaming out behind her, when a voice asked mockingly: "Undine, is it? I could have sworn it was Elizabeth Sheri-dan . . ."

Twisting in the water and treading while she shaded her eyes because the voice came from the sundeck, she saw it was Dan Godfrey, standing on its topmost step, regarding her smilingly.

"Skinny-dipping, are we?" he drawled negligently, coming down the stone steps toward her. "There's a closet full of swimsuits in each cabana . . . or do you prefer swimming nude?"

Her body was a pale shimmer in the blue water. "I just prefer swimming."

He obviously preferred riding, because he was in palest beige jodhpurs and a
pure silk shirt, a foulard silk cravat thrust carelessly into its open neck.

"Mind if I join you?" he asked, his hands going to the buttons of his shirt.

"I've had my swim . . ." She turned to do a powerful crawl away from
him in the direction of her clothes, lying in a straight line from the bottom
step to the pool's edge. Placing her hands flat on the tiled top she vaulted
herself up and out of the water in one lithe and easy motion, scooped up her
clothes without breaking her stride, then made for one of the cabanas, disappearing inside, but not before leaving him with an impression of magnificent
nudity: broad shoulders, firm breasts, an enticing rump and endless legs, all
marble white but faintly tinged with the flush of her exertions.

A natural blonde, he noted. And a good swimmer. One of those tireless,
powerful water-babies. Obviously she possessed physical as well as mental
strength, but was in no way inclined to let him join her, which was interesting.

"You'll find brushes, combs, hair dryers—all you need," he called, strolling
toward the cabana she'd chosen.

When she came out again, dressed once more in shirt and slacks, she was
toweling the tangled mass of her hair. "Here, let me," he offered, reaching
for the brush she carried, "it's all tangled up . . ."

But she moved away from his hand. "I prefer to do it myself, thank you."

And doesn't like to be touched, he thought, salting that fact away too.
Prude? You are on to something here, Dan, my boy . . .

"It will dry quicker in the sun," he suggested. "Come up onto the sundeck."

It had a striped awning, cushioned stone benches, canopied swings and sun
loungers, all upholstered in primary-colored canvas duck edged in white. The
broad brick wall which overlooked the airstrip was lined with hibiscus and
oleander in pots.

"If you go without a hat your hair will soon be lint white," Dan observed.
"The sun is very strong here. Don't let those trade winds fool you . . . How
about a cold drink?"

He went to a massive icebox, brought out a tall pitcher filled with liquid
that was faintly pink.

"Our famous Marlborough fruit punch . . . oranges, lemons, pineapple,
passion fruit, papayas . . . all liquidized and spiced with rum . . . most
refreshing." He poured her a highball glass full.

She drank deeply. "Mmm . . . delicious . . ."

"Fresh every day; if no one drinks it the servants do . . ." The eyebrows
lifted. "You'll get used to the rich life," he advised tolerantly. "Everything

here is changed every single day, whether anyone uses them or not; towels, brushes, combs . . . even the water in the pool . . . seawater, by the way, as you will have noticed. In fact, you will not only become used to it, you will expect it." He stretched out in a canopied swing. "So, what have you been doing with yourself—apart from work. Cass tells me you are a glutton for that."

"I've been taking my bearings, mostly in the gardens. I only just discovered this."

"You are a good swimmer."

"I like the water."

Reaching to a shelf behind him he handed her a large bottle of oil. "I would anoint yourself," he said, "and liberally . . . you have a very fair skin."

His voice was casual but his eyes filled with meaning. He saw a faint downcurve of—distaste?—bend her lips, as though he had introduced a totally unnecessary twist to the conversation. She took the bottle, laid it to one side.

"That's a very good oil . . . it will prevent you from burning. Would you like me to rub you?"

"No, thank you."

Yes, the distaste *was* there; a definite *frisson*. No doubt about it; she definitely did not like to be touched.

"I take it you like lotus land, then?" he asked comfortably.

"I have no complaints."

"What about the natives?"

"Harmless."

Bitch! He drained his glass, refilled it, feeling the rum warm.

Leaning back in her own lounger: "You never stop trying, do you?"

"If at first you don't succeed . . ."

"We had a motto at Henrietta Fielding: 'Thriftiness is next to Godliness.' Waste was pointed out to us as the eighth deadly sin; to do without was a virtue and a strength."

"So that's where you get it from," he murmured. "But in that case, does not the thought of all that money lying around going to waste not grieve you?"

"But it is not going to waste, is it? It is earning interest—apart from yours, of course."

Riding that one: "Which is in you. I never knew anyone brought up in a Home as distinct from a home . . . What was it like?" He was viciously polite, ostensibly sympathetic but reminding her mercilessly of her background.

"Things have changed since Oliver Twist."

He persisted. "It must have been very—hard—for you; your mother dying when you were so young . . ."

"I don't remember."

"Not remember your own mother?"

"Not at all."

I wonder, he thought. True or because it suits her to say so?

"But surely when she died—she must have left something of herself behind?"

"Only me."

And that is all that matters to you, he thought. He had never met such a self-absorbed woman. Her world began and ended with herself. She had no interest in anyone else. Self-reliant unto making her own clothes. Still, that went with the rest of her. She herself was an original. Look at Margery. Everything she wore had a designer label. Take them away and she did not exist. She was what her clothes made her. This one made her clothes.

All part of her structure, he mused. She knows who she is and is quite happy with it. Probably resents all this as an intrusion. Look at the way she is dealing with it. Quite unemotionally. Not feeling it, only thinking it. Which was, he thought, the key to her. She rationalized everything. Probably had a lot to do with why she did not like to be touched. Would not swim naked with him; would not let him brush her hair; would not let him apply suntan oil. This, he reflected, deprived him of his weapon—or the use of it, anyway. Women who did not like to be touched usually had a fear of men. And this one had brought her ten-foot barge poles with her. I think, he mused, I have stumbled on my first clue. A hang-up about sex, maybe? That sort of thing would go with her ice-maiden appearance . . . This bore looking into . . . Then he saw the book she had been carrying, now laid on the cane table beside her. He turned his head to read the spine. *The Tempests: A Family and Its History*. And that gave him his idea.

"I see you are interested in your antecedents," he observed casually. "But that is a dull old tome . . . If you want to know about your forebears, I know of a much more interesting way."

"Oh? What?"

"Would you like me to show you?"

"Yes, please." He was under no illusions. It was what he was going to show her which sparked her interest; not the fact that he was going to show her. Another clue.

He had pondered how to get her alone. Now the perfect opportunity had been offered. He took her back into the house, into the vast library, sixty feet long and forty feet high, crammed with books and a couple of long leather chesterfields on which to lie and read them. On a table almost as long as the room were laid out a plethora of the latest magazines, indicating the interests of their readers, ranging from *Time* and *Newsweek* to the *Spectator* and *Economist* via *Vogue, Harper's, Women's Wear Daily* (Margery's bible), *Town and Country, Field and Stream, Opera,* and the *Connoisseur.* But Dan went straight to the shelves at the bottom by the windows, where he lifted down half a dozen big photograph albums, beautifully bound in fine calf and tooled in gold with relevant dates.

"The very thing," he announced. "A photographic history of the Tempests, from the earliest daguerreotypes to the latest David Bailey. They will tell you far more than that boring old tome . . ."

But he did not lay them on the table. He carried them to the long chesterfield, dumping them in one corner and calling: "Come on . . . these need two laps." That way he could get real close; body contact was an infallible sign. But when he laid the spread volume across their joint laps she was sitting well away from him. There was no body contact whatsoever. Knew it! he thought delightedly. Frigid as hell, solid all the way through. But to confirm it, as he turned the pages he did so in a manner that brought his left arm into contact with her right breast. But only the once. Next time she had moved. No doubt remained. In this permissive day and age, Elizabeth Sheridan was a twenty-seven-year-old virgin or he had not ceased to be at the age of fourteen.

But he gave no sign. He merely gave her an amusing running commentary on who was who.

The first volume was Victorian: bearded men and chignoned women, posing artfully on terrace balustrades or with dimpled cheek on well-turned wrist. They played croquet or picnicked on the lawns, or sat holding the reins of pony traps while a groom held the horse's head. They gave way to Edwardians: the women with tight corsets and frizzed hair, billowing bosoms spilling laces and pearls, the men with pomaded hair and waxed mustaches. They, in turn, gave way to the twenties: shingled hair and skirts above the knee, men in flannels and striped blazers; and the thirties: women with marcel waves and pure silk stockings, the men at the wheel of Lagondas or MGs or three-liter Bentleys. It was not until they came to the war and its aftermath that Dan really came into his own.

"That was Margery's first husband . . . he was a duc. I'm afraid she came down in the world afterward; nothing but marquises and counts since then

. . . He was her second—a White Russian prince—and the only one worth a light. A great sportsman, Dimitri Galitzin. The trouble was, he hunted women too and Margery would not stand for that . . ."

Lightly he touched on the character of each face, usually leaving his sting behind. Dan had a malicious tongue hidden under a froth of sweet smoothness, but Elizabeth Sheridan gave no sign either of appreciation or otherwise. What interested her were the photographs themselves, though not enough to prevent her from moving away when he got too close. Fascinating, he thought gleefully. A woman who looks like she does? It was another layer peeled away, but hidden in between the others was the reason why. A bad experience, perhaps? Rape, even? Or that self-absorption of hers? But why? What had turned her off men and into herself?

While she was gazing at the photographs he was surreptitiously gazing at her. She *looked* unawakened. There was about her the air of something untouched, unused. Women who weren't virgin had a certain glaze about them . . . moved differently, were aware of their bodies in a different way. And this one ignored hers. Fed it and dressed it and kept it clean. But no more.

He compared her to Margery. When you looked at her you *knew*. It exuded from her like perspiration; a definite sheen. This one was cool, chaste . . . Frigid, he thought, just as coldly. Which only made him the more convinced that the answer to Elizabeth Sheridan lay in her childhood. That Home, for instance, and the five years she had spent elsewhere before entering it . . . He found he was becoming impatient to be away, to start digging. Instead, he sat on and talked.

"Yes . . . that's Cass. A real carrot top in those days." He could see she was fascinated by the young, beardless David, whose mouth under the beard was revealed as being as soft as a woman's. And the young Margery, when her hair was still brown and her figure undisciplined. And Helen, thirty years ago, shy and vulnerable and fragile.

She examined with care Richard Tempest's two wives. The one a little brown wren, the other a bird of paradise.

"You are very like your mother," she observed, glancing up at him.

"Only to look at."

Angela Danvers lounged in a hammock under a tree, surrounded by adoring young men. Her blond hair was exquisitely coiffed, her body veiled in semitransparent chiffon; it was only when you looked closely that you saw the flawless breasts displayed with cunning lubricity. Dan stared at his mother, a curious flatness in the glittering, water-colored eyes, and turned the page.

She lingered longest over the photographs of Richard Tempest, going back, again and again, to contrast the man with the boy, poring over every photograph in which he appeared. Until, "Who is that?" she asked, laying a forefinger on a certain face. Dan looked.

"Oh . . . him! That's Dev Loughlin . . . he used to be Richard's blue-eyed boy. But first the honeymoon ended, then they got a divorce . . . then Richard banished him from Paradise." Dan's voice was savage with glee. And then deliberately, just to see her reaction, "But catnip to the ladies. He just has to appear on the scene and they can't get enough."

And there it was. A faint *frisson* of distaste, a more gelid set to the features. She did not ask why, but she closed the book reluctantly. "That was indeed informative . . . thank you."

"My pleasure," he demurred, tucking away the information she had all unknowingly handed him. "My pleasure indeed."

Helen Tempest cleared her throat. "It has occurred to me," she said, lying in her teeth because she had thought of nothing else for days, "that I have not shown you over the house."

Elizabeth Sheridan laid aside her book. "No hurry," she said easily. "I have lots of time."

"Nevertheless"—having nothing else, Helen clung to the rules—"I should have asked you sooner." As she had done in her mind, rehearsing the words over and over in front of the mirror, staring at a death's head. Remember who you are, she had told it, and heard the evil echo back: "And what you are." As she had been doing so much, lately. Remembering things she had thought long forgotten, put away in the attic of her mind. Since Elizabeth Sheridan's arrival it had been brought out into the light, covered with dust but still hideous. But she could not hide her head in the sand forever. "You realize there is far too much to see in just one visit. Perhaps if we started with a walk-through? That would give you an idea of its size and layout. Once you know your way around you can revisit at your leisure."

Elizabeth rose to her feet. There were only inches between them, to Elizabeth's advantage. Helen turned away.

"We will begin in the Great Hall . . ." Their footsteps echoed on its tessellated flags. "We call it 'Great' because it is the largest of the five in the house and because it houses the family portraits."

It was big, high, echoing, the floor a chessboard of gleaming marble. On either side of the massive front door, with its enormous brass lock and bolts, polished like mirrors, stood twin Georgian sedan chairs of brass-studded crimson leather, in which footmen had once sat. Above the door hung the Island flag, which was of the colors and arms of the House of Tempest, powder blue and scarlet, with the motto I WILL SURVIVE embroidered in gold. In the center of the floor stood a vast marble console on which rested a superb Ming bowl massed with lilacs; in front of it, the heavy, leather-bound visitors' book and a brass tray filled with pens. Hiding the green baize door to below stairs was a magnificent coromandel screen; above it, on the walnut panels of the wall, hung an ornate Chinese Chippendale mirror complete with candle sconces. Placed at intervals was a set of eight Jacobean chairs with intricately carved backs and crimson brocade cushions fringed in gold. And everywhere sunshine poured down from the dome of the cupola on the roof; light falling like torchbeams to highlight the glitter of the Waterford chandelier, bounce gleams from polished brass, and make the colors of the portraits which lined the wide staircase glow.

Helen halted before the first, a full-length portrait of a Jacobean gentleman wearing green velvet slashed with gold, with a ruby in one ear and another on a finger of the hand resting on his jeweled sword hilt. He had green-gilt hair and bold green eyes and a haughty expression. "The Founder," Helen said, with a gesture of the hand that was pure pride. "The Honorable Richard Tempest the First. He was a friend of James the First, who made him a land grant in Virginia, where he founded the dynasty and built the first Marlborough, burned when the family left America after the revolution." Reaching out a hand she pressed one of the roses carved on the frame and the portrait swung out, revealing the cage of a small seat-lined lift. "My mother found it difficult to climb the stairs later in life so we had this installed." She let the portrait swing back again. "And this is his wife, the Lady Arabella . . . and here is their son, Francis . . ."

The portraits ascended in chronological order and changing fashion, but so often with the same face, especially the hair and the eyes. They were always green, always brilliant. Each was sumptuously dressed, dazzlingly bejeweled. As their power and wealth increased, so did their magnificence. Helen knew each one. Name, history, position in the family hierarchy. To her they were not just painted faces; they were people who had lived in this house, walked its corridors, slept in its beds, eaten at its tables. Their blood ran in her veins, and her attitude, her carriage, the look in her eyes, proclaimed her pride.

As they ascended the stairs, that pride stiffened her backbone, tilted her head up, lightened her face and bearing, so that at last, when they reached the Upper Hall, and progressing round it came to the enormous Sargent which dominated one wall, she flung out a hand and announced: "My grandparents Nicholas Tempest VI and his wife Charlotte, with their children, Francis, who was my father, and Victoria. It was painted on the occasion of the tercentenary of the Founding, in 1903."

They stood grouped before the portrait of the Founder, which had been placed on an easel in the Great Hall. Nicholas Tempest, a tall, blond man with a quiet but proud face; his wife, plain but undeniably elegant, her hair piled in a pompadour, wearing a sweeping scarlet-velvet gown embellished with finest lace among which the gleam of priceless pearls could be glimpsed, a diamond fob watch pinned to her bosom, a sable stole trailing from her shoulders. Their son, Francis, was a reprint of his father, while their daughter, Victoria, was plain like her mother, but sturdy and high-colored.

"My grandmother was much loved on the Island . . . she established the hospital here, which my brother rebuilt and greatly enlarged."

Helen moved on, pausing before the last of the portraits. "And this"—she gazed at the portrait with eyes suffused with love—"is the portrait Philip de Laszlo painted of the last Tempest Family. My parents and their children. My brother Richard, my twin brothers Charles and Nicholas, and myself . . ." Her eyes, as she gazed at the portrait, were somehow sad, suffering, filled with a longing to be part of that family still. "It was painted in 1931 on the occasion of my brother's coming of age."

Francis Tempest, fully adult now, stood holding the hand of his ten-year-old daughter, Helen, demure in a crisp white lawn dress tied with a blue satin sash, matching bows tied around her fat ringlets. She leaned against him shyly, one foot crossed over the other, in white stockings and patent leather slippers with flat bows. Her mother stood between her twin sons, their arms around her waist. Her blond hair was marcelled in the style of the period and she was wearing a Fortuny Delphos dress of fine silk velvet, a golden girdle around her waist and a long strand of pearls to her knees. On his father's right stood the heir, Richard Tempest, at twenty-one. Already head-turningly handsome, he leaned negligently against the portrait of the Founder, so that the astonishing likeness to a man dead three hundred years was thrown into startling prominence. The two could have changed clothes and no one would have remarked on the change of identities. His hair was just as greenish gilt, his eyes as green, his expression as haughty, but lightened by a sardonic glint to the eye, a mocking tilt to the smile. He knew who he was; he knew he was handsome; he knew it was his face you were looking at.

"The last Tempest Family," Helen repeated, and her voice was full of longing.

"What happened to your twin brothers?"

The unexpected question seemed to startle Helen from a reverie because she jumped visibly. "Oh . . . they were killed in the *Hindenburg* crash. They were returning from a tour of Europe with their tutor." Her sadness made her voice low. "They were only eighteen years old. My mother never got over it; it affected her health and she died not long after the war began. My father . . ." Helen's voice constricted and it was obvious that he had been adored. "My father was killed in London when a buzz bomb destroyed the Old Tempest Building . . ." Her voice was a whisper. "He was only fifty-seven, and I—I was left only with my brother."

"There were no other Tempests?"

"In England, yes . . . but not here, in the Bahamas. My father's sister has a son but, of course, he is not a Tempest." Helen turned slowly, almost reluctantly, as though forcing herself to face, not another portrait, but flesh and blood. "You are . . ." She sounded puzzled, as though she could still not quite believe it.

"I know. I've been looking at my own face all the way up the stairs." Elizabeth turned, her gaze sweeping past all the long-dead but not-forgotten faces of her ancestors. "They all look so totally sure of themselves."

"They were." The pride was back in Helen's voice. "As members of a great family. It was their destiny, and as individual members they dedicated themselves to its continuing greatness. How else are great families made?" Helen's pride turned to bleakness. "Now it is all finished . . . now there is no Family, merely a collection of individuals."

Helen's head came round slowly, and her beautiful aquamarine eyes met Elizabeth's emerald gaze. Her voice was bitter when she said, with another gesture toward the de Laszlo: "Yes. *That* is the last, true Tempest Family . . ." She gazed at it somberly.

"It has always seemed to me," Elizabeth observed, "that pride in oneself came first." She smiled faintly, turned back to the portrait. "Do *you* think I look like him?"

"You are his image," Helen answered in a stifled voice. She began to fiddle restlessly with the enormous aquamarine she wore on her right hand before turning away and walking toward a pair of carved and gilded double doors set between the last two portraits. She placed one hand on the handles, which were shaped in the form of plumes. There she waited until Elizabeth joined her, then pressed down slightly until the door gave instantly, silently on oiled hinges. Helen took one step inside, inhaled deeply, then motioned Elizabeth forward, before closing the door behind them.

But as she turned to her once more, her mouth opened in astonishment. Elizabeth Sheridan was transformed. She quivered like a pointer which had just found. The gelid control had melted; she was flushed, bright-eyed, radiant with delight. Helen was astounded. Until she realized what had happened. Her own warmth, that of relief and joy, released a spontaneous, transfiguring smile, for she knew her fears had been foolish. Marlborough was pleading her cause for her. Silently, Helen took station behind Elizabeth as she began, like some awed acolyte, to walk slowly, almost drift through the Aladdin's cave that was Marlborough.

The light that filtered through drawn jalousies was aqueous; you felt that at any moment gorgeously hued fish would glide silently by. Helen threw them back and golden light flooded in, striking dazzle from crystal and silver, making porcelain glow and fabrics glisten. There was no sound, but the silence was soothing; footfalls were hushed by the thick pile of magnificent carpets. The house had a presence, benign, indulgent, like some great beauty who knows she will always be the most beautiful of them all.

With unerring taste Helen had distributed the results of countless forays around the world by members of the family. From the treasure houses of the storerooms she had chosen only the best, and set them into a pattern of beauty that dazed the eye and stilled the tongue. Never had she been so glad that she had done so.

There was not a speck of dust. The maids had already been through, and Helen had done her flowers. Each morning, two footmen pushing great trolleys behind her, she went round the house placing fresh-cut flowers in porcelain bowls and vases, silver epergnes, crystal flutes. Already they had scented the air.

Helen could see that Elizabeth was stunned. It was evident in the parted lips, the shining eyes, the ecstatic expression, as she gazed with unbounded delight and pleasure at a palette of the most exquisite colors: soft, faded rose, delicate silvery blue, faintly flushed cream, sharpest, singing lemon. Great mirrors hung on silk-lined walls, reflecting fabulous French furniture and the patina of fine old woods: rosewood and satinwood, walnut and mahogany. Ceilings matched carpets, everything in sumptuous harmony, an incomparable wealth of Louis XV and XVI furniture disposed on Aubusson and Savonnerie carpets under Beauvais tapestries and Spitalfields silk or carved boiserie panels. There were giltwood cabinets filled with Sèvres soft-paste and the baroque jewel figures of delicate carvings in ebony and gold, silver gilt and jade.

There were paintings everywhere, marvelous English paintings: Gainsborough and Reynolds and Lawrence and Stubbs, and they too were hung with an eye to the furnishings, so that the Gainsborough of Lady Sophia Tempest wearing a liquefaction of French blue satin matched the Lyon silk of chairs and hangings, the yellow roses in her straw hat echoed in the flower arrangements.

The impact was one of stunning, overwhelming beauty, and it broke through Elizabeth's controlled calm.

Helen had not expected such a response. She walked slightly behind, only going ahead to open doors, allowing Elizabeth to float through carved and gilded lintels into vista after vista of breathtaking beauty. She watched as Elizabeth touched, caressed, smoothed, trailed, bent to inhale the fragrance of roses massed in brilliant Chinese vases whose enamel was so fresh it seemed to be liquid. Without exchanging a word they drifted round the house, Helen and her captive audience, whose ecstatic response was, though made in total silence, more eloquent than any words.

Helen's heart was at peace. She felt, for the first time since Elizabeth Sheridan had come to Marlborough, once more in possession of herself. But all she could find to say, inside herself, was a litany of "Thank you, thank you, thank you," both to Marlborough and whoever or whatever had concealed, at the heart of a coldly beautiful jewel, a molten center and an acute, almost agonizing, response to beauty. All her worrying, all her fears . . . how could she have doubted Marlborough? Had it ever failed? But never had she *felt*, as if it were her own, such a total, overwhelming response. And from Elizabeth Sheridan of all people! Helen took it unto herself and rejoiced. She knew, knew with an ineradicable confidence, that Marlborough was safe, that she was safe, that nothing would now ever be changed. Not by this woman. Not by this acolyte who was a total believer.

When finally, after a couple of the most fantastic hours Elizabeth Sheridan had ever spent, they emerged into the Upper Hall again by means of the double doors on the other side of it, Helen closed them behind her, placing her palms flat against the carved wood as though trying to express, by touch, all she felt in her heart. But when she turned back to Elizabeth her warm smile froze. The impassioned response had congealed once more into classical calm. It shocked Helen speechless.

"And you did all this?" Elizabeth asked.

"The means were there . . ." Helen faltered.

"Perhaps, but you have done something incredible with them. I have seen all that England has to offer but this . . ." Elizabeth let out a long breath.

"I am glad you like it," Helen murmured, deeply gratified. "I come often just to walk around it. It has a presence. You noticed? It soothes and restores."

"Yes." Elizabeth's voice was remote. "We all have our religions."

Hesitantly, greatly daring, Helen ventured: "I think—perhaps we share the same one?"

"Beauty in all its forms." A faint smile. "I was brought up in an atmosphere of brown paint and polished lino. I had no idea what a house could be like until I went to Uppark one summer. Since then I have seen every one it is possible to see."

"And I," exclaimed Helen delightedly. "When I was creating Marlborough I went round all of them myself." She clasped her hands in excitement, "And now you will be able to go round this one whenever you like."

"Oh, I shall like," Elizabeth assured her.

Helen glowed, only again to be taken aback when Elizabeth asked practically: "It must cost the earth to run?"

"Half a million pounds a year."

She expected Elizabeth to wince, but she only asked: "Is that enough?"

"Everything is costed. My brother did a time and motion study some years ago . . . I have the fabric surveyed every year and the contents checked. I always clean every piece of porcelain and crystal myself, and a specialist firm comes here to clean carpets and fabrics when necessary. The house is kept at a constant, thermostatically controlled temperature and I protect the rooms from the sun. It is very strong here, you know, and can play havoc with color and fabric." Helen felt the need to explain, to share. "The contents are cataloged, of course, so if you would like to study them . . ."

"Oh, I would. Please."

They were walking back across the hall, but slowly, Elizabeth obviously reluctant to leave.

"And you do it all yourself? No housekeeper?"

"I run the house myself . . . Moses, our majordomo, assists me, and I am fortunate in having a large staff . . . but, yes, I do it all. My brother left it all to me."

Elizabeth Sheridan turned her head. "Oh, no," she corrected coolly, "he left it all to me."

"I would not have believed it had I not been there to see it," Helen told Cass later. "It was *the* most astonishing thing. She *can* feel, Cass; she *does* feel—and deeply. If you had seen her response!"

Cass looked impressed, but her mind was occupied with other things, and she was only giving Helen half an ear, even though—the result of long practice—her attention appeared to be fixed. What was on Cass's mind was the sudden departure of the heavenly twins. The fact that they—ever an unholy alliance—were going their separate ways didn't mean a thing. Dan was his usual, flat-calm self, but all of a sudden Margery was full of the joys of spring, and considering that ever since the reading of the will she had been suffering her own winter of discontent, the change at once registered on Cass's barometer. She knew of no reason why Margery should undergo a spring change; true, she still had her allowance, but it was nothing compared to what she had expected. So it had to be something else. Andrea Farese? Cass had heard he was a prime stud, was reputed to have laid everything but the railroad tracks, and that Margery had at last found someone up to her every trick. And she *had* said she was going back to Italy. But . . . would a woman, going back empty-handed to a lover to whom she had promised the earth, look so all-fired smug? Dan never gave anything away—unless he had no use for it; but Margery's brains had never been much in evidence, and they had long been scrambled by sex and sybaritism.

Italy my foot, Cass was thinking, as she saw a procession of footmen coming downstairs carrying bags. Dan's had already been loaded; he was probably airborne by now, bound—he said—for Nassau. Margery was using the Jetstream luggage. "I have to go carefully now," had been her reason. Yes, but where? Cass thought.

". . . and I am to go on running everything as before," Helen was saying with a dazed sort of happiness. "She *asked* me to, Cass. She said no one else could . . . She even asked me if I needed more money."

"Fine. I'm really happy for you, Helen . . . Now, if you'll just excuse me . . . I want a word with Margery."

She was just coming down the stairs, groomed to the nth degree in an ice-cream-white Yves St. Laurent pants suit, a rakish trilby set aslant her lion's mane of hair.

"A word in your shell-like." Cass strong-armed her to one side. "Once you are off this island, don't get the idea you are off-limits. One word of any of this and I'll have her cut off your allowance."

Margery jerked her arm free. "I never bore my friends by talking about my family!" she snapped.

"Really! And here was I thinking that you didn't have one or the other!"

Margery bridled and Cass stared hard into the mascara-laden eyes. "I mean it, kiddo. If you so much as tell it to the breeze . . ."

Margery could only bluster: "You've changed your tune, then; not that I haven't noticed you playing hers. Sucking up to her." Quaking before Cass's hard stare, she hurried on: "You needn't worry! I have better things to do!" and ran.

Cass was still standing there, gnawing on a thumbnail, when Helen stopped by her.

"Cass . . . have you seen Nieves?"

"Huh! Oh, no. Why?"

"Well, Moses tells me she took one of the powerboats over to Nassau early this morning and is still not back." Helen was uneasy. "Nieves never goes across to Nassau alone . . . or anywhere unless she tells me first." She hesitated. "But she has been very antagonistic to Elizabeth."

Cass noticed the use of the first name but gave no sign. Only then did what Helen had been telling her fully sink in.

"Friends?" she asked, smiling crookedly, and feeling annoyed for no good reason.

"Well . . ." Again Helen hesitated. "I think we have reached—understanding," was all she would commit herself to.

"And she really liked the house?" Now she really *was* remembering what Helen had said.

Helen shook her head wonderingly. "If I was speaking of anyone but Elizabeth Sheridan, I would say more a falling in love."

Cass repressed a frown. That was out of the character impression she had formed.

" 'Whatever you want,' she said to me, 'whatever you need.' "

Cass felt that hit home. "And why not?" she asked lightly, reaching for the common sense. "She's no fool, you know. She knows she could never run a house like this."

Helen shook her head again. "I think she could do anything she put her mind to," she said seriously. "She is going to run the Organization."

"You in your small corner, me in mine," Cass observed. Then, unable to resist it: "But you do realize that we are privileged only because we can *do*. I don't believe for one moment she'd have any use for us otherwise."

"I know," Helen said, giving Cass the surprise of her life. "She has not much use for people, but she loves—things . . . beauty, craftsmanship, elegance." She shook her head again, still having difficulty in coming to terms with her good fortune, and the way it had come about. "There is a lot going on beneath the surface, Cass. I saw it this afternoon. It was as though I had unlocked a secret door . . . and out of it came an Elizabeth Sheridan I did not recognize; warm and—and *feeling* and—and—"

"Human?" asked Cass.

Helen's face lit up. "Yes, that was it. All of a sudden she came alive."

Which was how Nieves was feeling. Filled with excited anticipation, even though she felt sick with nerves and queasy with guilt. It had been so easy. She had taken one of the powerboats and asked one of the boatmen to take her across to Nassau. Once there, she had sent him back to the Island saying she would call when she wanted to return home, because she intended to spend the day shopping. After seeing the boat out of sight, watching from behind a pile of bales, she had made for the British Airways office, where she had bought herself a one-way ticket to Dublin via London.

She had purloined a fat roll of bills from Helen's household drawer and had carefully checked airline timetables so as to be sure of making the connection without too much hanging about. She had her passport safe and a big pair of sunglasses, donning them when she bought her ticket. Then she went along Bay Street and bought herself a bag and some underwear, some short-sleeved T-shirts and a thick sweater, as well as her first pair of jeans.

She changed in the lavatory at the airport, then, feeling strange and oddly shy, she had hid herself behind a copy of the *Bahamian Review* while she waited for her flight to be called. She had reasoned that if they came after her, they would not be looking for a teenager dressed like any other teenager instead of the prim and proper Nieves Boscombe. And she had brushed out her hair and let it hang about her face, in the manner of current teenage fashion, instead of her usual neat ponytail. She also provided herself with a big straw hat which, when pulled down, half-hid her face. With that and the big sunglasses obscuring the upper half of her face, she felt reasonably disguised, but she knew she was hectically flushed and was convinced that everyone was staring at her. When she joined the throng flocking together for her flight, she scuttled along, head down, and lost herself in the middle.

On the plane, she was just another passenger in the tourist section, which fascinated her, as she had never before traveled other than as a passenger in a private jet, usually one belonging to the Organization. This was different, uncomfortably crowded—and she had a large, fat lady next to her, the fat flowing into her own seat.

Once airborne, the lady brought out her knitting, while Nieves waited for the dreaded conversation to start. Then she noticed the pattern the lady was following was written in German, and from the way the lady tried to talk to the flight attendant, she had little English. With relief, Nieves relaxed in her seat, and the release of tension was so great she drifted off to sleep.

When she got to Dublin, it was raining and cold. She pulled on her sweater and went looking for a taxi. The driver eyed her up and down: the jeans, the long hair, the single bag, which did not go with the cultured accent, and said disapprovingly: "And isn't that all of sixty mile!" when she told him her destination.

"I can pay," Nieves told him haughtily.

"And it's awful late for a young lady like you to be goin' off into the wilds of Galway!"

"But I'm expected!" Nieves lied quickly. "I called them just now and they said to take a taxi and they would be waiting up for me."

" 'Tis to be hoped somebody is. Where was it you said—Kilmarran, was it?"

"Yes . . . it's Mr. Dev Loughlin's house. The film director," Nieves added helpfully.

"Dev Loughlin, is it, now? And didn't he do a fine play at the Abbey Theatre last year . . ." He opened the cab door.

On this, the last lap of her daring and exciting journey, Nieves found her excitement turning to apprehension. She looked back at what she had done and was astonished. She had not realized desperation could drive you to such lengths. Well, I am desperate, she thought defiantly. But guilt was beginning to undermine her resolution at the thought of the worry she must have caused. Dev will explain, she thought. He'll know what to do, he always does.

As the driver turned off the main road, she peered out and recognized, even in the darkness, the familiar lane. "It's not far now," she said excitedly. She sat on the edge of her seat, face pressed to the window. "There it is . . . those big gates—that's Kilmarran!"

They were open, as always, and as the cab drove through them and up the long, straight drive toward the lights of a big house, she squirmed on the edge of the seat, her hand ready on the handle, and even as the cab stopped under the peeling stucco of a large portico she was out and lifting the big iron knocker to send it thundering. Almost at once the front door opened and she fell, in a welter of frantic tears, into the arms of the tall, dark man who stood there.

"Dev . . . oh, Dev!"

The taxi driver dumped Nieves's bag at her feet. "That's thirty pound you owe me."

Nieves fumbled through her tears until Dev took the roll of notes from her hand and paid the man, adding a good tip.

The driver grinned. "And a good night to *you!*"

Inside the big hall, lit by a fine but dirty Waterford chandelier, Dev Loughlin took a handkerchief from his trouser pocket. "Here . . . it's a wet-enough night."

But Nieves would not loosen her clutch on his shirt, her face pressed against his chest. "I had to come. I had to! It was the only thing left to me . . . Oh, Dev, I've been so unhappy."

Dev raised her face with one finger, mopped away tears with the handkerchief.

"All right . . . you can tell me all about it. It surely must be something terrible to make you do a bolt."

"It is, it is! You just don't *know.*"

"No, but I am sure you'll tell me . . ."

Nieves sniffed waterily, looking adoringly up into the dark Spanish face with its intensely blue Irish eyes. "That's why I came . . . because I knew I could."

"Come on then. I've got hot coffee and sandwiches."

"Oh, lovely! The food on the plane was *awful!* Do people actually eat that stuff?"

"People who aren't rich do. You never have seen how the other three quarters live, have you?" But Dev's smile, which lit the dark face, made Nieves giggle, weak with relief. He was not angry. He looked kind and safe and secure as ever.

She looked up at him nervously. "Have you heard from Marlborough?"

"I have. Three times."

Nieves flushed. "I suppose they are worried . . ."

"Naturally. When a meek and mild miss, like Nieves Boscombe, takes it into her head to fly the coop—on a scheduled flight, no less—they worry. And wonder why."

Nieves hung her head. "I didn't know what else to do."

"Then let us call them and tell them what you have done. *Then* you can tell me why."

He walked her into a vast and sparsely furnished room, of a faded grandeur, where a big wood fire burned. Only one lamp—above a big, badly scarred table—lit the room. It hung over a moviola machine which was surrounded by thousands of feet of 35-mm film. Nieves darted toward it, exclaiming: "Oh, Dev! Is this it?"

"Yes. I'm just doing the editing—or trying to. When Cass will let me."

Nieves looked shamefaced. "I'm sorry," she whispered. Seeing the fire, she went toward it, held out her hands, then turned her back to it, rubbing her enticingly curved rump, numb from so many hours of sitting, as she looked round the room. "The Lawrence!" she exclaimed. "It's gone!"

"To Sotheby's." Dev was pouring coffee from a battered silver Georgian pot into a cracked Rockingham cup.

"Oh, Dev, soon you'll have nothing left at all!"

"Only my self-respect." He grinned, showing very white strong teeth. "Here . . . get this down you, and Thomas has made you some sandwiches."

They were roast beef, sliced thick, in bread cut like doorsteps, and Nieves fell on them. "Mmm, I do love Thomas's sandwiches . . . we never have them so thick at Marlborough." Her face, her voice, were childishly happy. "And I love Kilmarran; next to Marlborough it was always my favorite place." Her face shadowed. "Now it *is* my favorite place . . . I hate Marlborough now—hate it!"

Dev glanced at her from under absurdly long lashes, as thick and curling as a woman's. "Come now," he said mildly, pouring himself a cup of coffee and remembering he was hungry and had not eaten all day; food went by the board when he was working: "It can't be *that* bad."

"It's awful!" Nieves was vehement. "You don't know . . ."

The door opened and a leprechaun of a man in ancient butler's garb peered round it. "So it's arrived, then!"

Nieves dropped her sandwich to run forward, arms outstretched. "Thomas, oh, Thomas!"

He put his arms round her, patting one shoulder. "Runnin' away is it, then?" he asked gruffly.

"Only to you, Thomas, only to you."

"Beguilin' miss! You'll not be gettin' round me like that one does!" This with a jerk of the head at Dev, munching peaceably.

"Thank you for the sandwiches," Nieves said placatingly. "I was just saying to Dev that no one makes them like you do."

"When I've the makin's," Thomas said, scowling at Dev. "But why wouldn't we be killin' the fatted calf for you, missy?" He pinched her chin with a grimy hand. "I've made up the bed in the Blue Room," he said to Dev. "The sheets is not a pair but the bed's the least damp!"

Nieves gazed sorrowfully round the bare, faded walls, hung with what had once been red damask, now splotched with damp and showing brighter patches where paintings had formerly hung. The scrollwork ceiling had lost its chandelier; only a bare bulb showed. The house was dying from lack of money. Nieves sighed, her eyes filling with tears. "Oh, Dev, every time I come you have sold more things. I hate to see Kilmarran looking so shabby."

Not only the Lawrence of Dev's great-great-grandmother on his father's side had gone, but so had the Goya of his great-great-grandmother on his mother's side. And the silver wall sconces, and the Grinling Gibbons wall carvings.

"*Why* didn't Gramps leave you some of his money . . ." she mourned.

Dev looked at Thomas.

"And it's us reduced to sellin' off bit by bit!" Thomas said bitterly. "Your sainted mother would never forgive you! All them beautiful things she brought from Spain when she came here as your father's bride, and even your

Grandfather Tierney's guns! And as for the horses!" Thomas raised his hands as if about to clasp them in prayer.

"I don't shoot," Dev said, "and I can't afford to keep the horses."

"And what about this house? Soon you'll be sayin' you can't afford that! More than three hundred years the Loughlins have lived here, even Cromwell's men couldn't destroy it, but you're lettin' it fall away into the bog!"

"Needs must," Dev said shortly.

"That *thing* needs, you mean!" Thomas jerked his head at the moviola machine. "Eats money, it does! And the electricity bill not paid!"

"Don't scold, Thomas," coaxed Nieves.

"Somebody has to. We'll be in the streets soon, and he doesn't care just so long as he can feed that benighted thing!" He patted Nieves's cheek. "Now you eat up your sandwiches like a good girl and I'll be puttin' bottles in your bed . . . We'll talk about things in the mornin'."

Nieves sighed. "He's right, you know," she reproached Dev. "I only wish I could help. If I had any money I'd give it all to you!"

Dev smiled; it was soft, strangely sweet. "I know you would, *guapa*, and in return I'd give you a piece of the profits—if and when I make any!"

"But—" Nieves broke off as the phone rang. Her face paled. "That will be Cass!" she whispered in fright. Dev was picking up the receiver. "Cass? I was about to call you . . . Yes, she's here."

"Tell her I'm all right!" Nieves hissed frantically.

"No . . . Absolutely fine. Tired—and hungry." Dev grinned at Nieves. "No, well, she does now . . . No, I sent her straight to bed . . ."

Nieves heaved a relieved sigh and settled back to her sandwiches.

"I think a few days R & R," Dev was saying. "Then I'll bring her back myself . . . if that's all right with you?" Nieves could hear Cass's squawk, heard Dev laugh. "That's kind of you . . . Yes, in about a week . . . Oh, that would be nice . . . I don't think Nieves cared for public air transport . . . Yes, it's almost finished . . . Sometime next year, I hope . . . if I can line up a distributor. Well, we'll have to see about that. How are things at Marlborough?"

He listened, sipping coffee. Then he laughed again. "Not you . . . I'm sure you've covered all eventualities . . . Tell David I'll see him in a week and tell Helen not to worry. Nieves is safe and sound—and penitent. I'll read her the riot act in the morning . . . Yes . . . Fine . . . 'Bye." He hung up. "You are consigned to my custody for a week, then Cass will send a plane for us."

Nieves clapped her hands. "A whole week." Scrambling from her chair she hurled herself at him, hugging him hard. "Oh, thank you, thank you!"

"Now you can tell me about it."

Leading her back to the battered old leather sofa he sat down and she knelt beside him. "It's awful!" she began dramatically. "You have no idea."

That's what you think, Dev thought, remembering David's long and detailed letters.

"She's horrible, Dev! Horrible! Cold and hard and—and unforgiving! Everything has changed since she came . . . everything is spoiled."

"Not because of her, surely," Dev said mildly. "All this is your grandfather's doing!"

Nieves looked taken aback, before saying defensively: "But she is nothing like him! He was so warm, so loving . . . he was like a fire; she's a block of ice! He took you in . . . she fends you off." Her eyes welled. "Why did he do such a thing, Dev? Didn't he love me? I thought he did, and he knew I loved him. It is not as if he ever knew her. She was as much a stranger to him as she is to us. You don't know what it is like seeing her here, there, and everywhere you look. Nothing is the same. Everybody walks on tiptoe—even Cass!" Nieves's shock showed plain. Then her face and voice broke up. "And Daddy . . . he goes around trailing her with his eyes like she was some divinity." Her hurt and bewilderment made Dev reach for her, hold her in the curve of his arm, where she curled like a motherless puppy. "I was so unhappy . . . I just couldn't stand it anymore, and there was no one to turn to but you." She burst at last into wretched, unhappy tears. "If only you knew . . ."

But Dev knew a great deal. Thanks to David's long, graphically detailed letters, and a photocopy of Richard Tempest's dossier, he knew exactly what had been happening at Marlborough. As seen, of course, through David Boscombe's eyes, which were incapable of seeing anything else but Elizabeth Sheridan. Weak as water himself, David had always been a sucker for strong-minded women, obtaining some sort of masochist's delight from being able to do no more than worship from afar, which satisfied something in his deeply romantic nature. Women had always looked down on him from pedestals.

Dev had always thought David had been born several centuries too late. He belonged to the age of courtly love, when jongleurs had poured out their passions in songs and verse. David had poured out his to Dev in his letters. It was obvious that his imagination had taken wing since the advent of Richard Tempest's daughter. Who must, reflected Dev, be quite something to have caused all this heartburn. Except, of course, it was Richard Tempest's own, inimitable recipe. If it was me, Dev thought, holding Nieves comfortingly, I'd be on my guard too. I'd need to be, considering I was the cause of some major surgery—and without anesthetic—on the rest of my father's "family." She would need to be calm and controlled to deal with that lot, because they were anything but. She had been delivered into a den full of deliberately starved lions.

He remembered her dossier, its careful details as to the living of her life, her habits, her choices, her friends. She seemed to have lived like a nun. In the list of her addresses, where she had lived and with whom, there had never been mention of any man. No male-female relationships at all, in fact. No wonder she appears to have no humanity, he thought. She doesn't seem to be a human being. Yet Richard Tempest had chosen to pluck her from her self-enclosed convent and chuck her right into a gambling hell. Why? It was a puzzle, he decided, but a fascinating one. It would be interesting to meet this strange, inhumanly cold woman. He had met just about every other type . . .

Nieves stirred, sniffed, mopped her eyes and blew her nose. "I knew you would understand," she sighed happily. "I'm so glad I came."

"So am I." Dev smiled back, the blue eyes holding her with an expression that made her quake. "But all the same, doing so has caused people who love you a great deal of worry."

Nieves hung her head, stared fixedly at Dev's jean-clad knees. "I always meant to call them when I got here," she mumbled. Dev raised her face to his with his hand, and she caught it with hers, holding it to her cheek with a trust and confidence that made him want to knock David's head from his shoulders. "Running away is not the way to solve problems," he said gently, but in a way that made her bite her lip. "Facing them, handling them, is what being grown up means." Which again brought him back to David, who had never managed to do so.

"I'm sorry," Nieves whispered forlornly.

"Then you must tell them so, when you call them—yes, you must." She had flung up her head in agitation. "Especially your Aunt Helen. Cass told me she was very upset."

"But so was I," wailed Nieves.

"So is everyone," Dev returned remorselessly. He saw that sink home and left it at that. "Now I think it's time you went to bed."

Even the word made Nieves yawn, but deliciously. The aftermath of her tension-ridden flight and her abandoned bout of weeping had left her feeling boneless. But she was content in the knowledge that she had done the right thing—even if it was only for herself, she thought guiltily. Dev would sort it all out. He always did. She yawned again. For the first time in days she felt safe and secure because there was someone she could turn to for love and protection.

"I do love you, Dev," she said drowsily, curled up against him, her hand in his, warm and strong and comforting.

"And I love you, *guapa.*" He dropped a kiss on her hair. But above her head his face was grim. It was as well he was going back to Marlborough again. There were things to be said to David.

"Come on, then."

He took her up the wide, straight stairs and along to her room, a huge, echoing chamber dominated by a vast four-poster bed hung in faded, and in places tattered, blood-red brocade. Thomas had lit a peat fire which glowed in the grate, and the outlines of several stoneware hot-water bottles could be seen through the bedclothes.

"Oh, I could sleep for a week," Nieves sighed, eyeing the bed.

"Into it, then, and if you are a good girl, we'll go riding tomorrow morning."

"Oh, can we?" Nieves was ecstatic, standing in front of him, hands clasped on her breast. "Can I ride Firefly?"

"Why not? He's getting fat and lazy . . . do him good to work some of it off."

"Oh, yes, let's!" Nieves hopped up and down in excitement. "Do you think he will remember me?"

"Ask him tomorrow."

Nieves flung her arms around him, standing on tiptoe to rub her cheek against his, before she drew back with an "Ouch! You're all bristly."

Dev rubbed a hand along his unshaven jaw. "Too busy working."

"Is it good, this one?"

"I think so."

"What's it called?"

"*The Unknown.*"

Nieves's face darkened and she buried her face against his chest again "Don't talk about *that,*" she shivered. "That's how everything has become suddenly . . ."

"No, you only feel it has," Dev said gently. He dropped a kiss on her hair "Good night, *guapa . . . Duermes bien.*"

"*Buenas noches.*" Nieves yawned, and when the door had closed behind Dev she stripped off shirt and jeans, bra and briefs, and dived under the covers, feeling for one of the bottles with her feet, wrapping her arms around the other one, the third shoved into the small of her back. She sighed once, deeply and contentedly, closed her eyes, and was asleep.

Dev heard the phone ringing as he went back downstairs. It was David.

"Just thought I'd say thanks," David said. Then: "She's okay?"

"Yes . . . tired, and emotional and upset—but okay. What the hell are you playing at, David? Are you blind and deaf as well as dumb?"

David's defense mechanism triggered a blustery "You know damned fine how things are here!"

"With you I do! I noticed your letters—while very descriptive of Elizabeth Sheridan—didn't say a word about your own daughter!"

Silence. Then: "Wait until you meet her," David said sulkily.

"I can't wait!"

"She's all I said—and more! When are you coming, anyway?"

"In about a week."

"Movie all finished?"

"I'm on the last stretch of the editing."

"Good?"

"I think so."

David sighed. "Let's hope the distributors think so . . . Maybe now that Richard is dead his dread hand will let go its grip."

"We'll soon find out."

There was another silence, then David said abruptly: "My allowance is okay. She's going to go on paying it, so there is still money available . . ."

"Then let's hope that with this one I can start paying you back!"

"I don't want it back," David said roughly. "I only want that you should make something more than awards out of it . . . what the hell have I got to spend money on, anyway?"

"Watch it, David, your self-pity's showing."

The silence crackled, then David laughed. It was harsh. "I can always count on you, you Irish-Spanish son of a bitch!" But it was said with deep affection. "Thanks for looking after Nieves," he continued awkwardly.

"You know I'm happy to do so—but I'm not happy about the fact that she feels it necessary to come to me in the first place!"

Another silence.

"It's been far too long, David . . ."

"Some things you never get over."

"I don't recall you ever trying."

There was a strangled sound and then: "And the hell with you too!" David snarled, and hung up.

Dev sighed, replacing the receiver. David Boscombe was his old and good friend but he could be a pain in the ass. His solution to problems was to run away from them. If he had bothered to look over his shoulder, he would have seen that they were keeping pace with him.

Dev ran his hands through his thick black hair. Work, he thought.

He was placing a roll of film into the viewing head when Thomas came to clear the tray.

"Is it still workin' ye are, then? And at one o'clock in the mornin'!" He began to clatter cups. "Fine goin's on!" He sniffed disapprovingly. "More money than sense, the lot of 'em. Why is it that them as can put money to its best use never has any?"

He paused by the table, tray in hand. "You'll need to be takin' care with that one." He jerked his head upward. "Haven't I seen the way she looks at you! Like the sun was shinin' out of your aspect! That's a child—and don't you be forgettin' it!"

"I never do," Dev answered, raising his eyes to meet Thomas's worried concern. Searching their vivid blueness, Thomas nodded, satisfied. "I'll be off to me bed, then . . . and as for you—you'll not be forgettin' there's still the electricity bill to pay!"

The door banged behind him. Money, Dev sighed. Always damned money. Money he owed. Money he didn't have. Money he couldn't make. And all because of the pernicious influence of one vengeful man . . . Well, now that he was silenced perhaps things would change, get better. Worse they could not get. This last film had been two years in the making. Several times he'd had to break off and hire himself out as an actor or find work as an editor or cutter.

Who knows, he thought, setting the film running, maybe Elizabeth Sheridan could be persuaded to invest in him . . . It would be worth a try. Through David's hyperbole the fact that she was nobody's fool had stood out strongly. And he had nothing to lose.

Margery was already seated at their table in Le Gavroche when Dan joined her.

"A martini—double," he ordered the hovering waiter. He looked uptight, upset.

"Well?" Margery demanded.

"No—it is not! The same old runaround. Nobody knows a damned thing. Now the hospital records are no longer in existence. Every which way we turn the records have vanished. Well, the death certificate won't. Thank God for Somerset House! What about you?"

"Nothing. Nobody who knows her knows anything about her past. And I can't get too nosy because they might get suspicious."

"Damn!" Dan scowled ferociously. "Which leaves us with the Henrietta Fielding Home for Foundlings."

"That's gone too." Margery referred to a scribbled note. "It is now owned by Kent County Council and it's been turned into offices."

Dan's martini came and he downed it almost desperately, ordered another.

"If you ask me," Margery volunteered, "everything has been erased—and we know who rubbed it out!"

"Yes—time! The trouble is that it was all nearly thirty years ago." Dan's forehead corrugated. "So he must *always* have known . . . kept tabs on her from the beginning. And told us only what he wanted us to know. Which only convinces me beyond doubt that there is much more to find out."

His second martini came and he sipped, thinking hard. "Okay . . . so the next stop is Somerset House. And that's a hell of a job because all we have to go on is the year. Still, we know when the child entered the Home, so if we concentrate on the period immediately before then . . ." Dan's eyes were cold as glass. "It's there, I *know* it is. The fact that it doesn't seem to be only makes me more convinced. The deeper we go the more obvious it becomes that the answers we have been provided with are not the true ones."

"Richard was covering up while seeming to reveal everything?"

"Didn't he always? It's his style, all of it. He always kept the vital clue to himself. But I'll find it, by God, if I have to use bloodhounds!"

Margery eyed his vindictive face. "You really hate her guts, don't you?"

"I'd hammer in the nails at her crucifixion!"

"After she has signed *her* will!"

Dan's grin was wolfish. "In her own blood . . ." He picked up the menus and handed her one. "Let's order. All this digging makes me hungry."

SEVEN

"How is Miss Arden, today?" Helen asked the nurse.

"No change, I'm afraid."

"Hasn't she said anything—anything at all?"

"Not a word. She hears, and she is aware—but she never makes any response."

The nurse was opening the door to Mattie's private room. "Visitors, Miss Arden." Her voice was cheerfully bright. "And look what lovely flowers they have brought you."

Helen followed the nurse into the room, followed by a trepidatious Cass, whose first visit it was. Nieves's flight had brought home to her the other responsibilities she had been neglecting, and on hearing Helen was making her every-other-day visit, she had virtuously tagged along. But she was not prepared for what she saw. Helen had warned her Mattie looked awful, but the last thing Cass had expected was a zombie. Mattie Arden had always been done in glowing colors, a Titian, perhaps, or maybe a Rubens. Flaming hair, milk-and-roses complexion, double-lashed pansy-purple eyes, all glossed with the electricity of vibrant health. "The constitution of a horse!" Mattie had been wont to say proudly. What confronted Cass was a gaunt, skeletal frame with a death's-head out of which stared, sightlessly, two purple stones. Even the bright hair was dulled. The rest was shrouded in apathy.

Jesus Christ! Cass had to swallow the words. But she did what Helen had done and bent to graze the gray cheek with her lips. Mattie gave no sign of response.

Cass sank down shakily into a chair by the bed, Helen on its other side, and they looked at each other. Helen shook her head slightly at Cass's shocked face.

"Mattie, my dear . . . how are you today?" Helen's voice was warm, and she began to talk inconsequentials, giving Mattie the news she thought she would want to hear.

Cass sat numbly. Christ, this is horrible! she thought, appalled. It was like talking to a corpse. Thank God, David had not come . . . something had sent him off on another drunken binge.

She tried to take her cue from Helen, to chatter easily, without sounding too shriekingly false, feeling her smile stiff on her lips, unable to move around her shock, which blocked every view. Nothing they said or did produced the slightest response. Mattie just lay and stared into nothingness. But Helen sat for fifteen minutes, talking steadily, easily, giving no sign of Mattie's inertia. At the end of that time, Cass could only think of escape, and as soon as they got outside the door, she shuddered and gasped, "Jesus, that was horrible! I need a drink!"

Once in the Rolls, she leaned forward to push the button that slid back the panel to reveal the bar, poured herself a stiff slug of whiskey and downed it at a gulp. "I'm all shook up! What in God's name has happened to her?"

"Richard died," Helen answered. She spoke into the intercom. "All right, Henry, you may drive us back now."

Cass stared sightlessly out at the busy village. All she could see was the lump of gray matter lying on that hospital bed.

"We can't leave her like that!" she said. "We can't!" She turned to Helen. "Something *has* to be done."

"What?" asked Helen helplessly. "The doctors have done all they can."

"I don't mean the doctors. I mean *us!*"

"What can we do that they cannot do?"

"I don't know yet—but I'll think of something . . . We just can't leave her there wasting away, for God's sake!"

"She has no reason to want to live," Helen said tonelessly. Then, softly: "I know how she feels . . ."

Cass set her glass down with a jerk. "That's it!"

"That's what?"

"What we do! We tell her about Elizabeth."

Helen gasped. "The shock would kill her!"

"Or cure her."

"We couldn't do that!" Helen looked terrified. "The doctors would never allow it . . ."

"Doctors! You leave Louis Bastedo to me! Mattie has got to be galvanized back to life—and the one sure way is to tell her what has happened."

Helen was a-quiver with fright. "Cass, you must not."

"Somebody has to! You know how all-fired temperamental Mattie is. If she was to be told what Richard has done she'd be fit to die! Her ego would never stand it. She always had to be number one—on and off stage—but this time she has been upstaged. She'd come back to life with a vengeance, if only to reap it somehow!"

Helen's eyes threatened to swallow her pale face. "Cass, it would be so cruel . . ." The very thought made her heart wrench. She had known cruelty, suffered it in silence. But Mattie never suffered in silence. She made everybody suffer with her. "I don't like it, Cass . . . we cannot take the responsibility."

"Would you rather we just let her lie there and waste away, then?"

"She has already suffered one massive shock. Another might do her in." Helen firmed her voice, became Miss Tempest of Marlborough. "I forbid it, Cass. I absolutely forbid it!"

Cass met the agitated, imperious sea-green eyes and said no more, but she continued to think about it. She was damned if she was going to let Mattie Arden die of willful self-neglect.

Helen, in her fright, went straight to Hervey, who added his condemnation and ordered Cass not to interfere. But it was David, feeling very badly

done to, still smarting from Nieves's flight and Dev's recriminations, who
seized his chance to turn the accusing finger on someone else for a change.

"Are you out of your mind?" he blustered.

"It's Mattie's mind I'm concerned about."

"Then let those who know best take care of it! Must you *always* interfere?
You love to make waves, don't you? Just for once, leave things alone."

David was very fond of Mattie. She had always been kind to him,
mothered him. Now he felt he had to protect her. And he had his own score
to settle with Cass after the tongue-lashing she had given him after Nieves's
flight. "I am as fond of Mattie as anyone," he said now, "but what you are
proposing to do is crazy—and highly dangerous!"

"So's smoking—and I'm not prepared to give that up either."

David's face congested. As always, he felt frustrated rage build in the face
of Cass's superior word power.

"It's tit for tat," he managed. "All you really want is to get your own back
on Richard for what he's done with the Organization."

"Trust you to think that! Can't you see there is no *need* for Mattie to
waste away? I know her too, you know. I am as aware as you that this started
as one of her self-dramatizing little ploys, but it's gone too far, don't you see?
She can't stop herself anymore! Well, by God, if she can't then I will!" She
eyed him scathingly. "Unlike Nieves, Mattie has no Dev Loughlin to run
to."

David's face was purple. "Mind your own business!" he stuttered. "Christ,
how you do love shoving your nose into other people's business! I'm warning
you—keep it out of my affairs!" Too late he saw how he had laid himself wide
open.

"Ha!" Cass said. "It would do you a hell of a sight more good to have one
now and again instead of wearing away your knees in worship! Don't think I
haven't seen the way you moon around after Elizabeth."

David wanted to run. As always, Cass was hitting the conversational ball to
where he could not return it. "Watch your mouth!" he blustered.

"The way you watch hers? Hoping for a kind word? Jesus Christ, David,
what is it with you? Isn't it time you stopped this nowhere drift of yours and
got back on course? So somebody rocked your dreamboat. So take a firm
hold, hoist yourself up, climb back in again and set sail for *somewhere!* Retreat, retreat, always retreat! What's the matter, frightened to show your
back in case somebody sticks another knife in it?"

David was shaking with rage and terror.

Cass was in full flow. "Can't you do anything else but stand around and
wring your hands? I am sick to death of you and your self-pity! If you find this

world so cruel and nasty, then get yourself off to a monastery. Your daughter is already thinking in terms of a nunnery."

David blanched and retreated a step, but Cass followed, her face red, the blue eyes like lasers, well away into her own rage. "Surprised are we? You shouldn't be. Since when have you ever shown her any signs of fatherly love —I mean the earthly kind? No wonder the poor kid ran away—and to the one person she has left to rely on! Where were you when she felt lost and lonely? Mooning over Elizabeth Sheridan, that's what! You know damned well you haven't a hope in hell—but that's why you do it, isn't it? Then you can point the finger and say, 'See . . . failed again,' and go fetch yourself another bottle of bourbon!"

"Jesus!" David said the word prayerfully, almost tearfully. He had not bargained for this. He wanted to run, but Cass had backed him into a corner.

"It's time you took off those bourbon-colored glasses and saw things as they really are instead of how you would like them to be!"

"Get off my back! You nosy, interfering bitch!" he stuttered, his tongue thick, his body trembling, hearing his voice wavering all over the place. He was never any good at rows; they always resulted in humiliation and rout.

Cass's face was mottled. "You soft-centered lump of blubber! Did you ever think that all I was trying to do was help?"

To his total undoing, David saw that the cornflower-blue eyes were bright with tears. He had never seen Cass cry in his life. It was like seeing Niagara crumble and totally did him in. Doing what he always did when faced with a problem, he ran.

Cass put up a furious, trembling hand to dash away the tears. Worry, rage, and dismay were churning in her stomach. She needed a drink to steady it . . . It was only when the bourbon hit that she almost choked at the thought that she was doing exactly what she had just belabored David for. Making straight for the crutches. But what he had said hurt. That he should see her—Cass van Dooren—as a nosy, interfering bitch . . . Somebody has to prop them up, she argued with herself, and I just happen to be the nearest sucker with a soft spot for the woebegone and the misbegotten. But there was no getting away from the fact that he had unwittingly hit home. She did like the feeling of importance it gave her . . . She needed their need. Which brought her up smack against what she had been avoiding: the purely surface thinness of Elizabeth Sheridan's need. Not of Cass herself, but only of her knowledge and expertise. And once she had acquired her own . . . She poured herself another stiff slug and tossed it back.

She also swallowed her intention—in no way lessened—to drag Mattie back from the brink. Helen had forbidden her to act, Hervey had backed her up, but, Cass reasoned, if you were going to go by the book, and when it suited her she could, then the logical person to ask, since she was the one, next to Mattie, most concerned, was Elizabeth Sheridan.

But all she got was a polite but firm "It has nothing to do with me."

"It has *everything* to do with you! It is about you I'm proposing to tell Mattie, and on you she'll come down—and I wouldn't let that happen to anyone without due warning."

"Thank you," Elizabeth said politely and returned to her book.

So Cass bided her time. She said nothing, gave no sign of the preparations she was making, like taking copies of the will and the dossier. These she put into a plain brown envelope. Then she let a whole week go by. She visited Mattie twice, keeping Helen company, and each time she saw her she felt her resolve harden. She was damned if she was going to let Mattie give up on life. She would prize those dead fingers from around her throat if she had to break each one separately.

And then one afternoon, while Helen and Hervey were attending a meeting of the Hospital Management Board, which comprised the two of them and Louis Bastedo, who was Chief of Staff, she got out the little red Sprite and drove herself to the hospital. Mattie was lying as if she had not moved for weeks. She still stared at nothing, gave no sign of being aware of anything, but Cass knew her well enough to know that Mattie Arden was quite capable of making a drama even out of this. Life, to her, was grand opera anyway. And underneath the Turkish delight was a layer of hard candy.

Mattie had been born in a Polish ghetto; had worked for her living since she was fourteen. More to the point, she had fought for it. Mattie loved a fight. Her life was a series of them; there was always some shindy going; with a fellow singer, with the press, with her manager. She thrived on scenes and gave of her best when she had managed to best someone else.

Cass was convinced that her present apathy was because the fight had gone out of her. Her spirit level was at an all-time low. What Cass intended to do was send it to the top. And in all fairness, she *had* warned Elizabeth . . . Well, she thought, eyeing the gaunt death's-head, it will either kill or cure . . . but she's dying anyway so what's to lose . . .

Helen, Hervey, and Louis Bastedo were in Bastedo's office, going over the appropriation for the coming year, when the door was flung open and his head nurse said, "Dr. Bastedo, all hell is going on in Miss Arden's room. She's out of bed and demanding to be driven back to the House."

Hervey was on his feet instantly. "Cass!" he said. But Louis beat him to the door, and they were followed by Helen. All three ran for the stairs.

They could hear Mattie as they ran down the second-floor corridor: ". . . no, I will not get back into bed! I want my clothes and if you know what is good for you you will fetch them! Take your hands off me!"

They fell in through the door and there was Mattie, struggling ineffectually but with surprising strength in the grip of two nurses, Cass dancing around in front, saying "Now, Mattie . . . for God's sake, Mattie!"

"Cass!" thundered Hervey, white with fright, "I thought I told you . . ."

"Never mind what you told her!" yelled Mattie, catching sight of him. "Why the hell didn't you tell me?"

She was hectically flushed, and the pansy-purple eyes were snapping like teeth.

"You were in no condition to be told anything," Louis Bastedo said calmly. "Let Miss Arden go, please."

The nurses released Mattie and she swayed slightly, putting out a hand for the bed, but she was spitting mad, adrenaline pumping away furiously.

"All right," Louis said quietly. "You can go," he said to the nurses.

"Now then," Louis said, turning to Cass, who had gone to stand by and a little behind Mattie, the two of them against the rest. "Playing doctors and nurses?" he asked pleasantly, but Cass flinched.

"Playing God, more like!" Hervey began furiously.

Louis quieted him with a hand. "I didn't know your ambitions ran so high, Cass," he went on, raising shiny black eyebrows. His eyes traveled to Mattie. "But if this is the sort of miracle you perform, perhaps I should offer you a job."

Cass grinned, relaxing. Louis Bastedo was one of the few men she respected, especially his authority, but he was obviously not about to throw it at her right now.

"I thought it was high time Mattie was brought back to life," she said bluntly. "I told them"—she nodded at the furious Hervey, the alarmed Helen—"that I thought Mattie needed to be shocked back into it. They didn't agree. So I took it upon myself."

"As usual!" Hervey snapped furiously.

Mattie had been standing with closed eyes, breathing deeply. Her anger had drained her sudden flare of strength. Now she opened her eyes, straightened, swayed, and Cass put out a quick hand to steady her.

Mattie put a hand on Cass's shoulder—she was feeling a good eight inches taller—and said: "And thank God she did!" She swept Hervey and Helen with a baleful stare. "Why didn't you tell me?" she demanded menacingly.

The famous voice rose. *"Why didn't you tell me?* Why didn't you tell me about *her?"* She swept the photograph from the bed and brandished it wildly.

"You were so ill," faltered Helen, "in no fit state . . ."

"Well, I'm in one now, and—Get your hands off me!" She tried to fling off Louis's hand as he picked up her wrist, put his fingers on her pulse.

"Doing the three-minute mile," was all he said, mildly. But her pulse was stronger, very much stronger.

"It's what's waiting twelve miles away which interests me," rasped Mattie. "Now get my clothes. I have a score to settle."

"Doctor, you cannot allow . . ." appealed Helen, but Louis said, "By all means."

He rang the bell above the bed. "Miss Arden's clothes," he said to the nurse who appeared. Then he stood with his hands thrust in the pockets of his white coat, his heavy-lidded eyes looking sleepy, almost bored, but no one was deceived.

"Really, I do not think Miss Arden is well enough," began Hervey.

"Yes, she is," Louis said. "She has lost an alarming amount of weight. You'll have to put it all back before you can even think of attempting Wagner," he advised Mattie kindly, then turned back to the others. "But it was shock she was suffering from—that and a death wish. Physically she checked out sound."

"See!" Mattie was triumphant.

Hervey tightened his lips but Helen looked relieved.

"However, I would like to know what you intend to do once you get back to Marlborough," Louis went on affably. "There is a limit even to your resolve."

Mattie was all of a sudden dangerously placid. "Oh, just see someone," she said negligently, but her eyes boded ill.

"Now, Mattie . . ." began Hervey.

"Don't you 'Now, Mattie' me! You—you fink! You let me lie there while all hell was let loose! You would have let me just fade away and never said a word!" She was wrathfully indignant. "If it hadn't been for Cass here . . ."

Cass smiled blandly into Hervey's furious face.

"Really, Cass, it was very remiss of you—but I am so glad you did it!" Helen said, switching from reproach to delight.

"She's the only one who gave a thought to my feelings!" Mattie glared, then yelled—conveniently forgetting that she had decided she had no use for them anymore—*"Where are my clothes?"*

The nurse came running in with Mattie's clothes on a hanger.

"We'll leave it to the ladies, shall we?" Louis took Hervey by the elbow. "Ring when you're ready," he said to the ladies.

Outside the door, Hervey shook his arm free. "Well," he snorted down his nose, "I always knew you to be anything but an old-fashioned GP, but this is going some, even for you!"

"Hervey, one has to know when to bend with the wind. Whatever Cass has told Miss Arden is obviously what she needed to hear—even if it was not what she wanted."

Hervey met the bland brown eyes with a flat stare. "You know very well what she told her," he said grimly. "I am well aware that there is not a soul on this island who does not know."

"What goes on up at the House is far better than any soap opera," Louis agreed gravely, "but we both know that this is a closed community—and that goes for mouths, too."

Hervey nodded, frowning. "*Is* she well enough to leave hospital?"

"Oh, yes. What ailed her was not physical. She's had every test. Her heart is a steam engine and her lungs are bellows. She's lost far too much weight, so I'll put her on a rich diet, but that's a tough cookie, as we say where I come from. She'll survive."

Hervey reflected briefly on what would happen when fire met ice, and hoped so. On the other hand, when he was through with Cass . . . Really, she was far too much of a law unto herself. Richard had always allowed her far too much license. But he *had* made her co-executor . . .

"Cheer up, Hervey," Louis said breezily. "Miss Arden in a tizz is something I have only read about up till now."

"That's where she spends most of her time," Hervey answered glumly.

"But preferable, surely, to the despair she was in," Louis went on softly.

Hervey sighed, looked shamefaced, and said grumpily, "It could have gone the other way. Then what?"

Louis smiled, shook his head. "When it comes to reading people, Cass van Dooren is usually word-perfect."

But that only made Hervey feel even more disgruntled, because it shoved him in with the backward readers.

The bell rang, and they went back in to find Mattie dressed—or hung—in her clothes. She was engaged in making up her face, applying blusher high on colorless cheeks, skillfully highlighting eyes which were so large they threatened to drown her face, and outlining her lips in a zinging vermilion.

"God, what a mess!" she snorted at her reflection, tugging at the cowl neck of her dress so as to conceal empty saltcellars.

"Will you get a wheelchair?" Louis said to the nurse.

"I can walk!" Mattie was outraged.

"All right," Louis agreed easily, "show us."

Mattie tilted her head, swanned forward, and almost fell off her high heels. "Whoops!" Louis caught her. "My damned legs have been boned!" she gasped.

"The wheelchair," Louis said again to the nurse, who whisked herself out.

Louis lowered Mattie into a chair. "Rich food and plenty of it," he ordered briskly. He turned to Helen. "Rich soups, lots of eggs with butter, lashings of cream . . . Feed her up. Basically, that is all she needs. And rest. No"—he held up a hand—"I don't mean bed rest. I mean in a chair, on a couch. Your physical resources are low, but Marlborough can provide you with just as good care as I can give you—and in the style to which you are accustomed."

Mattie eyed him, then grinned. "You are a cocky son-of-a-bitch but you know your business."

The nurse opened the door, wheeled in the chair.

"Right." Louis swung Mattie easily into his arms and deposited her in it, then proceeded to wheel it away, a little procession forming behind: Cass trotting on one side, Helen walking on the other, Hervey and the nurse following.

The bright sunlight made Mattie blink. She waved a queenly hand as she was pushed through the small crowd of nurses gathered to see her go and bestowed her most dazzling smile. The car had been brought round. Louis, assisted by Oscar, the chauffeur, got her into the back, Helen next to her, and Cass hopped into the jump seat with Hervey. As Oscar got into the driving seat, Mattie pressed the button to lower the window, stretched out a hand to Louis, which he took. "Thanks, Doc . . . You run a great hospital but what I need right now is not your kind of medicine."

With a flourish, Louis bent to kiss it. "Just don't take an overdose," he returned affably, and stood waving until the car had turned out of the gates. Then he turned to the nurses. "Okay, girls, show's over. Back to work."

As Oscar drove into the village, passersby, noting the Marlborough car, nodded and smiled, the women bobbing curtsies, waving when they saw it was Mattie. She was much-loved on the Island; always took a leading part in the annual carnival, when she gave them for free what other, richer people paid a hundred dollars a seat for. And as much as they wanted.

But Hervey wore a disapproving primness. "I hope you're satisfied," he snapped at Cass.

"Aren't you?"

"Fortunately, it has turned out well, which in no way alters the fact that you took a grave risk. I wonder Louis kept his temper."

Cass didn't. She knew Louis would not let it rest there and was fully prepared for an eventual confrontation. But she could take that. She had been proved right, hadn't she?

"She *is* at the house?" Mattie asked suddenly, threateningly.

"Where else?" Cass asked.

Mattie subsided, staring moodily out of the window. Well, thought Cass, I did warn Elizabeth . . . But she doubted if she had ever met anyone like her. They had all indulged Mattie, Cass thought, from Richard on down. She had been as proud to be *maîtresse en titre* as she had been to be the Divine Diva. In Mattie's eyes, the one went with the other, and just because Richard was dead made no difference to her stature in her own eyes. She would just have to learn the hard way. Which was the only way Mattie ever learned.

As luck would have it, as they came up the last flight of terrace steps, Elizabeth was just rounding the corner of the house. Mattie, leaning heavily on the supporting arms of Hervey and Helen, stopped dead. Cass, bringing up the rear, saw the stiffening back, the instant defiant tilt of the head. She saw Helen glance nervously at Mattie, take a firmer grip on her arm. Hervey cleared his throat apprehensively.

Nipping round them, Cass called brightly: "Hi! Look who we've brought home . . . Come and meet Mattie."

Elizabeth walked toward them. Out of the corner of her eyes, Cass saw Mattie shake off the supporting hands, draw herself up in a Medea-like stance. But as Elizabeth came nearer, and Mattie saw the physical reality, Cass also saw her react to it like a blow. In navy slacks and a white shirt, her hair drawn back from her face, Elizabeth's resemblance to Richard was total and terrifying. Cass watched Mattie realize the height, the presence, the composure, and gather her own together.

Elizabeth came right up to them. "Miss Arden," she said, smiling, "I am delighted to see you here." She held out a hand, but Mattie made no move to take it. She looked Elizabeth up and down slowly, prima donna assoluta noticing a member of the chorus. It was insolent, superior, quelling.

"You will understand if I am unable to return the compliment," she replied haughtily.

"I should be surprised if you did," Elizabeth returned calmly.

Mattie's eyes flashed. "If we are going to talk about surprises . . ."

Now Elizabeth's eyes moved candidly and deliberately over Mattie, making her gaunt, hectically flushed face glow like a stoplight.

"When you are up to it we can talk about anything you like, but for now I do not think you *are* up to it. When you are, I am at your disposal."

She bowed, before walking off.

Mattie made a strangled sound and took a step after her, but Helen, with a frantic "Now, Mattie, please . . ." held on to her, while Hervey, on her other side, pinned her fast, and added grimly, "You are wasting your time, Mattie."

"The insolent bitch!" burst from Mattie's lips like a bullet. "Who does she think she is?"

"She knows," Cass said succinctly. "And you," she added, "will find out."

But Mattie, her flushed face losing its color, was watching Elizabeth disappear into the gardens. She sagged suddenly.

"Let's get her inside," Hervey said quickly, and between them, they half-carried the tottering Mattie into the house, where they sat her down in one of the sedan chairs while Cass rang for Amos, Moses's eldest son and the first footman. When he came he swept her gently, easily, into his arms and carried her up the stairs to her suite. There Marta was hovering, and she proceeded to fall on Mattie with squawks and frantic mutterings in Polish, running before Amos to open doors so that he could place her on her bed. Then she waved him away.

"Let's leave her for now," Cass said quickly. "Marta knows what to do."

Outside, she forestalled Hervey's onslaught by saying, "All right, before you start . . . They've taken each other's measure and Mattie now knows what she's got to come to terms with. Let's leave her to it, shall we?"

But Hervey wanted the last word. "It always was kill or cure with you, wasn't it?"

Cass fixed him with a hard stare. "When I had a choice," was all she answered.

They were having tea when Louis Bastedo was announced.

"I thought I'd check and see that everything is all right," he said affably.

"Well, if silence is anything to go by . . ." Cass allowed.

"Will you have some tea, doctor?" Helen asked, reaching for a cup.

"That would be nice, thank you."

"Do sit down, and let me introduce you to Miss Sheridan. Elizabeth, this is our Island doctor, Louis Bastedo."

They shook hands.

"We are very proud of our hospital," Helen went on. "Dr. Bastedo has made it into one of the best in the entire Caribbean—if not *the* best."

"Any time you would like to see it," Louis offered, "just let me know."

"Thank you," said Elizabeth.

They sat and chatted pleasantly, while Louis drank two cups of tea and ate a large chunk of the famous Marlborough angel cake. Then he said, "I'll just go up and see Miss Arden"—he turned to Cass—"and I'd like a word with you, if I may."

Cass rose. "I'll come with you."

"So that's her," Louis said thoughtfully, with an admiring glint, as they went out.

"That's her."

"How did Miss Arden take her?"

"Bad medicine," Cass answered laconically. She eyed him and sighed. "Now I suppose you are going to administer mine?"

"I *am* the doctor. And the next time you feel like taking over, do me the courtesy of saying so first. You never did fear to rush in, did you, Cass."

"Somebody had to," Cass defended herself stubbornly.

"Did it not occur to you that I might be of that same opinion? All you had to do was ask."

Cass looked meek. "I thought you might have run me off the grounds." Then: "Were you? Of the same opinion, I mean."

"I was as aware as you that something had to be done. You were ahead of me in that you knew what." Drily: "You had Miss Sheridan up your sleeve . . ."

Cass gurgled. "She'd never fit there!"

Louis's eyes gleamed. "Splendid creature, isn't she?" He fixed Cass with a resigned stare. "No wonder Miss Arden took a conniption fit."

"I knew she would, you see . . . That was what was bugging me—Mattie Arden has never taken *anything* lying down!"

"As her doctor you still owed me the courtesy of asking my cooperation in getting her on her feet."

"Sorry," Cass said, meaning it. "It won't happen again." They looked at each other and Cass nodded guiltily. "Promise."

"To which I will hold you! Now, let's go see Miss Arden."

Mattie was in bed, surrounded by copies of the will and the dossier.

"Three weeks you let me lie there and never a word!" she threw at Cass, as she came through the door.

"You weren't taking notice of anything *anybody* said!"

"You knew damn fine I'd take notice of what was said about her!" She glared at them both, but let Louis take her pulse. "That bastard!" she hissed. "That conniving, cheating, double-crossing lying bastard! I'll never forgive him for this! Never! How dare he do this to me! To me! Mattie Arden! Twenty years I gave that man and he tossed me aside like some two-bit whore!"

Definite signs of a return to normal, Cass noted. Mattie's ego was being blown up to its normal inflated size. But she also noted that Mattie's reaction was anger. Fury at being scorned. Fury at not being remembered as "special." It would be later, when the fury had subsided, that the pain would start. And the real trouble. Mattie upset meant everybody else upset too. The tears would flow and she would throw a scene in which bits and pieces of her most famous roles would be incorporated: Medea's fanaticism, Norma's rage and grief, Isolde's tragedy. It was her way of working them out of her system. Her rages were phenomenal, her scenes legendary. The toughest managers had been known to lock themselves in their offices when the Divine Diva went on the rampage. Afterward—when she had got her own way—all would be sweetness and light. Then she would be generous and tolerant and giving. And in that mood she would give you her last cent. It was if you tried to cheat her that she lost her cool.

She and Richard Tempest had shared a boisterous relationship, on-again, off-again, but that Mattie had adored him had never been in doubt. More than once she had flounced off in a huff when he had shown a partiality for a certain woman, though when he married a second time—without telling her —her resilience, founded on supreme confidence in herself, had kept her buoyant, and when, not three weeks after the honeymoon, Richard was once more pursuing her, she only made him wait a day or two. Lovers she had had by the legion, but love she had known only once. And losing its source had almost killed her.

Now, eyeing the furious face, Cass knew she was on the way to recovery. *This* was the Mattie she knew, not that lifeless, hopeless "thing." She had no fears for Elizabeth Sheridan—she could handle herself. In fact, Cass thought pleasurably, that ought to be a world-championship bout. Which was why, when Mattie demanded imperiously that Elizabeth be brought to her, Cass shook her head and said: "No way, Mattie. Things have changed around here. You don't demand anymore. None of us do. We are all her pensioners now. We *all* got tossed aside. She doesn't take orders, Mattie. As you will find out. You met her, didn't you?"

Cass saw that sink home, could almost hear the hiss of air as Mattie sagged back against the pillows. But Mattie had a native shrewdness which always warned her when she went too far. She shrugged and said, "At that it is probably a good thing. Right now I admit I'm not up to her. But let me get back my health and strength . . . then watch out!"

"Well?" Cass asked anxiously, as she and Louis went back downstairs.

"I'll say one thing," Louis observed dryly, "life is going to be anything but dull around here."

Margery and Dan met at the bar of the Dorchester Trader Vic's. Both looked disgruntled. Dan ordered double whiskey sours.

"Hours of wasted time," he announced. "There is no such thing as a death certificate for a woman named Elizabeth Sheridan who died early in 1952. I went right through two quarters. I even checked the following year just in case. Nothing. Whoever Elizabeth Sheridan's mother was, that was not her name." Then a slow smile appeared. "And it's my belief she's not dead, either." His eyes were a-glitter. Margery's mouth dropped. "I think the child was dumped. Which brings us to who did the dumping. The mother? Richard? And why the false trail?"

"But—according to the old records of Henrietta Fielding, the child's mother was named Elizabeth Sheridan and she did die!"

"Records can be fixed. And we are talking of Richard Tempest, remember?" Dan's voice was positive when he went on: "There is a cover-up here. For some reason Richard did not want anything known about the mother of his child. What we have to find out is why. If she is still alive, there has to be a damned good reason to pretend she's dead. There's no death certificate. Not for a woman named Sheridan. Not for a woman named Tempest, either. I checked that too. And I looked under Dysart and Innes, just in case. Nothing. God knows what her name was, but I do know one thing: when Elizabeth Sheridan was taken into Henrietta Fielding she was neither orphan nor foundling . . ."

Margery's face was uneasy. This was turning out to be more than she had bargained for. But Dan was obsessed. He would not be dragged away from the maze, no matter how many dead ends he ended up at.

She was tired, too, of all this cloak and dagger. On top of which she had not been feeling too good these last few days. A nagging pain in the pit of her stomach, which sometimes seemed to be trying to dig its way out of her back, had been dragging her down. And she was bleeding at the wrong time of the month. She drank her whiskey sour gratefully.

"Those records were falsified," Dan was saying. "That again is typical of the way Richard worked. You know how he taught us that everybody has a price . . ."

"Well, that Superintendent woman who was in charge at the time is dead."

"Marion Keller," Dan said.

Margery shivered. "Everybody connected with this is dead."

"I've wondered about that too."

They looked at each other. "You don't think . . ." Margery's voice trailed off.

"Why not?" asked Dan. "Did he *ever* let anything stand in his way?"

Margery shivered. "I don't like this. The deeper we go the murkier it gets."

"It's always darkest at the bottom. But we've got one small gleam of light. Elizabeth Sheridan's mother is not dead and we—Goddamn it!" He turned angrily. Someone had jogged his arm, spilling his drink.

"Oh, I say, sorry!" apologized a male voice, then: "By all that's holy! Dan Godfrey!"

Dan looked up, then smiled delightedly. "Freddy! Freddy Tempest!"

The two men pumped hands. "The very man!" Dan exclaimed delightedly. He noticed Freddy's eyes on Margery.

"You don't know my stepsister, do you? The Contessa di Primacelli. Margery, this is Freddy Tempest . . . one of the *English* branch," he added meaningfully.

Tall, blond, horsefaced, with a chin that faded once it left his mouth, Freddy smiled and said diffidently, "We did meet once, years ago . . . when I stayed at the Cay. I don't suppose you remember . . ."

Margery, who did not, lied sweetly: "Of course . . ."

Freddy remembered very well. He had been only seventeen and she the hottest thing in the Caribbean.

A weed, Margery dismissed. All teeth and try-ons. From the look of him, one of the lower-echelon Tempests; down on his luck and bemoaning the fact to anyone who would lend him a fiver. Margery had never cared for her stepfather's English relations—too high and mighty for her taste. It was Dan who had cozied up to them; not for the money, which they no longer possessed, but for their title and connections.

". . . just going down to Tempests for the weekend," Freddy was saying amiably. "I say, why don't you come . . . It's been absolutely ages and everyone would love to see you . . . Uncle Dick has never stopped talking about the funeral." Uncle Dick being the twenty-first Earl who had represented the English branch at the funeral, an amiable eccentric who dressed like a tramp and had difficulty remembering the names of his children.

"Love to!" Dan answered promptly. "I could do with a weekend in the country . . . Still got a goodly supply of horses, I trust?"

"About all we have got," said Freddy mournfully. "But what are you doing over here, anyway? Come to spread a little of all that fantastic wealth around?" He was frankly envious.

"Oh, just looking up old friends," Dan answered easily. "A weekend with a few more would be just the very thing."

"I'm afraid you'll have to count me out," Margery said, sounding hollow with regret. "I've a prior commitment in Venice."

"Oh, I say. Pity, that . . ." Freddy cursed his luck. From what he had heard, the Contessa was generous with more than her body, and he was only going down to Tempests to dodge creditors anyway. "Perhaps another time." He smiled winningly.

Dan glanced at her. He had noticed she was twitchy of late. She never had been able to go long without sex. So let her go to Venice; she could get herself screwed into the ground for all he cared. She was useless anyway. Margery always had been one to let everyone else do the work while expecting her share of the results . . . if they were good, that was. He would do far better on his own. He had intended to drop in at Tempest Park, but this was heaven-sent. Since he had found out about the close connection between the Tempest Family and the Henrietta Fielding Home for Foundlings nothing had clicked. Meeting Freddy, fatuous fool though he was, was his first piece of genuine luck. He could snoop to his heart's content all weekend.

"So join us," he invited affably, "sit yourself down. What are you drinking?"

Mornings Elizabeth spent with Cass. After lunch, she walked; by the end of the first week she had covered the Island, knew the layout, understood how it was run. She liked to walk. It was good exercise and her thoughts kept pace with her feet. She also swam every day. The food at Marlborough was superb, but there was far too much of it. Breakfast, lunch, tea, and dinner. At least an hour's energetic swimming was not only a pleasure, it was a necessity. And once she had been shown the house, she visited that every opportunity she got.

But this particular afternoon she felt heavy with food, and somewhat restless. So she decided to swim over to the small island where she had first heard the bell tolling for Richard Tempest and, though she did not know it then, for her.

She came out of the water breathing hard. That half mile had been hard going the last couple of hundred yards. She was getting soft. And eating too much. She resolved to cut out tea, that stately ceremony: Helen behind the silver Georgian spirit kettle and teapot, dispensing Earl Grey or Darjeeling and tiny, luscious sandwiches, hot scones bursting with raisins and oozing butter, and angel cake which melted on the tongue. Now, she fell back on the hot, sugar-fine sand. She would get her breath back, then do the return trip. That ought to burn up the calories. Closing her eyes, she let the hot sun wrap her in its warmth.

The sound of a plane woke her. An Organization twin-engined jet, wheels down, was just about to touch down on the strip. She watched it race— engines screaming in reverse thrust—away out of her sight and wondered who was arriving. Then she remembered. Cass had said Nieves was being brought back today by Dev Loughlin. Spoon-fed, the lot of them. Wrapped in cotton wool spun from gold thread. Once she got into her stride there would be some changes made. She had not gazed every day, from her place at the table, at the example of Miss Henrietta's handiwork proclaiming that Waste Not meant Want Not, for nothing. Money was not spent so much as thrown. Not that it had made any of them any happier. In fact, she thought, sitting up to grasp her ankles and rest her chin on her knees, as families went, this one could not be classified as a happy one. None of its members could be used in the pack with which she had played as a child. That pack had not contained Contessa di Primacelli the Whore, or Mr. Godfrey the Gigolo, nor yet Mr. David the Drunk. Which makes me what? she thought. Elizabeth the Heiress? The thought made her smile. No, the games played here were much more deadly. More in the line of sudden-death play-offs. Idly she wondered what it was that Richard Tempest held over the heads of his stepchildren to prevent them from contesting his will. Something so unpleasant it had stayed their hands. Well, that was their concern. Just so long as they did not expect to become hers. She had no intention of allowing them to hang about her neck like the Old Man of the Sea . . .

Which reminded her. She had no idea of the time, but judging from the position of the sun, still hot and high in the west, it must be at least five o'clock. She had left her watch with her clothes, in a tidy heap on the sand just in front of the beach house. Dev Loughlin's beach house. How come he, of all of them, was privileged to own a piece of Tempest Cay? He must indeed have been the blue-eyed boy, as Cass had said. Well, he *was* talented. He made the most marvelous movies.

Why had *he* been cast out of Eden? Cass had acted, this morning, as though the Prodigal Son was coming home. So had David. Even Mattic, according to Cass, intended to mark the occasion by leaving her suite. Mattie the Mistress. *La Grande Maîtresse*, if her attitude was anything to go by. Elizabeth sighed. Now there would be her to contend with. Bent and determined on retaining her place as favorite. No doubt, during the past week, holed up in her suite, she had been preparing her plan of campaign. The way she had done her *volte-face* had been an indication of things to come. One minute prepared to join her lover, the next demanding her old place back.

Elizabeth got to her feet, stretched. Time for another game of Unhappy Families.

After the swim back, the muscles in her thighs fluttered and her heart pounded. Flopping onto the sand she lay there, eyes shut, drawing deep lungfuls. She felt, rather than heard, someone walking toward her, stop just in front of her. Raising her head she looked straight up into the sun; a tall, masculine shape. Craning her neck she shaded her eyes, squinting upward. The sun was behind him, outlining him in radiance, and for a moment all she could see was his flaring shape. Then, as he came into focus, she saw a very tall, very black-haired man smiling down at her. He had a dark, Latin face but the bluest of blue Irish eyes, intense and vivid, and as they met hers, she felt her stomach plunge and her skin prick. Awkwardly she gazed up at him, held by the domination of those eyes, all motion stilled, as though caught in a freeze-frame. Her mouth had dried and she could feel the beat of her heart pound against the sand. Unable to move, she waited for him to release her. He bent, held out a hand, and with one easy motion had her on her feet, his hand still holding hers. She could feel it, all the way up her arm to her throat, tightening it, making her flesh tingle.

"Hello," he said. "I'm Dev Loughlin."

EIGHT

"Isn't he gorgeous?" Cass asked besottedly, gazing up at Dev with unaffected delight in his handsomeness. Her glance at Nieves was teasing. "You taken an option on him, honey?"

Nieves blushed.

"And no need to introduce you two?" Cass asked, looking from Dev to Elizabeth.

"I've already introduced myself," Dev answered cheerfully. "When she came out of the sea like a mermaid . . ."

"You took tired," Helen said concernedly, noticing Elizabeth's silence. "It's a long swim out to Sand Cay and back."

"I'm all right," Elizabeth said abruptly. "If you will excuse me, I will go upstairs and change."

"We are not bothering to dress for dinner," Helen called after her. Then, with her own, besotted smile at Dev: "This is a strictly informal weekend."

"Great to have you back, boyo!" David boomed, slapping Dev on the back.

"Great to be back," Dev answered truthfully.

"How long can you stay?" asked Cass hopefully.

"As long as I can . . . Right now I have no plans."

"Good, because I have . . . It's been far too long."

They were all gathered on the terrace, all clustered round him, eager to have him back, to know how he was, what he had been doing. Cass had hold of his hand, Nieves hung on to one arm, and Mattie had slipped her own through his other, while Helen hovered. Even Hervey was beaming, and Harry, whose last weekend it was before leaving for home, was delighted to see Dev again.

"How long has it been?" Cass was asking.

"Too long," Dev answered promptly.

"Thank you for looking after Nieves," Helen murmured gratefully. Her glance at the culprit was reproachful. "We were so worried."

Nieves went to hug her. "I'm sorry, Aunt Helen. I'll explain later . . ."

Helen nodded, smiled, relieved to see Nieves as well as happy to see Dev.

"Did Elizabeth really come out of the sea and fall at your feet?" Mattie asked wickedly. She sighed, fluttering her long, false eyelashes. "Just like all the rest of us . . ."

"True," broke in Cass. "Nieves has had the beach house ready for ages. Did you know she sweeps and cleans, takes fresh flowers?"

Nieves blushed once more.

Cass grinned up at Dev. "Still laying them in the aisles, or wherever?"

"The last one laid an egg!"

"I want to talk to you about that," David said, moving in to detach Dev from his female escort, taking him away, farther down the terrace.

"Glad to have your boyfriend back?" Cass teased Nieves, noticing how her eyes never left Dev.

Shyly: "He's not my boyfriend." Nieves denied, but glowing.

"No? You could have fooled me . . ."

She gazed down the terrace to where the two men had their heads together, David talking, his face eager and, for once, alive, Dev, head bent, listening gravely. That one could fool any woman, she sighed. An absolute male powerhouse . . . It was not just the long, lean body, the endless legs and what you were aware, instantly, he carried between them; it was not the dark, hawk-like Spanish face with its intense, Irish-blue eyes, which, when they looked at you, sent your stomach plunging and set your heart to thump and your skin to prick; it was not the thick, Latin-black of the hair through which you longed to slide your fingers, nor the brilliant warmth of a smile

which lit his face from within and not by strong, almost blue-white teeth. It
was not even the potent combination of Spanish macho and Irish charm. It
was the power, pure and absolute, of a man who was one hundred percent
male. Dev Loughlin was the most masculine man Cass had ever encountered,
and it was not because he either cultivated or flaunted it. It was merely part
of him; a sexuality that took you by the throat and shook you, ever so gently,
making you heart-thumpingly aware that this man was capable of that most
exquisite, brutally tender impalement; the kind you read about in sexy paperbacks and fantasized about when your husband had rolled off you and gone to
sleep. Women adored him. And not because he was the personification of
their every waking dream. It was because they knew they could lean on him.
Cass, who trusted no other man, would have handed over her life in complete
confidence. Dev had immense strength. You just knew that he would never
fold. Not only could he charm the birds off the trees, the women leapt from
the branches, but it was always into arms that never let them fall . . .

With Nieves, he shared top billing with her God. Watching her now, Cass
felt the old sense of unease at the almost ecstatic expression on the child's
face. Nieves was too damned pure . . . She did not see Dev for what he
really was; the sex had not penetrated the shield of her innocence. To Nieves,
he was the father she had never had. And what luck it should be Dev, Cass
thought. He was not the kind to take advantage. Never had Cass seen him
put Nieves down; in any way demean or mock or show boredom at her
obvious adoration. His attitude had always been just right. He gave her, Cass
thought, exactly what she needed. Emotional reassurance, a hard rock to lean
on, an ever-ready and receptive ear, and an understanding heart.

Damn David, Cass thought. It's all his fault. Look at him now . . . She
could see, on David's face, all that Dev meant to him. But even that was
ambivalent. On the one hand, David loved Dev for his strength, his integrity,
his acceptance without judging. On the other hand, he hated and resented
his sexuality, his never-ending and total success with women—wherein David
had only failed and abysmally at that—his power, his charm. Cass was well
aware that while David was deeply grateful for the concern Dev showed
Nieves, he also resented his assumption of it in the first place. Where Dev
Loughlin was concerned, Cass thought glumly, David Boscombe was a seething mass of conflicts and hang-ups so tight they were strangling him.

As if he felt her eyes, David glanced round and met them. Then, quite
deliberately, he turned his back and drew Dev farther down the terrace.
That's right, Cass thought savagely, turn your back as usual. Refuse to see
what you don't want to see; your daughter's crush on a man old enough to be
her father; a man with whom she could never cope. For God's sake, David,

she's having trouble coping with herself! She needs a father—*that's* why she
turns to Dev, although she doesn't know it. She could get hurt, David. Not
because of any intent on Dev's part but because she just doesn't yet understand what he is. I know that with you it is a case of out of sight, but for
God's sake don't let it become one of out of mind . . .

When Janna ushered Dev into the room, Mattie opened her arms wide and
cried joyously: "Dev Loughlin, as I live and lust!"

"Mattie, my love!" He lifted her bodily from the chaise longue and bussed
her soundly. She returned his embrace enthusiastically.

"Oh, you are a sight for these sore old eyes!"

"Let me look at them," Dev commanded and Mattie lay obediently in his
arms, relishing their strength and power, and let herself be scrutinized. She
knew she was looking, if not exactly good, a hell of a lot better. She had eaten
everything put before her over the past week; poured double cream wherever
possible and stuffed a second helping down if there was still room. She had
gained a whole seven pounds. She had had her hair and her nails done, and
hidden her gauntness under one of her gorgeous Chinese mandarin robes.
That Dev was dismayed by the wasted lightness when he was used to a heft
and weight, he hid under a bantering: "Just-opened pansies, as usual . . ."

Mattie kissed him again, her mouth lingering on his appreciatively. "I
knew I could count on you." Her face darkened. "At that, you are the only
one . . ."

"Want to tell me about it?"

It was obvious she was having trouble keeping the lid on. But they were
close friends of long standing. Dev sensed at once that some deflection was
called for if they were not to have shrapnel ricocheting all round the dining
room.

He sat down on the sofa, Mattie still on his knees, holding her hands in
his.

"Have you met her yet?" Mattie asked abruptly.

"Briefly."

"What did you think?"

"She's the image of her father."

"That bastard!" She flounced off Dev's knees as the energy of her anger
surged. "How could he do such a thing to me! To *me!* Twenty years I gave to
that man! And what does he leave to me? Nothing! Not even a mention in
passing! God, if only I had him here! I'd kill him!" Her fingers, with their
newly varnished nails, curled into talons.

"That would defeat the purpose, surely," murmured Dev.

Mattie whirled, met the look in the bright blue eyes and laughed. "Oh
. . . you!" But there was still hurt in her eyes.

"Nieves told me you were hammering on death's door . . . Now look at
you! You ought to be grateful!"

"It was Cass who let the cat out of the bag!" Mattie retorted grimly. "The
rest of them just sat tight."

"Well, they all had to hang on," Dev said practically.

Mattie came to sit down by him again. "But why would he do such a
thing? *Why?* I would have sworn I knew him as well as anyone, but this—"
She shook her head bewilderedly, sounded forlorn. "A daughter, Dev!" The
pansy eyes welled. "And not mine!"

She fell forward into his strong, hard arms and wept.

"You'll ruin all that makeup," Dev warned lightly, at which Mattie sat up,
blinking away the tears which sat like dewdrops on her false eyelashes. "But
what am I going to *do?*" she asked tragically.

"Do? Why should you *do* anything? Whatever else has changed, you are
still Mattie Arden, the Divine Diva."

"Yes, but . . . I shall look such a fool when all this gets out. They'll all
laugh themselves silly. Oh, how they will love the sight of me tossed aside in
favor of some other woman's bastard!"

Mattie's pride was deeply hurt. Of her two titles, she had been as proud of
one as the other. To be the Divine Diva *and* Richard Tempest's favorite had
made her one up on all the other women. They had both played at tit-for-tat,
but after twenty years everyone had *known* that Mattie was and always would
be Number One. Now she was not so much as included. It hurt. She felt she
had been publicly humiliated.

"Nobody's going to know for some time yet. And by the time they do, who
knows what might have happened?"

"But I shall never be able to face them, never!"

"Of course you will. And with your head up."

He was looking at her with his warm, intensely blue eyes, and she smiled
back at him uncertainly. His hands enfolding her own were strong, warm,
encouraging.

"But I won't have him," she whispered, realizing that was what it all came
down to. Under all the rage, the hurt, there was still the desolation of knowing she would never have him again. She was angry, but most of all she was
sad. Each time she worked out her anger, ranted and raved, swore and threatened, trying to burn it away, it seemed to grow. That was why she had stayed
in her suite, because she did not feel able to confront the last, terrible sadness: Richard Tempest's daughter by another woman.

"Who was she, Dev?" she wept miserably, unable to stop the tears this time. "Who *was* she?"

Just someone he used, as usual, Dev thought, like he used everybody. "Whoever she was, she was long before you," he said gently. "Elizabeth Sheridan was born in 1947; you didn't even meet Richard until 1954 . . . She was over and done with by the time he met you."

Mattie sat up slowly. "I never thought of that." He saw her face undergo a change. "Of course," she said, relief making her smile dazzle. "It was long before me, wasn't it." She sniffed, flicked away tears with her fingers. "That does make a difference, doesn't it. Before, not after, I mean. No one can say he threw me over for her."

"You were the only one who lasted," Dev said gently. "Until the day he died . . ."

Mattie's eyes filled again with tears, but this time they were of pride. "I did, didn't I."

He saw her take a deep breath, her head go up. "I have twenty years' tenure," she proclaimed dramatically, her voice vibrant. "That gives me some rights!"

"Every right," Dev assured her.

She sniffed, flicked away tears again, and he knew she had put them away, if not for good, then for the time being.

"Go on," he encouraged. "Make yourself beautiful. Then we'll go down and make a grand entrance!"

Mattie clapped her hands like an excited child. She never could resist making an entrance.

"Just think of it as grand opera," Dev urged, his grin flashing again. "God knows, it's no more improbable than anything Verdi or Puccini ever set to music."

Mattie gurgled. "The cast-off mistress and the unknown, illegitimate daughter. You're right! Puccini could have done wonders with it."

"Come to that, you do look like the Princess Turandot . . ."

He saw her hand go to her throat; that was one of her greatest roles; the appallingly difficult great aria of the Princess when sung by Mattie Arden was absolutely unforgettable; but he saw fear flicker in her face and eyes. He knew she had not tried her voice since Richard's death. She turned away and her shoulders were bowed. She was facing the triple mirrors of her dressing table, and in them he could see her biting her lips, face pale, eyes anguished. He knew she was afraid to try.

She saw him looking at her in the mirror, tried to smile.

"Princess Turandot, remember?" he pressed gently.

He saw the smile tremble. "I've only sung the role . . . by all accounts we've got a real one downstairs."

"Who *can't* sing," Dev said.

Again she underwent one of her swinging changes of mood. "One singer in this family is enough!" she said, eyes sparkling.

She went forward to her dressing table, picked up a hare's foot, dipped it into a box of pink powder and began to brush it over her cheekbones. As she did so, he heard her begin to hum. Her eyes were intent on her cheeks, and her hum ostensibly absentminded, but Dev knew, from the way she held herself, that she was listening to herself, feeling her voice. Only when she was sure did the hum become a softly sung rendition of the last part of the famous aria. Carefully, she highlighted her cheeks, the hare's foot trembling slightly in her hand, but as she heard her own voice issuing from her mouth seemingly unimpaired, he saw her courage and confidence burgeon, and the careful motion of the brush take on a dramatic sweep even as her voice swelled and rose.

"That's my girl," Dev said softly, in a way that made her smile at him even as she sang. She was still not unleashing the full power of her voice, which could ride the full volume of a Wagnerian orchestra; husbanding it, moving it along cautiously, not forcing it, not yet ready to unleash those crucifyingly difficult high notes which many a lesser singer had failed to scale. But the sound was there; that honeyed, full, goldenly rounded tone which so ravished her admirers, and she was content to let it drift back into its wordless hum as she applied fresh lipstick, finally fading altogether as she sat back, turned her face critically this way and that before cocking an eye at Dev in the mirror and asking, "Will I do, then?"

Dev rose to his feet and her eyes traveled upward to his face as he came toward her, placing his hands on her shoulders and pressing firmly, all the while holding her eyes in the mirror. His smile released her own, happily relieved dazzler. "You'll do," he said quietly, and her hand came up to squeeze his.

"Right," she said confidently. "Let's go downstairs and do her . . ."

Everyone turned as Mattie and Dev came out to join the gathering on the terrace. Mattie clapped her hands once more, in that gleefully childish way of hers. "Oh, we're dining out here like old times!"

Helen smiled. "It is such a beautiful evening. And when we heard you were coming down . . ."

"Champagne too!" Mattie's eyes held their own bubbles.

"Well, you downstairs, and Dev with us once again . . . what else?"

Helen asked happily. "But you must take care . . . I have had this brought out for you."

She led Mattie to where a couch, upholstered in glowing topaz velvet, had been placed in the center of its surrounding chairs. There, Mattie bestowed herself comfortably, cushions at her back, her small feet—she was very vain about them—in brocade slippers protruding from the barbarically embroidered hem of her robe.

"Well, and isn't this nice," Mattie sighed happily. "Dev, come and sit by me." She patted the chair next to her, and Dev good-naturedly sat down beside her, Nieves moving to the chair next to him. "Now then, everybody here . . ." Her eyes darted round the gathering.

"Elizabeth will be down in a moment," Helen said. "If someone will open the champagne . . ."

The table had been laid in the center of the terrace, its white lace cloth graced with glittering crystal and gleaming silver, tall white candles burning in engraved storm lanterns against the drift of the soft evening breeze.

"Oh, how lovely." Mattie sighed happily. "Just like old times." She took that as her theme for the evening, and proceeded to keep it in her firm grip. Old times—in which Elizabeth Sheridan had played no part.

Quite deliberately, even when Elizabeth joined them, having, in spite of Helen's reminder, changed into a short rather than long dress, Mattie kept the conversation in areas of which Elizabeth knew nothing and could play no part, so that she sat silently, able to do no more than listen while Mattie held center stage right under the center spot. Now and again Cass smiled at her encouragingly, well aware of what Mattie was doing but also confident that Elizabeth would not demur at being relegated to the chorus. That Mattie was herself—well, almost herself—again was all that mattered, and to that end they were all prepared to indulge her, just as Mattie was quite content, indeed expected, to be indulged.

Even Caesar, the chef, had entered into the silent conspiracy, producing a dinner consisting of Mattie's favorite dishes. Tiny mushrooms stuffed with truffles and served on a bed of artichoke hearts, stuffed squab and wild rice golden with saffron, even her favorite devil's food cake lavished with fresh cream. Mattie had a very sweet tooth. She ate heartily, and drank champagne with reckless abandon. The dinner table, set under the stars, was bubbling like the wine; there was much laughter and good-natured banter.

As they left the table, Cass settled herself in a cushioned lounger with a comfortable sigh, stuffed to the gills with food and contentment. Mattie was back on form, Dev was back at Marlborough and all, for once, was right with her world. This was how Marlborough could be; as Elizabeth had never seen it. Knives put away, teeth bared only in smiles, all tensions smoothed away, all tight knots untied. Squirming comfortably on her cushions, she smiled fatuously round.

Helen too was happy, beaming with an almost tearful gaze at the relaxed, smiling faces. Oh, if it only could *always* be like this. Easy and comfortable and happy. Mattie had put a match to the evening and it glowed, brightly. Everyone was so delighted to see her looking so good, obviously feeling so good, that their indulgence had preempted all other emotions.

I knew I was right to send Dev to her, she thought, gazing contentedly at his dark, smiling face, listening to the deep, temple-gong voice as he talked to Mattie, falling in easily, as was his way, with Mattie's mood, fetching and carrying and being as supportive as the cushions behind her back.

Even David was quite sober; she had heard his rumbling laugh boom out several times. He was even being affable to Nieves! She caught Hervey's approving smile, returned it before sweeping her gaze on past Cass, her nose buried in her snifter, on to Harry, chatting amiably to Elizabeth. She had her head bent attentively, yet there was something about her . . .

She was not relaxed. She sat in a fan-backed cane chair, wearing a chiffon dress of palest, coolest green. The full skirt frothed around her knees as she sat with her back straight, her legs crossed, the bare, gleaming legs tanned and silky in high-heeled strappy sandals. But she was twisting the stem of her glass restlessly between her fingers. Surely not Mattie? Helen thought, disturbed. She had taken over, as was ever her way, and she had perhaps harped a little too strongly on times past . . . Did Elizabeth see her as making a challenge, perhaps? To what? Helen thought bewilderedly. After all, Mattie was only demonstrating her right to be included as a member—albeit ex-officio—of this family.

Cass held out her cup as Moses came by a second time with the coffeepot. "Yes, please . . . and a little more Armagnac, too." She smiled up at him as he moved in his stately, placid way through the group, dispensing coffee with one hand, liqueur with the other. Stretching out a hand, Cass helped herself to some tiny ratafias and nibbled deliciously. She shouldn't really . . . Ah, the hell with it, she thought, dredging up another handful. Not tonight.

Sinking into the cushions she closed her eyes. She could smell the jasmine in the big stone troughs under the windows, mingled with the heady drift of the magnolias set like stars amid the leaves of the big old tree at the corner of the house; the rich aroma of Hervey's cigar mingled with it, and the good, mouth-watering fragrance of coffee. This was living, she thought comfortably. This would show Elizabeth that it was not armed warfare all the time. And she could cope with Mattie . . . She took a swig of her brandy. The

two of us can cope with anything—and anyone—else, she thought drunkenly. But, thank God, Dev was here. She opened her eyes to smile at him—
and froze. He was listening to Mattie rattle on, an attentive smile on his face,
but he was looking at Elizabeth Sheridan.

Cass sat up with a jerk. Jesus! she could ride that look. Her eyes darted to
Elizabeth, who was in the act of draining her glass, after which she leaned
forward to place it on the glass top of the table in front of her. But as she did
so, her eyes met those of Dev Loughlin and Cass saw her freeze, held by
those eyes as they stared at each other. Cass felt her heart plunge sickeningly
as a queer sense of terror squeezed it between icy hands. She wanted to leap
forward, impose herself between them, break the contact. But then Mattie
put a hand on Dev's arm and he turned his head, breaking the contact
himself. Cass saw Elizabeth's hand jerk, and instead of the glass hitting the
table it missed and fell to the terrace, shattering. At once, Harry was picking
up the pieces and Elizabeth was saying, "Sorry . . . that was clumsy of me."
But her voice was mechanical, her expression blind.

"Don't worry," Helen reassured, though the glass was of Russian crystal
and one of a set that had belonged to Catherine the Great. Moses saw that
all the pieces were collected before bearing them away in a napkin.

Christ! thought Cass, almost moaning out loud. Jesus Christ! She gulped
her brandy, feeling it burn but also hearing the glass chink against her teeth
as her hand shook it. For God's sake, she told herself furiously, don't be a
fool! Since when were you Madame Zsa Zsa who sees and knows all? But she
knew, even as Dev answered Mattie, saying something that made her laugh,
her eyes sparkling up at him, that even though he was not looking at Elizabeth anymore, she was conscious of him with every nerve ending. It was all
there in the look she threw him. Jesus Christ, Cass thought, I've got to put a
stop to this. "How about some music?" she asked loudly.

"Oh, yes," Helen came in warmly. "On such a night as this . . ." She
turned to Nieves. "Play for us, darling?"

Nieves blushed. She was a good pianist, often spent hours at the piano.
"Yes, do play for us," Mattie commanded. But Nieves was looking at Dev.
He smiled directly at her. "Yes, Nieves . . . play." The deep, resonant voice
made Nieves shiver. Cass, her eyes elsewhere, saw the way Elizabeth moved
in her own chair, as if that deep, masculine voice had laid hands on her.

Oh, Jesus. Cass could have screamed.

"All right," Nieves said.

"And Moses shall open the windows so we can all hear," Helen said,
nodding at Moses, who followed Nieves from the terrace.

"She plays very well," Helen assured Elizabeth proudly. "And you love music, don't you. What a good idea, Cass." She bent an approving smile in Cass's direction. Cass's own smile felt as if it would snap.

The windows of the white drawing room were flung open, and soon the sound of the Bechstein grand floated out to them. Nieves played with fluency and feeling, but she sounded rather nervous until she got into her stride. She gave them Debussy's *Clair de lune*, then his sad little waltz *La plus que lente* to which Mattie hummed softly, and finished off with a rippling Chopin study. When she came out again, shyly acknowledging their applause, her father said, "Don't stop."

She said, still shy, "I thought Dev might play his guitar . . ."

"Even better!" exclaimed Mattie.

"I don't even know if it still will play," Dev said. "It's been a long time."

"Oh, I've kept it tuned," Nieves said naïvely. "I've got it all wrapped up."

Mattie chuckled. "That's not the only thing you've got wrapped up, if you ask me!"

Nieves went scarlet, but when Dev said, "That was a nice thing to do," her blush changed to radiance and she ran back inside the house.

Mattie patted Dev's hands, fluttering her lashes at him. "I don't know how you do it," she remarked innocently, "but I've never known it to fail."

Everybody laughed, but all Cass heard was the sound of Elizabeth Sheridan's chair as she turned it so that its spreading fan back removed her from Dev's gaze and put her four-square to that of Cass.

Nieves came back reverently carrying a silk-wrapped bundle, watched anxiously as Dev unwrapped it to reveal a beautiful, classical Spanish guitar, tried its strings, made a few adjustments, and said, "Absolutely perfect," to Nieves, who hopped from one foot to the other with delight, before exclaiming, "Oh, you'll need a footstool!" Bringing one back she set it reverently at his feet and he propped one foot on it, flashing her another smile, which again sent her pink with pleasure.

"All right," Dev asked, "what shall it be?"

"Something Spanish, of course!" Mattie said reproachfully. "One of those lovely gypsy things."

"Like this?"

Dev began to play, the throb of the guitar accentuated by the rhythmic thud of his fingers on the wood.

"That's it!" Mattie began to snap her fingers in time.

The beat made feet tap, eyes sparkle.

"A multitalented man," Harry whispered softly to Elizabeth. "If he did not make films he could always earn a living as a concert artist."

Elizabeth said nothing.

"That was lovely," Helen said, when the applause had died down. "But won't you play us one of those lovely, sad things? . . . I forget what they are called."

"*Soleares,*" said Dev.

"Yes, that's it. Please, Dev?"

Her great eyes beseeched and her sadly tremulous smile begged.

"For you—anything," Dev said, and Helen rewarded him with one of her burning looks.

This time, as the first notes of the guitar fell plangently onto the soft, sweet air, limpid, crystalline, hanging for a moment before dissolving, in a diffusion of shimmering beauty, Cass was conscious of an answering quiver from Elizabeth. She felt sick. It was as though he was playing *her.* The notes rippled through the air in a plaintive sadness, the guitar throbbing passionately, as eyes were closed, cigars burned away unsmoked in lax fingers. But Cass was stiff and straight in her chair, her eyes fixed to Elizabeth, who had pushed back her chair into the shadows of the poinsettia bush. The bright moon found its way through the heavy foliage and glimmered about her face, and what Cass saw there made her bite her lips on a moan.

Elizabeth was transfigured. Cass would not have believed that this enraptured, agonizedly ecstatic face was the coldly composed, unemotional one she had come to believe was the only one Elizabeth ever wore—or could ever wear. She *could* feel.

It was there, for all to see. But a quick look round told Cass nobody was noticing anything. They were all sitting with their eyes closed. Except Dev. And he was once again looking in Elizabeth's direction. Then, with further horror, Cass saw he had moved his own chair so that she was again directly in his line of gaze. Cass wanted to blurt out, "No! No! You mustn't look like that!" to Elizabeth, and to Dev, "And you mustn't make her . . ." Used as she had become over the past weeks to Elizabeth's negative responses, this positive, anguished one made her recoil, as though she had unwittingly stumbled on something intensely private and personal.

Cass's tough exterior hid a finely honed perception. That same inner radar which warned of approaching disaster also communicated inner feelings to her, but until now she had never felt anything emanating from Elizabeth Sheridan except a chill wind. As they had worked together, talked together, established a working relationship, so Cass had also become, almost without her knowing it, emotionally involved. Her admiration of Elizabeth's capability, the way she assimilated and the speed with which she did it, had done more to make Cass warm to her than anything else. That there had been no answering warmth had not lessened it. This was a worker! Why, the two of them could take on the world! It had excited her, given an extra edge to her days. And when, by dint of careful but casual remarks, she had found out that there was nothing either in Elizabeth's life or on her mind to distract her from the task in hand, she had found her warmth turning to heat. In her mind, the two of them had formed a partnership: two strong-willed, independent women—neither with much use for men—who directed the spotlight of their force and energies on work and accomplishment.

In her mind, they were already a force to be reckoned with. Their single-mindedness merged into a shared commitment: the Tempest Organization.

Now Cass stared stupidly at the pieces of her broken dreams. Dev Loughlin had done it again. But to Elizabeth! *Elizabeth Sheridan!* No, it was not possible, it could not be . . . She wanted to weep. Elizabeth was immune to men; never once had she talked about them, about any particular man. Even when Cass had said jokingly, "You realize running the Organization is a full-time job? If you are thinking of marriage and children . . ."

"No, I am not," Elizabeth had returned flatly. "That is not for me."

"Now it isn't, but you can never be sure about the future," Cass had demurred, wanting to be sure herself.

"I can," Elizabeth had answered. "That is not for me," she had repeated.

"What's the matter?" Cass had asked lightly, daringly. "Don't you like men?"

The green eyes had regarded her dispassionately. "What can any man do for me that I cannot do for myself?"

Which meant, Cass had thought triumphantly, that they don't do anything!

Wrong, she thought wretchedly now; wrong, wrong, *wrong!* Why had she not paid more attention to Elizabeth's abrupt coldness, her near-rudeness to Dev when they had come back together from the beach house? She had spoken to him only when spoken to, and then at arm's length. Because she had been conscious of him even then.

Cass transferred her gaze to Dev, and it was rancid with hatred. It's all your *fault!* You and that damned animal thing you carry around with you! She felt on the one hand that he had betrayed her by directing it at Elizabeth, and on the other that Elizabeth had betrayed her by succumbing to it.

And as if on cue, Elizabeth's eyes flew open and she looked straight into Dev's. Cass could have swung from that gaze. It was almost a visible connection; it seemed to Cass she could hear it humming . . . Then she realized it was Mattie. Dev had begun one of Granados's songs, and suddenly Mattie was singing the words, her Spanish—in which Dev had coached her—sounding authentic and guttural. Lightly her voice overlaid the guitar, skipping over the top of the tune and ending in a bravura exclamation.

Everybody burst into spontaneous applause, Helen, in her enthusiasm, getting up to embrace Mattie delightedly.

"It was there—so I just let it come," Mattie demurred, wide-eyed, triumphant.

Everyone buzzed and hovered round, but Cass dared not take her eyes from Elizabeth, whose face had once more set into its normal, scrupulously composed expression. Cass blinked. Elizabeth got up from her chair, walked past Dev Loughlin as though he did not exist, and the little group fell back expectantly. Mattie's face as she gazed upward was wary, defiant. But Elizabeth's voice was reverent when she said, "No wonder they call you the Divine Diva."

Mattie burst into tears.

Cass started when someone asked, "What's up, Cass?" It was Hervey, looking concerned.

"Nothing," she lied, adding quickly to forestall the disbelieving look and any further questions: "I've got a headache . . . that's all." And that was no lie. It was splitting in two, the ax that had fallen still sticking out of it.

"You smoke too much," he said distastefully, looking pointedly at the cigarette in her hand and the other one burning in the ashtray, which he stubbed out with a sigh and a shake of the head.

Helen came over to join them, sitting down beside Cass. "What a nice thing that was to say to Mattie," she said, referring to Elizabeth's comment, after which Mattie, in a highly emotional state, had been borne away by Dev, her arms about his neck, her face buried in his chest, Nieves trotting at his heels.

"Oh, well, I happen to know she is a music lover," Hervey said importantly. "When I visited her flat I noticed she had a first-class stereo and a large collection of LP's."

"Yes, I know," Helen agreed. "I showed her Richard's collection and she was most enthusiastic."

"When was this?" Cass asked suspiciously but eagerly.

"Oh . . . some time ago," Helen answered vaguely. She gazed round at the depleted group. "What a pleasant evening this has been," she said happily. "And crowned by Mattie sounding unimpaired . . ."

Which is more than I am, thought Cass. She looked round too. "Where's Elizabeth?"

"Gone up," Helen answered, rising. "And I'm going up too . . . This has been an exciting evening."

Hervey promptly rose. "Allow me to escort you." He offered her his arm and they went off walking close.

Cass got up and went over to the brandy, poured herself a double and tossed it back.

"All bestowed?" she heard David say, and turned to see Dev coming back alone.

"Yes. She's in bed—but floating."

"You played that song deliberately, didn't you?" David asked admiringly.

Dev only smiled. "Well, it is one of her favorites . . ."

David punched him on the arm. "Sly devil!"

Cass sauntered toward them. "So how's the movie business?" she demanded truculently.

"All disaster and demonic possession," Dev answered lightly.

"Still having trouble shaking the money tree?"

"What do you mean—still?"

Nonchalantly, never taking her eyes from his face: "If it's any help—why don't you try Elizabeth? She's a movie buff. Seen every one of yours a dozen times . . ."

"Is that so," Dev answered pleasantly but inscrutably, helping himself to a drink.

"Is it so! I should know . . . I'm closer to her than anybody!"

David laughed. It was like glass breaking. "That's still at the end of a ten-foot pole!"

"What did you think of her, anyway?" Cass pursued.

"She's very beautiful."

"Isn't she, though?" David's face lit. "Did you ever see such a face?" He sighed. "I'd love to paint it."

Cass almost dropped her glass. Not you too! She had seen the way he followed Elizabeth with his hang-dog expression; something Elizabeth failed to see. But the expression on his face now was besotted, dreaming.

"Then why not do it?" Dev said calmly.

Now David's jaw dropped and he flushed, squirmed. "Well . . ." They could see him delving desperately for an excuse. "She never seems to have any time . . . what with working with Cass and all."

"Mornings only!" Cass said ruthlessly, blocking that exit. "The rest of the day is her own."

"Yes . . . well . . . I've only been *thinking* about it," David said hastily.

"So ask her," Dev said, the bright blue eyes pinning David firmly to the wall. "She can only say no."

David flushed. "Yeah," he muttered, "but in such a way . . ."

He turned and though appearing to wander off was, in reality, running.

"He's gone and done it again," Cass said scornfully. "Worshiping at the shrine." Then, with deliberate casualness: "Of course, she really is stunningly beautiful . . . don't you think?"

"Yes. She's beautiful," Dev said, in a voice that added nothing to that fact.

"I could put in a good word for you, if you like," she offered.

The blue eyes were thoughtful, then he smiled and his face changed. "You know me, Cass. I may not allow myself to be bought, but I can still sell myself . . ." He set down his glass. "Now I must go and give some time to David. See you in the morning. Good night."

"Good night."

Cass watched him catch up with David, saw them disappear down the steps in the direction of the beach house. Thank God, she thought, he's not in the house, just down the corridor from Elizabeth. She'd have sat up all night watching his door . . . not waiting to see him come out but who went in. It had been done before. With Dev, it was par for the course.

Elizabeth was in the shower. Cass waited until she came out, wrapped in a toweling robe.

"Hi!" Her voice was brightly breezy. "Just thought I'd say thanks for being so nice to Mattie."

"I didn't do anything except tell her the truth."

"Maybe, but it came from you, and that was all she wanted, really. And don't mind the way she came on so strong tonight . . . the King may be dead but it's still 'Long Live the Queen.' "

Then, as Elizabeth sat down at her dressing table to brush her hair, "What did you think of our other visitor?" Cass asked carelessly.

"I didn't."

"Didn't what?"

"Think of him."

Liar! Cass raged. She had given herself away.

"He plays a good guitar, don't you think? He's a man of many talents, our Dev."

"He does make marvelous movies," Elizabeth said slowly. She was brushing her hair with long, sweeping strokes, almost as if she was giving herself a beating.

"Want me to do that?" Cass asked, straightening.

"No!" It was quick, almost a reflexive recoil. "No . . ." Elizabeth repeated, more calmly. "I don't like anyone touching my hair."

Cass watched her in silence. Her face was empty, the cat's eyes unblinking. It was as though in the shower she had deliberately washed away all expression.

Abruptly, wanting to provoke a reaction: "I told Dev you were a movie buff," Cass said. "I thought perhaps you might be interested in providing him with financial backing."

"Did he ask you if I would be?"

Cass's heart sank. That was a wrong answer. The right one would have been: "Why should I?"

"No. Dev does his own asking," she answered. "I just thought . . . Well, you've run that documentary a dozen times and you did say you agreed with Pauline Kael that it would be a tragedy if lack of the necessary wherewithal prevented him from making what she called 'marvelously consistent works of art.'"

A faint smile appeared on Elizabeth's chiseled lips. "Greater love hath no fan?" It was sardonic, honed to a fine edge.

"Well, aren't you?" Cass bounced back sharply.

"But he never makes any money." Cass recognized the evasion.

"Only because he can't always get a distributor. The big companies have that all tied up." And Richard had them tied up, she thought, but did not say so. "I thought you approved of talent!" she accused.

"I do." Elizabeth lifted her arms to fasten her hair with a barrette.

"Well, then! God knows Dev is talented . . . in more ways than one," she added in a nudge-nudge, wink-wink tone of voice. And if he is going to exercise it in your direction I want to be there to see him, she thought. Out loud she urged, "You'd have nothing to lose."

Elizabeth rose to her feet. "That," she said, "depends entirely on what he wants. Good night, Cass."

It was dismissal. Leaving Cass still swinging by the short hairs.

It was beginning to grow light before she managed to fall asleep, and by the time she got downstairs, not having solved a single problem in spite of devoting every brain cell to them, she was as sour as curdled milk. She had overslept; God knows what had happened while she had not been there to see. Suppose Dev had already made his approach. Suppose Elizabeth had let him. Suppose they were even now, the two of them, off somewhere alone . . . and she not knowing where.

She all but fell down the stairs, not encountering a soul on her way. The

South Parlor was empty. The cloth was still laid and what smelled like fresh coffee was on the hot plate. There was only one place. Her own, no doubt. Which meant that everybody had been and gone . . . Frantically she trotted through rooms, failed to find anyone, until at last, going out into the dazzlingly bright sunshine, she came across Elizabeth stretched out on a lounger on the terrace reading the London *Times*.

"Where is everybody?" Before she could order her day she had to know its content.

"I have only seen Hervey and the Count. Miss Arden is not down yet, and Helen is doing her flowers."

"And the others?"

"I believe they have gone sailing."

And don't care, said the voice. Cass felt her heart lift. "Of course! The first thing Dev does whenever he comes back is take out the *Pinta* . . ." Her gloom evaporated. Suddenly the sunshine was true instead of jaundiced yellow. He had gone sailing! And without Elizabeth! See, she scolded herself, you do *not* see and know all.

"In which case," she said happily, "why don't we play hookey too? It *is* the weekend."

"I was expecting we would work this morning, as usual."

As usual! As though nothing had happened! Cass felt her heart soar.

"Okay . . . whatever you say . . . but I'm going to have some breakfast first."

"I'll see you in the office, then—in half an hour?"

"That you will," agreed Cass light-heartedly, almost light-headed with relief. "That you will!"

And when she did join Elizabeth, she saw at once that her attention was, as always, wholly on the task in hand. Dev Loughlin had not distracted her. Indeed, she really went at it, Cass thought with satisfaction. It was she who looked at the clock to exclaim, "One o'clock already! Where did the time go?"

There was no sign of Dev, David, or Nieves at lunch. Helen informed them they had departed before eight, taken a picnic basket. "They said they would be back for dinner."

See, Cass scolded herself, if he can go off for a whole day, and if she could not care less . . . ! It was the *music*, she told herself, the night and the magic of it and Mattie and all . . . and my overblown imagination.

So comforted did she feel, so secure, that she decided she would have a siesta. Now that she knew Dev was safely out of reach she had no qualms about leaving Elizabeth alone.

"So what are you going to do with yourself this afternoon?" she asked her indulgently.

"I'll think of something . . . I think I might swim."

"Go carefully if you go out in the sun," Helen said concernedly. "I have an excellent cream . . . I will give you some. Use it lavishly; you have a very fair skin."

Toiling back up the beach about six o'clock, having left Dev and Nieves at the *Pinta*, back early because, while heeling sharply before a sudden buffet of the trade winds, one of the sockets had broken, David became aware of something in his line of vision. Nearing it, he saw it was Elizabeth Sheridan, flat on her back, one arm thrown over her eyes, the other lying limply on the hot sand. She was wearing a silky-sleek black maillot, its straps undone, against which the oiled sheen of her skin gleamed like satin. She seemed to be asleep, unaware that the tide was coming in, straining up the sand, eager to reach the long, narrow foot only inches away. David stood still, staring.

He had been aware of her body many times, through the thin material of a shirt, the silk of a dress, but had always viewed it abstractly, as a work of art. Now, in the closely fitting swimsuit, he saw it fully revealed for the first time. It was magnificent. Full and rounded hips, firm, columnar thighs, breasts larger and deeper than he had imagined, all rosily gilded under the sun.

There was something pagan about the way she lay, something abandoned and not in keeping with her controlled character, as though she had flung herself down in exhaustion after some violent bout of activity—like making love.

He had a sense of voluptuousness, of sensuality—things he had not hitherto associated with her. She compelled his eyes. He stood and stared, unable to bring himself to wake her, or to leave her to the burning sky. The cloth of her suit was quite dry; she must have been there for some time. If she didn't move she would soon find herself awash. But he just stood and looked, all sorts of wayward thoughts taking possession of his mind, forming images which excited and aroused him. For the first time he was conscious of her sexually. Eyeing her lustfully, he was instantly, ravenously, aroused.

When, suddenly, she moved her arm from her eyes, regarded him from them with chilling clarity, he knew she had not been asleep at all. He felt himself flushing guiltily and sullenly, as though he had been caught doing something he shouldn't.

"Tide's coming in," he said brutally. "If you don't move you'll get soaked."

She sat up, moved backward, shaking her hair, exciting him still further.

"How was the sailing?" she asked.

"Fine—until a socket broke. That's why we're back early."

"*Pinta* was the name of one of Columbus's ships, wasn't it?"

"Yes. It means painted . . . she's red, you see—but no political connotations. Dev is from the *Emerald* Isle."

She was reaching for her dress, folded beside her, taking a small brush from its pocket, and some pins, which she held between her strong white teeth as she brushed her hair up and back. "He is part Spanish, isn't he?"

"Mother. Irish father. Born in Galway."

"He is a good friend of yours?"

"My best . . . Why so curious?"

He lowered himself to the sand beside her, to sit, knees up, concealing his erection.

"He seems to compel everything from curiosity to concupiscence."

David's jaw dropped. He had never heard anyone use that word in his life. But it was the sort of thing she *would* say. Even sex was reduced to a word.

"You admire him very much, don't you?" she asked suddenly.

David shrugged defensively. "I hadn't realized it showed," he answered shortly.

"Like the Scarlet Letter."

At the tone of her voice he flushed just as red. "Which one?" he asked savagely. "F for Failure or C for Compromise?"

"Well it certainly isn't S for Success."

His mouth was open, his eyes those of a wounded deer. What had brought this on?

"Except, of course," she went on, "his artistic successes are commercial failures."

"That's not his fault!" David leaped to the defense. "He has trouble getting them distributed . . . If you can't get people to pay to see your movies you can't make any money, can you?" He picked up a handful of sand, let it trickle through his fingers. "Maybe things will be different now . . . Not that I'm worried," he added hastily. "I've got a percentage in just about every one of his movies and I know they will pay off one day."

"Dev pays all debts?"

"He will, when he can," he answered doggedly. "I know Dev . . ."

"For long?"

"Almost twenty years."

"How did you meet him?"

"In Spain . . . I was following a certain bullfighter and he was making *The Moment of Truth.*"

"Your wife was Spanish, wasn't she?"

Silence, then: "Yes. She was Dev's cousin."

His tone was flat, expressionless.

"What does the name Nieves mean?" she asked next. "It is a Spanish name, isn't it?"

"Yes. It means snow . . ." David stared at the sand. "She was born in a snowstorm in the Sierra de Guadarrama."

Elizabeth eyed his tightly closed face and turned away from what was obviously a closed subject back to the one she really wanted to know about.

"How does it come about that Mr. Loughlin owns a piece of this island?"

"Richard gave it to him." David threw a handful of sand into the wind. "They were very good friends. Once."

"Is that why he hasn't been back here for so long?"

"Yes." He turned on her. "I thought you didn't give a damn about anybody." Then he smiled. "But Dev's different, isn't he? Women *always* think so." Cynicism corroded his voice.

"Is that why you envy him?"

Again David was astounded. "Who wouldn't?" he defended. "He's got this magnetism about him; it draws people—women—like iron filings."

"And he makes *you* feel inadequate."

David's mouth opened again, but before he could think of an answer: "Is that why you drink?"

Again, David's face slammed shut. "I drink, therefore I am," he answered jeeringly.

"What—a drunk?"

Christ! he thought, mortified. What have I done to deserve this? His dismay at her accurate reading was equaled by his anguish at her doing so aloud.

"We all have our crutches," he answered surlily. "What's yours?"

She took it seriously. "Not having one."

"Jesus, that's too complicated for me!"

"Is that why you don't paint anymore?"

Now, he thought. He licked his lips, swallowed, and said: "Well, as a matter of fact"—he spoke in a rush to get it over and done with—"I was hoping you would let me paint you."

She turned her head and he forced himself to meet the green eyes and the surprise in them. "Me?"

"Why not?" he asked lamely. "You are worth painting."

"Of course . . ." she said, with the air of one remembering. "Portraits are your specialty, aren't they."

At her tone of voice he flushed. "I didn't know you'd seen any."

"I haven't. Cass told me. She said you were once a very fashionable portrait painter."

In a strangled voice: "I did a few." Then, as if he felt it necessary to explain: "I did one of Richard, you see . . . and it sort of took off from there."

"Where is that? It's not here."

"No. It hangs in the lobby of the Tempest Building in New York. It will come here, though. Then it will be hung with all the rest." He made it sound like an execution. One he would pay to watch.

"Ah . . . I see. You want to paint me for posterity." She was being gently sardonic.

"I want to paint you for me," he said, and flushed deeply and nearly fell over backward when she said, "All right."

"You mean you will sit?" His excitement made him almost stutter.

"Yes."

"Oh . . . well . . . fine . . ." It had been so easy he couldn't believe it.

"When?" she asked.

"Well . . ." His mind worked feverishly. "I have to get a few things ready first." Like canvas and paints, for instance.

"All right," she said again. "Let me know when you are ready." And with a lithe movement she was on her feet, picking up her dress and sandals, and went loping off up the beach in her long, easy stride, leaving him gaping after her. He started violently when a voice asked, "What did you do? Frighten her off?"

He blinked up into the sun to see Dev, Nieves by his side, holding his hand. David held out his and Dev heaved him up.

"I asked her if she would let me paint her, and she said yes—just like that," he said dazedly.

"Oh?" said Dev, and Nieves looked up at him quickly. "You haven't lost the urge, then?"

David studiously refused to meet the knowledgeable blue eyes.

"I told you when I wrote," he said vaguely. Then he changed the subject. This one wasn't something he wanted to share with anyone just yet. Not even Dev. "Did you get the socket fixed?"

"No. It's cracked right across. I'll go down to the boatyard and get a replacement."

That evening, before dinner, Cass was looking through the *Chronicle*, the weekly newspaper of the Island, when she exclaimed, "Guess what's playing at the Bijou tonight!" The Bijou was the Island cinema.

"Surprise us," Dev said.

"The Marx Brothers' *Duck Soup!* Oh, I could just go an hour with Groucho! What do you say we all go? Make an outing of it."

"Oh, yes—let's!" Mattie clapped her hands.

"What time does it start?" asked Nieves.

"Nine-fifteen . . . We could make it if we dined a little earlier."

"Of course," Helen said at once, reaching out a hand for the bell rope.

Dev was the only one who didn't go. He wanted to go to the boatyard for a replacement socket so that they could sail again next day.

"Where to this time?" Cass asked.

"I thought we'd make for Cat Island . . . maybe picnic there."

"Oh, that would be lovely!" Nieves said happily.

"Want to come?" Dev asked. He turned to Elizabeth. "You too."

"Cass is a lousy sailor!" David protested. "She always has to go over the side because she gets seasick!"

"Not if it's flat calm!" Cass flared.

"Tomorrow should be hot and very calm," Dev said easily. "Have you ever sailed?" he asked Elizabeth.

"No."

"Then why not come along? The *Pinta* can squeeze five."

"I'm sure Elizabeth would enjoy that very much," Helen said warmly. "The sailing hereabouts is marvelous. You should try it at least once."

"Do *you* get seasick?" asked David.

"No."

"And I won't either!" Cass said quickly, determined that, if she had to hang over the rail all the way there and back, she was not going to be left behind this time.

"Oh, yes you will!" David grunted. "You always do. You used to retire to your stateroom even on the *Tempestuous.*"

"So I'll take pills! I'm coming and that's that. And if we are going to the movies we should be on our way."

There were eight, so they used the big Rolls. Three in the back, three in the jump seats, and Nieves beside David, who drove. Dev followed in the Mercedes sports. At the village, he turned off one way with a wave and they went the other.

It was almost eleven when they came out, along with the throng of villagers, who greeted them smilingly. Helen paused to talk to several of them.

"Oh, there's Dev!" Nieves darted off toward where he was leaning against the Mercedes, talking. "You should have come, Dev. It was a scream!"

"Just so long as *you* enjoyed it." He smiled down at her.

Afterward, Cass could still not quite work out how it happened. They were milling around, groups of villagers talking to one or other of the Family as they moved toward where the Rolls was parked. She got in, and after a few moments, Hervey, Helen and Mattie following, David heaving himself into the driving seat. When Cass peered out of the back window for Elizabeth, she saw that Dev had stopped her, with a hand on her arm, but was saying something to Nieves, who turned, disconsolately, and came with dragging feet toward where the rest of them waited.

"Where's Elizabeth?" Cass asked sharply.

"Dev is driving her back. He says he wants to talk to her." Nieves got in beside her father and sat stiffly, obviously not happy.

"You did tell him she might be interested in backing him," David reminded, making Cass think: So he told you . . .

"All here?" asked David, turning round. Cass craned her neck. As the Rolls turned the corner of the street, Dev and Elizabeth were still standing there. Then they were out of sight.

Why that devious son of a bitch! Cass raged. Money, my ass! He doesn't have to get her all to himself in a two-seater sports car to discuss an investment! He could do that tomorrow, on the *Pinta*. He's up to no good . . . But didn't he say he could still sell himself? And weren't you the dum-dum who planted the suggestion? You and your fast mouth! She kept looking out the back window so often that Hervey said impatiently, "I think, my dear Cass, you may trust Dev to deliver Elizabeth safely."

Yeah, thought Cass. But from what—or to what?

There was never any sign of the Mercedes. When she got out of the Rolls she pretended to be taking in deep breaths of the fragrant night air, but her eyes were scanning the hill and its road like radar. It was bare and white in the moonlight. She had no choice but to trail the rest of them into the house, where coffee and sandwiches were waiting. She ate most of them, one eye on the door and the other on the clock. And as the time went on, and on, her uneasiness grew. When Dev finally walked in through the door he was alone. Her eyes raked him. He looked no different. Still brought into the room the same, powerful presence before which Mattie sat up, a hand going up to pat her hair, and Helen smiled brightly, while Nieves ran to him eagerly.

"Where's Elizabeth?" Cass asked sharply.

"Gone up. Any coffee left?"

"Oh, this is cold," Helen answered. "Let me ring for fresh."

"You escaped with your virtue intact, then?" Mattie observed innocently, her eyes sparkling maliciously.

"It is supposed to be its own reward," Dev answered gravely.

There was absolutely nothing to tell from his voice, his bearing. He could be a bloody clam when it suited him, Cass thought furiously. But she had counted the time: exactly fifty-two minutes. Time enough for God knows what to have happened. And right now, she had to find out what.

"No more coffee for me," she said, rising and manufacturing a vast yawn. "I'm bushed . . . all that laughing." She made for the door at a walk. Mustn't run. Hand on the handle she paused. "What time tomorrow?" she asked Dev.

"I want to leave at seven," Dev answered. "We've a long way to go."

"I'll be there!" Cass promised, adding truthfully, "I wouldn't miss it for the world."

Elizabeth's bedroom door was locked. Cass knocked. "Elizabeth? You all right?"

"Yes." But it was not a voice Cass recognized.

"I just wanted to tell you . . . Dev wants to leave at seven o'clock."

Silence.

"Elizabeth!"

"Yes. I heard you. Seven o'clock."

The voice was flat, toneless.

Cass pressed her ear against the wood. "You still want to go?"

Another silence.

Cass rattled the knob. "Elizabeth! Are you sure you're all right?"

This time the silence went on for so long she rattled the knob again, aware that her heart was thumping and she was in the grip of a fear that made her want to weep.

The door opened abruptly so that she fell in against Elizabeth, clutching at the towel wrapped high and close about her body, her fingers clawing at it so that it loosened, gaped, and Cass saw, burned into her eyes even as the bruise was imprinted lividly on the white skin, the dark discoloration on Elizabeth's left breast, the darker red of the nipples, looking inflamed and swollen, and, as her eyes lifted to the face, the matching pulpiness of the mouth.

It lasted only a microsecond before the towel was back in place and Elizabeth was saying in a violent voice, "I'm not deaf. Seven o'clock you said and seven o'clock I heard! I'll be ready, all right? Now will you let me get some sleep!"

Cass had to hang on to the doorjamb. "Oh . . . yes . . . sorry . . . I just wanted to make sure." Then she fled.

In her own bedroom, she flung herself down on her bed, thrusting her face against the pillows to muffle her bitter, screaming words. "Bitch! Liar! Whore! They've been fucking each other blind!"

She screamed her rage and pain into the thick feather pillows, feeling her throat hurt and a sour bile-sickness rise into it as she acknowledged what she could no longer deny, a fact she had put away from her for days now. The worst had happened. She had fallen in love with Elizabeth Sheridan.

NINE

The *Pinta* came back over the heavy swell of a purple sea under an almost black sky. The heat had become lowering and oppressive. Lightning flickered a forked tongue along the horizon, reached greedily outward, followed by the menacing rumble of distant thunder. Eyeing the threatening darkness, Cass prayed terrifiedly that they would make Tempest Cay before the weather broke, and as its lights appeared in the distance she hung on to the rail, weak with relief. But even as she felt the relief, the lightning reached the boat and licked at it greedily, lighting it eerily white, and an earsplitting crash of thunder sent Cass cowering with her hands over her ears. Storms terrified her. They were the one area where she felt herself to be at the mercy of elements over which she had no control and no defense. She hung on to the rail with a terrified grip, but a sudden heave of the sea sent the *Pinta* bucking and she was tossed against the cabin housing, hitting her shoulder an almighty thump.

"Get below!" bellowed David, lending his massive strength to that of Dev in hanging on to the wheel, but Cass paid him no heed. Being below and hearing but not seeing was even worse. If they were going to be swamped, she wanted to see it before she felt it. Nieves was tying herself to the rails. Elizabeth had her arms wrapped around the mast. She was drenched, water streaming from her, and Cass slid, as the deck tilted, toward her, ending up, with another thump, against her legs. She seized the sodden denim with fingers like claws and hung on frantically. She was feeling ill as well as terrified. She was, as David had said, a bad sailor.

She felt Elizabeth prize her grip loose and drag her upward, then squeeze Cass in front of her body, her long arms wrapping themselves round the mast again. Cass could see white-frothed mountains of an evil green dipping and rising in front of her, and she closed her eyes with a moan. As the *Pinta* dipped headfirst into a trough, she gave up all hope.

Dev was heading for the cove where the beach house was. It was the nearest landfall and a couple of miles downshore from the private harbor.

"Best make for the cove!" he shouted to David, above the scream of the rapidly rising wind. "We'll never make it round the airstrip to the harbor!"

Rain suddenly fell like a curtain, drenching them in seconds, but the lights of the jetty were suddenly nearer because the *Pinta* was being driven onshore. As Dev held the boat steady in a sea that had Cass giddy with its motion, he shouted, "Make for the cottage . . . As soon as I get her alongside the jetty —jump for it!"

David left the wheel to come and help, taking a firm grip on Nieves as she untied herself and helping her to the rail, where she clung as the jetty, rising and falling like a seesaw, loomed in front of them. As the *Pinta* fell, Nieves climbed onto the rail, he holding her, and as the jetty rose to meet them, jumped, falling onto her knees but safe. He turned to Cass. "Come on!" he roared. With Elizabeth's help, peering through the curtains of rain, they got Cass onto the low rail, teetering frantically, and, as the boat and jetty met, Cass launched herself, eyes shut, only to fall on top of Nieves. Then she felt the solidity of wood beneath her. Instantly her seasickness left her and she was on her feet. Both she and Nieves were ready to receive Elizabeth, who leapt nimbly.

"Make for the cottage," bellowed David, and turned back to help Dev.

"Come *on!*" screamed Cass, but Elizabeth was standing staring at the *Pinta*, at Dev struggling with the bucking, leaping boat. Cass seized her arm. "Will you come *on!*"

The three women, bent double under the driving rain, ran for the beach house, set back under its overhanging rock. Dodging the waterfall streaming from the captain's walk, they fell in through the door.

"Thank God!" Cass shivered. Her teeth were chattering and she was a squelching, sodden mass, but she was on dry land, able to control, and at once began to do so. "Put a match to that fire, Nieves, then out of those wet things. Elizabeth—you'll find towels in the bathroom—get them, then wrap yourselves in them. I'll start coffee . . ."

Nieves knelt to put a match to the big pile of brushwood stacked in the fieldstone fireplace. It took light instantly, crackling into a bright, warming flame. Squelching as she went, Elizabeth got the towels. Cass left a trail of water as she went into the kitchen and shiveringly filled the coffeepot.

When she came back, Nieves was huddled in a towel, modestly undressing beneath it. Elizabeth was stripping off her jeans and T-shirt, tossing aside her bra and briefs before wrapping herself in her own sheet-sized towel, but not before Cass had seen the magnificent body, puckered and goose-fleshed but still enough to make her catch her breath, eye hungrily the fleece between the long legs, the exact color of her hair. The bruise on her breast stood out lividly. Then all was covered by the towel. Cass took her towel into the kitchen. Suddenly she was ashamed of her own, overweight, suet-dumpling body. She rubbed herself briskly, then wrapping her towel about her toga-style she padded up the stairs to the bedroom to fetch a couple of robes. "Here . . . that should fit you." She tossed down a short toweling robe. Nieves took it and put it on over her towel, which she then dropped to the floor. "You'd better have this one." Elizabeth caught the thin, navy-blue silk garment.

"Bless you, Nieves, for keeping this place ready." Cass shivered as she came to the fire, picking up the sodden clothes and spreading them about the stone of the fireplace, draping the jeans over the fire irons and hanging the T-shirts from the stone shelf above, pegging them with the brass clock and a vase of flowers. "God knows how long they will take to dry . . . We'll probably have to have clothes sent from the house"—she glanced up at the steaming windows—"if and when this lets up."

Barefooted, the blue robe fitting her perfectly, its belt wrapped twice around the indentation of her waist, Elizabeth toweled her hair. Her cold-stiffened nipples were sharply erect under the thin silk, and Cass ordered her forward to the fire. "Come and get warm." She was not having her thrust *them* at him when he came in. Taking a couple of logs from the basket, she added them to the already bright blaze. Then she sniffed. "Coffee." She trotted back into the kitchen, and shortly they heard the chink of china and cutlery.

The door flew open, letting in a squall of wind and rain—and David, who banged it shut.

"God, what a blow!" He sniffed. "Is that coffee I smell?" He trod water into the kitchen. "What's to eat?"

"Out of those wet clothes first," Cass ordered. "God knows what you'l find to put on . . . Where's Dev?"

"Coming . . . He's making sure she's well tied."

Picking up a towel, David disappeared into the bedroom. Cass came out o the kitchen with a tray of mugs and tin of shortbread. They were all sitting munching and drinking when the door opened again and Dev appeared, hair flattened, shirt clinging, jeans pasted onto the long legs. Nieves got up at once. "Oh, you're soaked! Here . . . take this towel."

He squelched into the bedroom, but not before Cass had seen his eyes go instantly to where Elizabeth was sitting hunched over the fire, her back toward him, wearing his robe. "We raided your closet," Cass called after him.

"Feel free." He shut the door.

He came back in a fresh shirt and jeans, carrying a kimoni, which he tossed as Cass. "Not your size, but better than that toga."

David, behind him, bellowed when Cass came out of the kitchen again. "Madame Flutterby!" He grinned. The kimono was meant to come to the knees. On Cass's five feet nothing, it reached her ankles.

"Needs must!" Cass answered with dignity, proceeding to collect the mugs.

"I'll call Helen," Dev said.

She was very relieved. "I was so worried when the storm came up."

"We'll ride it out down here," Dev said. "We've got dry clothes and Nieves has the kitchen well stocked." Nieves looked pleased. "We can spend the night here, if necessary."

"Steaks all right?" Cass asked, poking her head out of the kitchen door.

"Fry on!" David assured her heartily.

"No, the *Pinta* isn't damaged; knocked about a bit, but that's all . . . All right. If the storm doesn't let up, we'll see you in the morning."

Dev hung up as Cass came back with coffee for him and David. "Got anything to put in it?" David asked hopefully.

"In the cupboard in the kitchen," Nieves told him quietly, in a voice which made him stump as he went to get it.

"Do you think we'll be here all night?" Cass asked dubiously.

"There's no sign of a letup," Dev answered, holding out his mug so that David could add a slurp of scotch.

"Put another couple of logs on, then," Cass ordered Elizabeth. She went to feel the steaming clothes. "Still wet. So's your hair," she added maternally, putting out a hand to touch it, only to miss when Elizabeth jerked her head away. "It's so thick," Cass went on casually, putting the hand in the pocket of her kimono and holding it clenched there.

Lowering himself to the rug in front of the roaring fire, David drank deeply of his heavily sweetened coffee. "Best part of the day," he grunted.

"It was a lovely day—until the storm came up," Nieves flared indignantly.

Cass shuddered. "Don't remind me!"

"I told you you'd be seasick!" David said witheringly.

"In that sea! Who wouldn't be?"

"Elizabeth wasn't," Dev said lazily.

"Oh, but Elizabeth would never let herself succumb to a *minor* thing like that!" David said nastily. The glance he threw at her was narrow-eyed, resentful.

You too? thought Cass. She too had been conscious, from the moment they set sail, of the sizzling feeling, almost an antagonism, emanating from Dev and Elizabeth. Even Nieves had been aware, but puzzled, not understanding its cause. Her own relationship with Dev was so innocent, so platonic, that though she was aware of the antagonism to the point of being disturbed by it, she had not understood it.

But Cass had. And so had David. You couldn't help but feel it. It was gut-real, highly charged, wholly sexual. Cass had been appalled. Dev *had* got to Elizabeth. Somehow he had thrown her switch; the empty negative had become the dangerous positive. How? thought Cass, agonizedly. *How?* Oh, she knew of old of Dev's own magnetism; she'd seen women make fools of themselves because of it. Margery creamed her pants every time he came within scenting distance. But never had she thought to see Elizabeth succumb. Yet she had. And was handling it badly. For her. She was brusque, insolent even. So much so that at first, until it finally penetrated even his slow understanding, David had murmured to Cass, "No love lost there."

No, stupid! Cass had thought vengefully. Love *found*, more like!

It was because she could not handle what she had found, she was sure, that Elizabeth was so uptight. She gave off the outrage of a woman who had suddenly found herself confronted by something she could not control. Try as she might. And she was trying. Boy, was she trying, Cass thought. It was the only comfort she could draw from a situation that she herself was finding harder and harder to handle.

She mourned the loss of the Elizabeth she would have sworn—on any Bible you cared to produce—was immune to men. To sex. Never once, for instance, had she so much as indicated that she was aware of David's dog-like devotion, of the way he worshiped from afar. But her attitude to Dev was so charged with awareness it crackled.

Cass had not worked daily and closely with Elizabeth for a month now without learning something about her. Her outwardly tough-cookie façade was designed to conceal a highly sensitive interior. Working with Richard Tempest had taught her that first, hard-learned lesson. So, with Elizabeth, she had looked hard, listened closely, and learned—she had thought—a lot. Only to find out she had not even begun to learn. Like everybody else, Cass thought sadly, Elizabeth Sheridan was not what she seemed. But *that* bastard —she shot a look at Dev that would have felled him had he met it—had spotted it at once. And he'd been pressing on the spot ever since. Cass was aware of his silent pressure; knew that David was too, but whereas it made him puzzled and uneasy, it made her angry. How *dare* he draft Elizabeth into the battle of the sexes. Because that was what he had done. Worse, he had made her aware, for the first time, of the battle itself. Which was why Cass had monitored them all day; every sense stretched, every whisker of her interior antennae tuned in to their frequency. She measured every glance, weighed every word, which was how she knew Elizabeth was fighting it. And long though she might to offer her help, she knew that would be fatal. Instinct warned Cass that Elizabeth would never forgive her for even *knowing*. Worse, her laser brain would instantly want to know how. Cass shivered. There was no way, now, that she could ever tell Elizabeth. Dev Loughlin had put his spoke in that wheel too. Cass threw him another rancorous glance. That bloody thing he carried between his legs had no conscience—but it made every woman he met spine-tinglingly conscious of *him*. Bastard! Sexy, womanizing, magnetizing bastard!

Cass slumped back against the sofa. She felt miserable, aching, and what she had not felt in a long time, had been careful to make sure she did not feel: lonely. Elizabeth was steadily, remorselessly being drawn out from under her influence. And she mourned, even as David must be mourning, she knew, the sight of those unmistakable feet of clay. Dev Loughlin, the supreme awakener, had brought the statue to life. Cass had seen it last night. That animal, mouth-drying sensuality of his had melted the ice.

She had seen the glances—puzzled, hurt, then bitterly envious—that David had directed at Dev on and off all day. He too had caught the quality of the two voices as they spoke to each other, the way Elizabeth moved under those hot, vividly blue eyes, hooded under the absurdly long lashes, flatly predatory. He had seen the way those same blue eyes could pin Elizabeth down, so that she was held, awkwardly, until he turned them elsewhere. And David's own eyes, when they looked at Elizabeth—who never, ever saw him —were so hurt they made even Cass feel it through her own torment.

You and me both, she thought heavily, looking at him now, gazing at Elizabeth with baffled longing.

She dragged herself up. "I'll go and cook those steaks . . . they should have thawed by now."

"Can I help?" Elizabeth asked.

"Yes," Cass answered quickly. That at least would get her out of range of those deadly eyes.

The steaks went down, accompanied by tomatoes in a spicy dressing Elizabeth made, and some frozen french fries. "Thank God for a freezer," Cass said fervently. Dev opened a couple of bottles of wine, and, after piling the dishes in the sink, they once again sat round the fire, not talking much, each one occupied with insistent thoughts.

It was Cass who roused herself to say: "Listen . . . the rain has stopped."

They all cocked an ear. There was only the sound of the dripping eaves and the heavy boom of the surf.

"Ten o'clock," David said, stretching. "We can get back to the house, then."

"These clothes are dry enough to wear," Cass said relievedly. "Not bone-dry, but they'll do us no harm for half an hour."

When she turned to Elizabeth with the still slightly damp jeans and T-shirt, she found her fast asleep with her feet on Dev Loughlin's lap.

"Leave her," he said lazily. "She's dead tired. She did a lot of swimming today."

Yes—to get away from you, Cass thought viciously.

"I'll stay too," Nieves offered quickly.

"No, sweetheart. You go on back to the house, have a hot bath, and go straight to bed. You got a soaking and I don't want you to catch cold."

Nieves hesitated, torn between his obvious concern and his order—for order it was—to leave him. With Elizabeth Sheridan.

"I'll bring her back," Dev went on easily. David opened his mouth, closed it again, silently took the clothes Cass handed him, and lumbered heavily into the kitchen. Nieves went silently upstairs. Cass dressed in the kitchen when David vacated it.

"Look—I'm sure Elizabeth would as soon come back with us," she said, unable to stop herself making one last try.

"She's dead to the world," Dev said. "Let her sleep."

He was right. Elizabeth was heavily, deeply asleep, her face buried in the cushions. Dev had hold of her ankles, the long fingers dark against the pale gold skin. Cass could have cut them off at the wrists.

It was a beautiful night. The air had cleared, though heavy clouds still rode high, fitfully covering the moon. The trees dripped and the beach was strewn with seaweed and driftwood. There would be enough light to enable them to pick their way up the beach, although Cass insisted David take a torch, just in case. Once they reached the path it would be all right, because that was lit.

Dev carefully lifted Elizabeth's feet away and accompanied Cass and Nieves and David to the door.

When Cass looked back, from the gap in the rocks, the door was closed again. She had the feeling that she had been shut out of Elizabeth's life.

Elizabeth moaned silently in her sleep, moving her head from side to side, arching her body, mouth opening, tongue searching—and came awake with a shock, heart thumping, mouth dry, breath coming like that of a panting animal.

She was in the beach house, flat on her back, the room dark but for one lamp. Raising herself stealthily, she peered over the back of the sofa. Dev Loughlin was writing at his desk by the window. Silently she lay down again, looked up at the ship's clock on the mantel. One o'clock in the morning. Her dream had been so vivid . . . so real. Not a dream. Memories. The ones she had deliberately suppressed ever since . . . She pinched off the thought before it could bloom.

It was enough—too much—that he should dominate her waking thoughts. That he had invaded her dreams was disastrous. It showed just how great his impact was; had been ever since she had squinted up into the sun and seen nothing but blue, blue eyes, heard a deep voice say: "Hello . . . I'm Dev Loughlin."

She had been unable to look away from him then; had been unable to get away from him since. Not only her mind was no longer under her own control. He had her here alone. The others had gone . . . She cursed herself for falling asleep. But she had been both physically and emotionally drained.

She closed her eyes again. All she could see was him. The long length of him, the intense blue of his eyes, the absurdly long lashes, the way his gaze probed her with a knowledge that terrified.

You should have paid more attention to what Cass told you, she thought for the thousandth time. Didn't she say he was the male principle on legs? Didn't you see it that first evening? It had been the old case of the fox among the chickens. He only had to stand there for the befuddled birds to run themselves right into the lazy jaws . . .

Which led her to the remembered look, the feel of his mouth. Her stomach dropped and her skin pricked, her nipples hardening into thrusting peaks. She turned over, pressing her body into the resilience of the firm cushions, feeling the swell of her breasts, the bones of her hips, the length of her legs. The thought of being touched by him swamped her in a wave of desire.

She heard a rustle as he got up, lay absolutely still as he came over, stood for a moment looking down at her. She pretended she was still asleep. But her heart was knocking and her whole body was tense. Only when he moved away did she relax with a silently shuddered sigh, feeling the sweat trickling down between her breasts. She forced herself to breathe deeply and evenly. Control, she thought. This will not do. It will not do at all. He had not only violated her body; he had violated her mind . . .

Once more she reminded herself remorselessly that she did not *need* him. It was greed. Sheer sexual greed. And that could be controlled. The thought of not controlling it was even more terrifying than the pleasure she knew, now, was to be obtained from yielding. That had totally done for her control. It must not happen again. She dared not let it happen again. The trouble was, he had dominated her from the beginning.

He had come out of the sun like a solar flare and the touch of his hand had burned into her even as his eyes had left a trail of fire as they moved over her face and body with the slow sureness of the successful male. She had been held by them, awkward, stiff, trembling, and aghast. For the first time in her life she was afraid of a man.

She had been on the defensive from the beginning. All night those eyes had stalked her, making her clumsy, nervous, unsure. While his hands, when they had played the guitar, had somehow played *her* . . .

She had not slept that night. All she had done was think of him. And then, in the morning, to come down and find him gone! She had been furious, and appalled at her fury. And had taken it out on David. She had watched, with savage satisfaction, the humiliation and confusion chase each other across his defenseless face, yet, on a deeper level, ashamed of the fact that she needed to. Never before had she felt a need for revenge.

And then, to see him in the distance; no mistaking that height, the long-legged ease of movement—she had fled, only to pace up and down her room like a caged animal, raging at herself, telling herself she was no more than a bitch in heat! It was sex, nothing more. Raw, greedy, sleep-and-composure-destroying sex. Daddy, buy me that . . . It had made her laugh hysterically. God knows she had the money . . . Except this one was not for sale.

It had reduced her, for the first time since childhood, to a frantic, single, repeated thought: What am I going to do? Dear God, what am I going to do? She didn't know. She just did not *know*.

Nothing like this had ever happened to her before. She had not believed it could.

Yet she had found herself dressing for dinner with care, in spite of Helen's warning. She pondered over the right dress . . . finally chose a drift of thin chiffon, the color of lime juice and a long drink to a thirsty man. She belted it tightly at the waist, let the flimsy bodice fall so as to hint tantalizingly at her full, firm breasts. She had left her hair down, sprayed it with a perfume that was warm, sultry, provocative; done her face with care, using all her model's tricks. Some strange new force had control of her, compelling her to make of herself a presentation . . . She knew it when she saw the look in those blue eyes; the way the focus changed, subtly, turning their Irish blueness into something which dried her mouth and set her hands to tremble—and yet loving it, exulting in it, diving headfirst into it . . .

All night it had padded between them, breathing softly, yet tensed, ready to spring. And under her own tension she had been aware of his; of the vibrantly special sound to his voice. She wanted to do to him what he was doing to her; stretch even tighter the already unbearably tight awareness between them that was so keen she could feel what he felt, hear his unspoken thoughts, register every degree of his desire. It was the most exciting yet the most terrifying thing she had ever known. And she knew why. For the first time in her life, she was experiencing what it felt like to be a *woman*.

Never before had she been so conscious of her body. Every cell had been sensitized. Her hands were supple, her fingers abnormally tactile. The smoothness of a glass, the tip of a cigarette; she handled them as if they were priceless. Every line and curve of her body she carried as though they too were beyond price, hinted at by the close confines of her dress, carried on her high-heeled sandals.

She felt honed to a hollow eggshell fragility. Her mouth, when she drew on a cigarette—she was smoking now, with a sensual enjoyment—seemed to draw the smoke inside her skull, where it writhed and curled. She was sure that if someone were to strike her, lightly, she would give off a chime like a bell.

When he had declined to come to the Bijou she had been both relieved and resentful. He knew damned fine that she, who adored movies, would sit there and stare at a screen containing nothing but his face. But when they came out and she saw him waiting . . . Exultant triumph lanced from her slow-curving smile as she looked at him and saw the flicker there; the jolt of his breath. Now they would see who could play games . . . But as she moved past him with an insolent sway of the hips, he put a hand on her arm and she could not have moved. It was light, but it held her paralyzed.

"I'll drive you back," he said, a command, not a suggestion, and obediently, tranquilized into subjection, she said, "All right." He had introduced her to two men; she had not heard their names, not heard anything, and all the time his hand was on her arm, holding her wrist as he might a dog on a lead, or a butterfly in a net. She felt she was a specimen he had trapped; awaiting the hands that would lift her, precisely and delicately, placing her in position, spreading her, then pinning her down forever.

She felt drugged; everything had slowed and magnified. When she put up

a hand to brush away a questing insect, it felt heavy. She was conscious only
of a will-sapping lassitude which proceeded to drain her of everything but the
knowledge of its cause.

When he opened the car door, she got into it like a sleepwalker. He did
not speak as he got in beside her. Nor did she. She stared ahead bemusedly.
The Rolls had long gone. He started the engine, put the car into gear and
moved off, waving a hand at the watching men. Only when they were out of
the village and on the straight bone-white road did he increase speed. His
hand on the gear lever was decisive, controlling casually but totally. On the
middle finger was a crescent-shaped scar, white against the Latin-dark skin.
As he moved the gear lever up through its changes, it was only inches away
from her bare leg. She drew away instinctively. The thought of its touching
her totally demoralized her.

The window on her side was open; the wind blew her hair over her face.
She put up a hand to capture it. Glancing across: "Too windy?" he asked.
"Close the window . . . that button there."

But, stupidly, she could see no button and she leaned forward, hand hovering helplessly. Slowing the car, he leaned across to do it for her. As his hand
moved, so she followed it, and saw what he was aiming for. She leaned
forward, and even as his hand pressed the button so did her breast press into
his arm. She could not restrain her gasp. His face was only inches from hers.
Helplessly she stared into the flame of his eyes. His foot hit the brake and the
car slewed to a tire-screaming halt, crossways on the road. He was cutting the
engine with one hand even while he was drawing her to him with the other.
Then they fell on each other.

It was violent, quite out of control, entirely without tenderness. It was a
raging hunger, and they devoured each other. Mouths wide, tongues deep,
fingers gripping, teeth nipping, nails digging. They made incomprehensible
sounds; breathed as though they were running; they touched, bit, gripped,
sucked, mouth to mouth, body to body, welded to each other except when
his mouth left hers to trail hotly down her throat and the deep vee of her
dress, his fingers insistently pushing aside her dress so that he could take her
nipples into his mouth, causing her to moan as she felt that tongue sucking,
pulling, and the answering tug deep, deep inside her. He lifted her bodily so
that she was across his knees, cramped in the small confines of the car; so he
used one hand to open the door, his other still holding her to him, and when
the door swung wide, he slid, still holding her against him, out of the car and
onto his feet, only to take three steps to the side of the road, holding her just
off the ground before sinking with her down onto the grass which edged a
lush plantation of sweet corn which rustled in the sea breeze. As easily as

shucking one of the ears he had her naked, and her own hands frantically aided and abetted his own stripping until their bodies, hot and slippery, were pressed together over every straining and quivering inch.

Her moans were deep in her throat and she thrashed her head wildly from side to side until he pinned it with his mouth, his fingertips trailing down her body, making it arch, until they found the golden fleece and caressed it, making her shiver convulsively, but open her legs to his probing, insistent fingers. Her own hands, acting entirely on instinct, slid over his chest, down the muscled thighs, over the firm, tight buttocks before sliding between their bodies to grasp what lay pulsing between them. She kissed him passionately, biting his tongue, her mouth wide and gasping as his fingers played skillfully and teasingly on that most sensitive part of her, making her shiver and moan and urgently seek his own mouth again.

When it left hers, to travel slowly and erotically all over her body, pausing at her breasts, she thrust them into his mouth, moaning as the gentle tugging of his lips and tongue caused an answering tug deep within her body. As he continued downward, probing her navel, making her cry out inarticulately, she began to tremble as the hot, arousing mouth paused for a moment as he parted her legs, then she felt it; a needle point of unbearably pleasurable sensation as she stiffened, quivering, then fell, with a wrenching sense of losing everything, through the first of a series of helpless, shuddering orgasms. The first in her life. Time after time she came until she had to gasp, in a voice that was hoarse and pleading: "Please . . . I can't . . . no more . . . please . . ."

"Yes, you can . . ."

His voice, tight, ruthless, made her open her eyes. His were staring into hers. Helplessly she gazed as she felt him take her ankles, push her knees up and back until he had them over his shoulders. The blue eyes licked along her like flame. "Yes, you can," he repeated, and proceeded to prove it by entering her in a long, delicious slide that filled her, impaled her, drove her wild, every inch of him pressing on nerve endings that shrilled, screamed with delight, overwhelming her with waves of agonizingly pleasurable feeling and sent her grinding, twisting, undulating against him, her inner muscles clamping and squeezing. But he did not move; he held off as she gyrated madly, violently out of control, her arms clamped about him, her body pressed up, up against him as if to take him entirely into her, feeling him hot and hard inside her.

Only when she had once more come, powerfully and uncontrollably, did he begin to move, thrusting deeper, harder, in a remorseless, driving, pulsing rhythm, timing his thrusts to hers so that their bodies slapped together, moist with heat and her suddenly pouring secretions. She began to make sounds

that were wild, like sobs, and once again she began to plead: "Oh, please
. . . no more . . . I can't. I can't . . ." As she fell through yet another
series of tumultuous, exploding orgasms.

"Yes, you can . . ."

And she did, coming yet again and again, multiorgasmic, all molten and on
the peak of a wave that lifted her up, carried her forward, only to throw her
down with a crash before picking her up once more to sweep her up to the
next crest before casting her down again, and again, and again . . .

His breath was harsh in his chest and his thrusts quickened, became so
agonizingly exquisite that she screamed, mouth wide, the cords of her neck
standing out, nails digging into his shoulders until she felt his body clench as
he gathered himself, and through the slits of her eyes she saw his head go up
and back and felt him convulse and then the stunning shock of his own
coming, which carried her high before flinging her down so hard she lost
consciousness, coming back slowly to find herself limp and thready of breath,
he collapsed against her, chest heaving, mouth open against her as he fought
for breath.

She became conscious of the gritty feel of sandy earth beneath her back, of
the dampness of her hair, felt the wind cooling her heated body. And yet
dazed, floating, no longer unconscious but not yet conscious. Only empty,
drained, replete. And very, very tired. There was no sound but for their
laboring lungs and the sound of the wind in the corn. She drifted with the
sound, hovering above the deep drop of sleep before falling right over its
edge.

It was the moth which woke her. It drifted across her face, its wings
brushing her eyes. She put up a hand to drive it away and awoke with a start,
feeling suddenly disoriented and panicky. She was naked, her dress over her
but not on her, and as she sat up, startled for the moment, memory returned
and she turned her head slowly, carefully, to see Dev Loughlin, fully dressed,
sitting beside her, ankles crossed, smoking a cigarette. Their eyes met.

Instantly her face flamed and she flung herself away from him in a roll that
left her in a crouch, hands supporting her, her horrified face regarding him
from the tangled thicket of her hair. He saw the dazed eyes clear like fog
before a wind, and her voice was laden with shock, shame, and hatred when
she hissed, "God damn you to hell for doing this to me!"

She was bone-white. Her eyes were incredulous. He had never seen any
one look so shocked. As though they wanted to be sick. He could see her
trembling. She did not believe what had happened. She could not and still
believe in herself. He could all but hear her thoughts: What have I done?
What *have* I done?

But he said nothing. It was important that she knew not only what she had done, but why she had done it. And that he had known, not only that she could—but would. He had not planned it this way, or so soon. But it had happened. And because it had, he had learned a great many things. So, he hoped, had she. Not about him. About herself.

She was still staring at him. Incredulous, shocked beyond anger. Aghast at a self she had not known existed. No, he thought, would not allow to exist. It was always there but suborned, driven underground as far as it would go. He had somehow triggered it off. No, not somehow at all . . . he *had* triggered if off. He had known it even as he took hold of her hand, helped her up, unable to look away from those incredible, terrified eyes, those same eyes that were now filled with loathing. But not for him. For herself.

"It's not what I did. It's what you did. I told you that you could, remember?"

Her face flamed once more as memory played back her own hoarse, agonized voice and his remorseless denial. As if he read her thoughts: "This was inevitable. We both know it. Which was why you refused to admit it."

His dispassionate dissection both shocked and terrified her. Nobody had ever seen so much so quickly—or so deeply. How? She felt stripped of so much more than her clothes. Her self-protection had gone too. He had taken everything; seen her as no other human being had ever seen her. An animal. Wild, out of control, greedy, frantic. Worse, it was he who had made her so.

"I had a hunch there was a woman inside the igloo."

Anger produced an ice-cold voice. "And you were arrogant enough to believe you could bring her out!" Her eyes slid away from the unfalteringly blue gaze.

"I did," he said softly.

Her jaw clenched. "I want to get dressed." She sounded petulant.

"I'm not stopping you." But he made no move to toss her dress toward her. She remained crouching, hiding behind her hair. The thought of standing up, revealing her naked body, walking toward him, to where her dress lay in a crumpled heap on the sand, curled her insides to writhing snakes, but crawling across would be even more demoralizing. She knew she would have to go to him. This man would never make it easy for her. That thought inflamed her enough to rise to her feet and walk, staring steadfastly at her dress, to pick it up, feeling his eyes on her. Her hands were trembling so badly she dropped it, had to pick it up again. And still he sat silently, looking, looking.

She dropped the dress over her head, fumbled with the zip, only to feel the long, now cool fingers push hers away, draw the zip up with a sibilant hiss. As he did so, his hands grazed her flesh and she could not repress her sudden convulsion.

She bent to pick up her sandals and to her horror saw her strapless bra and briefs lying where he had flung them. He bent to pick them up, held them out to her. She snatched them, wondering wildly how she was going to put them on, knew there was no way she was, and crumpled them into as small a ball as she could and held them in her hand. She heard him sigh. "You've a long way to go," he said, "and I don't mean the rest of the way back to the house." She felt him turn her to face him and she gazed steadily at the top button on his shirt, focusing her eyes on it and not on the flesh that had been so silken under her hands. She clenched her teeth and waited.

"You are not what you think you are," he said, in a voice so gentle she felt tears prick. "You have made that abundantly clear. To me. But what matters is that *you* accept it. Think about it—and you will, because that's what you've trained yourself always to do. Then, when you have, we'll talk again."

"I have nothing to say to you," she said, dismayed to hear her voice tremble.

"I think you will find you have," he said mildly. "But even if you decide not to say it, I have a great deal more to say to you."

He put a finger under her chin, in such a way that she had no choice but to raise her face to meet his eyes. "Remember that," he said. Then he turned to walk back toward the car. The door was still open as he had left it, and he got in and leaned across to open the other one. In silence she settled herself, slamming the door, wrapping her skirt around her. Then he started the car, turned it back onto the road, and once more headed for Marlborough.

She was out of it before he could cut the engine, taking the steps two at a time, vanishing into the House. By the time he entered the hall there was no sign of her, only the sound of a slamming door.

For the first time Elizabeth locked her door behind her. She leaned against it, eyes closed, for a long time. Finally, she dragged herself away from it, found herself still holding the crumpled ball of lingerie and hurled it violently away. Then she strode into the bathroom, turned on every single one of the six shower heads, until the force of the water sounded like Niagara, before stripping her dress over her head—she would never wear *that* again—and flinging it into a corner. But as she prepared to step into the shower she caught sight of her replicated self in the mirror-lined walls and her leg went down and her arm lowered and she stood looking at herself; saw her hands come up to touch the bruise on her breast and then slide, fingertips trailing, all the way down to the fleece of pubic hair, still damp. She stood that way for a long time. Then, slowly, she reached in and switched off the shower before slumping onto the cool tiles of the floor, head hanging, eyes shut.

And she was going sailing with him in the morning.

By eight o'clock the *Pinta* was well out at sea, butting through its sparkling blueness before a brisk breeze; scarlet paint wet and shiny, teak deck smooth and glassy, brass gleaming, multicolored sails taut. But by midday the breeze had died, exhausted by the heat, and the *Pinta* lay becalmed in a hot, breathless silence.

"Oh, never mind Cat Island," Cass had said, sounding relieved. "Let's just laze . . . it's too hot to do anything else."

So they had brought out the picnic basket, eaten what Helen had ordered prepared. Delicious cold *gazpacho*, because Dev loved it, thick wedges of *tortilla española*, redolent of onions and garlic, a mixed salad, all washed down with a crisp, beautifully chilled Lambrusco, followed by fresh fruit and perfectly ripened Camembert.

But she had not been able to eat, to force food down a closed throat. Cass, wolfing almost desperately, had asked, "What's up?" the blue eyes keen, and when Elizabeth had answered, "Not hungry," replied, "I am," and eaten Elizabeth's share too.

Then, afterward, they all lay about the deck, almost comatose from food and heat. David had brought out the cassette recorder and played a medley of slow, trumpet blues, followed by Miles Davis's *Sketches of Spain*, which had made Cass mutter irritably, "Jesus, what is this, a fiesta?"

The mournful trumpet had echoed across the empty silence like a wail, but it had been worse when David had put on Debussy's *L'Après-midi* . . . music Elizabeth normally adored. The sensuous, gauzy music wreathed itself around them like the heat haze in the distance; languorously exotic, shimmeringly enticing. It had made her even more aware of the long legs that lay only inches away from hers, the heat-glazed skin of his chest, the sun behind him highlighting the ridiculously long lashes lying on cheeks she had seen sunken in passion the night before. She had to force her mind away from him, from what had been straining at her leash ever since.

All through the long night she had lain sleepless in her bed, struggling with herself, trying—and failing utterly—to analyze what had happened, unable to bring her normal rationality to bear on something that was as ephemeral as instinct. She had put it under the microscope of cold reason only to find she could not bring it into focus. Her eyes were somehow unable to see; everything was blurred, strange. Even her mind was sluggish. Never before had it failed to dominate her feelings. Now, here she was, infected by a raging fever for one particular man's body and quite unable to bring down her emotional temperature.

She had only been able to reveal one mystery, or, rather, have it revealed to her. Now she knew what it was those other models had talked about so endlessly. Now she understood what they had meant by fulfillment. And yet she felt betrayed by her own body. The one she had believed incorruptible. It had played her false; been not dead, but sleeping. Waiting for the *right* man; the right mouth, the right hands, the right body. Now she knew what that meant. The throbbing, deliriously sensitive *life* they could bring . . .

Which was, she realized—lying only inches away from it—what was so vital about Dev Loughlin. He was so alive. Right in the middle of it, embroiled, involved, so much a part of its complex pattern that he seemed to have been woven into it. Everything she was not. A participant, not a spectator; filled with that vibrancy of strength which took on life and exulted in the struggle. It was obvious from his films, which throbbed with a singing vitality, filled with people, colors, all the myriad flavors and intricate strands of life. As he had filled her, last night. And not with the turgid piece of dead flesh she had expected, but with a part of himself that was as alive as he was, an extension of the self he was. Even now, she could remember her delighted amazement. She had handled it not obediently but instinctively, lovingly, and she distinctly remembered wanting to touch it with more than her hands and his pushing her head away gently and saying, "No . . . not this time . . . this is for you, not me."

She had done those things? *She?* Elizabeth Sheridan had thrown her inhibitions off with her clothes and launched herself, mother-naked, into a sea of unbridled, unashamed sensuality. It was not possible. It just could not be. But it was. As hard as she tried to push away, she only went round in circles. At the center of which, watching and waiting without impatience, was Dev Loughlin.

The *Pinta* lay becalmed all afternoon, lying motionless on a sea that was an empty expanse of shimmering turquoise, draining all the color from the sky, leaving it pale, exhausted, sickly. The burning disk of the sun moved inexorably across the sky, but the heat did not lessen; rather, it increased, and gradually the line where sea met sky became smudged by brushstrokes of purple shadow which stained its paleness like a bruise. There was no swell; they lay under a gigantic inverted bowl where sound echoed hollowly. Elizabeth felt that if she shouted, made any sort of violent movement—as she longed to do—the silence would crack, split, and fall apart. Her nerves were tightened to the last notch, and when she knew she could stand it no longer —this silent, relentless pressure he was exerting just by *being*—she leapt up and dived over the side like a seal, the water parting to receive her like oil, affording her no shock of cold to lower her temperature. Head down, she went away from the boat in her fast crawl, surfacing only every third beat to breathe, then pounding on until her arms were so heavy they would not lift and the muscles of her thighs were fluttering like the wings of a trapped bird. Which, she reflected as she floated face up, getting her breath back, she was.

There was something implacably ruthless about him. He said things in a perfectly ordinary voice that cut her to the heart. "You are not what you think you are," he had said. All right, so she wasn't. She had only just found out. But how—*how* had he known.

"This is for you, not me," he had said. And he had foregone what she sensed would have taken him to the far reaches of pleasure to take her there instead. What sort of strength was *that?* It made her shiver. Here, in the bathwater of the Bahamas, it made her feel cold with dread. For above all, above the revelation of self, the things she was learning, almost minute by minute, about herself, she had known one incontrovertible, absolutely certain thing from the very start: she was afraid of *him.*

The faint sound of a voice dragged her back to the present and, treading water, shading her eyes, she could make out the distant figure of someone waving frantically, beckoning her to return. She did so more slowly, reluctantly; heard, when she was within earshot, David bellowing, "Come *on!* The glass is dropping and Dev wants to start back."

He had to use the engine, and its noise brutalized the thick, soft silence. As they chugged on, the sky deepened slowly from palest lilac to a deep turquoise which gradually changed to an ominous mauve before turning into a threatening purple.

It soon became a race to see which would reach the Island first. It was a tie. Even as Dev turned the *Pinta* through the reef the storm struck, and by the time they reached the cottage her clothes were sticking to her.

When Cass tossed the navy robe at her she knew as soon as she grasped it who it belonged to. It brought the remembered smell of his skin back to her in a swamping wave of feeling, and the feel of the thin silk against her own skin made her shiver deliciously. It was not cold that made her teeth chatter against the thick china mug as she drank her coffee. Her taut emotions, the quick heat of the blazing fire, and her exhaustion, coupled with her sleepless night were too much for her. She slept heavily, deeply. And dreamed.

Now, as she lay flat on her stomach, listening to the plop! plop! of the dripping gutters and the soft fall of ashes in the fireplace, she was once more conscious of the fluttering wings of panic. Once again he had arranged it so he had her alone. Oh, God, she thought, closing her eyes and forcing herself to breathe deeply. Now what?

Never in her life had she felt so helpless, so vulnerable. She had not known it was possible for one human being to have such a devastating effect on another. And she had not believed it would ever happen to her. She must have moved involuntarily, her body making the physical protest she was feeling mentally, because she heard him get up again.

"You look rested," he said, from his great height. "Good. Now we can have our talk."

She looked at the clock. Almost one-fifteen. "It's late . . . I'd better be getting back to the House."

"They know where you are. Now we can find where you are at."

His voice was calm, easy, but it filled her with dread. That was when he was at his most dangerous. He was not a man who would ever raise his voice. He did not have to. "You were restless in your sleep," he went on. "Bad dreams?"

She did not need to answer.

"Who were you fighting? Me—or you?"

She was silent.

"I've been thinking about you," he continued, coming round the sofa and making to sit down. Hastily she drew up her legs, drew the robe tightly about her, and retreated to the corner of the enormous couch. "In fact, I've been thinking of nothing else."

"I didn't ask you to," she refuted quickly.

"What has that got to do with it? Or is that something else you only allow on your own terms?"

Oh, God, she thought, feeling her blood drumming through her body. He's going to start and I can't stop him. There was no stopping this man. He came on inexorably. She had noticed it that first night, when he kept Mattie steady on the pinnacle she had leapt for, mastering, without seeming to, the little group of people, his long, dexterous fingers ready with a lighter or a cup or a glass, tossing a comment to this one, answering a question there, agreeing pleasantly somewhere else. She had noticed the radiant submission of Nieves, the glowing happiness of Helen, the sexually incited sparkle of Mattie. Only Cass had seemed to glower, and that she had put down to having her nose put out of joint. He had affected everybody. Even Hervey, who had coughed, cleared his throat, and said, not looking at her but ostensibly out at the view, "Good chap, Dev. You must not believe all you hear about him . . . women, I mean," he added vaguely. "There's a lot of jealousy . . ." he had finished, apropos of nobody in particular, then nodded and returned to his chair by Helen.

Yes, *women*, she thought. And then it hit her. This strange, new, inexplicable emotional upheaval, her loss of identity, was because she had become . . . a woman. Her status had altered. This uncontrollable, clamorous awakening was because he had changed her. That was why, she realized, falling into belated insight headlong, she had not been able to wash him away last night; had not wanted to lose the smell, the remembered feel, the taste of him. The old self would have stepped under that water unhesitatingly, deliberately. This new one was unable to do that.

Wide-eyed, startled, she gazed at him, realizing too that she was seeing him through eyes whose vision had cleared. Never before had she noticed the fine dusting of hairs on a man's forearm, the strong bones of a wrist. Fascinated, her eyes wandered over the dark shadow on his jaw, the way the high cheekbones were set, the way his thick black hair grew to a widow's peak on his forehead. She could see the little lines that fanned out from the corners of the brilliantly compelling eyes; the longer, deeper ones at the sides of the thin-lipped yet sensual mouth. She was seeing things close, so close they blocked everything else.

This emotional eruption of nonrational feelings had left her vulnerable and no longer under her own control. He had made her question herself deeply. He had said she was not what she thought she was. Now, she knew he was right. He had somehow managed to probe her secrets, but what frightened her was how he had known they were there in the first place. She had always been terrified of losing control, not only of the situation but of herself. Now she knew why. Last night had shown her. *He* had shown her. He had said she could, and made her prove it.

Eyes wide with shock, she sat dumb.

"What's the matter?" he asked.

She shook her head.

"You are afraid, aren't you?"

She nodded. It was useless to lie.

"And have been ever since we met . . . I felt it the instant our eyes met. It happens like that, sometimes. Too much, too soon—that's why you fought it."

Another nod.

"But it has begun now. It's too late to stop it. You know that, don't you?"

She did not answer, only stared at him silently.

"Nothing like this has ever happened to you before, has it?"

"You know it hasn't." It came out bitter, bewildered.

"Or to me," he said.

Her head came up quickly and she searched his face disbelievingly. Now he nodded. "Truth between us. No lies."

"But—"

"But what?"

Confused, she tore her eyes away. "Well . . ." She took a deep breath, said it quickly to get it over and done with. "I was given to understand you do this sort of thing all the time."

"What sort of thing?"

"Women," she answered bluntly.

"I like women. They are one of the great joys of life. And women like me. That makes it even better."

She was staring at her hands; anything rather than look at those eyes which drew the truth from her like a drug.

"But you have not had much—if anything—to do with men, have you?"

"No."

"Because you were afraid of yourself."

Again her head came up with shock at his perception.

"I have a theory about that," he said. "That's what I wanted to talk to you about."

Warily: "Oh?"

"Yes. You remember I told you last night that you are not what you think you are? Well, I have spent most of my time since then thinking about what you *really* are."

"How would you know?"

"Oh, I knew all about you long before I met you. David wrote me reams. Nieves told me her version. And as soon as I got here I heard it from all sides."

She flushed. "Oh, I see, you are going to explain me, put me right, is that it?" She could feel anger building and seized it; anything to help her beat him off.

"I'm going to try."

"Very generous."

He smiled and again she flushed, moved restlessly. "If you have something to say, then say it!"

"Oh, I have. And I intend to."

He crossed one leg over the knee of the other, holding his ankle. "It's a fascinating story," he began. "That's what I've been doing while you slept. Putting it down on paper."

"Of course," she murmured, eyes downcast. "You are a *writer*, aren't you?"

"And people are what I write about. Then I make the story into a film. But you've seen them all, haven't you? Cass tells me you are a movie buff . . ." No answer. "This particular script concerns a particular woman."

"Naturally!"

"No, this one is not natural. A strong-minded, self-generating, self-sufficient woman of unknown parentage. Brought up in a Home. Well fed, well cared for, strong, healthy, wealthy now, but far from wise. Especially about herself. She thinks she has got it all together; all of a smooth piece; no tears, no holes, no snags. A beautiful ivory tower. A real pleasure to look upon. Especially to men. Which is all they ever do. Because it is surrounded by a force field of such negative power that anyone who tries to get through gets frozen to death. Nobody has ever got close enough to see what lies inside. It never *does* anything; it only stands there, the most beautiful of whited sepulchers. So beautiful that people who see it can't help but say, 'How beautiful! How exquisitely constructed! How strong, how unshakable!' Never 'How dead!' " She was very still, her head bent, staring down at her hands, but she was listening. Intently.

"What no one knew, of course, was that inside it was a terrible charnel house! Stuffed to the ceiling with incarcerated emotions, all clubbed unconscious, flung, jammed, shoved into every available cupboard and dark corner, to starve or freeze to death. They were dangerous. They could hurt. And the whole reason for the ivory tower was to protect her from hurt, from all the pain and associated grief that human flesh is heir to. Because, a long time ago, so long it was beyond conscious memory, she *had* been hurt. So badly, that even the thought had been buried. And having buried that, she had to bury anything else that might conceivably remind her, no matter how indirectly. They all had to go. Which meant she had to gut herself, become an empty shell. Or so she thought. Oh, she looked like a living, breathing human being. An unbelievably beautiful woman. She had a face that caught the breath and a strong, beautiful body that stood tall and walked proudly. She had a way of moving that was a challenge to men, all of whom she walked over. Which convinced her she could walk over anybody. That she was invincible, unconquerable. But all these thoughts did was provide another layer of ice. Until the exquisite ivory tower was constructed of it. A marvelously beautiful white stalagmite; unbelievably smooth and silky to the touch, but so cold it blighted every hand that touched it.

"But she didn't care. Serve them right, she thought. She had to get rid of every feeling, you see. Not to care, not to feel, not to want, not to need—this was what mattered to her. Oh, and things. Dead things. Like pictures and books and furniture. And pictures of people on a screen, because they were

not real, you see, so had no power to hurt her. Music she loved—so much it
made her suffer, but in a pleasurably painful way . . . not in the hurtful,
really painful way that people could hurt. It could move her, but without
touching her. She felt it in her mind but never in her heart."

Her face was bone-white, the lashes standing out like scratch marks on her
colorless cheeks. She sat very still. Only the rapid rise of her breasts under the
thin silk of the robe betrayed her.

"She walked, she talked, she breathed—but she did not live. She was dead.
She had no life support, you see. Because she had no life. She had become
what her fear had told her she must be: a nothing. Without feelings, without
emotions. She did not really know why, had never questioned her mind's
authority. It had told her that emotions were deadly; that anything to do
with them, in any shape or form, was forbidden. That if she did allow them
to touch her she would suffer. Love was death. Involvement with another
human being meant pain and suffering; emotions meant danger. They were
not to be trusted. So she had never allowed hers to move.

"Until one day, one man came across this beautiful but soulless piece of
architecture and thought: 'How beautiful.' He was so caught by it, so intrigued that he went to take a closer look. And a very strange thing happened. Instead of being driven back by the icy force field, something in him
rendered him immune, so that he was able to get right up close and look deep
inside. And was appalled. What a waste, he thought. What a terrible, tragic
waste. So he determined to do something about it. And broke in. But the
moment he got inside, all these emotions began to clamor for their freedom,
with such force and strength that they overwhelmed him. He had never
known anything like it in his life, but he was glad, because it meant they
weren't dead. And so he let them run riot, brought them all out, but when he
turned to go back inside he found the doors locked again."

He paused. When she did not say anything: "That's as far as I've got," he
said. "I'm not sure how it should end. Any suggestions?"

Her voice was harsh, but it trembled as she asked, "Dr. Freud, I presume?"

"Don't presume anything." He was unruffled. "You presumed you had no
feelings and look how wrong *that* was." He was implacable.

"Oh, I forgot to add, this woman is also a miser; unwilling to let one small
particle of self escape her total control—her real, imprisoned self. Because
she does not trust it, and that is because she doesn't like it. Self-denial usually
springs from self-hatred. How can you love other people if you cannot first
love yourself?"

Her voice was low but vibrant with anger when she sneered: "Analysis as
well as sexual therapy? Spare me the instant diagnosis, if you please!"

"I'm much better at sex than psychoanalysis. Much more practice. But I read a lot. Since meeting you I've read a lot more . . . You are strangling yourself with your hang-ups and will have to be cut free. And don't knock the sexual therapy. It worked wonders with you last night." The embarrassed flush stained her throat and face again. "But tonight all you can see is your own shocking lack of self-control, which you're telling yourself was disgraceful and degrading, right?"

"You forgot to add unnecessary!"

"Ah, yes. You would see it like that."

"I can see you for what you are: a sexual opportunist!"

"You would not recognize what I am if it came up to you in the street and spat in your face! You can't even recognize what I am offering. So I'll tell you. To help make you face yourself. Let loose, you don't *have* any inhibitions. That's what is scaring the hell out of you."

It was in her face, the painful knowledge that she was hearing the truth and a hopeless, helpless vulnerability that had her cornered. But she had to find her own answers the hard way. It was the only way she would believe them. To shove her along he went on: "You were incredible. Because it was all there, only waiting to be released. I'm only grateful it was to me you released it."

She writhed at the truth of his words. How did he know so much? Experience, she answered herself. *Women,* remember?

She studied his face, as if looking for answers there even though she knew, from what had not been said as much as from what had, that what he was doing was forcing her to find her own. Who *was* he? She brought forward the facts. Thirty-nine, artistically acclaimed, commercially disastrous. A man who radiated a sexuality that had thrown, hog-tied, and shackled her the first time their eyes met. A man still nine-tenths unknown. She knew *of* him; in her usual methodical way she had made it her business to, but she had not dreamed he would overwhelm her so; make her look at herself—and in the magnifying mirror of his own eyes, which had seen so much and so deeply. Right inside the ivory tower he had said she had made of herself. She had known this to be true as soon as he said it. Which again brought her back to *how?*

She should have paid more attention when Cass had said he was something else again . . . She should have perceived, by the way he was talked about, his presence anticipated and looked forward to, that he was *different.* She had never met a man like him. Had not known there even were such men. Men who saw so finely, so intensely. Or a man who could make her see too. And feel. And think. And she had to *think.* He had given her so much to think about.

"*Will* you let me help you?" he repeated.

"By helping yourself?" She was using the only weapon she had against him.

"Of course!" It failed utterly. "I am as self-interested as the next man. When I see a woman as stunningly beautiful and as fascinating as you I have a case of the plain, old-fashioned urge to possess. Except the next time I want us both to know what we are doing and do it deliberately, not because we can't help it."

Again she felt the hot flush as her body responded even to the memory, but she beat it back. "Your nobility overwhelms me! You take me to bed, work me over, and before I know it I am being written up in Masters and Johnson. While you have made the unmakable. Anything to enhance an already legendary reputation."

"All I want is to make you over . . . into the woman you really are."

"You keep saying that! I am already the woman I want—and always intended—to be!"

"Liar. *That* woman only looks like one . . . it takes courage to be a real woman."

"You mean one who would say yes to you!"

"Not only to me. To life."

She all but ground her teeth.

He went on, relentless: "You need to have what has festered far too long cut out of you; give room to those feelings, the passion you showed me last night. That was instinct, pure and simple; the rest you learned as you went along—and the ease and speed with which you learned proves that you want to."

He was always there, waiting for her, whichever way she turned.

"We have to find out *why* you are; *why* you are so afraid of letting go; *why* emotions terrify you; *why* you have deliberately if unconsciously frightened away men. There is always a reason for that kind of self-protection and yours is the fear of being hurt. What we have to find out is what hurt you, so badly and so deeply that you have gone in fear and trembling ever since. It's my theory that the answers lie in those missing five years of yours, the ones you cannot remember."

"Who told you that?"

"Hervey . . . And that you have no memory of your mother . . . that's a vital clue. We tend to forget what we find too painful to remember."

White-faced she leapt to her feet, off the sofa and away from him. His implacability, his immovability, and his very tangibility were unnerving her. She felt she had to get away, that her composure was eroding like her character before his remorseless exposure.

"I do not need your Samuel Smiles treatment, thank you! How I live is my concern."

She swept her clothes from the mantel, and the clock with it, so that she had to grab at it, set it back with a thud. Then she stalked into the kitchen. He heard her banging about in there. She came out fully dressed, flung the robe at him. "Send me your bill!" she flung after it. "But don't make any more appointments!"

The door slammed behind her.

When Cass, who had been pacing restlessly up and down, up and down, said finally, "I'm too restless to sleep; I think I'll go for a walk," Mattie, whose nose had instantly scented a situation when Cass came back minus Dev *and* Elizabeth, said, "I'll buy you a collar for Christmas! Have it engraved: '*My name is Cass van Dooren and I belong to Elizabeth Sheridan.*' "

Cass's face flushed a painful red.

"I know you!" Mattie laughed theatrically. "You've got the hots for that snooty bitch, but she's got the hots for Dev—and he for her! Oh, yes, I saw them playing their silent little game last night. He stalked her from the word go!"

But Cass had gone too. At a run. Serve her right! Mattie thought spitefully. Let's see her stub her toe on *that* snooty bitch! She herself was feeling trodden on. Since that one sentence, Elizabeth Sheridan had not so much as looked her way. Now, she had also spiked Mattie's plans regarding Dev.

As soon as she had heard Dev was coming back to the Island, she had decided he was just what she needed. God knows, she had always wanted him but had known, the first time she set eyes on him, that this was one man she could not allow herself; not while she was Richard Tempest's mistress. He would allow her others—as she allowed him—but not Dev Loughlin. She had known it instinctively from the way Richard said his name, and, of all of them, had been the only one not surprised when the Great Schism took place. She had always known it was only a matter of time. And Richard's jealousy.

But Richard was dead. And she had come very much back to life, a life in which sex had played a large and important part. And she was not getting any. Dev would put that right.

But that bitch had taken him too! Mattie felt she was being elbowed right off the stage. And she was used to being right smack in the center as the star.

It was just too much! She felt betrayed once again. How he could pursue that frozen-faced bitch was beyond Mattie's understanding. It would be like going to bed with an ice pack. Except she knew Dev would not waste his time on a fruitless exercise. So he had seen something. Those blue eyes of his always saw through any false façade. They had seen right through Richard, hadn't they? Which still did not make it any more palatable. And now, here was Cass, obviously just as jealous! Nothing was going right. Everything was hideously, miserably wrong . . . She felt neglected, overlooked, and over-ruled. Cass had warned her things were different, but this was unsupportable! Something would have to be done.

Cass was halfway down the beach when she saw, in the bright light of the moon, Elizabeth striding toward her.

"Oh, there you are. I was just coming to see if everything was all right."

She took a step back before the look Elizabeth threw her. "Let loose the leash, Cass! I am not your property either!"

Either? "Now just a minute . . . *I said just a minute!*"

She trotted after Elizabeth, already past her on up the beach.

"What the hell has got into you?" She did not dare ask *who?*

Elizabeth stopped, whirled. "Mind your own business! And stop dogging me! I will *not* be followed, I will *not* be spied on! Do you understand? Nobody owns me! Nobody!" She went off again at her long-legged lope, her voice floating behind her. "Just—leave—me—alone."

"Well!" gasped Cass. Then again: "Well!"

TEN

Devlin Alejandro O'Loughlin Ruiz y Alarcón had been born, thirty-nine years before, of a passionately loquacious, incurably romantic, hopelessly im-practical Irish father and a hot-tempered, hot-blooded, ruthlessly practical Castilian mother. Patrick O'Loughlin had gone to a reception at the Spanish Embassy in Dublin, where he had met the Ambassador's eldest daughter, Conchita, and fallen strickenly, hopelessly, in love. Six hard-fought months later he had taken his Concha back to the great, drafty Galway mansion which dominated the stud where he raised purebred Irish hunters; once there, he had proceeded to raise, on the trot, three daughters. It was in his drunken pride at having fathered, nine long years later, the long-hoped-for

THE RICH AND THE MIGHTY

son, that he set his iron-mouthed, vicious-tempered gray at a stone wall known locally as the Mountains of Mourne and been thrown against it instead, sailing over it with a last triumphant yell of "I've done it!" And he had. As well as doing for himself. The whole county—the whole country— mourned. Patrick O'Loughlin had been the greatest hunt jockey of his generation, especially with the drink taken. What a pity, they said sorrowfully, that this time he had taken one too many.

The young Dev was therefore raised in a house of women, spent a childhood divided between them and horses, for his mother proceeded to do what her husband had never managed: establish a world-class stud. He thus learned, at a very early age, what made both of them so high-spirited, so contrary, so stubborn; acquiring on the way a vast knowledge and great skill with the one, and a deep love and understanding of the other.

His first memory was of his mother's big four-poster bed; of sitting beside her as she breakfasted there on hot coffee, black as sin, and warm croissants, and afterward smoked a long, thin, black Spanish cheroot. His first remembered smell was of that bedroom; of his mother, warm and voluptuous in a billowing white lawn nightgown, her black hair hanging down her back, her billowing breasts soft as cushions, smelling of cologne and female, all mixed up with the fragrance of coffee and black Spanish tobacco.

Afterward, he would sit up in the big bed and watch her dress for the day; always in her habit, for mornings were spent with the horses. He would watch, fascinated, as the bed-warm, billowingly maternal figure of his mother was changed into a tightly corseted, black-serge, hourglass martinet, booted and spurred, the wild black hair tamed and coiled and netted under a severe black bowler, her snowy-white stock pinned with the emerald shamrock which had been her husband's first gift. This taught him his first important lesson. That how a woman looked was not always what she really was.

This was further reinforced when, spoiled and indulged by his older sisters, they allowed him to sit and watch while they got ready for hunt balls. Once again he saw the change from horse-mad hoyden to sleekly groomed beauty, from casual girl into elegant woman; hair sleek and shiny, young, firm breasts —so different from his mother's voluptuous cushions—cradled in wisps of satin, long legs glossy in nylons anchored to frilly suspender belts, freckled arms concealed under long, white gloves. Suddenly they were unrecognizable, but he knew who they *really* were; so from the start, women never awed or mystified him. He knew what they were, and loved them for it, in all their moods and vagaries. Which was why they loved him.

His sisters' tears, as they mourned a lost beau or a carelessly inflicted defection, made him into the tenderest of men; one who, when he was old enough, never knowingly inflicted pain. This only served to enslave more than ever the women who were instantly attracted to him by his all-pervading sexual magnetism. Even when an affair was over the woman remained a friend. So it was that no matter where his work took him, there was always a woman waiting with open arms.

They knew he was married to his work, that he loved their sex generally rather than one particular woman, but they also reveled in a single-mindedness that meant, when at last he came to them, his time was for them and them only; a distillation to a concentrated essence of a man whose presence was intoxicating.

He was happy to be back at Marlborough again, while they were deeply delighted to have him back. It was his first break for many months, and there was a lot to catch up on. Mostly about Elizabeth Sheridan. He listened with grave intentness to what each one had to say about her. Her impact had hit like a meteor and the resultant explosion had wreaked havoc. So it was that the word portrait painted by David, embellished by Nieves's acid touches, was further enlarged by Hervey's approval of her capability and intelligence; by Helen's still surprised but wholehearted appreciation of Elizabeth's own appreciation of Marlborough; by Cass's gleeful anticipation of a soul mate with a drive like a camshaft and a bludgeoning self-confidence; by Mattie's fear and jealousy.

When he put it all together, he was left with an in-depth portrait of a coldhearted, hard-eyed, unemotional, and ruthlessly practical woman who was all brains and no understanding. Who did not suffer fools gladly and was only prepared to suffer anyone else provided they did not waste her time. Who had no use for emotions and took everything with a liberal application of salt. Who had no memory of the first five years of her life or the mother who had borne her; whose creed was "He travels fastest who travels alone" and ruthlessly cut loose those who could not keep up with her. They all poured out their grievances or their hurts or their praise or their resentments, even their bewilderment in Helen's case, so that he was prepared for an Amazon wearing armor plate, and alive with a curiosity as to why she should feel the need to wear it. Of all men he had proved, time and time again, that what a woman seemed was not always what she was.

When he saw her come out of the sea, every instinct told him this one was no different, and he knew, the instant their eyes met, that he had caught her unawares, with all her guards down.

Curiosity, and Nieves's hissed: "That's her . . ." had propelled him forward to see the reality of the photograph David had sent; the very stuff of which the dreams of his romantic nature were made. Inhumanly beautiful. Not a woman but a statue. The gilt-blond hair, heavy with water, was swept ruthlessly back from a face whose bones were classically perfect, while the plain navy-blue swimsuit only served to exhibit the sumptuous abundance of a body that was all female. Truly, he thought, she is all David said she was. Until, bending down to offer her a hand, she looked up at him and their eyes met. It was a sudden, stunning fall into nowhere and then the breath-robbing shock of two consciousnesses colliding. For a moment, there was no one in the world but the two of them. He fell right into eyes as deep as the sea and felt himself drowning.

And then suddenly, as if she had put both hands on his chest and pushed, he was outside again and the eyes were closed, even as she was. He had a sense of a door slamming somewhere. It was only as he held her hand, cold from the sea but alive with tension, like a high-voltage cable, that he also sensed, as powerful as the salt scent of the sea which clung to her, an almost palpable current of fear. She dropped her hand and wiped it on her leg, as though he had left traces of himself on it, and under his eyes he saw the image she projected take form. It was then that he realized it was a hologram. Reach out, as he had unthinkingly, instinctively done, and you went right through it.

He had to admire the way she did it. Long practice. It was as though she had plucked from nowhere an invisible coating of liquid glass, the kind that gave you back a reflection but from behind which she examined you with great care. Had he not felt it, known she felt it too, he would not have believed it. But he did. She was the one who did not. Her every word, her whole attitude, refuted it. It had not happened, her body, her eyes, were saying. Therefore we will not think of it. Strange, he thought. Why? It—she —fascinated him. She was a monumental fake. Again—why?

Under his eyes, which he was unable to take from her, he could see her burning resentment, yet he was aware she was sealing every entrance, blocking every hole. She was not even willing to let him see her anger. Her manner polite but distant. She did not smile. As they walked back along the beach, he did all the talking. When she was required to answer she did so, but she volunteered nothing.

On his other side, he was conscious of Nieves's stiffness, a taut wariness he could feel vibrating through the hand he held in his. Elizabeth Sheridan walked apart, so that there was no possibility of physical contact. She looked straight ahead, never turned her head to glance at his face, was careful never to meet his eyes.

Fascinating! he thought, totally intrigued. Fascinating! She did not walk so much as stalk, and her head was up. Defensive, he thought. Every hackle raised . . . He had got to her, all right. As she had to him. Even when, as they reached the path and took the shortcut up the rocks, she did not take the hand he held out to help her. She made her own way. Yes, he thought, always has, always will. But why is she so defensive? A woman with her face. It did not make sense. She must be used, by now, to men's reaction to it. Yet she acted as though it was not a compliment but an insult. Strange. Very strange. As strange as she was. And she had put on her dress as though to walk under his eyes in her swimsuit was embarrassing. Perhaps her size? She was only inches shorter than he; very tall for a woman, and in this thin-is-beautiful age, she was sixty years behind the times. The Edwardians had prized bodies like hers—full-breasted, wide-hipped, long-legged. David had said she was magnificent and he'd been right. Yet she acted as though she was not beautiful but just plain big. Yes, *plain*.

And then, suddenly, it hit him. She did not believe in her own power. Here she was, possessed of the most potent weapon a woman could have in a world ruled by men, yet totally uncertain of it. Why? He had known—and had—many beautiful women who had never, ever failed to capitalize on it. As a weapon, as a source of power, as a means of livelihood. This one not only did not use it, she had no idea of it. Another why. It was only later, thinking about her, that he finally understood. The fraud she perpetrated on others was her particular form of truth. Control had become second nature, and had been applied from an early age. Since losing her mother? That sort of shock was known to produce amnesia; it was the only way some people could cope. Which meant, then, that she had once been deeply sensitive, even painfully feeling. Which also meant she was a coward. Hervey had said she was a coper, but it was only of *things*. People she never allowed near enough for the need to arise. Because once it had all but done for her?

One thing stood out like a red light. She was totally inexperienced with men. She had no idea how to handle what had happened. The sophistication was a veneer, consciously and endlessly applied. She took cover and cowered there. Which meant she was frightened of sex too? He knew she was, when he played his guitar. It was the strangest thing, as though he was playing her. He could feel each quiver; the thrum of the guitar was the thrum of her blood. And when she bolted—because that, in spite of the deliberately calm way she moved, was what she did—he knew it was from him. He had caught that blazing, hate-filled, desperate look she had thrown him.

That night he could not stop thinking about her; could not sleep because of her. She unreeled inside him like a film as he played back every look, every gesture, stopping now and then to freeze the frame so as to examine her face, her attitude, the sound of her voice. Knew, as he finally heard the clocks in the house strike four, that his decision was made. He had to do something about her. Not that it was a conscious decision. He knew he had no choice. So he went to see Louis Bastedo.

He left them as they went off to the cinema and visited the boatyard, where he ordered the new socket, then he went to the hospital. Louis pumped his hand, slapped him on the back. "About time, you old reprobate! Let's go kill a bottle and talk a blue streak."

They were old friends. Louis had been running the hospital for seventeen years and he and Dev had taken to each other at once. In the years they had not seen each other they had corresponded, managed to meet up once when Louis was in New York attending a medical seminar, but at once took up the old, easy relationship as though it had never been put down.

"I'm not taking you away from anything?" Dev asked.

"Nothing to be taken away from . . . they're a healthy lot around here. My time is your time. So tell me, how's the movie business these days?"

Louis, too, held a piece of Dev's last two movies, but apart from his financial interest, the entire business of filmmaking he found vastly interesting. So for a while they sat and talked movies.

"Who knows," Louis commented finally, refilling their glasses, "maybe now that the old fox is dead things will change. I mean, what can he do from the grave?"

"You mean you haven't heard?"

Louis grinned. "It was all over the Island within hours," he admitted.

"People can talk of nothing else."

"Have you met her?"

"Once." The brown eyes gleamed. "Quite something . . ."

"That's what I want to talk to you about."

Louis sighed. Pure envy. "Already!"

"I want your professional advice. I think she's one hell of an emotional mess."

Louis's interest was fixed.

"I want to put a thesis to you," Dev went on.

Louis grinned. "Will it hurt?"

Seriously: "Well, I rather think it will."

Louis frowned. Dev was really serious.

"I know your discipline isn't psychiatry, but I also know your reading is as vast as your knowledge in all fields of medicine. I want expert confirmation."

"About what?"

"Her state of mind."

"She seemed sane enough to me."

"That's not the trouble. It's her *kind* of sanity."

"Well, you know what they say . . . the crazies hold all the keys to the padded cells."

"That's what she's in, I think. A cell of her own making."

Succinctly he gave Louis a rundown on what had happened from the moment he had seen Elizabeth come out of the sea.

Louis sighed. "You may not have met any, but there are women, you know, who can't even stand the thought of sex."

"But there is always a reason, isn't there?"

"Y—e—s . . . What, in your opinion, is hers?"

"I think it all lies in those missing five years of hers. Not only has she forgotten them, but she has absolutely no memory of her own mother. Hervey told me that's what she told him. Not so much as a single memory. She has no idea of anything that happened before she found herself in that foundling home. Which means she could have suffered some traumatic shock, right?"

"Could be." Louis picked up his glass. "Five is a dangerous age at which to lose your mother."

"That sort of shock can stultify?"

Louis nodded. "It has been known."

"I think that's what happened to her."

Louis took out his pipe, began to fill it, always a sign he was thinking deeply.

"It all makes for her unnatural control, her negation of emotion; her eagerness to embrace pure reason rather than—"

"You?" Louis's eyes were twinkling.

"All right, me. We collided, Louis. I've had my share of women but nothing like that ever happened before. Never."

"And she's been running scared ever since?"

"Terrified." Dev leaned forward across the table. "But more of herself than of me."

"We know that a child, separated from its mother at an age when it is too young to understand why, can be—again depending on that child—damaged, sometimes irreparably. It can lead to deep feelings of insecurity and instability, which in turn make for a passionate protection of self; sometimes a total preoccupation; one which leaves no room for seeing any other point of view."

"I think that's her," Dev said.

"Which is probably why she has taken all this without so much as a flicker;

it hasn't really touched her emotionally. And because she doesn't expect it to
last. Nothing does, is what they usually believe, allied to a conviction that
they are surrounded by hostility and misunderstanding. This is why they are
always in a state of constant alert . . ."

"That *is* her," Dev said again.

"Sounds like a classic case," Louis said finally, sorrowfully.

"Of what?" Dev asked.

"Deprivation. At a particularly vulnerable age she was deprived of her
mother; of probably the only love she has ever had. It killed all her emotional
responses because they mean pain and suffering. *Not* to feel, *not* to need, *not*
to be hurt; these are usually what motivates emotionally damaged people
such as—from what you tell me—she would seem to be. But I am adding to
your thesis. To establish any of this beyond doubt I would have to see her,
talk to her."

"She would *never* agree to that. I told you, she has not the slightest idea
that she is not whole and perfect; just—different."

"Then she needs help."

"Which is why I'm asking yours."

"I can't give her that kind of help, but I could pass her on to someone who
could."

"Louis, you have a knowledge and understanding of human nature that
makes you an instinctive psychiatrist . . ."

"But not qualified to treat her. That could be dangerous, and not only to
her. I will not take risks with my job or my hospital."

"I know that—but I would."

Louis surveyed Dev in silence. Finally: "She's really got to you, hasn't
she?"

"I told you: we—collided."

Louis sighed again. "Well, if as you say it's the first time it ever happened
to you, this . . . collision you talk about, we can make another assumption
and say it has never, ever happened to her."

"Obviously," Dev said impatiently.

Louis scratched his ear with his pipestem. "Tricky," he said.

"That's why I came to you."

"You really want to help her?"

"Yes. And . . . melt her, if you like."

Louis's smile was affectionate but tinged with envy. "I've never known you
to fail."

"Neither have I," Dev answered honestly. "I was born lucky enough to
have something women want. That's what gets me, you see. I *know* she wants

it too. But she's tearing herself apart trying to deny her own nature . . .
There's a woman at the center of the iceberg, Louis. I know it; I felt it that
first time . . . She's not what she believes she is. What I want to know is—
how do I show her? She's put up every barrier she can find . . . I have to get
through them. I need to."

Well, well, thought Louis, both surprised and envious. He had seen his
friend cut a swathe through women like a combine harvester through a
Kansas prairie, but while Dev loved women, there had never been one particular woman. Until now. And she had to be off-center. Probably why, Louis
thought shrewdly. Dev had had so many women that the offbeat, the unusual, would have a fresh appeal. Which was not being uncharitable, Louis
thought. Dev Loughlin, in spite of his rampant masculinity, was no macho
stud: he had an understanding heart and a wellspring of tenderness that
never ran dry, no matter how much of it he gave to the women who needed
it. They were never women, *per se.* He was always as deeply interested in
their minds as their bodies. Louis had often envied his particular brand of
sexual therapy and the fact that he hadn't even *trained* for it! Now he said
reluctantly: "Well, then, it's up to you . . . Having got this far, you have no
choice but to take it further."

"I know that! What I want to know is how?"

Louis thought, sucking on his pipe. "Well, you have established some sort
of contact. All you can do is keep it up. Talk to her; get her on her own; find
out what makes her tick; how she sees things, people, her whole attitude to
life. What you've told me is what you have learned from other people. Now
you must find out for yourself and, if you can't handle it, tell me. In the
meantime I'll get in touch with an analyst friend of mine in Miami and pick
his brains. I'll find out what else I can. But for God's sake go carefully . . .
this is a girl already off-balance. Don't push, but on the other hand, keep up a
gentle pressure . . . the kind she is already feeling."

The brown eyes were bland but Dev read them true and nodded.

"And if you need any more help . . ."

"I don't doubt I will," Dev answered honestly. "Thanks."

"A very beautiful woman, that," Louis said, almost absently.

"Isn't she, though! But I'd swear she doesn't think so, not consciously
anyway. Yet at the same time she uses it to intimidate . . . she's got David
going round in circles."

Louis sighed. "Ah, well, David . . . But her attitude is probably not that
of challenge; rather, to prevent any man from threatening her by making
one."

"Which is what gets me! All that beauty going to waste! She's not living,

Louis, she's existing—and doesn't know any better. For me, *hell* is life without living."

"Which is why I counsel caution. You know what cornered animals are like. A soft voice and a warm smile. Don't shove yourself at her but *be* there . . . if you know what I mean," he added vaguely, knowing full well Dev did. Usually all he ever had to do where women were concerned was just stand there.

"Okay," Dev said, much more cheerfully. "I'll start tonight. She's gone to the Bijou with the others. I'll see if I can get her alone and take it from there."

He had honestly meant to do no more than follow Louis's advice. Talk and get her to talk. But the moment he saw her it hit him again; knew by the way her own eyes changed focus that she was feeling it too. And once he had her in the car he was conscious of nothing but her nearness; of the scent of her, the shape and powerfully female current emanating from the soft chiffon of her dress, the fast rise and fall of her magnificent breasts; the way her hair, heavy and soft as silk, swung about her face. So nerve-tinglingly acute was his awareness that he had to concentrate hard on his driving, clenching the wheel tightly when what he wanted to do was reach out and grab her. But that, he knew, would be the worst thing he could do. She was obviously teetering, and he could not bear to send her falling the wrong way. Away from, instead of toward, him.

But the mutual awareness was so tense, so suffocating, that when his arm brushed her breasts their mutual flashpoint exploded. It was at once totally out of their control. The only thing he could think of, when he could think at all, was that he had been right. She had been repressed. He had let loose the whirlwind. What she had been born knowing broke its shackles and overwhelmed him; long-submerged instinct now wholly revealed. Her body told him everything. Underneath the tightly battened-down lid raged uncontrollable fires, and when he opened it they seared him, left him drained as he had never been drained. And marked—with her mark—for life.

He cursed himself. He should have *known* that once the fire had died all she would be conscious of were the ashes and dust in the mouth. She was horrified; not only by what had happened but that it had happened at all. But he did what he could. And afterward, thinking about it, unable to think of anything else, he had comforted himself with the thought that he had proved to her that what he had told her was the truth. She was not what she thought she was. The trouble was, she was not what he had expected, either. But he could cope with that. What mattered now was that *she* did.

All next day on the *Pinta* it hummed and throbbed between them. She had come aboard with her ten-foot pole (but at least she had come aboard—though that fitted: she would not acknowledge his power by admitting to it) and kept it thrust firmly at his chest. But it was wearing her down. By the end of the day she was glazed with emotional exhaustion and the desperation of her inner struggle. That, too, worked in his favor. And when she fell asleep he seized his chance. *Now* they could talk. Except that he did most of it, unable to help himself, so intense was his own desperation. It hit her hard. He saw her flinch, but she did not go to pieces. There were no hysterics, no wild accusations, no tears. Her face was white and her eyes were bruised but she came back fighting, and he knew, even as she did so, that he would not have her any other way. Which was when he also knew that he loved her. Somebody, somewhere, had said that love was being obsessed by another human being. And he *was* obsessed. He recognized that he had committed himself to saving this woman from herself even if he lost his own self in the process. Except of course it was done. He *had* lost himself. To her.

ELEVEN

Elizabeth Sheridan fled from Dev Loughlin as from the furies, afraid as she had never been before. It was only in her room, the door locked, as though that would protect her, that she went over what he had said, scrutinizing every word in her search for flaws. She failed utterly. Every word made what she had always clung to: common sense. Her rationality forced her to accept it. So, in desperation, she tried to force aside the blackness that lay beyond her first, conscious memory: that of lying in a strange bed, in a strange room, in a strange house that smelled of polish and boiled cabbage, afraid and lost and lonely. There was nothing. The only clue she could find was one he did not know about: her fear of cemeteries. That had to spring from those lost years. And it was only when she assimilated that, that she also realized, with stunned shock, the reason why, in more than a month on Tempest Cay, she had never in all her walking around the island gone within a hundred yards of the Old Burial Ground to visit her father's grave. It was not because she did not—was not able to—think of him as her father, did not care whether he had been or not. It was because she was afraid to.

It made her cold with horror. He was right! She *was* a fake. She was not ruled by rationality and logicality because of a deliberate contempt for messy emotions; she embraced them as a bulwark *against* those very emotions. A memory, no longer consciously recalled, held sway over her.

Utterly appalled, she sat and stared at a self she had tried all her life to subjugate. The one Dev Loughlin had released last night. One she had run from in terror. The self who could feel; intensely, passionately, agonizingly. No, she was not what she had thought she was. That woman would not have done what she had done; would never have gloried in what it had always considered overrated. Unnecessary. Dangerous.

That was why she had fled from it, the old subconscious fear dominating. Retreat was the better part of valor. And she was a coward, wasn't she? Preferring to be unfeelingly dead than feelingly alive. Oh, God, she thought, wrapping her arms around herself because she could not stop her convulsive shivering. Oh, God . . .

She sat hunched and cowering amid the ruins of her life, wincing as the pieces hit her. She was still sitting there, when she became aware that some-one was hammering at her door.

"Elizabeth! Will you for God's sake open this door!"

Cass.

"I have to talk to you." The knob rattled. "I know you are in there."

"Go away," she said dully.

"This is too important . . . please, open the door. Elizabeth?" Cass's voice was raised, sharp, brooking no argument. The door thudded once more, the knob turning angrily. "It's important," Cass called pleadingly. "Dan's back . . . from London."

Elizabeth raised her head. London?

When she opened the door Cass all but fell in. "About time!"

"What's the matter? Why is it important?"

"Because he says it is. He's up to something . . . looks like he's swallowed a whole cageful of canaries! He says he has something of absolutely vital importance to tell us—especially you!"

Elizabeth frowned. "Like what?"

"He won't say until we are all downstairs . . . yes, everybody! He's so full of himself he's running over—which means he intends to run right over us!" Cass paused dramatically. "I think he's been dustbin-dredging! *In London,*" she drummed in.

But Elizabeth was still standing there. She looked awful. What *had* hap-pened in that beach house? Well, that would wait. Right now, all her in-stincts told her that what Dan had to say wouldn't. "Come *on!*"

Everyone was in the white drawing room. Helen, in a cloud of sea-green ruffles looking both surprised and none too pleased, Hervey as ever by her side. Mattie was frowning at her reflection, tidying her hair, while David was scowling at Dan, who was standing with his back to the fire—newly mended —obviously happy to be back. Only Nieves was missing. And Dev at the beach house. Where he can stay, Cass thought.

"Ah . . . the lady herself." Dan smiled, sighting Elizabeth. "Now we can get down to brass tacks."

Cass looked pointedly at his feet, elegantly shod in handmade shoes. He grinned. "So sit, then. Come to that, I think you all should sit down."

He ceremoniously flourished a chair at Helen, who said dubiously, "I cannot think why you should get us all out of our beds."

"But that is what I intend to tell you!"

"About what?" demanded Cass.

"The past, of course!"

"Whose past?"

Dan turned to Elizabeth, glittering eyes filled with an unholy glee. "Who else?"

"So that's why you left in such a hurry!" Cass exclaimed, light at last shining on that particular dark corner. "Margery too?"

"Oh, she's long gone back to Venice . . . couldn't keep away from that Venetian stud of hers, especially when she heard he was all ready to sign himself over to Barbara what's-her-name . . . you know, the cosmetics queen. Margery was off like a shot. Not that she was much use to me anyway. As Richard always taught us, never leave anything to anybody; always do it yourself."

"So just what *have* you done?" Hervey demanded suspiciously.

"Why, solved the puzzle, of course!"

The look on their faces told him they were still struggling with their own. He laughed. "Oh, this is *so* nice . . . to have you all sitting on the *sharpest* of tenterhooks." His glance at Elizabeth strung hers up tighter. "How does it feel?" he asked softly.

"Oh, for God's sake, you've pulled all the wings off all the flies! Get down to it, will you!" Cass's impatience was steaming.

"Patience, patience." He drew up his own chair, disposed himself comfortably, first punctiliously drawing up his trousers, crossing his legs.

"Well, now, as I said, I have been in London. I went there to conduct an investigation. You all know that Richard's will did not please me. The more I thought about it the less pleased I became. It left so many questions unanswered. So I decided I would see if I could answer them."

"Like what?" Cass demanded.

Dan ignored her. "While I was there, I happened by great good chance to run into Freddy Tempest—you remember Freddy, Helen? Lionel Tempest's boy?"

Helen nodded obediently. "Yes, of course, but what—?"

"I am getting to it. Allow me my own good time. It was all *I* was allowed." Another razor-edged look at Elizabeth, who was sitting with rigid spine and forbidding face, staring at nothing.

"Well, he invited me down to Tempest Towers for the weekend, and *what* a fascinating weekend it was. Sad, in a way. You have no idea just how straitened our English relatives are, my dear Helen. Two lots of death duties on the trot. They are having to sell off an awful lot, and while I was there, a man from Sotheby's came to appraise some paintings . . . one a particularly ravishing Corot, by the way. But among them"—he rose from his chair to go over to one of the sofas, reached over and came up with a flat, brown-paper-wrapped parcel—"was this little gem."

With great care and nail-biting deliberation he untied knots, folded string, carefully stripped away paper to reveal a gilt-framed portrait, about twenty-four inches square. This he propped up against the base of a lamp on a small table, which he drew forward as a sort of stage, the light illuminating it to their assembled gaze. "There . . ." He stood back admiringly. "Now isn't that a pretty thing?"

Heads craned as everyone crowded to peer at it. It was David, acting in his capacity as the "art" expert, who went forward authoritatively to bend down, hands on knees, in front of it. "Why . . . it's Helen!" he exclaimed.

"Pick it up," Dan encouraged. "Take a good look."

David did so, holding it under the lamp. "Not bad . . . nice brushwork . . . lots of detail, and I like the tempera . . . good technique." He peered closer, then said in a thunderstruck voice: "R.T.! Not Richard Tempest!"

"No. *Not* Richard Tempest," Dan agreed smugly. "*Rupert* Tempest . . . an English cousin." He turned to Helen, who had fumblingly donned her glasses. "You remember Rupert, don't you, Helen? You knew him very, very well, didn't you?"

David held the painting out to her. Helen took it, looked at it. Her expression was puzzled, and her eyes were wide as she stared at herself when young. She was sitting on a swing suspended from the branch of a big elm; she was dappled with sunlight and in the act of flying upward, hair and dress streaming, head thrown back to reveal the line of her throat, eyes wide with excitement, mouth open and laughing, hands gripping the thick rope. She was

wearing a pretty silk dress and she looked alive; alive as none of them had
ever seen her. And happy.

"Painted at Tempests in the spring of 1946—April 1946, to be precise. By
the then son and heir to Tempest Towers and all its debts: Rupert Dysart-
Innes-Tempest, Viscount Dysart . . . *your* Rupert, Helen . . . the Rupert
you wanted to marry."

Hervey, who had been bending over Helen's shoulder, moved away instinctively as she snapped upright. Peering concernedly into her face he saw it was
ashen.

"That ring on your finger . . . see it," Dan helpfully pointed to the hand
wrapped around the rope of the swing, "that is the ring he gave you. Such a
pretty, sentimental little thing. Victorian, of course; they did so love anything with a message, and this one spells out a very special message. You can't
see all the stones but I know what they are. A diamond, an emerald, an
amethyst, a ruby, another emerald, a sapphire, and a topaz. All first quality,
of course. All you do is take the first letter of each stone, put them together
and, hey, presto—the word 'DEAREST'. Now isn't that nice?"

His smile was glittering, honed to a deadly edge as he turned it onto
Elizabeth. "You know all about it, don't you? You have a ring just like it,
don't you? Exactly like it, in fact. Now isn't that a coincidence?" He beamed
round at their stunned faces. "Two people, living thousands of miles apart,
both members of the same family, both possessing identical rings . . . *quite*
a coincidence. Except Helen does not have hers anymore, do you, Helen?
Lost it, did you? Gave it away, perhaps? I mean, you couldn't very well give it
back to him even if you did not eventually marry—because he was killed,
wasn't he? Such a tragedy! So that the ring was all you had."

Cass's forebodings laid cold hands on her spine. "What are you getting
at?"

"Patience, patience . . . Allow me the pleasure of getting there in my
own good time. I have already devoted enough of that to this little quest.
Helen knows what I am getting at, don't you, Helen?"

His words were daggers, but Helen was feeling no pain; she wasn't feeling
anything.

All eyes, out on stalks, swiveled her way, but she was staring at the painting, eyes wide and fixed.

"You can see she does," Dan murmured happily. "She recognizes that door
to the past. And if you will bear with me, I shall take you through it"—he
laughed again, exultant—"just like Alice. But first . . ." He turned to Elizabeth, who was now looking at Helen with a slight frown. "That ring of yours
—would you fetch it, please?"

"Why?" she asked.

"Because, I assure you, it is an important—perhaps *the* most important—piece of a puzzle of which Richard was very careful to lose what he thought were the vital parts. But I found them." His voice sharpened, became an arrogant command. "The ring, if you please."

He held her stare insolently, smiling slightly, something in his attitude radiant with spite. Silently, Elizabeth got up and went out of the room.

"What has Elizabeth's ring got to do with the one Helen is wearing?" Hervey asked uneasily.

"Everything," Dan answered succinctly and with relish. Hervey subsided, his uneasiness increasing, worried by Helen's reaction and disturbed by his own. Helen engaged to be married! He had never known that. Why had she never told him? Why had she never explained? His glance, under the concern, was reproachful, but she did not see. She was not seeing anything but her young, happy self. Her attitude began to alarm him. Her glance was too fixed, her body too rigid. And there was something about her eyes . . . If she had made any sound he would have said she was screaming.

"How do you know Elizabeth has a ring like the one in the picture?" Cass asked dangerously.

Dan met her deadly eyes with a shrug. "I made it my business to—again following Richard's hard-learned lessons. Know thine enemy."

"That's why you are doing all this, isn't it? Because from the beginning you have regarded her as yours!"

"I have regarded her exactly as Richard intended I should regard her," Dan replied swiftly. "*I* had nothing to crawl for . . ."

Cass flushed, opened her mouth, but Elizabeth came back into the room, followed by a sleepy Nieves.

"What's going on?" she asked, looking instantly round for Dev and frowning when she realized he was not present.

"Fun and games," Dan answered smilingly. "*Do* join in." He turned to Elizabeth. "The ring."

He held out a hand, palm up, but she did not hand it over. He dropped his own. "All right, then show it to the others . . . but show it!" His voice sharpened vindictively.

Cass held out her own hand. "Yes, let's have a look." She smiled at Elizabeth, who did not smile back as she dropped the ring into Cass's palm, where it lay, winking in the light.

"Describe the stones, if you please," Dan commanded.

Slowly, Cass turned the hoop of stones, set into a ring of gold. "A diamond, an emerald, an amethyst, a ruby, another emerald, a sapphire, and a topaz." Defiantly she shrugged. "So what? If it is Victorian, then there must be dozens like this . . . a keepsake, probably."

"Look inside, at the shank. Read out what is carved there."

With another sharp look at Dan's smiling face, Cass did so. "Initials, an H and an R joined, and a date . . . 1946." Cass's voice trailed away. Slowly, as if afraid to, she looked up into Elizabeth's face. It was carved from marble.

"Where did you get this ring?" Dan asked softly of Elizabeth.

"Miss Keller gave it to me." Her voice was as rigid as her face.

"When?"

"When I left Henrietta Fielding."

"Why?"

Pause. Everybody waited tensely, shivered when Elizabeth said, reluctantly, helplessly: "She said it had belonged to my mother."

The silence shuddered. Then Dan pounced, twitching the ring from Cass's nerveless hand to hold it up between finger and thumb and advance toward Helen, still sitting numbly, before thrusting it in front of her face.

"Remember this ring, Helen? Your engagement ring? How you had your initials carved into the gold . . ."

Helen shrank, eyes wide and terrified, mouth trembling. She put up a hand as if to ward away evil.

"No." Her voice was harsh, strained. "No . . ."

"Oh, but yes! This is *your* ring; the one Rupert Tempest gave you; the same ring that was given to Elizabeth Sheridan by the Lady Superintendent at the Henrietta Fielding Home for Foundlings with the information that it had belonged to her mother!"

"No!" It was a moan, terrified, anguished. "No . . . it cannot be . . . they told me I had dreamed it all . . . they said I was mad." Her voice rose and she clapped her fingers over her mouth, one hand holding the other as if to prevent any more words escaping.

Dan continued ruthlessly: "But I am not mad, nor is Elizabeth. This ring was yours . . . now it is Elizabeth's"—his voice lowered, became a soft, vicious hiss—"and we know why, don't we?"

"No . . . no . . ." Helen's voice rose even as she herself wavered unsteadily to her feet. Hervey put out a quick hand but she shook it away to retreat, eyes wide and terrified, head shaking endlessly. "It was not real . . . I imagined it all . . . there was no baby . . . it was all in my head." Her hands left her mouth to clutch at it, squeezing as though trying to exude those imaginings.

"Ah, but there *was* a baby." Dan's voice stalked her, would not let her go. "The one Rupert Tempest fathered on you: your little girl, remember? Only now she is a great big girl, and there she stands, Helen, the baby you lost, all grown up: Elizabeth Sheridan!"

Cass felt the hair on the back of her neck prickle. Jesus Christ! she thought, rocked back on her heels. Helen had come to a standstill; she had lowered her hands from her head, now held them clasped in an attitude of prayer on her breast. Her eyes, fixedly wide, were pinned to Elizabeth, who was staring back into them, her own dilated and incredulous.

"It's not *Richard* she looks like—it's you!" Dan proclaimed dramatically, flinging out a hand, playing his role to the hilt. "Look at that painting!" Everybody else looked obediently but Helen and Elizabeth had eyes only for each other. "That could *be* Elizabeth! But Richard made us look at *him* . . . and you were his sister and all the Tempests have a pronounced physical likeness. That's what he hoped would blind us, don't you see? She is not Richard Tempest's daughter and he knew it! She is yours! The daughter you conceived by Rupert Tempest! Your baby, Helen . . . the one you were told was only a figment of your imagination . . . she is real, Helen! Flesh and blood!" He seized Elizabeth's hand, dragged her, slackly unresisting, forward in a way that made Cass rise from her chair and reach out a hand. But Elizabeth went by her, right up to Helen, who had not moved. Now Dan took Helen's hand, ruthlessly placed it against Elizabeth's face. *"Feel* it, Helen! *Look* at it! *Your* face! *Your* child! *Your* baby!"

"For God's sake!" Hervey was up and out of his chair, only to be stopped in his tracks by the eerie, banshee howl of Helen's voice, feeling his own hair bristle. "No . . . no . . ." It was cut off suddenly and she swayed, and her face changed, seemed to slide off in a trance. "My baby." Her voice was high, thin, an empty singsong. "I lost my baby . . . they took her away and I could not find her. I looked everywhere but they said she was not real . . ."

Hervey took another step forward, his hand going out, his own face white and suffering.

"Helen . . . my poor love." His voice was full of pain.

Slowly she turned to him. The eyes were blank, blazing queerly as they stared into his, not seeing him, not seeing anything. "Help me find my baby," she said, in the same singsong voice. "You will help me find my baby, won't you?" She smiled then, and her eyes seemed to recognize him. "You will help me find my baby, won't you . . . because you love me." It was pathetically innocent, helplessly cruel.

"Yes," Hervey tried to steady his voice. "I will help you."

"I knew you would . . ." The smile, a rictus merely, made her mouth a gash, then it dissolved even as she did, like a melted puddle, into a heap on the floor.

Pandemonium erupted. Cass leapt at Dan, fists pummeling, feet kicking. "You bastard!" she shrieked. "You sadistic son of a bitch! You greedy, self-loving, misbegotten, knife-twisting—" Her voice strangled on her rage but she continued to punch and kick until Dan took hold of her wrists and held her, raging and futile, out of reach.

Hervey was down on his knees instantly, face anguished, raising Helen's head, holding it against him, while Mattie rushed to Cass and dragged her off Dan.

Shouldering through, David shoved Hervey aside and picked Helen up in his arms to carry her tenderly across to a sofa and lay her down.

Elizabeth had not moved. People passed her, knocked into her, but she merely moved as they did, not of her own volition.

It was Nieves, confused and frightened, who ran to the telephone. "Dev? Oh, Dev . . . please come . . . everything's awful . . . Aunt Helen . . ." Her voice choked. "Oh, come, please!" She listened, nodded, breathed a fervent "Thank you," and replaced the receiver.

Everyone was still milling around confusedly, mostly where Helen lay still and white. Only Mattie noticed Elizabeth, who seemed to have taken root. Brusquely she dragged up a chair, pushed her down into it. Elizabeth folded like a pile of clothes, sat unmoving. Mattie turned to the sofa, where Helen lay wide-eyed and staring.

"Let her breathe!" she said irritably, pushing them away before bending over what looked like a wax dummy. "Good God, she's stiff as a board! Somebody call Louis Bastedo."

This time David made for the telephone.

"Are you happy now?" Cass flung at Dan.

"I will not be happy until I get what is mine—for certain it is not hers!" He jerked a virulent nod at Elizabeth, and for the first time Cass became aware of the rigidity, the congealed attitude of shock. Rushing over, she bent to put a hand on Elizabeth's, lying limply in her lap. They were cold. Raising a ravaged face to Dan: "Oh, you *bastard!*" she hissed.

"Not I! She's the bastard—and not Richard Tempest's! She's Helen's daughter. The ring proves it! The will is a fraud! But if you are still not satisfied, then I will go further."

Something in his voice made even those clustered round the sofa turn their heads.

"You heard Elizabeth say the ring was given to her by one Marion Keller, Lady Superintendent at the Home? Well, a lady named Marion Keller was employed as companion/nurse to Helen Tempest back in 1946; what is

more, she accompanied Helen when she went to Europe that spring. Cast
your mind back, Cass . . . Remember her? Tall, brisk, no-nonsense type?"

Everyone looked at Cass, whose face had gone first red then white. "Oh,
my God," she whispered.

"Now you remember!"

Hervey stared at Cass. "Is this true?" he asked incredulously.

Cass bit her lip, but nodded.

It was Mattie who said it: "So it *is* true . . ." She sounded delighted.

"Of course it's true!" Dan sounded angry. "Unpalatable it may be, but
then, so many truths are—especially Richard Tempest's truths! And I swallowed more than my fair share of them, along with every dirty lesson he
taught me! Like never letting a man up once he is down. You'll only have to
fight him all over again. Lie to anybody, everybody—but never to yourself;
never show pity—it will always cost more than you can afford; how to take—
because if you wait, you will *never* get it. I practiced what he preached,
because he always promised me I would eventually enter his Kingdom of
Heaven—the one where he kept all his money. But he left me standing
outside. *She"*—another vicious jerk of the head at Elizabeth—"was the only
one allowed in. Well, I've just blown the gates. Now I'll take what's mine no
matter whose hard feelings!"

"You've just murdered any we might have held for you!" Cass spat.

"Sticks and stones . . ." Dan's tone was indifferent. "It's money I'm after."

"How did you find out about Marion Keller?" Hervey interrupted.

"A witness, of course. Of the most reliable kind. An old family retainer.
You know how the English are about them; pensioning them off with a little
cottage in the grounds. Well, down at Tempest Towers lives a little old lady
called Nanny Baines; eighty-seven years old but spry as an elf and with such a
remarkable memory! She was Mr. Rupert's nanny and he was her angel. She
was only too happy to talk about him, to tell me how he and Miss Helen fell
for each other like a ton of bricks. Love's young dream, according to her.
Everybody was delighted—especia!!y the old Countess, because even then
the English branch was short of money. The only person who was not delighted was Miss Helen's brother. And he absolutely forbade the marriage.
Miss Helen, he said, was not—and I quote—'fit for marriage.' She was, he
gave them to understand—and again I quote—'not quite right in the head.'
In fact, he said that if it was not for him, she would be locked up in a lunatic
asylum."

The silence quivered with shock.

"That is why she had a nurse-companion. A respectable title for a keeper!

But Mr. Rupert would not have it. Not his sweet, beautiful Helen. So what does he do but elope with her—aided and abetted, says Nanny Baines, by that same Miss Marion Keller. Sneaked off in the middle of the night, they did. Mr. Richard was fit to die! He had such a go at the old Countess that she took to her bed while he chased after the elusive pair. One week later, Mr. Rupert comes back alone. Very down. Very bitter. Says Helen has been spirited away by Richard and he recalled to his regiment. So back he goes to Germany, where he gets himself killed on some army maneuvers. Consternation! All hopes of that lovely money gone! The Countess prostrate, a rift in the friendly relationships between the two branches, the son and heir dead, and gloom and despondency rampant. It was Black Monday at Tempest Towers. Nanny Baines remembers it *so* well."

"How do you know they did not get married?" It was Hervey, still trying.

"Because Nanny Baines told *me* that Mr. Rupert told *her* they didn't. You don't run off and find a judge like you do in the States, not in England. Even a special license takes time, and you have to have papers and such. And when you are a Viscount Dysart and Miss Helen Tempest, you have to be very careful about the whole thing. No, they never actually got to tie the knot— only to consummate it." He flung out a hand in the direction of the graven image that was Elizabeth Sheridan. "And there's the living proof. We were all so busy looking in the direction Richard pointed us that we overlooked the fact that she is also a dead ringer for Helen—who also has the Tempest foot."

"Richard and Helen were brother and sister and very alike!" shot Cass.

"It's no use, Cass. The ring confirms it all . . . The one in the portrait is the one Marion Keller gave to Helen's daughter as the only thing left belonging to her mother. For God's sake, they had a whole week together before Richard caught up with them. And Marion Keller was sent packing in disgrace, while Helen was spirited off to where, nobody knows to this day. Only he was too late; she was already pregnant—with that baby she just now asked you to help find, Hervey."

It was so out of character that Hervey's flying leap took them all by surprise, so that he had his hands round Dan's throat before they could come to and haul him off. The two men fell to the ground, sending furniture flying. David sprang forward, but before he could reach them Dev Loughlin was bending down from his great height to hook hands in the collars of the two men and haul them up and apart, while Dr. Bastedo, who had followed him into the room, went straight to Helen.

"Well, well . . ." Dan croaked, fingering his throat. "I never thought the day would come when I'd be glad to see you." His smile at Dev was thin, furious.

"What the hell is going on here?" Dev asked, raking them with a hard glance.

Everybody began to talk at once, but it was Nieves, who had darted forward to clutch Dev's hand, who said: "Dan says Gramps is not her father—that Aunt Helen is her mother!"

At once, Dev's eyes went to Elizabeth and with one stride he was across to her chair.

"Somebody call the hospital," Louis Bastedo said from where he bent over Helen. "Tell them I want an ambulance—on the double!"

Hervey clutched at Louis's sleeve. "Hospital? Why the hospital? She has only fainted from the shock."

"But a nasty one," Louis answered soothingly. "I'd like her where I can do some tests . . ."

"Tests? What tests?"

"Just a checkup," Louis lied, still soothingly.

"She's stiff as a board," Mattie volunteered with relish. "That's no ordinary faint, if you ask me."

"Nobody did, Miss Arden," Louis said pleasantly, but in such a way as to make her flush and shrug sulkily.

"Ambulance on its way," David reported, hanging up the phone.

"I really cannot see . . ." began Hervey.

"But I can." Louis said, still pleasantly, and this time Hervey subsided. "I should like to know, though," Louis continued, "what it was that caused her to faint."

Dan laughed. It was exultant. "She saw a skeleton," he said. Louis turned to look at him. "I confronted her with her past," Dan felt constrained to explain.

Louis turned back to Helen, a thoughtful look on his face.

Hervey cleared his throat. "She seemed to"—he swallowed—"to—lose contact with reality," he finished evasively, still needful to protect. "Let me explain . . ." He took Louis's arm, walked him out of earshot, and proceeded to recount, in a low voice and with many a rancorous look at Dan, what had happened. Cass, who was nearest and straining her sharp ears, heard him murmur urgently: ". . . beyond these four walls, you understand? It is a matter . . ." His voice dropped again and she could hear no more.

Dev had dropped to his knees by Elizabeth. "It's all right," he said in a calm, easy voice. He turned his head. "Somebody pour her some brandy."

Cass leapt for the decanter. When she handed the glass to Elizabeth, it was Dev who took it, raised it to Elizabeth's mouth, and said, "Go on, drink." Obediently she did so. Mattie, who had been watching with great interest, murmured, *sotto voce*, but loud enough for Cass to hear, "What did I tell you." Nieves also heard, and she glanced quickly at Mattie and then, with stricken, dawning comprehension, back to where Dev had one arm around Elizabeth's shoulders, the other still holding the glass to her lips.

"Listen!" David cocked his head. "There's the ambulance." Its thin wail could be heard, nearing rapidly. "I'll go open the doors," he volunteered.

Nobody spoke as the stretcher was wheeled in at a run and Helen was lifted onto it and covered with a red blanket.

Hervey said, in a voice brooking no argument, "I shall accompany you," to Louis, who answered only with a polite "If you wish," before nodding round and following the stretcher out.

At the door Hervey paused, looked back at Cass. "I'll call you," he said.

Cass nodded dumbly, and Hervey shut the door behind him. Then she fell into a chair. "Jesus Christ!" she muttered in a voice that was almost a screech. "Somebody get *me* a drink!"

"Let's all have one," David agreed.

Dev rose to his feet. "Now, will someone please tell me what has been going on here?"

"We've been playing consequences," Dan answered sardonically.

"Cass?" Dev turned to her. But she downed the large brandy David handed her before launching into a concise exposition of the night's events.

Dev heard her out in silence. Only when she finished, and had handed her glass to David for a refill, did he ask, "The picture and the ring—may I see them?"

Mattie grabbed them from the table where they had been put aside in the confusion. Dev took them both to a lamp, examined them carefully in its light. Then he asked, "Did anyone try the ring on Helen's finger?"

Dan looked furious. It was the one thing he had forgotten. "Oh, come on," he ridiculed. "That won't wash! Too many other things have already come clean."

"Well, she's only gone to the hospital," Mattie said practically. "It can still be done."

"All right, let's leave that for now," Dev said. "Let's go back to 1946." He turned to Cass. "You were here then, weren't you?"

"Only just."

"So you can tell us."

"It's all a very long time ago . . ."

Dev gave her a look. "We all know about your memory, Cass."

She was not sure whether to be flattered or furious.

"Yes, come on, Cass," Mattie urged. "That trip to Europe . . . you must have been along."

"Yes. I was."

"Well, then."

Cass reached for the cigarettes. "I know nothing about either the portrait or the ring. The first time I set eyes on them was tonight."

"All right. Tell us about the rest."

Cass inhaled deeply. "I'd only been with Richard about three months when he decided on the trip to Europe. He wanted to buy up some bankrupt companies, bring them into the beginnings of the Organization. He took Helen along because he thought she needed the holiday. The intention was to leave her with her English relatives while we—he and I—went to the Continent." Pause. "Marion Keller came with us as Helen's companion."

"Just why *did* she have a companion?" Dev asked.

Cass did not answer at first, then, reluctantly: "Richard's explanation was that Helen was subject to irrational behavior at times; he said she was epileptic—*petit mal.* She would go off, sort of, like into a trance . . . something like the way she went tonight. He said he had been advised by her doctor never to leave her alone."

"Who was her doctor?"

"Old Doc Walters."

"Louis's predecessor?"

"Yes."

"What kind of irrational behavior?" Dev asked next.

"Well, she used to get very upset. Used to have screaming fits, throw things, refuse to eat, refuse to speak . . ."

"Often?"

Cass thought. "Well . . . looking back I think it was every few weeks or so. That was when she walked in her sleep."

"You saw her?"

"I met her, the first time I was working late. When I finally went up to bed I came across her wandering the corridors . . ."

"What did you do?"

"Took her back to Marion Keller."

"She was here then, when you came?"

"Yes."

"And what did she say?"

"Nothing much. Just that she would look after Helen." Another pause. "At that, Helen was kept pretty much—apart."

"What was Marion Keller like?"

"Tough. But charming with it. No-nonsense type. And Helen was very attached to her. She to Helen, come to that."

"So you all went on this trip to Europe," Dan interrupted impatiently.

"Yes. We sailed on the *Queen Mary*, and when we arrived at Southampton, I went on to London while Richard took Helen and Marion up to Kent, to Tempest Towers. He joined me in a couple of days. Then we flew to Germany. First Frankfurt, then Munich. It was while we were in Munich that he got the call from England and told me he had to fly back there. Helen had been acting very strangely, he said. He was gone about three days. When he came back I knew something was wrong. You know how he could be. Everything wrong, nothing right . . . Anyway, we went on to Berlin and then to Vienna. After about a week he got another call from England. This time he was gone a week. When he came back, he told me Helen had suffered a complete nervous breakdown." Cass ground out the stub of her cigarette, making dust. "I never saw her again for five years."

"Where was she?"

Cass reached for another cigarette. Her hands were unsteady. "I presumed some—mental home. He never said. He made it plain it was not a subject for discussion. And I was new then, so I never brought it up."

"Did he ever see her?"

"He always said he did. Every time he went to Europe he would go off for a few days and I always assumed it was to see her."

"But you never went with him?"

"No."

"Did he ever talk about her?"

"No. I got the impression that it—upset—him."

Dev's eyes were on Elizabeth, a steady, watchful, protective stare that made Cass glower sullenly, wiping her face clean when he turned to ask, "When did she return to Marlborough?"

Again Cass thought. "That would be in 1952 . . . yes. It was when I had a bad case of shingles. We had no hospital here then and I had to be taken to Nassau . . . When I came back, there was Helen."

"What was she like?"

"I didn't see her at first. She stayed in her suite. When she finally did come downstairs Richard warned us all not to be shocked by her appearance."

"Was it bad?"

Cass's voice was strained. "She was so thin . . . arms and legs like a stick insect. And they had cut off all her beautiful hair . . ." Tears dripped off her chin and Mattie dug into the pocket of her robe, handed across a tissue which Cass blew into fiercely. "And so damned pathetic. She flinched if you so much as threw her a look." Cass's voice rose, wrathfully: "And instead of Marion Keller she had an old bat of a nurse. A real gorgon! Seraphine hated her. But Richard insisted she be with Helen at all times. She even slept in the same room. He told us that he had only been allowed to bring Helen home on the understanding that she had a—a keeper." Cass reached for another cigarette. "He said she had tried to kill herself."

"What did Dr. Walters say?"

Cass's mouth curled. "Whatever Richard told him to say."

"Were no psychiatrists called in?"

"No. The only doctor who ever attended Helen was old Doc Walters—until he died and Louis Bastedo came."

"But Helen recovered, obviously."

"In time," Cass said. "For a long time she was apathetic, only left her suite to sit in the gardens or walk there—and always with the old bat."

"When did it start to change?"

Again Cass pondered. "Well . . . it was about the time Richard married Angela Danvers in 1957. He was going on a world trip—a combination honeymoon/Organization inspection—and would be away about three months. He suggested to Helen that she do something with Marlborough. Gave her *carte blanche*. She'd always been interested in furniture and things."

"And Helen agreed?"

"Like a shot. She took Marlborough to pieces and put it together again. It wasn't then like it is now, you know. What you see today is all due to Helen. God, there were some ugly bits and pieces then. She got rid of all the heavy Victoriana and Edwardiana and had the decorators in and all the paintings and the old fabrics cleaned by specialists. She really threw herself into it, and I remember it seemed to give her a new lease on life, too."

"Of course!" Dan laughed. "Richard was a crafty devil! He redirected her maternal instinct. How many times have we all heard Helen say, 'Marlborough is my baby'?"

Mattie's mouth formed an O.

"I'll bet he was making sure she wouldn't go around asking where her real baby was."

Watching Cass's face, Dev asked, "Is that what she did?"

Cass nodded. "When she first came back. She still walked in her sleep, but not like before. Before, she had just drifted around like a ghost . . . just—standing there sometimes. I think that was the *petit mal*. But afterward . . ." She drew fiercely on her cigarette. "She used to weep and moan,

wringing her hands. Scared me half to death the first time I saw her." Cass
shivered at the remembered shock. "I went up to her, asked what was the
matter, and she wrung her hands and looked at me so piteously . . ." Cass
swallowed hard. " 'I can't find my baby,' she said. 'They have taken away my
baby. Please, help me find my baby. She will be so upset . . .' Then the old
bat came tearing up and when I asked what was all this about a baby, she told
me it was none of my business but, when I threatened to tell Richard about
her rudeness, she said it was all part of Helen's illness. She'd been subject to
delusions, one of which was that she had a baby."

"You see!" Dan slapped his thigh. "It all fits perfectly."

But Dev was thinking again. "What proof was there that Helen was in a
mental home?" he asked abruptly.

"Only Richard's say-so."

"You handled all his finances. Did you ever pay any nursing home bills?"
Cass shook her head.

"Any sort of medical bills?"
Another shake.

"There you are!" Dan was triumphant again. "If Cass didn't pay it, then
there was nothing to pay. She handled all Richard's personal stuff . . . even
to the bills for the jewelry he bought Mattie!"

"I always assumed he paid them himself," Cass said, almost apologetically.
"The whole thing about Helen was under wraps; he just didn't want anyone
to know. When people did ask, he always said Helen was in a private sanato-
rium in Switzerland; that the doctors had recommended against her living in
a tropical climate."

"I'll bet he did!" Dan laughed jeeringly. "He didn't know where his sister
was, is my bet. And the time he spent 'visiting' her was in reality searching
for her! There are far too many coincidences here. Two people, the image of
each other, both missing five years of their lives—and exactly the same five
years. From 1946 to 1952—well, six years in Helen's case—but we have to
take her pregnancy into account. And that Marion Keller should figure in
both those lives is far too much of a coincidence. And another thing"—he
was warming to his theme—"who just 'happened' to be the Chairman of the
Trustees of Henrietta Fielding? That same Countess Tempest who was the
grieving mother of our own dear Rupert! How's *that* for a coincidence?"

"And she let her own granddaughter—complete with the Tempest foot—
live as a Foundling in a Home subsidized by her family? Come off it!" Cass
snorted.

"Oh, I asked Nanny Baines about that too. Nothing was known about any grandchild. Who would connect a child named Elizabeth Sheridan with Helen and Rupert Tempest?"

"You keep on pointing out the incredible resemblance!" Cass shot back.

"Now, yes! But then? A five-year-old? Just another child; one face among many—and probably not seen all that often. No, Marion Keller kept *that* secret to herself. Again, according to Nanny Baines, she was nobody's fool. She knew that if the Countess knew, Richard Tempest would find out and *that* was something she was determined he would *never* know."

Dan whirled on Elizabeth. "Did you ever meet Countess Tempest face to face?" he demanded insistently.

Elizabeth looked up at him. "No."

"There, see!"

"She only came to the Home once a year," Elizabeth went on, in a voice devoid of expression. "The only other time we saw her was in church."

"What better place to hide a child than in full view of everybody!" Dan trumpeted triumphantly. "She must have read *The Purloined Letter* . . . Nanny said Marion Keller was a highly educated woman."

"She went to Girton," Elizabeth said, still in the same toneless voice.

"I take it she is dead now," Dev said to Dan, contemplating him from thoughtful blue eyes. "Otherwise, you would be flourishing her at us too."

"She died in 1968," Dan said shortly.

"October 1968," Elizabeth amplified, still in the same mechanical voice.

"Were you at her funeral?" Dev asked quickly.

He felt her hand tighten on his; saw the shudder that ripped through her but did not leave her any less rigid. "No," she answered.

"Did you ever see her after you left the Home?"

"A few times. She kept in touch."

"But she never told you anything more about your mother?"

"No."

"I don't suppose you ever asked," Dan said scathingly.

"No," Elizabeth answered. "I didn't."

Something in her remoteness seemed to anger Dan. Snatching up the portrait from where Dev had laid it on the table, under the lamp, he went to thrust it in front of her face. "Look at this painting! Go on . . . take a good, hard look! Doesn't that face mean anything to you? It's your mother, for God's sake! Your *mother!* Nobody ever forgets their mother!" At the savagery in his voice Dev put out a hand and compelled Dan upward and backward, but Elizabeth had taken hold of the portrait with her free hand to regard it with a concentratedly intense stare that seemed to be straining for something.

"The colors . . ." she said, in a strange, now hesitant voice.

"What about them?" Dev put his other hand on her shoulder, pressed encouragingly.

"They remind me . . . other colors." He saw her grope after some elusive memory. "On a floor . . . a pool of them . . . I used to play with them."

"Where? When?" It was Dan.

Again she seemed to strain herself to the limit, then she slumped. "I can't remember."

"At the Home?" asked Dev.

"No." Her voice was firmer. "There was no stained glass at the Home." Her face changed. "It was a window, a big, square window, a ship . . . a galleon in full sail." They saw her squeeze her eyes shut in an effort to grasp total recall. Then she slumped, failing. "That's all I remember."

"Why can't you remember?" Dan asked furiously. "I can remember back to when I was a hell of a sight younger." He sounded as if he blamed her for it.

"I think it has to do with the . . . death of Elizabeth's mother," Dev said quietly.

"She's not dead—" began Dan angrily.

"We know that—now. But Elizabeth did not know it then."

"You mean . . . that was when Richard somehow got Helen back into his clutches again?" Cass asked slowly.

"Probably. We don't know what happened, but obviously Helen disappeared suddenly. How else could it be explained to the child except as a death?"

Cass caught her breath, only to hear Elizabeth say, in a voice unlike one Cass had ever heard from her, resembling the singsong of Helen's chant: "Perhaps that's why I can't stand cemeteries . . ."

Dev bent to look into her face. "Tell us," he said, his own voice making Nieves bite her lip and Cass clench her teeth.

"They . . . upset me, frighten me . . . I can't even walk down a street where there is a cemetery . . . I feel all panicky and can't seem to breathe, and my legs won't move . . ."

Remembered terror was in her voice, her face, her eyes. Cass stared aghast at this new, frighteningly strange Elizabeth; one who made her want to hold her close and say: There, there, it's all right, Cass is here. But she sat tight, said nothing. Dev had the controls. She saw that Elizabeth's hands were squeezing Dev's hard; she could see the bloodless skin flare against the tan of the rest of it.

As she watched, as through a microscope, she saw his press hers reassuringly. "If I so much as see a cemetery I feel it . . . something I can't control . . . and I have to get away before I make a fool of myself." Elizabeth's struggle with her voice was too much for her and she lost it. She closed her eyes, sat white-faced and trembling.

Cass was aghast. The very idea of Elizabeth Sheridan even feeling out of control was treasonable, unthinkable. But she could see it was no news to Dev. She felt her anger start to boil.

David, who had not said a word so far, only sat and listened, growing more and more amazed, said timidly, "Perhaps you went to your mother's funeral?"

"How the hell could she do that when her mother isn't dead?" Dan asked testily. "Helen is her mother!"

David scowled. "I'll believe that when Helen says so."

"For God's sake, what more do you want? I've given you chapter and verse and a damned good bibliography!"

"There is still a lot as yet unknown," Dev answered shortly. "Like where Helen lived during those five years."

"In the house with the stained-glass window, of course," Mattie answered promptly.

"Maybe—but where was that? And how come Marion Keller found out Helen was . . . no longer around, so as to take the child into the Home?" He shook his head. "We're still holding an awful lot of loose ends."

"So we get Helen to tie them up," Dan insisted.

"When?" David asked sourly.

"And there's another thing," Mattie interrupted. "Why would Richard claim Helen's daughter as his own?"

Nobody had that answer.

"There had to be a reason," insisted Mattie. "Find that and you find out everything else . . . you mark my words." She glared round defiantly.

"Oh, now, come on!" Dan said disbelievingly. "It's right up his street! He must be laughing his head off! He drives his sister round the bend, keeps tabs on her child being brought up in a Home, then makes that same child *his* heiress—without anyone knowing or even suspecting the truth. It bears his evil brand all the way through. You know how he loved tying you up in knots."

"Yes, and he also knew how you loved to wriggle out of them," Cass retorted, then caught her breath as she saw where that led to.

"So? Perhaps this was his last, final game . . . After all, what has he got to lose? He's dead."

"And we've come to a dead end," David said gloomily. "Well, until we can get Helen to open it up," he added hastily.

"That was no faint," Mattie put in, shaking her head and very definite. "She was stiff as a board. When you faint, you go all limp and heavy."

"Which is why Louis took her to the hospital," Dev answered absently. "Anything we want to know will have to go through him . . ."

"The hell it will! He's only a paid servant of this family!" Dan said angrily.

"He runs the hospital," Dev said, unmoved.

"And we run him!"

Dan stalked angrily back and forth in front of the fire. "Helen holds the answers and we've got to get them out of her!"

"*If* she remembers," Mattie murmured.

"Then we *make* her remember!"

"How?"

"There are ways . . ." He was irritable. "What about that truth drug, what's its name . . ."

"Sodium pentathol," Dev said.

"No, not that one." He clicked his fingers. "Scopolamine! That's it! A shot of that and everything comes out."

"You'll have to shoot Hervey first," Cass pointed out grimly. "Not to mention Louis Bastedo."

"He runs his hospital on *our* sufferance," Dan retorted. "We have to know," he insisted. "By whatever means we can use . . . That will must be proved to be a fraud."

"We don't know that," Cass denied. "Hervey would know."

"Hervey! His specialty is company law! We have to consult someone who specializes in probate."

"Over Hervey's dead body!"

"Over anyone's dead body!" Dan said, in such a way as to make them all look at him in horror. "You think, having come this far, I'll sit down and shut up?" Dan asked, derisively. "No way!"

"The only way is through Helen," Dev said, ending the discussion.

"Which means there is nothing more we can do tonight. In any case, Elizabeth has gone through enough already."

"I'll take her up . . ." Cass rose.

"No. I will," Dev said.

Cass sat down again with a thump, watched in burning impotence as Dev raised Elizabeth to her feet, moving like her spring had broken.

"You too," Dev said to Nieves, whose face, at being noticed once again, sprang to life even as she sprang to his side. "Take her other arm," Dev instructed, and obediently, because it was what he wanted, Nieves slipped her arm through Elizabeth's stiff one and between them they walked her gently from the room.

"Poor bitch!" Mattie said, without any sympathy at all.

Dan laughed. "Bitch is right . . . they're all bitches where that one is concerned."

Cass leapt from her chair, her open palm cracking across his face, the full force of her arm behind it. "You shut your mouth!" she snarled, gobbler red and dangerous.

Hand to his cheek, reddening fast, Dan first stared, then grinned evilly. "Well, well," he said softly. "So that's the way it is . . . I might have known."

Mattie watched with bright eyes, while David, as always the last to know, looked sick.

Cass's mouth trembled. "You don't know anything," she said, "anything at all . . ."

Then she made a run for it.

Nieves helped Dev up the stairs with Elizabeth, who walked between them like a zombie. In Elizabeth's bedroom, Dev said, "Thanks, love. I can manage now."

Biting her lip: "Are you sure?"

"Yes. You go along to bed. Go on," he repeated, as she hesitated. Seeing her desolate face: "I'll be along in a minute . . . when I've got her to bed."

"Oh . . . all right, then."

Elizabeth made no response as Dev undressed her. She had the glaze of shock. There was no light in her eyes; they were as dull as her movements and, when he had her at last in the bed, under the covers, stared upward, wide, fixed.

"My poor love," he said tenderly. Then again: "My poor love . . ."

She did not hear him. For a moment, he remained looking down at her, then with a decisive air left her lying there and went along the corridor to Helen's suite.

Seraphine opened the door. "Mister Dev." Her smile was warm.

"I need your help, Seraphine . . . You know what has happened here tonight?"

The smile vanished. "Yes."

"I want to talk to you about it. But right now, could you make one of your tisanes for Miss Elizabeth. She's in a state of shock—and there's more to come. I want her to have a good night's sleep."

Seraphine nodded. "Of course." Her eyes scrutinized his face, probed the blue eyes, registered their intensity and worry. "I will bring it to her," she said.

Dev's smile was wide with relief. "Thank you."

When Seraphine returned, they raised Elizabeth, and while Dev held her, Seraphine put the cup to Elizabeth's lips. "Drink," she said, in a crooning, massaging voice. "Drink . . ." Obediently Elizabeth drank the steaming, fragrant liquid, not conscious of what she was doing but obeying the voice, until the cup was empty.

"She will sleep," Seraphine said, satisfied. "For twelve hours at least."

"Good. That's what I wanted."

Gently, Dev laid Elizabeth back on her pillows, covered her. Her eyes were still open, but as he gazed he saw them flutter once, then close.

Seraphine stood, the empty cup in her hands. Her gaze was enigmatic, hooded, as it brooded on Elizabeth's face.

"You understand why I want to talk to you?" Dev asked.

She nodded. "Of course." She turned her unfathomable eyes to his. "I will wait for you," she said, bowed, and floated silently away.

Dev bent to put his mouth to Elizabeth's. She did not move. He smoothed back tendrils of silky hair.

"I'll be here in the morning," he said out loud, feeling his heart twist. She had been reduced, rendered more vulnerable than he could have wished. Her whole world had just fallen in on her. But wasn't that what he had wanted? The chance to help her rebuild on new foundations? He hoped to God his specifications were the right ones.

Nieves was on her knees in front of the candle-lit statue of the Virgin, wearing a nightie that was frilled to the ears and fell to her feet. She turned, smiled radiantly as she saw who it was, then turned back. He saw the rosary in her hands move once more, her eyes closed, her lips moving silently. He waited until she kissed it, crossed herself, then rose to her feet.

"Oh, Dev," she said, and it was a frightened wail, "it's all so horrible." She ran to him, burying her face in his, her hands clutching at him. "What is going to happen to us all?"

"Dan has set the wheels in motion," Dev said. "We are along for the ride, love."

Her eyes were wide and dark. "How he hates her," she said disbelievingly. Then beseechingly: "I didn't like her but I never hated her like that, honestly I didn't."

"Of course you didn't," Dev said. "You couldn't." He led her across to her four-poster bed, all frills and dotted swiss canopy. Climbing into it, she regarded him solemnly. "We must all help Aunt Helen, mustn't we?"

"Yes."

She moistened her lips. "And—and—Elizabeth too."

"Yes, her too."

"Is she—all right?"

"Yes. Sleeping."

Nieves shivered. "She looked horrible . . . all stiff and—and white."

"She has had a bad shock—they both have."

Nieves's eyes welled. "It was cruel, horrible . . . I hate him!" she said vehemently. "He's horrible and spiteful!" Piteously: "It's not true, is it? Gramps would not do such terrible things."

"That's what we have to find out," Dev said gently.

"He couldn't—not Gramps!"

But the desolation in her eyes said she knew he could. Had done.

"Oh, I'm so glad you are here . . . I couldn't have borne it if you hadn't been."

"Yes, I'm here." Gently he forced her down into the bed, drew up the covers.

"It will all come right, won't it, Dev? In the end, it will all come right?"

Her own foundations were clearly quaking.

"We'll do all we can to see that it does," he said, his voice soothing.

"I won't sleep," she warned, her face miserable. "How can I sleep? I can't stop thinking about it." Her hand clutched his. "Must you go? I feel better when you are with me."

"Yes, I must," Dev said, gently remorseless. "There are things to do." Then, seeing her desolation: "But not until you are asleep." His hand went to the lamp, switched it off.

"Hold my hand." It was a child's voice, frightened of the dark. She felt him take it. Her own curled inside his, feeling its warmth and comfort. "That's better." Her voice was content. He sat on, in the darkness, until the hand slackened, and its limpness and her breathing told him she was asleep, before stealthily withdrawing it, putting it under the covers. Then, quietly, he left her.

Seraphine had a tisane waiting for him too. It smelled of lemon and tasted indescribable, laid soothing hands on the tension at the back of his neck. "*Are* you a witch?" he asked, smiling crookedly.

The black eyes gleamed. "They say many things about me."

"But you always know whatever happens on this island."

Inscrutably. "I am *of* the Island."

"And how long at Marlborough?"

"I was fourteen when I was brought to sit by my lady's crib and watch her."

"And you have been watching ever since."

The tisane lifted the tension which had held him, easing the impact of the night's events, reducing them to a sensible size, easier to handle. But he drank a second cup before he told Seraphine all that had happened, she saying nothing, only holding his eyes, her own watchful, guarded.

Only when he had finished did she speak. "The portrait and the ring. I should like to see them."

He had retrieved them from the drawing room, now handed them over. Taking a pair of rimless spectacles from her apron pocket, Seraphine examined both at length. Then she sighed. "Yes . . ." Her head nodded as though in confirmation. "Yes."

Dev waited.

"She was different when she came back to me," Seraphine began, right where Dev wanted her to. "No longer a girl but a woman. But thin, frightened, with scars under her head and a body I saw at once had changed. Breasts fuller, larger, no longer pink-tipped and firm, but softer, with that sag that only comes after they have held milk. And she did not have her terrible monthly misery. Always she had been forced to spend days in bed, suffering terrible cramps. Old Dr. Walters had said the only thing that would cure it would be a child. So I gave her one of my tisanes, and while she was sleeping I examined her. There was no doubt. There had been a child. Before we had a doctor I delivered the babies. I knew."

"But did she?"

"No. She knew nothing. Did not even remember me, at first. She had to be told . . . so many things. And it was after she knew, that the dreams began."

"Dreams?"

"Every night, always the same one. She would walk in her sleep and search, weeping and wringing her hands, then stand, her head cocked as though listening. And when I went to her she would put a finger to her lips and say, 'Shh . . . can't you hear? My baby is crying for me . . . I must find my baby . . .'

"And she would not be satisfied until I helped her search. Night after night this went on. And in the morning she would remember nothing. When I asked her where she had been, what she had done, she could not tell me. Always the answer was the same: 'I don't remember,' and questions upset her. It was only in her sleep that I found out bits and pieces. That the baby was a girl, that she had long, blond hair, that she loved it desperately, needfully, and that it had been taken from her. But when I asked who had taken it she would look round fearfully and put her lips to my ear and whisper, 'Them,' but I could never get her to say who they were. And when I asked her who her baby's father was she would say only, 'It is *my* baby,' and weep again. And I had to be careful because *that woman* was always watching and listening; I knew she had been set to spy. She was not needed; I looked after my lady. There was nothing for her to do but listen and watch and report back to *him.* So I saw to it that she always had a tisane before she went to bed; that way she never heard my lady when she walked at night. And I took good care to keep the doors of the suite locked, so that there would be no danger of anyone else knowing I did that because one night my lady got downstairs and Miss Cass found her. But when she came to me, told me what my lady had said, I told her it was all part of her illness . . . That Mr. Richard had warned me of it."

"And had he?"

"Yes. He said the doctors had diagnosed her as schizophrenic; that the baby was a fantasy, the product of a world into which she had retreated when she was mad. So when he asked me, I told him she had walked once or twice, but that my tisanes always gave her sleep. And that satisfied him."

"Did you believe she was mad?"

Seraphine's face blazed into a beacon of scorn. "She was never mad! She was made to believe she was—something entirely different."

"What makes you think so?"

"Because the only doctor who ever saw her was old Dr. Walters—and he said what he was told to say. He was afraid for his nice, easy life, even more afraid of losing his drug supply."

"He was an addict!" Dev was shaken. This got worse.

"Morphine. My nephew Solomon was his houseboy. It was he who said my lady was mad when she got upset, behaved strangely. He who said she should be kept locked up—but only because he was told to say so."

"What was Mr. Richard's explanation for her absence?"

"That she had had to be put away for her own good. When I asked him if I could go and see her he said she was kept in seclusion, that visitors upset her . . . even him."

"How was he able to bring her back?"

"He said she had tried to do away with herself; thrown herself down a flight of stairs, fractured her skull. He said the accident left her—docile—but that she would always have to be watched. That was why she had that *woman* with her." Scornfully: "She was no nurse! She was his spy—his eyes and ears on us at all times . . ." Seraphine's smile was hooded. "But I fixed her. She loved my tisanes, so I saw to it that they were ones which made her sleep heavily at night . . . most of the day, too. I said I would administer the drugs she was supposed to give my lady—but I did not. I squirted them away. And then one night I gave her a tisane that made her seem as if she were drunk . . . and he found her so." The smile was faint but inimical. "He had to send her away."

"So you had full charge of your mistress?"

"Yes."

"He—allowed—that?" Dev asked delicately.

Seraphine's smile twisted contemptuously. "Oh, yes. He knew he had no choice."

Something in the impassive face kept Dev from asking why, but he thought he knew. Richard Tempest may have been 'king' of Tempest Cay, but Seraphine was its high priestess.

"And after old Dr. Walters died, the hospital was built and Dr. Bastedo came."

"That must have changed things," Dev said.

"Yes, he found out what really was wrong with my lady. He was shocked at her treatment and told Master Richard so in no uncertain terms. He said Dr. Walters had been old and out of touch. My lady was the very first patient in the new hospital and Dr. Bastedo did all sorts of tests. And he called in a specialist doctor from New York. He said she should be given a new, still-experimental kind of treatment—hormonal injections." Another smile. "And Mr. Richard had no course but to agree, since the doctor was a very famous, very eminent one. And Dr. Bastedo had called him in while Mr. Richard was away on one of his trips . . . Oh, he was so angry, but there was nothing he could do because it would have brought out the truth. Oh, he said he was shocked, that he had always trusted old Dr. Walters implicitly, that he had been the family physician for years and years. But he said Dr. Bastedo should have waited to consult him first."

"And what did Louis say to that?" Dev asked, eyes gleaming.

"That when someone was sick you did not wait to be told what to do; you did it. That he had been brought to the Island to act as its physician; that he had acted in that capacity in getting a second opinion on my lady. And that he had written up the case for a medical journal . . . no names."

"And did it work, this new treatment?"

"It was a miracle. Almost overnight my lady changed; no more tantrums, no more sleepwalking, no more moods. She had never been mad, Dr. Bastedo said. Never. It had been physical—a hormonal imbalance. He said it was something doctors were only just finding out, that Dr. Walters would not have known."

"Is she still under treatment?"

"Yes. But much less now—because of her age," Seraphine said. "Now she goes only once every six months to the hospital for a hormone implant."

"I see," said Dev, who now saw so much. Then: "Louis Bastedo knows about the child?"

"Yes."

Reading her face, her voice: "But Mr. Richard did not know he knew?"

"It was never discussed."

Thank God for Louis Bastedo, Dev thought. A man who always knew when to keep his mouth shut.

"You have no idea—even now—where Miss Helen was, all those years she was away?"

Seraphine shook her head. "None. She could not tell me. Only the child remained in her memory . . . always the child, because she had loved it." Silently they stared at each other and the monstrous thing that had been done to a woman they both loved.

"Does she still sleepwalk?"

"No. Not since she was cured. Nor does she dream." Seraphine sighed. "She is convinced it was all part of her illness . . . Dr. Bastedo explained to her what was wrong, but I think—inside herself—she was convinced that she *had* been mad. Tonight would be the most terrible shock; it would bring back all the terrible things she had forgotten."

"Brainwashed," Dev said quietly. But Seraphine heard.

"I think so. She did tell me they had put things on her head, things with wires."

"Shock treatment."

"I believe so . . . but not to help her recover her memory. To obliterate it."

"But why? Why should he do such a thing to his own sister?"

"Because he hated her."

"Hated her!"

"He was jealous."

Again, Dev could only repeat after her: "Jealous?"

Why should a man like Richard Tempest, who had it all, be jealous of a shy, withdrawn, gentle soul like his sister?

"Of the child," Seraphine said quietly.

Dev could only stare.

"He had none of his own," Seraphine reminded him gently. Her eyes, hard and bright, held Dev's implacably.

"Dear God," Dev said. He had to get up, to move. "He wanted the child?" He swung to face her. "An heir . . . of course! All he had were stepchildren." He walked a few paces one way, turned and repeated them the other way. "It fits! By God how it fits! He always knew where the child was but said nothing because there was always the chance he might have his own. His will is only three years old. He must have made it when he knew there *never* were going to be any of his." Dev took a deep breath. "And to be able to appropriate Helen's child, he had to make sure she had not even the faintest memory that she had ever had one." Dev shook his head. "It's right —but it's still not wholly right. Something's missing." He searched for it. "Why would he go to such lengths to ensure he could appropriate his sister's child as and when he needed to—wanted to . . ." His face changed.

Holding his eyes, Seraphine nodded. "He was sterile," she said.

Dev stopped his restless pacing and sat down again.

"Lady Eleanor told me. During her last illness, when she knew she was dying. She found it hard to rest comfortably so I used to massage her with oil I make myself. One day, when I had put her back to bed she took hold of my hands and made me swear a solemn oath that I would watch out for Miss Helen when she was dead. 'Promise me, Seraphine,' she said. 'Swear to me on my Bible.' She was so insistent that I swore, even though I knew I would go on doing what I had always done. And then she told me why. Years before, when Miss Helen was a small child, Lady Eleanor's cousin had come over from England with her children to spend the summer. They were of an age, but within a week of their arrival one by one they came down with mumps. And no sooner were they over it when Miss Helen caught it. None of them had it seriously, except Mr. Richard. When he took it he was very ill. He was fourteen . . . just coming into manhood. He recovered, but it left him sterile."

"How did they know?"

"It was not until years later. While Mr. Richard was up at Oxford there was a girl. She became pregnant and accused Mr. Richard of being the father. He swore that she had been with other men besides him. The girl had a rich and powerful family and so there were blood tests and other tests. That was when they found out. It was impossible for him to be the father—any child's father. It was all hushed up, of course . . . Rather than let it get out, Mr. Richard accepted the responsibility, but the girl had a miscarriage anyway, so there was no child. And after that—after he had seen every doctor who knew anything and none of them could do anything—he began to change. Lady Eleanor told me. She told me Mr. Richard blamed his sister. He had taken the disease from her, so it was all her fault . . . She had destroyed him as a man. There would be no heir, ever. Richard Tempest was the last male of the line." Seraphine paused. "Lady Eleanor told me she thought it had driven her son into a kind of madness. He never accused her, but Lady Eleanor knew her son . . . dearly though she loved him, she knew him. That was why she swore me to silence and protection. She said to me, 'Promise me she will never know . . . must never know. But you will . . . guard her, Seraphine, protect her from him . . . Never leave her at his mercy, never! I know him—and he has become a monster.' She wept, oh, how bitterly she wept. Never have I heard a woman weep like that."

There was a long silence. Finally: "So you knew, then, when Miss Elizabeth came, that she could not be Mr. Richard's child . . . Did it occur to you she might be Miss Helen's?"

"I knew she was." Seraphine was calm. "But how could I tell that to my lady? After all the terrible years, she had found peace . . . forgotten the fact that she had had a child. So I said nothing. I decided I would wait. And see."

Dev sat back in his chair, stunned. "Did Mr. Richard know that you knew?"

"No. Only the doctors—and they were in Europe. No one knew," Seraphine repeated. "It was not something he could stand anyone knowing."

"Miss Cass?"

"No. No one except his parents. And when they were dead, only himself." Seraphine smiled. "And myself."

And he dared not send you away, Dev thought. Richard Tempest held no fears for any man, but for this woman . . . He had heard the stories; that she was a witch, that she was skilled in healing; that long before Richard built the hospital, even though there was a doctor on the Island, it was to Seraphine the people went to. They said she could cast spells, could provide you with aphrodisiacs, with all sorts of medicines. Whatever she had given him tonight had totally relaxed all his tension. He felt clearheaded, calm. And whatever she had given Elizabeth had sent her into a deep and healing sleep. No, Richard Tempest would not dare send this woman away.

"Now my lady *must* know," Seraphine said emphatically. "Now the time is right for all to be made clear." Her imperious stare softened. "It will not be easy."

Dev sighed. "I know . . . but I don't want everyone to know about the sterility; not yet. Especially Dan Godfrey. That would really put him in the driver's seat." Dev moved restlessly. "Which is what I still don't understand.

Richard must have known Dan would not sit still under this kind of treatment . . . What he is, Richard made him."

"All of them," Seraphine said. "If only I had been able to accompany my lady to Europe. It was the first time she had gone anywhere without me. But I had an ulcerated leg . . . I knew I could heal it by my own herbal poultices but it took time and I could not walk. I am sure that is why Mr. Richard chose that time to take Miss Helen to Europe with him."

"Is that why he employed Marion Keller?"

Seraphine smiled. "She was supposed to wean my lady away from my influence, but she was a lady of good sense and knew better. And she did not trust him. She did not say so to me but I knew. And she was devoted to my lady; they liked each other, trusted each other. That was why I did not worry when they went off without me. I knew my lady was in good hands."

"Did Marion Keller never get some sort of message to you—to let you know what had happened, where Helen was?"

"No. I think she knew Mr. Richard would have me watched. It was too dangerous. And she was right. My lady's safety came first."

"Not even afterward—from the Home?"

"No. She would not dare. And I dared not go to Europe to search because he would have had me followed. My lady had to be safe."

"Did you believe she was safe?"

"I prayed that she was."

To what gods, Dev thought.

He frowned. "It's still not all of a piece. We know Elizabeth has no memory of her first five years—but how did he know? And he must. To have been sure enough to bring her here . . . set her down right under Helen's nose."

Seraphine said, "He had ways of knowing everything . . . That was why Marion Keller was so careful." She paused. "Miss Elizabeth remembers nothing?"

"Nothing—except for that moment downstairs, about the colors."

"That would be the shock," Seraphine said astutely. "That is the best time to probe further . . . when an opening has been made."

"Yes, but how do we get her to sit still under it? She has an iron will."

"She *had* an iron will," Seraphine corrected. "What we saw tonight was not the Miss Elizabeth who came here."

Dev sighed. "No . . . she was not." Thoughtfully, he scratched his jaw. "It's a risk, you know that."

"There is no other way."

Dev sighed heavily. "No . . . no other way."

"I will do whatever I can," Seraphine said, "to unite my lady with her child." Her eyes held his hypnotically. "Whatever," she repeated.

Dev nodded. "Thanks, Seraphine." He rose to his feet. "You have been of enormous help." He smiled. "I knew you would be."

TWELVE

Louis Bastedo was remembering. He was a thirty-eight-year-old New York Jew when, on coming off duty one night, after eighteen straight hours on the public wards at Bellevue, he had taken a dispirited look at the limp franks, the greasy beans, the dried-out hamburgers, and the wilted French fries, raised his world-weary brown eyes to heaven and demanded in outrage, "For *this* you chose me?" There had to be something better. There was. He found it in the back pages of the *AMA Review*. A small private island in the Bahamas wanted a doctor to run its brand-new hospital now being built. He had to be qualified in the disciplines of Medicine and Surgery; he had to be able to administrate; he had to be either English- or American-trained, possessed of no less than ten years' working experience in a major hospital. The salary made Louis reach for the sky, and there was even a house thrown in, with servants. He sat down and proceeded to compose a letter that would have them banging on his door.

After a week of nail-biting and no mail, he finally got a beautifully typed letter under a heading which made him utter a fervent "Oy vey!" signed by one C. van Dooren, bidding him present himself at the Tempest Building on Park Avenue at a certain time and date. He had his best suit cleaned, his dark, wavy hair cut, his Clark Gable mustache trimmed, and did as he was bid, turning up at the enormous, circular reception desk on the marble floor of the great glass tower, redolent of power and heady with the smell of money. A uniformed page took him to an express elevator which let him out fifty-one floors above the street into what he would have sworn was the concourse at Grand Central; any minute he expected to hear a sepulchral voice announce the departure of the Twentieth Century Limited for Paradise by way of the Elysian Fields. What he heard instead was the voice which had been described, in the issue of *Time* magazine which bore her face on the cover, as "cryptic, cutting and competent," and recognized at once the shaggy white chrysanthemum of hair, the pug-dog face, the pudgy, over-

weight body, even the dress—probably an old hand-me-down from Eleanor
Roosevelt—and knew he was in the presence of the right hand of God; more
to the point, by all accounts she held the keys to the pearly gates. So when
she proceeded to bone him, filleting him of every fact, he was glad he had
researched her, finally took his calculated risk by saying, as she precisely and
delicately laid bare the last fact, "Lady, you already know I'm circumcized
because that's my own medical report on your desk, along with what is no
doubt a libelous statement from my ex-wife, my bank statement, and straight
A's from the Chief of Staff at Bellevue, but if you want to count the hairs on
my head, I ought to warn you I'm on duty at six!"

The cornflower-blue eyes had widened, then narrowed. "No need," she'd
answered affably, "that's already been done."

He grinned. "I thought you might, seeing as how you are the C for Cass
van Dooren."

"There is another?"

"You mean I have to go through this again?"

That did it. He knew by the way she laughed that his gamble had come
off. And even though he did not get to see Richard Tempest that particular
day, he felt confident enough to surmise that his name would appear on the
very short list. It did. One week later he finally got to see the man himself,
who lived up to his legend. In the course of an hour's conversation, during
which not one direct question was asked—Cass van Dooren had done her job
well—he realized afterward, while sipping a restorative scotch on the rocks,
that he had been well and truly probed, down to those very hairs on his head.
It was no wonder Richard Tempest held the mortgage on the world. And me
a smart Jewish boy from the Bronx! he thought, discomfited.

The following Thursday he got a call from Cass van Dooren. Would he be
able to make it to Tempest Cay for the weekend? She was sorry for the short
notice and all that . . . He knew it was just another test.

"Lady," he told her gallantly but seriously, "to land this job I am prepared
to make even you . . ."

The bellow of laughter down the phone told him his luck was still holding.

But it was the Island which made him doubt that he, Louis Aaron Bastedo,
should be so lucky. It was not so much the (literally) out-of-this-world atmosphere, the private-bailiwick power, the marvelous climate, the tropical splendor; it was the hospital: shiny white, spanking new, and not only up to the
standard of any great teaching hospital but well beyond it. Richard Tempest
had spared no expense. As he explained, the Island was becoming industrial-
ized: the new fish-canning factory, the water desalinization plant, the electricity powerhouse, the new school—they would all need people, who got

sick, would need a doctor, perhaps even hospitalization. And all of it free. Louis was to recruit his own staff, and he deemed it not only politic but necessary to make it plain that a good fifty percent of them had to be of the Island. When Richard Tempest promptly and smilingly agreed, Louis knew his luck was still holding.

And when he entered Marlborough for the first time, he was quite positive that Somebody Up There did indeed like him. He had thought the Frick was a jewel; this house was Tiffany's—*and* Harry Winston's *and* Van Cleef and Arpels . . . And when he was introduced to a stunning blond lady, who played footsie with him under the table all during dinner and made it quite plain that she would be very interested in seeing his own jewels, his normally stickily retentive mind was by that time so befuddled that it was not until much later, getting his breath back in her gorgeous, silk-hung, emperor-size bed, that he managed to ask apologetically, "I'm sorry—but what was your name again?"

Now, seventeen years later, he sat tiredly at a table in his operating-the-ater-clean cafeteria, where the coffee was always good and always fresh, and reflected that she had changed that several times since. But he had changed too. So had his hospital. It was bigger, better, run by him with such precision and dedication that he could have staffed it with more doctors and nurses than patients, so many and regular were applications to be taken onto that staff. His Head Nurse he had filched from Columbia Medical Center, and his own scrub nurse had learned her trade at the great St. Thomas's in London. His interns were handpicked and he took the cream of the Island girls to be trained by his Columbia marvel. All in all, it had turned out to be a trip to Paradise, but it had its serpent. It had not taken him long to learn that the fairy-tale existence lived by the Tempest Family in their castle could have been, in reality, one of the grimmer little horror stories of the Brothers Grimm themselves.

Last night, he had no doubt that he had interrupted the telling of yet another one. Helen Tempest had been stiff as a board; in the grip of a hysteria that had blanked out her eyes and solidified her muscles. So he had injected sodium pentathol, spent most of the night with her, carefully drain-ing her mind of what had been festering there for years, thoughtfully taking notes which, after sedating her, he had carefully locked away with the rest of them in the file marked HELEN TEMPEST.

Then he had gone to catch up on his sleep, only to find he could not. What he had heard had left him wide awake and feeling sick. When he saw Dev Loughlin push through the swing doors, watched him sweep the room anxiously, smile with relief and come striding down the room toward him, Louis knew he had an epidemic on his hands.

"What kept you?" he asked.

Elizabeth awoke to a feeling of well-being and a sense of being wholly rested. She stretched until her muscles cracked and then, as memory surfaced, the events of the night before loomed up before her to obliterate everything else. She sat bolt upright, feeling her stomach drop sickeningly. The ring . . . the picture . . . Dan Godfrey's gloating voice . . . It all ran through her mind at high speed, pictures flashing by, voices shrill, rising until they became one high-pitched scream in her mind.

Oh, my God, she thought, looking at her hands and seeing the shake. Think . . . *think* . . . she commanded herself—putting a hand to her head, biting her fingers, clasping and unclasping her hands—and quite unable to.

She was sitting there, shocked and stupid, when the door opened.

"Good morning," Dev said. "How are you?"

The blue eyes were concerned, the smile warm as he came toward her.

"It is true, then." Her voice was slow, dull. That he should come here, now, confirmed it. "Last night . . . it did all happen?"

"Yes."

She put her hands up to her face. "Oh, my God."

"It's all right," he said, sitting down on the bed and putting his arms around her. "Hang on to me."

She did. She was trembling, though her body was still warm from sleep. And a lot else, he thought. The thaw has set in . . .

They sat in silence. It was obvious she was again in a state of shock, did not know what to say, was not able to say it anyway. When Loretta came in with a tray of coffee, set it down with a curious look from under downcast lashes before going out again, Dev poured a cup, hot, black, and sweetened it heavily. "Here . . . get this down you."

She gulped obediently, even though he knew she did not take sugar. Then she lay back, her eyes staring at nothing, but not the sightless stones they had been the night before. They were wide and fixed but alive. Dazed and incredulous, but a true mirror to her feelings. Oh, yes, he thought, exultant. The thaw *has* set in . . . But he had to rouse her.

"How about a shower?" he asked.

"What? Oh . . . yes."

She got up from the bed, did not even notice her nakedness as she walked into the bathroom. She was there a long time. When she did not come out,

Dev went in, found her standing under it, not doing anything, just letting the water run, her hair plastered to her head, her arms hanging, her eyes still staring. He turned off the shower, drew her out, wrapped her up in a sheet-sized towel, and led her back into the bedroom. There, he toweled her dry. She let him, standing obediently, letting him wrap it around her like a toga, waiting while he went to fetch a smaller one with which he toweled her hair. Then he took her hand, led her over to the triple-mirrored dressing table and sat her down before picking up a long-handled bristle brush. "I used to do this for my mother," he said, smiling at her in the mirror.

He put the brush to her temples, drew it straight back and down through the long, thick, damp hair. Carefully he lifted up tangles, brushed them out without dragging on them so as not to hurt her. When he had them all out, he once more swept the brush from temples to nape. Her head went up and back, going with the brush, and the face in the mirror was slack and dreamy, eyes closed.

"Nice?" he asked.

No answer, but the head came back even farther, so he paused for a moment to push her upright. "Don't stop," she said, making Dev do just that; freeze and feel the hairs on his own head rise stiffly. "You know that I love you to brush my hair, Mummy . . ." The voice was thin, piping, a child's voice, totally unlike her usual measured contralto. "Please . . . brush some more."

He did so, disciplining his hand.

"That's right . . . I love it when you brush my hair."

The eyes were still closed, the face dreamy, a little, satisfied smile on the lips.

"One hundred times, Mummy; are you counting?"

Dev did not dare answer, but brushed until his arm began to ache. When he stopped, she sighed once, deeply and dreamily. "That was lovely, Mummy . . . thank you."

She turned, raised her face, obviously for a kiss. Bending, he put his mouth to hers. But as she felt it she turned, bringing her body round to his, using the arms she slid around his neck to lift herself up against him. "I do love you, Mummy."

Again Dev did not answer, afraid his voice might break the spell. "You are supposed to say you love me," the childish voice reminded.

"I love you," Dev breathed, very softly.

Her eyes flew open. For seconds they gazed, terrified, into his and then she stiffened, made to thrust him away, and sagged, the eyes rolling up until all he saw were whites, as she slumped against him. Picking her up he carried her to the bed, laid her down. She was colorless, limp, but when he put a hand over her heart it was strong, if fast.

When she opened her eyes they were blurred, unfocused, as they had been that night on the beach, and as they had done then they cleared, saw him, registered him, and she said in a sharp voice, "What are you doing here?"

She realized she was lying on, not in the bed; that she was wrapped in a towel, which had come loose. Her face flamed and she rolled away from him and off the other side, wrapping the towel tightly about her. "What happened?"

He told her. The flush drained. "But I hate having my hair touched," she said in a strained, terrified voice.

"Now you do," Dev said.

"What—" she moistened dry lips. "What did I do?"

"You melted . . . went all soft and loose. Having their hair brushed does that to some people."

She squeezed her eyes tight shut. "Oh, God . . ." It was jolted from her.

"You had a bad shock last night—and it hit you again this morning. I think," he went on carefully, "that hating anyone to touch your hair was a form of protection against certain memories."

She turned her back on him. "No more parlor psychiatry, please!" It came from clenched teeth.

"No," Dev agreed. "From now on it has to be done properly."

She whirled on him. "Properly!"

He got up from the bed, walked toward her. She retreated. "I mean that we have to get at the rest of your memory through the proper channels. It is there; we know it is there. You have just proved it."

She put her hands to her head, squeezing it as though those memories could ooze out like toothpaste.

"It's the only way," Dev pressed, "if we are to get at the truth." He paused. "You remember last night?"

"Of course I remember last night!"

"Then think about what it all means . . ."

"I know what it means!" And sounded as if it terrified her.

"It means," Dev went on deliberately, "that what I said I thought you were is all true . . ."

"No," she denied, hands to her head. "No . . ."

"Yes." Once more he pressed relentlessly. "You are not what you thought you were. Your mother is not dead. She is Helen Tempest . . ."

"No!" Her voice rose. "No!" It was a stifled scream. He saw her sway and one stride had her in his arms.

"Don't fight it!" he urged. "Accept it . . . it *is* the truth."

She was shaking convulsively, teeth chattering. Dev wrapped his arms around her tightly, opening his jacket so that she could feel the warmth of his body. Her own arms slid beneath it and around him and she held on tight, as if for dear life.

"Accept it," he said again. "Helen Tempest is your mother, the mother you lost and somehow believed had abandoned and rejected you." He felt her stiffen. "Yes, you did . . . your child's mind could not accept anything else. One moment she was there and the next she was gone, leaving you alone."

"My mother is dead!"

"No . . . I think perhaps you were *told* she was, to stop your continuously asking for her . . . I think," he went on, very carefully, "that your fear of cemeteries stems from this . . . that perhaps you were taken to one."

"No . . . no . . ." Her voice was anguished.

"And shown a grave, perhaps . . ."

"No!" It was a howl. She beat against him with her fists and then burst into rending sobs. Picking her up again he once more went back to the bed and sat down on it, holding her on his knees, his arms around her, letting her cry. They came from the depths of her; her whole body convulsing under their strength and force. She cried for a long, long time, until all she was capable of were dry heaves, shuddering gasps of breath. Finally she lay against him, spent.

"Good girl," Dev said tenderly.

"I never cry . . . never," she said dully.

"No . . . that's why."

She blew her nose soundly on the handkerchief he gave her.

"Stiff upper lips have a habit of cracking," he observed with a smile.

"I seem to be cracking up."

"That's what happens when statues fall from pedestals."

Her head came up at that, only to meet and feel the warmth of the blue eyes, matched by the smile. For a moment she searched them, then managed a watery smile. "And you want to help me put the pieces together again."

"Venus de Milo *plus* arms," Dev answered gravely. She chuckled, and her glance from under her wet lashes was touchingly, oddly shy. "We are of a size . . ."

Dev laughed. "That's better," he said, hugging her.

Sounding surprised: "I feel better . . ."

"I told you. Better out than in."

She blew her nose again, then made a business of tucking the handkerchief back in his pocket, conscious of their position; her naked body under the towel, her perch on his lap, his arms around her. The marble whiteness, already tinged with pink, turned rosy red. She stared stiffly and fixedly at the top button of his shirt.

"Come over here," Dev said firmly, lifting her off his lap and rising to his feet, taking hold of a hand and drawing her over to the mirrored door of the dressing room, making her face herself, standing behind her, his hands on her shoulders.

"God . . . what a mess." She winced at the tangled hair, the blotched face, the rucked towel.

"That," Dev said, "is where you first went wrong. That's what threw me, when we first met . . . that a woman who looked like you couldn't handle a man's open admiration of it, until I realized that, to you, there wasn't anything to admire." He put his hands on either side of her head so that she had no choice but to look forward, straight at herself. "Take a good look," he said. "At a stunningly beautiful woman . . . red nose, puffy eyes, and all, you still take the breath away . . . *my* breath away. You—are—gorgeous—" he said with absolute authority. Then with a grin: "Take it from one who knows."

She stared at herself. "Am I?" It was doubtful, refuting.

"You are. No wonder the camera loves you." He paused. "But *you* never did, did you?"

She was silent. It was his answer.

"The Chinese have a proverb: 'He who would love must first love himself.' Whoever said that knew human nature. If we cannot love ourselves we can't believe that anyone else could love us. And that, my love, is where you put your first foot wrong . . . You took your mother's disappearance as rejection. But you had to find a reason for that rejection. And the only one your five-year-old mind could come up with was that she had not loved you enough, which finally got turned into never having loved you at all. That became an unshakable conviction that you were unlovable . . . which ended up staring into the mirror of self-hate."

She was staring at him. "What makes you so knowledgeable all of a sudden?" She sounded angry now.

"Not all of a sudden. I've been through the library downstairs for every book I could find on psychology; I've picked Louis Bastedo's brains and I called a psychiatrist friend of mine in Dublin. I spent last night thinking about you and only you . . . in fact, I have thought of little else since I met you." He turned her to face him. "I have spent more hours with only thoughts of you for company than I ever have of any woman . . ."

She shook her head.

"And I will get you to believe that, if I have to spend the rest of my life trying!" He sighed. "All right, so you still don't believe it, even now, but you will. And when you do—you are cured."

"Another case, Dr. Freud," she said bitterly.

"No. Dev Loughlin. Take a good look . . . go on."

"I know who you are," she answered quietly.

"Do you? I wonder . . . I think that what you really want to know is what I want with you?"

The sudden flare of her eyes told him he was right. He turned her round to face the mirror again. "There is your answer."

"But you said I was not how I looked," she reminded him triumphantly.

"No—but it was how you looked that got me into this state over you in the first place. And by the time I had found out the difference it was too late— and it didn't matter anyway."

He saw her eyes, frankly incredulous, do a wondering examination of herself.

"But I am so large," she said, "and I have a webbed foot . . ." Her eyes flicked at it and away.

Dev held her eyes in the mirror. "What law says that only small is beautiful? I am large . . . we are a fit, you and I. Yes, you are tall; yes, you are large, but splendidly so . . . you have a magnificent body." His eyes swept over it deliberately in such a way that she arched. "And so what if you have a webbed foot? That is what makes you a marvelous swimmer." He saw a smile flicker. "If you are not beautiful, why did they make you into a model?"

"In the swinging sixties anything went . . ."

"I refuse to believe you are the only model who is six feet tall."

Reluctantly: "No . . ."

"Well, then?" He shook her slightly. "You are beautiful. Believe it. I told you, didn't I—truth between us?"

Flushing slightly, she nodded.

"Then why won't you believe that I *am* telling you the truth? *Really,* look at yourself."

Once more he turned her to face him, tilting her chin with a strong hand that forced her to look into his eyes. "See yourself in *me* . . ." She could see her tiny reflection—and more. So much more. Wonderingly, held by those eyes, she stared up into them, drawn into them, as she had been from the first time she looked into them that day on the beach, when they had seen so deeply into her, into parts of herself she had kept covered for so long. Somehow they had begun her exposure to life itself.

"You *are* beautiful," he said, "you *are* lovable—and not just because of your beauty. You are all shot to hell emotionally—but there is a marvelous woman in there—hiding—and I want to help you set her free."

He saw her swallow. "How?"

"There is a way."

He walked her back to the bed, sat her down again, keeping his arm around her. "I went to see Louis Bastedo this morning." He felt her buck. "He knows all about you. I told him. I needed his help—asked him for it, on behalf of us both. We have to get at your lost five years—just as your mother has to recover hers."

"My mother," she repeated, testing.

"Yes, your *mother*. Because she is your mother . . . all that Dan Godfrey said last night is true. What we have to do now is bring you together by merging those lost years."

Uneasily: "How long would that take?"

"We don't have time for years of therapy. Dan Godfrey won't wait that long. We have to solve the mystery soon—but not only for his sake. For yours and for Helen's."

"How?" she asked again.

"Hypnosis."

This time she heaved herself off and away in an outraged, instinctive lunge. "No! Never!"

"It's the only way."

"Don't tell me Louis is a psychotherapist too!"

"No, he is not. But he is a jack-of-all-trades; on this island he has had to be. He is a very fine doctor, a first-class surgeon—and a totally unbiased and unprejudiced man."

"Never! Never!" Her voice was strident. "I will never allow my mind to be rifled by anyone!"

"That," Dev said forcefully, "is not the object of the exercise." He rose, took hold of her in a grip that held her fast. "Louis will not put you under and make you do stupid and embarrassing things. He is a doctor, not a puppetmaster. It is not like that, as he will explain to you when you see him."

"No! I won't!"

Well, Dev thought, I will have to go for broke . . . "Not even for your mother?" he asked in a cold, hard voice. He saw her flinch. She was wringing her hands, twisting and massaging them as though they were sore.

"Has it not yet sunk in? That woman in the hospital is your *mother*. Helen Tempest was the woman who used to brush your hair, the one you called 'Mummy'; the one you lived with, loved so desperately, grieved for so destructively . . ."

Her hands had gone to her head again, covering her ears. She was bent, as though under blows. "No . . . no . . ."

"Don't you want her to be your mother? Are you afraid of the fact? For a moment, think of *her*. If she, right now, at this moment, knew of you, do you think she would be afraid to accept *you?* Losing you did for her too, you know. You're not the only one in all this." He was being brutal, could see his words hitting her like blows, but he would bring her in out of the cold if it was the last thing he ever did.

"I can't," she moaned. "I can't."

"Why can't you?"

He could see her struggling with herself, both prosecutor and defender; willed her to come out with the truth. "Because I am afraid . . ."

"Of course you are afraid," he soothed, drifting toward her slowly. "But I'll be with you. You are not alone in this. We all want to help you . . . I know it's difficult for you to accept help; you feel it's an admission of failure . . . that obsessive desire of yours to be perfect goes back to your belief in an unlovable self; if you could not be loved you would be beyond its need." Before she could move he had her fast again, wrapping himself around her, all warmth and strength and confidence. "Every step of the way I will be beside you, holding your hand, whatever will help. I *want* to help you."

She was silent, but he could tell that she was at the end of her emotional tether by the feel of her body, all stiffness gone, sagging in a kind of defeat that thickened his voice when he said, "Will you at least talk to Louis? Let him explain. Not that it's complicated. It really is the simplest of things . . ."

He felt her heave a deep breath, and on it say wearily, "All right."

He was careful to release his own sigh of relief silently.

"Then let's get you dressed. He is waiting downstairs."

"I don't know about you, but I talk better on my feet," Louis said amiably, his sleepy brown eyes smiling at her. "Shall we take a walk?"

She studied him for a moment before smiling minimally. "All right."

She sounded calm, was giving a masterly display of indifference, but there was a tiny vibrato in her voice. And giving her the professional scan, his experienced, consulting-room eyes remarked other, subtle changes. Like the fact that there was a dull sheen to what had formerly been an icy glitter; that there were gaps in the invisible force field. Doubt had set in. And she held herself stiffly, with the rigid stance of someone struggling to support a mass that was breaking up. Pride, he thought. To hell and gone. Probably never asked for help in her life and finding it unbelievably hard to ask now. Some people just never learned how. Or were self-defeatingly convinced no one would ever want to. That he would have to find out for himself. He had already discovered what he could from other people. Dev had quickly explained, as they waited for her to dress, what had happened that morning. So, Louis thought clinically, she probably did think she was breaking up. That, coming on top of last night's reading of the book of revelations, was enough to be going on with. And now he had to convince her to undergo hypnosis. Well, he thought. By common consent she is a lady who never takes the bull by anything else but its horns . . .

They were walking, ambling, Elizabeth suiting her pace to Louis's slow, aimless stroll, in the direction of the rose garden, and as they descended the flight of shallow steps that led to it—Louis letting her go first and admiring from behind the swivel of hips that moved as if on ball bearings—he paused by a bush laden with saucer-sized blooms the color of clotted cream.

"Lovely bush," he observed, reaching forward to snap off a luxuriant blossom, "though I was never one to beat about *them.*" He handed her the flower. "But you can still profit from this one." She took it, her smile not reaching her eyes, bent her head to inhale its fragrance, taking a deep breath, on which she then said, "All right. What do you want to know?"

"Supposing you tell me how you feel about this. I don't mean last night, I mean everything. The whole shebang."

"I didn't. Not in the sense of actually feeling—except in control."

"Of things, or yourself?"

"Both."

"And now?"

They walked on in silence until she said, hesitantly, groping for the right words, "Open . . . wide open . . . like somebody had opened a door, letting in a light that—magnifies everything." Another silence. "I used to—see things from a long way off, like through the wrong end of a telescope. They were there, but far away; too far away to make any impact when they reached me. It was a feeling of—detachment . . . a sort of inability to become involved, to feel . . . touched . . . by anything."

"And now they are trampling all over you?"

A nod, then: "Yes."

"Well, you had something of a shock last night."

"Yes, but . . ."

"What?"

"Well . . . what I learned from Hervey Grahame was surprising, to say the least, but I wasn't shocked." She stopped, faced him. "If not shocked on learning who my father was"—again the slight hesitation—"why should I be so shocked on learning who my mother is?"

"Because you never had a father—to remember, that is. But you did have a mother. And her you remembered—even if unconsciously. The mind never forgets *anything*. It just buries some things deep in the files. Think of last night as someone bringing those files out of the basement."

She began to walk on, slowly, now fitting her stride to her thoughts. "Did —do you know what happened this morning?"

"Yes."

"How do you account for that?"

"Another old file. From the way Dev described it, having your hair brushed was something of a special thing between you and your mother. You loved having it done, she loved doing it. Perhaps she did it every night before you went to bed; perhaps when she dressed you in the morning. Whenever, wherever, it was obviously a form of physical contact that was both deeply felt and meant. One that would always—no matter who did it—bring your mother back to you. You had five years with her, remember—the most important five years of any life. Who was it said, 'Give me a child until he is seven and he is mine for life'?"

"St. Ignatius Loyola."

"He was dead right. It is during those first five years that we learn fastest and most; especially about love."

"Was that why I always hated having my hair touched?"

Carefully putting his feet in the footprints Dev had left, and grateful for them: "I think we can safely say yes. A protective barrier set up by the mind."

She was studying the ground, as if, should she not look exactly where she was going, she would fall.

"Would that—does that mean I was—damaged emotionally—by losing my mother?"

"It is not unknown." Louis, too, trod carefully. "Analysts' offices are full of people searching for the love they lost when they lost their mothers."

"But I have never done that." She was quick, definite.

"That's because the other half, having been, as they thought, rejected, they themselves reject to prevent rejection ever happening again. Sounds complicated," he added apologetically, "but human beings are, you know. And so is love," he amplified.

They walked on in silence. Finally: "I have never been able to do that. Love, I mean." Her voice was devoid of expression.

"Our minds dictate our actions. We don't, even now, knowing so much, fully understand the terrifying power of the human mind. We don't even use our brains to their fullest extent, only certain parts, and even then not at full stretch. But we do know that unconscious motivation is what *really* moves us."

"You mean that even though we do a thing for one reason, it is often for another?"

"On the nail again." She wielded, he thought, a very accurate hammer.

"So we are not necessarily what we think we are?"

"Usually not."

Again they walked on in silence for a while. "What you are saying is that we don't—even though we may think we are quite sure—really know what we are doing or why we are doing it. And that under hypnosis the real me will surface."

"I would not go so far as to say *that* . . . but what you *were* might. Like I said, the mind never forgets anything. The five years you don't remember are still there, like a photograph on a negative is still there."

"But memories can be erased."

Louis thought of Helen. "Yes. Brains can be washed like anything else."

"And is that what you want to do with me?"

"God forbid!" Louis stopped short. "Hypnosis is a release—rolling away the stone at the mouth of the cave, if you like, allowing memories to come forth. But once they do, that does not mean they will evaporate in the light of day."

He could see she was unconvinced.

"Let me explain it to you," he said, taking her arm. Louis was a great believer in bodily contact; it told as much as any temperature chart. "It is not the hocus-pocus of the nightclub act. People will not do anything which conflicts with their conscious beliefs. What it does is sharpen the memory, enable it to bypass the critical censor—a sort of mental guardian angel. It prevents buried feelings and memories from overwhelming us; it sifts and filters, then either rejects or allows through. All we do under hypnosis is give the angel a Mickey Finn; while it is out, the memories can tiptoe past."

"I would not be unconscious then?"

"No. Let me explain exactly what would happen."

Back at the house Cass was in high dudgeon. "You had no right to elect yourself president of this or any other fan club," she said furiously to Dev. "You have taken far too much unto yourself! And picked the wrong starring vehicle. Elizabeth Sheridan is the last person in the world to allow herself out of her own control."

"Not if she wants to get at the truth about herself."

"And we all want to get at *that,*" Mattie added.

"You mean you do! And we know why, don't we?" Cass swept them all—David, Nieves, and Hervey, who had returned from the hospital unaccustomedly wilted—with a thousand-watt glare. "All of a sudden everybody is putting an oar in and the only place we'll go is round in circles. As co-executors, it is Hervey and little old me who have the say-so. We steer this boat, and don't any of you forget it!"

"Elizabeth *is* the boat," Dev said.

"Dev is right," Hervey said, very subdued. "It is Elizabeth and Helen who count in all this."

"And we have been appointed to look out for them. You stick to Helen and leave Elizabeth to me!"

"You hope," Mattie murmured.

"Are you saying that you do not wish to attempt to get at the truth?" Dev asked.

"I'm saying no such thing! What I am saying is that some people seem to think they have the divine right to get at it."

"Oh, now, Cass . . ." Mattie, thoroughly enjoying this, looked shocked. "Dev is only trying to help. We all want to know the truth of this thing."

"And we all know why *you* do, don't we? So you can put Richard back on his pedestal. It would suit you just fine to prove he was not the father of a daughter by some other woman! Then you'd still be number one, wouldn't you? Have him all to yourself?"

Mattie's creamy complacency curdled. "Just as we all know who you would like all to yourself. You can't see any other color but green for jealousy—but at that it makes a change from black and white!"

"Listen who's talking!" Cass reared up on her hind legs. "You couldn't stand to think of the fact that she was Richard's daughter! That it was to some other woman's child he left his all! Don't you talk to *me* about jealousy!"

"It's always the same with you. *You* have to run things, own things, boss people around and tell them what to do. It's you who have appropriated the divine right!"

Cass's hand met Mattie's cheek in a brisk crack.

"Cass!" Hervey sounded more like himself. "You astonish me, you really do! What has come over you?"

"What has come over *me?* You can't talk either! When it comes to jealousy you're as green as any of us! You can't stand to think that Helen Tempest—the pure, the saintly, the *virginal* Helen Tempest—had another man's child out of wedlock!"

Hervey went up in flames. "How dare you! *How—dare—you!* I warned you once before not to sully Helen Tempest in my presence! Look to your own shortcomings before you complain of everyone else's! Mattie has the truth of it. I too have eyes. I have seen the way you—"

"Hervey!" Dev's voice was quiet but it cut Hervey's off in midsentence.

Dan, who had just sidled through the door, only to stand and listen pleasurably, was quite disappointed. Things were really taking off. Everybody making for their own plane and jettisoning everything except their own self-interest. But he saw Hervey's self-possession gain command again, heard him say stiffly, "I apologize. I am paying no heed to my own words. I will only repeat that this is no time for personal animosities. We have enough to contend with . . ."

Dan laughed, sauntered forward. "Dear me, right for once, Hervey. I do seem to have opened a very moldy can of beans. How the truth will out when it has nowhere else to go! Of course Mattie wants to rehabilitate Richard. Of course Cass wants to run everything—into the ground if need be; of course Hervey wants Helen to remain whiter than white—even if it only means another coat of whitewash. And as for you"—this with a vicious snarl at Dev—"you've got your eye on all that lovely money. Straighten this out and your financial worries are over! Well, for once I don't mind your I-am-the-great interference because it suits me too. Let's get down to this business of dredging up the past—and right now. Time's a-wasting!"

"Heaven forfend." It was Louis, sauntering into the room, Elizabeth, looking subdued and apprehensive, by his side.

"Well?" demanded Dan eagerly.

"Fine," Louis answered easily.

But Elizabeth was looking at Dev, as he was looking at her. Everybody held their breath. Nothing was being said, but everything was being understood. David felt himself dwindling away to nothingness while Cass had to bite her lip on a despairing sob.

"I'll do it," Elizabeth said quietly.

Bedlam. But David could only stand and stare at Dev. How did he do it? In God's name, how *did* he do it? He never failed. He only had to walk into a room and every woman was his. Where do I go wrong? Everywhere, he flagellated madly. He told you so, didn't he? He warned you about putting women on pedestals. He told you it was because you were terrified to death of a living, breathing, demanding woman with needs and a mind of her own. That you preferred the fantasy; always worshiped the unattainable ones *be-*

cause they were unattainable—and therefore safe. Out of reach and therefore touch. Easier to dream than risk the reality. That way you could worship without worry. Which was why you could never bring yourself to believe Inés . . . why you were so ready to accept Richard's version. It all comes back to your own self-doubt. Too unassertive, too diffident, too insecure . . . too shit-scared. But how can you acquire confidence when all life hands you is failure? He drained the glass of self-pity. The only thing you have ever suc- ceeded at is failure. Oh, yes. At that you are World and Olympic Champion. At the rest . . . He turned abruptly. He needed a drink.

Cass watched him head for his crutch. She felt crippled herself. She had lost. She knew it. It had all been there, in that look . . . Dully she followed David, understanding now, more clearly than she ever had, why he went where he did.

Mattie's pride was purring under a self-massage of triumph. Now they would see. Now they would find the absolute in proof that Richard had not fathered Elizabeth Sheridan. Why he had made her his heiress could be dealt with later. Probably because she was a Tempest. Of course . . . He had always been fanatically proud to be one. But all that mattered now was that she, Mattie Arden, would still occupy the number-one spot. Not rejected, not cast aside in favor of some other woman's bastard . . . A winner, not a loser.

Dan felt smugly self-satisfied. How he would enjoy seeing that frozen bitch reduced to a soggy puddle! Thought she was too good, did she? Arrogant cow. Who would have thought that in his search for something to topple her from that self-appointed perch he would find it in her very self. Now she would get hers. And he would get his. All that lovely, lovely money, the only thing worth having. *Then* he would be unassailable. *Then* they would not dare snigger behind his back: "Dan Godfrey, you know . . . Angela God- frey's son . . . but by whom is anybody's guess." He burned with the old shame, a feeling he had lived with every day of his young life when the other boys at school would inevitably taunt and jeer: "Your mother is a whore!"

"Liar!"

"Yes she is! My mother says she is! She says she's anybody's if the price is right!"

And there would be another fight. Totally out of control, he would unleash all his shame and anguish in violence, inflicting such damage that once again his mother would be requested to remove him. And he would go on to another school, where the same thing would happen again. No matter where he went, he took her reputation with him. The world in which she moved was small and tight; everyone knew everyone else, and the rich kids, mostly blasé and bored with stepfathers who changed with the seasons, nevertheless

still had the benefit of clergy. His mother was only kept by the men who paid
his school fees. And wherever he went, the gossip had got there first.

Time and again he had pleaded with her not to leave him in school, to take
him with her, but she had always been in the keeping of some man who did
not want a teenage boy on his hands.

"I can't, darling." The sweet smile that struck him as false; the faked
regret, the impatience on the lovely face.

"But *why* can't you?"

"Because, darling . . ."

"You don't love me, that's why! You only love yourself and what you can
get out of the men who pay to love you!"

And the rouged mouth would tremble and the big blue eyes fill with tears
and he would feel revenged, refuse to let her embrace or kiss him. She would
go off with her shoulders bowed, but it was always to get into some rich
man's car or plane.

Until she had married Richard Tempest. She had brought *him* to the
military academy where Dan had been at the time, the only place able to
discipline his ungovernable temper. She had turned up at Commencement
on the arm of this big, golden man, looking all fluttery and adoring and smug.
Had seen the looks, heard the whispers. "You know . . . 'King' Tempest
. . . they say he has more money than *anybody*. She's his latest . . . Wonder how long *that* will last." But it had. The big, golden man had actually
married her. Dan had been puzzled, uneasy. None of the others had gone
that far. But this man was different. He emanated a sense of power that
awed. The first time Dan had looked into eyes as green and brilliant as a
lion's, he had felt a chill of fear. And the voice, soft yet vibrant, made him
shiver. They had seemed to know exactly who and what he was—and why.
He had been removed from the academy and sent to Le Rosey, where many
of the boarders were the sons of mothers who passed, as in a game, from
hand to hand.

But he had gone to Tempest Cay for holidays and that had been a revelation. He had not dreamed there could be such luxury, so much endless
money. Or two stepsiblings: David Boscombe, a hulking, overweight twenty-
five-year-old with artistic pretensions, and his sister, a promiscuous slut who
had already had two husbands, and, setting eyes on the beautiful sixteen-year-
old adolescent, had proceeded to initiate him into the world of sex, teaching
him things he learned with rapidity and ease, which at first amused then
alarmed her as he caught up then passed her in depravity and perversion, so
that she came to both fear and hate him. Especially when he caught her in
bed with their stepfather.

He had known, then, once and for all, that all women were whores. They could all be bought. And there and then he made Margery his first victim.

He had stalked her, installed, with his mechanical bent, hidden cameras and tape recorders in the little beach house where she took her lovers; examined and evaluated the evidence and charged accordingly. She was a sex addict. Unless she had her daily workout she grew snappy. So he made her pay for the privilege.

The sort of things she did for kicks were something else, even in the set she traveled with. It was from her that he first learned of the secret and private world of swinging. He had pictures of her in combos, daisy chains, lesbian encounters—and worse. She was insatiable, quite capable of taking on two men at once and exhausting them both.

She had provided the basis of what was to become a sizable—but never big enough—bank account, all neatly squirreled away in a bank in Zürich. And once he grew old enough to enter, as an adult, the world where Richard Tempest ruled, filled with rich, bored, often desperately lonely women, he made them his prey, gaining not only a fortune but his revenge on a mother and a stepsister who had both betrayed him. In his turn, he used and betrayed every woman he could seduce.

When the plane in which his mother was flying to Europe for her third face-lift had flown into a mountain, he thought only: "Good riddance," thinking he was at last free, only to find her reputation lived on. As he discovered when he tried a little judicious blackmail on his stepfather.

He had eavesdropped, spied, listened, watched, copied certain documents and then confronted Richard with evidence of his complicity in an international cartel operated by several U.S. senators, the President of a South American republic, certain Army generals and a big man at the CIA, as well as certain top industrialists. But Richard had only laughed.

"Try it," he had invited lazily. "And I'll dig up your mother's bones and parade them around the streets. Oh, yes, I know how much you writhed under the fact that she was a whore." He had laughed again; that softly amused laugh without fear but with contempt, which meant he was onto you —and on top of you. "That, my dear boy, is why I married her. She was an amoral, empty-headed slut; but you . . . I had heard about you. All those fights, the deliciously vicious way you had with your detractors, and I thought —now there is a boy after my own heart, except that neither of us has one. You were exactly what I wanted. Devoured by hatred of her and all women." Another soft predatory chuckle. "Who do you think set Margery onto you to 'improve' your sexual education? Whose money was it she 'paid' over to you? I know all about you, dear boy. You and your paid perversions . . ." The smile had burned like boiling oil. "You have me to thank for your . . . shall we say, status?" The smile faded. "I have indulged you and let you wreak havoc for your own satisfaction. Now it is time you wreaked it for mine." A shake of the head and a benign reproof. "Always read the small print, dear boy, the line that reads: 'Nobody *ever* does anything for nothing. There is always a price to be paid . . .' with a little space and a few dots for the amount to be inserted. This is my price." The voice changed, becoming hard and cold and merciless, the smile changing to a numbing cruelty. "You will put your activities to work on my behalf. There are several—properties—I wish to acquire. They are owned by men whose wives should be child's play to you. You will therefore conduct your activities in areas I shall dictate. You may keep any money you make. That is not what I am after . . ."

And before he knew it he was in deep; enmeshed so helplessly there was no escaping from his role in the systematic wholesale looting of lives and property, all of it engorging the Organization so that it grew to a monstrous size, which crushed anyone who got in the way.

"And all for you, dear boy, when I am gone. Who else have I got to leave it to? Think of it as working for your old age." He had laughed again, roared with laughter, and Dan had joined in, because he had thought they were laughing together; joined in their hatred and contempt for *them*, the sheep who peopled the world. Only it had not been together. It had been Richard laughing at him. Like always. He had left everything to *her* instead. The first woman Dan was unable to classify as a whore. Which made him hate her even more. Determine to bring her down somehow, some way.

Now he sighed pleasurably, luxuriating in his satisfaction. He would not only have done for her, he would have done for Richard too. And his little game. Whatever that was. He shivered suddenly. Something nasty. His games always were; wheels rigged and decks stacked. But for the life of him Dan could not find a reason why. His own sister's daughter? Why would he do that to Helen? Because he hated her. He answered his own question unhesitatingly. He hated everybody. People were things to be used; bought and sold like an Organization product. It had been power he had loved. And used. To annihilate, destroy, crush, maim, after first acquiring the means. Like that deadly reel of film which showed his mother actually performing for a ring of slack-mouthed, drooling, pop-eyed old men, and doing such things . . . He pinched out the thought like a cigarette. Nobody would *ever* know that. Which was why he had to squeeze them of the money he craved before the will went to probate, and squeeze them until they gave . . .

By all means let Louis Bastedo ransack Elizabeth Sheridan's mind. It could only provide more proof. And Hervey, upright, moral, strictly legal Hervey, would not soil his clean hands by aiding and abetting a fraudulent will.

He sighed again, deeply, satisfyingly. Yes, at long last, he was about to come into his own.

THIRTEEN

"Right," said Louis. "Just let what's going to happen, happen. Expect it to happen—most of all, *want* it to happen."

Elizabeth nodded tensely.

They were in Helen's sitting room, a bower of peace and exquisite beauty. Louis had wanted an intimate atmosphere and this perfect little place, with the blinds drawn against the light, fitted his specifications exactly. The rain—which had come just after lunch—pattered soothingly on the terrace and rattled on the bushes outside the windows. It was cool, quiet, filled with the ineffably tranquilizing presence of Helen Tempest, who had brought to this small octagonal room the cream of Marlborough's treasures.

Elizabeth sat in a Louis XVI fauteuil upholstered in palest almond-green silk. Dev had drawn up another just like it and sat close to her. Louis was across from them, a small tape recorder on the delicate marquetry of a rosewood table. Around them, the walls were painted with *trompe l'oeil* representations of birds, forests, and waterfalls, while the carpet was a deeper shade of turquoise woven into the same pattern. Flowers were massed everywhere, scenting the air; roses, carnations, enormous shaggy-headed daisies with great golden eyes. Lacquered cabinets contained Helen's collection of tiny jade animals and Fabergé trinkets, while behind the ormolu guard rail of her spindle-legged writing desk stood her collection of miniatures, portraits of members of the Family. Meissen and Dresden figurines adorned small tables, and the wall sconces were of crystal drops that glittered in the watery light filtering through the drawn shades.

"Now then, I want you to be comfortable. That chair all right?" Louis sounded un-urgent, matter-of-factly relaxed.

Elizabeth nodded, but she sat bolt upright.

"Good. Now I explained this morning what I am going to do. You understand the procedure? Any questions?"

Now she shook her head.

"Good," Louis said again. "Now, I want you to look up at that beautiful chandelier above your head; that's right, tilt your head back and stare at it . . . That will induce a certain strain on the eyes and eventually your focus will blur. When that happens, close your eyes."

Elizabeth's eyes were fixed on the waterfall of crystal that hung from the carved and scrolled ceiling, but they were wide, strained, in no way showing anything but her inner, emotional disturbance.

After a while: "No use?" asked Louis. She shook her head again. "You're not relaxing." He leaned across, laid a hand over hers, sighed. "Stiff as a board."

"I'm sorry . . . it's just that . . . I'm nervous," she blurted.

"Of course you are, but unless you can relax we can't begin."

"I have an idea," said Dev. "Hang on a minute." He got up, went out.

"Why are you afraid?" Louis asked directly. "You said you understood."

"I do." He saw her swallow convulsively. "It's the thought of not being under my own control . . . relinquishing myself into someone else's hands."

"Of what you might do and say—like the incident of the hairbrushing?" Another nod.

"But that is what we are after," Louis said gently. "The *real* you . . ." Then, percipiently: "Perhaps *that* is what you are really afraid of."

Her eyes, wide and showing a much darker green, gave her answer. "I want to," she said in a voice she struggled to control, "but I am afraid."

"And your way with fear is not to confront it but to back off."

He hitched his chair nearer so that he could take a firmer hold on her hands.

"Don't you see . . . that is why you have this block. Because you were not willing to face—to endure—pain and suffering. Rather than fight them, you retired from the field. And what was begun as a child has continued in the adult. Your whole life seems to have been dedicated to avoiding any sort of involvement which could lead to your being hurt in any way. You set out to make yourself so incapable of involvement that you could never be touched, never mind moved by any sort of feeling. You wear that armor plating because inside you are possessed of an acute, perhaps even a hyper, sensitivity. And you have been careful not to expose it ever since you were able to do anything about it. That unconscious mind of yours is ringing every alarm bell to hand because that sensitivity is being threatened. You think that what we are going to do will expose it to more of the hurt and suffering which all but did for you once. But there always comes a point where retreat is no longer possible, because the end of the cul-de-sac has been reached—and that is what you went down, make no mistake. All that is behind you now is a wall. The only way out is to climb over it, and to do that you need help."

She was silent. He had illuminated her fears so clearly that even the sight of them, faced and realized, was a kind of relief.

"Facing oneself is never easy; most people run or hide from it all their lives. Your choice was made for you as a child, but the adult never questioned it; rather, you were grateful for it. I know it is hard to find that what you thought was a firmly constructed edifice is no more than a false façade, but we are here to *help* you. If it hurts, we are here. *You are not alone this time.* This is *my* hand," he tightened it on hers, letting its warmth flow into her cold one. "You have *my* interest, my wish to give aid, succor—whatever. And Dev's love . . ."

He saw pink creep into the pale cheeks.

He said dryly, "I know Dev. He has taken the big fall for you . . . oh yes, he has." He smiled. "He told me you didn't believe him, because you believe yourself to be unlovable. And do you know why? Because the barriers you put up prevented people from getting to you so as to be able to love you."

He saw her move, restlessly, as though sitting on tacks. "It's all so complicated . . ."

"Human relationships are. We all have our egos, you know. Why else do you think you labored to make yourself invincible—so you could set that ego in the middle and feel safe."

"Not anymore," she said bitterly.

"But that is where you are wrong. You are safe. For the first time in your life since you lost your mother. Because there are people here who care for you, love you, want the best for you . . . That's about as safe as any human being can ever get. Love is what most people spend their lives looking for, don't you know that? And here you are, surrounded by it, and can't even see it's there." He sighed. "Some people have all the luck . . . and the looks," he added.

"That's what Dev said."

"And he was right—as usual. My dear girl, there are women who would throw you to the wolves to be in your place! Make no mistake—step out of it and you'll be trampled in the crush to replace you. Dev is concentrated catnip where women are concerned."

"I know." It was shy, yet somehow proud.

"And by the end of this afternoon we shall know a lot more."

Silence. "It is the only way—this way?" she asked finally.

"If you want your questions answered—yes."

Another silence. *"All* my questions?"

"No. This is a beginning, not a conclusion. What we are after here and now is where you were, who you were with; if it was, as Dan Godfrey says, your mother, Helen Tempest. The rest will follow on from that."

She nodded. He could see he had answered her questions but not settled her doubts, but before he could say more the door opened and Dev ushered Seraphine into the room. She was carrying a tray on which was a teapot and a cup and saucer.

"I think Seraphine can help," Dev said confidently.

"I have made another of my tisanes," she said, entering on cue. "My lady always found this one very soothing to raw nerves."

She poured it out. It was pale green, smelled faintly of mint, and something else.

"You will find it will make you relaxed," she said, holding the cup toward Elizabeth, who looked up into the dark, impassive face and took it.

"It is a compound of various herbs," Seraphine said kindly. "It will not drug you, merely calm you." Her smile was encouraging, her eyes warm. "I have never known it to fail with my lady."

Taking it as a testimonial, Elizabeth sipped the hot liquid. She found she could not define the taste; it was aromatic, delicious; even its fragrance seemed to leave a healing path as it filtered into her head. She drained the cup. Taking it back, Seraphine placed it on the tray. Then she said, "There is another way." Stepping behind Elizabeth, she placed her hands, with their long, strong fingers, on the rigid muscles at the back of Elizabeth's neck and began to move her thumbs in a circular motion. "You are tense," she observed. She moved her fingers to Elizabeth's shoulders, probing, kneading, and Elizabeth closed her eyes as the magic of them spread a delicious warmth from her neck across her shoulders and down her arms. By the time Seraphine took them away she felt tranquil, every knot untied.

"Thank you," she said gratefully, aware she had yet another ally. Seraphine made her usual stately bow and bore the tray away.

"Better?" asked Dev, flashing his own white-hot smile.

"Much . . . she *is* a witch."

"Among other things," Louis said dryly. "I've used her in my time to calm down fractious patients. Sometimes I think she awes them into obedience."

"I'm ready now," Elizabeth announced, sounding confident.

"Good. Then let's take up where we left off."

Once again he made her look up at the chandelier, and this time, under the soothing drone of his voice, she did as he directed.

"I want you to breathe deeply . . . that's right, deep, deep breaths . . . all that lovely oxygen making your muscles even more relaxed . . . your head is beginning to feel heavy . . . soon it will tilt; when it does, just let it go . . . and your attention too . . . when that begins to wander, go with it . . . I can see you smoothing out . . . all that tight tension slipping away from you. Now your eyelids are feeling heavy, s-o-o heavy . . . why don't you close them . . . that's right . . . such a delicious feeling of relaxation, of sinking into a soft, feather bed . . . let it all slip away from you."

She was limp in her chair.

"Now . . . the little finger of your left hand is beginning to feel strange; it is tingling, twitching." Even as he said the words it began to do just that.

"The feeling is spreading to your whole hand . . . it wants to lift, float away, up toward your face."

The hand was drifting upward.

"The moment your hand touches your cheek you will be totally, completely relaxed . . ."

Her hand fluttered to her cheek, then fell, limply. She had entered fully into the altered state of consciousness.

Louis switched on the tape recorder.

"Now then . . . I am going to ask you some questions."

When Elizabeth opened her eyes she felt refreshed, as if she had slept deeply and dreamlessly for hours and hours. She stretched, feeling her muscles give easily and powerfully, as if newly massaged.

"How do you feel?" Louis asked.

"Marvelous!" Then, startled: "It is over?"

"And done with."

"But—"

"You responded marvelously. Went right under."

"What happened?"

"It's all on tape."

Her eyes went to the recorder. Reaching across, Louis pressed the rewind button and the reel began to whine.

"Was it—useful?"

"Hear for yourself."

". . . I am going to ask you some questions," Louis's voice, authoritative, came from the machine. "But they are about your past, so we have to go back there. I shall count backward slowly from your present age; when you want to tell me something that happened in any particular year, your little finger will raise itself; then I shall know and ask my questions. Twenty-seven . . . twenty-six . . . twenty-five . . ."

Slowly, steadily Louis counted off the years backward until, as he got to twenty-two, the little finger rose.

"All right, you are twenty-two years old. Tell me what is happening."

"Miss Keller is being buried today."

Elizabeth started as her own voice, sounding strained and short of breath, issued from the recorder. Leaning across, Dev put his hand over hers. She took it and held on to it.

"Are you going to the funeral?"

"I—can't."

"Why can't you?"

"I'm—afraid."

"Why are you afraid?"

"I—can't—walk . . . my—legs . . ." The voice rose, panic-stricken, struggling for breath.

"Why can't you walk?"

"Legs—won't—move . . . can't—walk—to—the—cemetery . . . I— must get away . . ." The voice was under pressure, being squeezed from a chest all but bereft of breath.

"Why?"

"Afraid . . . make a fool of myself . . . mustn't cry . . ."

"Why not?"

"Make—a scene—afraid . . ."

The voice sounded asthmatic as it struggled for breath, becoming choked with sobs and losing control.

"All right . . . we will leave the cemetery . . . twenty-one . . . twenty . . . nineteen . . ."

Elizabeth was rigid, staring aghast at the machine, but there was only Louis's voice as he counted steadily backward until he reached five.

"Mummy . . . I want my mummy . . . where is my mummy . . . please, please . . . where is my mummy . . ."

The voice was that of a child; thin, fluting, shattered by sobs.

"Why can't you find your mother?"

"I don't know . . . She has gone away . . . I hate this place . . . Please, oh, please, I will be good, I promise . . . Only take me to my mummy . . . I *will* stop crying if you take me to my mummy."

Elizabeth's eyes glittered with unshed tears but she said nothing. Her teeth were sunk into her lower lip; the hand that clutched Dev's was white with strain.

"Tell me where you are? What is happening?"

"In a big house . . . It is not my house . . . There are lots of children I

don't know and strange people . . . I want my mummy . . . please . . ."
The voice stopped. When it went on again it was filled with gladness and
relief. "You will! Oh, yes . . . see, I *have* stopped crying . . . I *will* be good
. . . I promise." Again there was a silence then suddenly the child's voice
screamed, again and again and again; terrified, frantic with terror and despair.

"Not down there! In the ground? You said you would take me to my
mummy . . . She is not in the ground—she is not!" The screams pealed
from the recorder, hysterical, abandoned, wholly distraught and out of control, becoming demented and then breaking suddenly, as if snapped in two.

"Four," Louis said quickly, commandingly, and then: "What is happening
now?"

"It's my birthday!"

The voice was now happy, excited, filled with pride. "I am four years old
and Mrs. Hawkes has baked a cake and it will have candles and Mummy has
made me a pretty dress."

"Where is all this happening?"

"At home."

"And where is home?"

"Number 23, Mackintosh Road, Camden Town." The child's voice said it
as an incantation.

"And who lives there?"

"I do."

"And who else?"

"Mummy."

"Who is Mrs. Hawkes?"

"It is her house. We live with her and Mr. Hawkes. Mrs. Hawkes looks
after me when Mummy goes to work and Mr. Hawkes is in the building."

"Which building?"

"I don't know. That's what Mrs. Hawkes says."

"Tell me about the house. What is it like?"

"Mummy says it's a doll's house. It has two rooms upstairs and two rooms
downstairs with a kitchen at the back, and there is a little garden where Mr.
Hawkes lets me help him."

"And is there a colored window in the hall?"

"Yes . . . it has a big ship in it. When the sun shines it makes the floor all
pretty."

"What sort of work does your mummy do?"

"She sews things for rich ladies . . . She made this dress . . . and Aunt
Marion bought me my ribbons."

"Who is Aunt Marion?"

"Mummy's friend."

"Does she come to see you?"

"Yes. She has bought me a doll for my birthday with long yellow hair like mine, so I can brush it like Mummy brushes mine."

"Does she do that often?"

"Every morning and every night. Mummy brushes my hair and tells me a story about a princess who had such long hair she could let it down from her window so that the prince could climb up it."

"Is yours as long as that?"

"Not yet . . . but Mummy said it will be."

"Do you go to school?"

"No. I have to be five. But Mummy showed me how to write my name."

"Would you write it for me?"

There was silence while the spool ran on and Louis picked up the pad by the recorder to hand it to Elizabeth. Printed on it, in the sprawling capitals of a child was the name ELIZABETH SHERIDAN.

"That is your name?"

"Yes."

"And what is your Mummy's name?"

"Mummy."

"No, I mean *her* name, like yours is Elizabeth."

"Oh . . . Helen Victoria. Mummy says there was a queen named Victoria. She took me to see the palace where she lived, and she said when she was a little girl she lived in a palace over the sea."

"And where is your daddy?"

"He died in the war."

"And what was his name?"

"Rupert," said the child's voice.

"Tell me about Mrs. Hawkes. What is she like?"

"She is fat and says the stairs will kill her."

"And Mr. Hawkes?"

"He has no hair, but he often gives me sixpence."

"And do you have friends to play with?"

"No. I have to stay in the house with Mrs. Hawkes, but she takes me to the shops and sometimes we go to the Heath and ride on the top of the bus if Mrs. Hawkes's legs are all right."

"And you are having a party because it is your birthday. With a cake?"

"Yes. Mrs. Hawkes has made it and it is all pink and has my name on it. She let me lick the bowl when she was finished."

"She is kind to you?"

"Yes, she calls me her little princess . . . like Mummy does. She is going to take me to meet the bus."

"Which bus is that?"

"The one Mummy comes on when she has been to work. Aunt Marion is coming and we will light the candles. Then I will blow them out and make a wish."

"And what will you wish?"

"That Mummy will buy me a pram for my doll."

"Do you think she will?"

"She says she will if she can . . . but she said she would not promise. Mummy says it is wrong to make promises unless you can keep them."

"And does your mummy keep her promises?"

"Oh, yes. Always."

"You love your mummy?"

"Oh, yes, best of all the world."

Again, the spool ran on silently for a while, then Louis's voice said: "All right. Now that we have been back, we will come forward again to the present, but quickly this time . . . six . . . eight . . . ten . . . twelve." Finally: "In a few seconds I shall count to five and say, 'Open your eyes.' You will easily leave the relaxed state and be wide awake but feeling refreshed and exhilarated, and you will keep this feeling with you . . . One, two . . ."

Louis reached forward to press the stop button.

There was a strained silence, until Elizabeth said in a sick voice, "Now I know why I hate cemeteries."

"Not without reason," Louis said. "Some well-meaning idiot, seeking perhaps to stop your endless crying—for which I think you must have been either punished or scolded, hence your fear of making a scene—took you along to a graveside hoping to set your mind at rest but only implanting a horror your mind refused to accept and so buried it. From what we have heard, I think there can be no doubt that you were deeply attached to your mother. You each were all that the other had, living with strangers. I think every emotion you had was invested in her, and when she 'died' you buried them with her; buried everything, in fact, because if you remembered her life you had perforce to remember her death. So your subconscious wiped your memory clean and implanted a new set of instructions: never again to become emotionally involved. And you followed that instruction to the letter, not realizing that that particular road led only to isolation. But as I told you, the mind never forgets *anything.*"

Elizabeth's silence had a brooding quality. What she heard had shocked her, and her face was white, but the feeling of calm and tranquility Louis had suggested she keep held her together.

"It was all there," Louis went on in his soft, totally matter-of-fact voice. "It only needed bringing out."

"But that is not all of it, is it?"

"No. And this is not the time to dig for it. We have what we need. We know where, and how and who."

"You mean the Hawkeses?"

"And 23 Mackintosh Road, Camden Town."

"Not far from where I live now . . ." Her abstracted voice changed as she raised her eyes, bright with sudden comprehension, to look at Louis. "Do you think that's why perhaps I chose to live where I do?"

Judiciously: "Could be . . . Why *did* you choose to live there?"

"I don't know. I just—felt I wanted to."

"Well, then . . ."

But she was brooding again, her eyes unfocused, looking inward and backward.

"I have to find them," she said with finality. "The Hawkeses."

Dev, who had not said anything, now commented: "It was more than twenty years ago. They might no longer live in Mackintosh Road." Pause. "They might no longer be alive."

"I still have to find out." She had arrived at a decision.

"Then we will," Dev said. She looked at him for the first time. "I'm coming with you," he said, having made his own decision.

She nodded.

"That's a good idea," Louis agreed, "but don't go at it like a bull at a gate." He smiled. "Open it first."

"It is open," she said, "and I am already through it because I *know* . . . now." She drew a deep breath. "Now I want to *see.*" She thought some more. "Will I begin to remember"—she gestured at the recorder—"consciously, now that I do know?"

"It is possible. In the natural progression of things, one prod can topple all the cards."

She nodded.

"When will you go?"

"Now," Elizabeth said.

Louis glanced at Dev, who said smoothly, "Why not? The sooner we know, the sooner we can straighten things out."

Elizabeth rose to her feet. The men stood too.

"That tape," Elizabeth said. "Could I have it?"

"If you want it."

"Yes. I do."

"Okay." Louis picked it up, handed it to her. She took it, looked at it, curled her hand around it. "Thank you."

"It wasn't so bad, was it?" Louis asked.

She shook her head. "No. It wasn't *bad* at all."

"How do you feel?"

Sounding surprised: "Quite calm."

"Good. That's how you are supposed to feel." Now he paused. "However . . . you might find your—euphoria—will evaporate. That's why I think you are wise to take Dev along. You will need support."

Which was what Cass instantly decided was her job.

"There is no need to take Dev," she said, unwilling to be a nonparticipating third in this particular triangle.

"Louis Bastedo advised it."

"And you actually took his advice?"

"He knows what he is talking about."

"True—but what *did* you talk about?"

"I told you. I remembered where I had lived, and with whom . . . Now they have to be found before I can find out any more."

None of this helped Cass discover what she wanted to know. Like just what exactly had gone on in the hour Elizabeth had spent closeted in Helen's sitting room with Louis Bastedo, Dev Loughlin, and a tape recorder. All Elizabeth had said when asked, "Is it all on there?" had been an uncommunicative yes. But it had been said in such a way that Cass had to stand chewing her nails *behind* the line. Not even Dan could get more out of her than the fact that the session had been helpful, had produced information she intended to follow up. Not even Hervey, pleading Helen's cause, had succeeded in getting anything out of her. And following her lead, Dev would say nothing. Everybody knew better than to ask Louis.

"So the sooner we get started the sooner we find out," Elizabeth was saying. "Will you make arrangements for the three of us to leave as soon as possible?"

"I still don't see why we have to take *him* along."

"Because I want him to come. If that does not please you, then do not come yourself."

"Oh, no, you don't! I'm co-executor. It's my duty to be there."

"Which is exactly why I want you along. Now let's not waste time, Cass."

Cass knew that voice. It meant subject closed.

It was raining when Elizabeth came out of Terminal Three; a steady, chill drizzle which boded ill for the coming summer but which made her turn up her face to its fine mist, beading her hair. Already, the tropical opulence of Tempest Cay and its insidious influence was more than three thousand miles behind her, and rain seemed to her to be a sobering shower, waking her up from that dreamworld and bringing her back to cold, gray reality. Hefting her suitcase, she made for the taxi rank.

Traffic was heavy and the rain slowed it. As she sat in the back of the taxi, she was conscious of a brisk freshening of spirits, a surge of her old, sandblasting common sense. She lowered the window. Even the smell of diesel oil and gas fumes and the faint waft of the brewery as they passed it all smelled of home, reality and familiarity, dispelling the cloudy fog of new emotions and both clarifying and distilling a potent sense of purpose.

At Waverley Court, the porter came out to take her bag.

"Nice to have you back, Miss Sheridan. Did you have a good holiday?"

"Yes, thank you. But it's good to be back."

He carried her case into the lift. As always, it smelled of polish and air-freshener. She inhaled it pleasurably. It was thinner than the cloying sweetness of the tropical flowers she had left; it did not clog the brain, drug the senses. She was glad to be home, knew she had made a wise decision to leave when she did. Whatever happened now, she needed to feel she was acting on knowledge, not influence.

The flat was exactly as she had left it, apart from smelling slightly stuffy after six weeks of closed windows. She went round opening them all, letting in the fresh air, not only to the rooms, but to herself.

There were few letters, mostly bills and circulars. She put the kettle on. A nice cup of tea, she thought. She was sitting sipping it, opening her letters, when the phone rang. It was Cass. "Hi! Just get in?"

"About ten minutes ago."

"Good flight?"

"Yes, thanks. You?"

"No trouble."

They had flown separately. Hervey, insistent as always on the status quo, had pointed out that for Elizabeth to be seen with Cass would cause speculation. All right for Dev to travel with her; he was known to be part of the scheme of things. Better for Elizabeth to fly back as she had come. Tourist.

"Lousy weather," Cass was saying. "But nice to be in London again. So, what's the schedule?"

"I'll call you," Elizabeth answered. "What's your number?" She jotted it down.

"What do you plan to do first?" Cass went on.

"Make plans—then I'll be in touch." She hung up.

Cass frowned at the phone. From where he sat, on the sofa next to it, Dev could hear the dial tone. Connecting that to Cass's frown he asked, "Cold front moved in?"

"And blowing briskly."

"Well, we are on her territory now."

Which, Cass thought, put them at a disadvantage. The Island had been theirs. Cass had the uneasy feeling that Elizabeth had separated herself by more than distance. The voice had been the coolly aloof one of early days on Tempest Cay. She had marked off their respective positions, but while it suited Cass to have her at a distance from Dev, it did not suit her to have to hew to the line.

"She says she'll call us. I suppose she is being as cautious as Hervey would have her be. And the press did pounce the moment we landed."

She sank back into the sofa. Dev put her drink into her hand. She smiled, but it was all surface.

"All we can do is wait," Dev said.

"And wonder . . . like what the hell Richard was playing at."

"Your guess is as good as mine," Dev said lightly.

"No guesses—that's what this game is all about." Her smile was crooked. "Find the lady."

"Two ladies."

Yeah, and I know which one you want, Cass thought. Casually: "Do you think Elizabeth has accepted Helen as her mother? Completely, I mean—in herself."

"She did on the Island. But Helen was there. Here . . ." Dev shook his head. "This is her territory."

"How did the little truth or consequences session actually go?"

"Very well."

"She produced the right answers?"

"The ones we need."

"Like the Hawkeses."

"Yes."

"I'd like to hear that tape sometime."

"Ask Elizabeth."

I shouldn't have to, Cass thought aggrievedly. She should have wanted me to hear it . . . I thought we were friends.

"God, how I hate all this waiting," she said pettishly.

"Then think how Elizabeth must feel."

Now he made her feel guilty.

"These Hawkes people . . . what did she say about them?"

"Not much. Mrs. Hawkes looked after her while Helen worked. It was their house they lived in, that sort of thing."

"Young or old?"

"I think middle-aged, from what Elizabeth said."

"I hate all this mystery," Cass complained jealously. "So she *must* be feeling even worse. She always liked everything cut-and-dried."

"Not this time. We are holding a long, wet, and convolutedly knotted string. All we can do is follow, untying as we go."

Cass sighed heavily. "I've got a feeling that says some of those knots are Gordian."

A bored female clerk in Camden Housing Department trailed over to where Elizabeth had been standing for several minutes.

"Yes?"

"I have just come from Mackintosh Road. I went to look up some relatives but the road no longer exists. I am hoping you can tell me where they have been rehoused."

"What was the name and number of the house?"

"Hawkes. Mr. and Mrs. George Henry Hawkes . . ." Even as she said it Elizabeth felt a *frisson*. The name had come easily, like that of old friends.

"I'll have to look it up." The clerk trailed away. Elizabeth waited impatiently. She had been feeling on the brink ever since she arrived, as though she was teetering but dared not dive.

The clerk came back. "All the Mackintosh Road tenants were rehoused on Heathview Estate."

"And where do the Hawkeses live?"

The clerk looked doubtful. "We are not supposed to give out that sort of information to strangers."

"I am not a stranger. I lived with the Hawkeses in Mackintosh Road as a child."

"The road has been demolished these ten years."

"I have been abroad."

Doubtfully: "You said you lived with them? Are they relatives?"

"Yes. Uncle and aunt," said Elizabeth, realizing with a shock that she had dredged up another truth. She had called Mrs. Hawkes "Auntie Hawkes."

"I'll still have to ask." The clerk went away again. This time a man came to the counter.

"It's not Council policy to disclose the whereabouts of their tenants to just anybody," he said snottily.

"I am not just anybody."

"Have you proof of that?"

Elizabeth took her passport from her handbag. "I told the girl, I have just come back from abroad . . . My mother and I lived with the Hawkeses when I was a child."

The man examined the passport, thawed a little when he saw she was a native but was still reluctant. "It is not Council policy . . ." he began again.

"But this has to do with a great deal of money," Elizabeth interrupted, and saw the expectant flare of interest. Taking Hervey Grahame's card from her wallet, she handed that over too. "This is the solicitor handling it."

The expensively engraved card impressed, as did the address.

"Well, in that case . . . If you would care to leave your address and telephone number I will get in touch with Mrs. Hawkes and tell her about you. Then it is up to her."

"All right." Elizabeth wrote her name and address and telephone number on the card the man gave her. "How soon?" she asked.

"I can't say. Someone will have to go and tell her. Might be today, might be tomorrow."

Bureaucracy's wheels refused to put on speed.

Back in her car, Elizabeth sat for a moment, feeling both disappointed and frustrated. She had come on at a run, expecting to clear all obstacles with inches to spare, only to fall at the first hurdle. There was nothing to do but go back to the flat and wait.

As she entered the lobby of Waverley Court, Cass and Dev got up from the leather couch.

"You didn't call," Cass accused.

"I had no reason to." Elizabeth avoided looking at Dev, led the way to the lift, which they rode in silence, Cass making a moue at Dev behind Elizabeth's back.

In the flat Cass prowled noisily. "So this is where you live . . . Nice view of the Heath and everything." Turning from the windows: "You could offer us a drink or a cup of coffee, or something."

"Which would you prefer?"

"Coffee, I think."

Dev followed Elizabeth into the clinically tiled kitchen, leaned against the worktop while she filled the coffee maker, ground fresh beans. After a moment he asked quietly, "What went wrong?"

"I went to Mackintosh Street. It's been demolished. And the Housing Department would not tell me the Hawkeses' address. They said they would ask her to get in touch with me."

"But that *is* good news," Dev exclaimed. "That means they are alive."

Elizabeth felt a slight shock. She had not even thought they might not be. As always, he managed to pick out gold from the dross.

"You didn't think of that?" Dev asked, noticing the momentary stilling of the hands.

"No. No, I didn't." She felt unreasonably annoyed. With herself for not thinking it and him for spotting it. She moved around the kitchen, setting out a tray with cups and saucers, adding a packet of chocolate biscuits, seeing as it was Cass. But Dev leaned across, picked one up, bit into it with strong, white teeth.

"Mmm . . . chocolate digestive. My favorites! How did you know?"

Silently she stared into the blue eyes. Beautiful eyes. Expressive eyes. Eyes that saw but did not judge—or condemn. They were smiling at her, but as she gazed she saw them reflect her own doubt.

"What's the matter?" he asked. "Second thoughts?" His voice was gentle, and in some strange way, the way she still could not understand, it lifted her spirits.

She nodded. "I feel—I hate all this waiting," she finished lamely, as if that would explain everything.

"I know. You want it all sorted out, classified, labeled, and filed."

"I can't help the way I am." She sounded mutinous. "It's just—" She moved her shoulders uneasily. "I hate unresolved situations." Not wanting to go any deeper just then, she lifted the tray, took it into the sitting room.

Cass pounced on the biscuits. "Mmm . . . goodies! So what's new?"

"Nothing except what I told you."

"Want me to wield my clout? I know a few choice names."

"No."

Cass tried again. "I called Marlborough. Helen is out of her shock, but no visitors. Hervey asked to be kept informed."

Elizabeth nodded. She was preoccupied, had a brooding air. The hot glow which had been so apparent after her session with Louis had all but died. She was once again very cool, very wary, eager to be convinced but not until she had seen, touched, proved.

They sat chatting desultorily, drank all the coffee, Cass finishing off the biscuits. Elizabeth kept looking at her watch. When the phone did ring, she leapt from her chair. "Yes, speaking . . . You did? Thank you . . . Yes, let me get a pencil." Cass had one in her hand. "137 Heathview Court, Chalk Farm . . . Yes, I can find it. And thank you again." She hung up. "Mrs. Hawkes is expecting us," she said.

"When?" asked Dev.

"Now."

Cass set down her cup, reached for her ancient mink. "Then what are we waiting for . . ."

Heathview Court was one of three tower blocks, each about twenty stories high, built of concrete slabs stained and discolored by the weather. Washing festooned the balconies, and the entrance hall was daubed with graffiti, littered with rubbish, and reeking of stale urine and cigarette smoke. The metal-lined lift resembled a coffin. Its smell made Cass wrinkle her nose, stand dead center on the grimy floor, her coat held tightly round her.

Number 137 was a plain black door with a shiny brass knocker and a nameplate engraved HAWKES. Above it was a small glass peephole. As Elizabeth raised a hand to the knocker, Dev asked, "All right?" She nodded, rapped once, heavily. They waited. Heavy footsteps came to the door and stopped. There was a silence and they knew they were being scrutinized. Then bolts were drawn and chains lifted before the door was finally opened to reveal two hundred pounds of massive old lady with frizzy white hair, wearing a virulently purple dress with a diamanté necklace, which matched the miniature chandeliers that swung from her ears. Shrewd, sherry-brown eyes examined them sharply before fixing on Elizabeth, who stood in the center of the trio. Then her face, which had taken on a slightly stunned look, broke into a beaming smile. Stretching her massive arms she exclaimed joyfully, in a ripe London accent, "I'da known you anywhere! Spittin' image of yer pore dead ma . . . And come to see yer old Ma 'Awkes after all this time."

Heaving herself forward, she enveloped Elizabeth in a patchouli-scented bear hug before holding her away again. "The spittin' image! You was just a mite when you was taken away and now yer a grown lady! Just like yer pore ma was, Gawd rest 'er soul . . ." Reaching into the square neck of her dress, she brought out a snowy white handkerchief with which she dabbed her eyes before blowing her nose soundly. "I got the shock of me life when the man from the Council called round. Ter think that after all these years! But come in, come in . . . tell me all about it."

She held the door wide and her eyes kindled as they lingered on Dev. "This yer 'usband, then?"

"No. A friend." Elizabeth's voice was bemused.

"Bring 'im in, then . . . let the dog see the rabbit! You another friend?" she asked Cass, who could only nod dumbly. "Come on in, then, all of yer. I've 'ad the kettle on fer ages."

"After you." Dev smiled in such a way as to make her simper before lumbering off down a short square hall and through a door which opened off. Following, they found themselves in a large, square living room, windows on two sides, a door opening into the kitchen on the third. It was crammed with furniture, all of it massively Edwardian, the centerpiece of which was a vast sideboard crowded with vases, pictures, bowls, and china figures. In the center of the room the table had been laid for what was obviously going to be high tea, even though it was just half-past eleven in the morning.

Plucking a pair of glasses from the mantelpiece, Mrs. Hawkes turned to survey Elizabeth through them once more, as if needing to verify what she was seeing.

"Oo'da thought it?" she mused. "After all these years! But I'm that glad to see yer . . . Many's the time I've thought of yer and yer pore ma . . . But sit down, sit down. Take the weight orf yore feet. I only 'as ter make the tea." She waddled off through the open kitchen door, her voice floating back. "Ain't often as I 'as visitors. Not like the old street, though I don't suppose you'll remember that! Still, you must 'ave remembered somethin' to come back and see old Ma Hawkes after all this time. The man from the Council said as 'ow you'd been in foreign parts?"

Elizabeth cleared her throat and in a voice that sounded rusty said, "Yes," then, in case Mrs. Hawkes, busy in the kitchen, had not heard her, again: "Yes."

"I thought you'd vanished orf the face of the earth when that Miss Keller took you away with 'er."

Elizabeth sat down on the edge of a green-plush armchair that was complete with beige lace antimacassar. Cass, looking frankly stunned, fell into the matching sofa, but Dev remained standing, looking with fascination around the crowded room.

The wallpaper was of fluorescent pink, covered in luridly colored pictures of simpering Edwardian nymphs. In one corner stood a whatnot festooned with plants in cachepots of bottle-green glazed china. Next to the kitchen door a china cabinet was filled with the remains of what was obviously the "best" china, the rest of it arranged on a tablecloth which, as Cass caught sight of it, made her sit up and do a double take. The carpet was shiny nylon, of a purple almost as virulent as Mrs. Hawkes's dress, and it matched the fiberglass curtains hung above others of Nottingham lace.

Over the sound of pouring water: "I never 'eard no more after you was took orf . . . though I did ask Miss Keller special to let us know 'ow you was. She never did, though, not so much as a word."

She came back into the room carrying a teapot under a knitted tea cosy, a china lady in a big picture hat, her skirts covering the pot.

"I expect you could just do with a nice cup o' tea," Mrs. Hawkes said. "And we'll use me best china seein' as 'ow it's an occasion, and me best clorth too . . . the one yer Ma sewed for me. Rare one with a needle, she was."

"May I look?" Cass asked politely but eagerly.

Mrs. Hawkes looked at her sharply. "American, are yer?"

"Yes."

Mrs. Hawkes snorted. "Take a good look . . . it still ain't fer sale."

Cass went over to the table, bent to pick up one corner of the heavily embroidered damask, examined the exquisite embroidery then, letting the cloth fall, said, "Yes. That's Helen's needle. There's no mistaking her handiwork."

Mrs. Hawkes was thunderstruck. "You knew 'er ma?"

"Yes. Very well."

"Well, I never! Not a soul come to see 'er when she was with us—'cept for Miss Keller, o' course."

"We, er—we lost touch," Cass improvised.

"Well, I'm ever so glad you ain't lost touch with me," Mrs. Hawkes exclaimed to Elizabeth happily. "You was only a mite when you left us. And that ain't a day I ain't forgotten, neither," she added darkly. "When that Miss Keller turned up on the doorstep and says as 'ow yer pore ma 'as been run over by a bus—well! I took one o' my turns, I can tell yer. And as fer you —pore mite!—you was that upset! Wouldn't be pacified when yer ma didn't come 'ome with Miss Keller like always. I ain't never seen a child in such a state before or since. Screamed and cried, you did . . . Wouldn't be comforted by nobody. You was that close, yer see, you and yer ma. Worshiped her, you did, and she you, come to that . . . always called you 'er precious." The handkerchief came out again. "She was a real lady, yer ma was. 'Awkes said that first time we set eyes on 'er. That's a lady 'as come down in the world, 'e says ter me. She ain't like the likes of us. And no more she was. But never a word of complaint . . . And 'er a pore widder 'ose man never come back from the war . . . or just after it, anyway." The handkerchief was restored to the capacious bosom. "Come and sit down, then."

"This all looks very nice," Dev said, holding out a chair for Cass, then another for Elizabeth. "You have gone to a great deal of trouble."

"Never! I told yer! I don't 'ave nobody come to see me nowadays . . . not since 'Awkes died, anyway."

"When was that?" Dev asked sympathetically, passing a cup filled with tea the color of oxblood over to Cass, who took it with a look that made Dev turn away.

"Ten years come this October. 'E'd just gorn down to the King's 'Ead for his pint. Just set down 'is glass and 'e was gorn . . . Not too strong for yer?" she asked Elizabeth, who was sitting with her cup in front of her lips but with her eyes closed and not drinking.

"No . . . no . . . Thank you."

Mrs. Hawkes looked round the table delightedly. "Well, this is nice, I must say. I likes a bit of company and to see my little Elizabeth again . . . Well, I'm fair done to a turn. Any friend of 'ers is a friend of mine . . . even if I don't know yer names."

"Forgive me," Dev apologized instantly. "This lady is Cass van Dooren and my name is Dev Loughlin."

"Pleased ter meetcha, I'm sure," said Mrs. Hawkes. "Irish, are yer?"

"Yes."

"Thought you was. It's them eyes." Mrs. Hawkes looked into them and giggled, covered her confusion by proffering him a plate of thickly buttered scones. "Fresh made. Don't take no more'n five minutes."

"Thank you." He bit into one. "Mmm . . . delicious."

"I was allus a good cook," Mrs. Hawkes admitted with simple pride. "Learned 'ow when I was in service." She bit into her own scone. "So now you can tell me 'ow you come to be lookin' me up after all these years. Like where've yer bin all this time."

Elizabeth, who had been sitting in silence, said, "When I left you I was put into a Home."

Mrs. Hawkes choked on her scone. "You was what? Well, I never! What did they want to do that for? I'd 'a looked after yer . . . I told that Miss Keller so. I know as 'ow yer pore ma didn't 'ave nobody . . . but a Home!" She was shocked to the core. "And 'ow long was you there?"

"Until I was sixteen."

"And where was this?"

"In Kent."

Mrs. Hawkes looked hurt. "And never a word did I 'ear . . . and not knowin' where you was I couldn't get in touch." She nodded shrewdly. "I knew as 'ow somethin' was wrong, I said to 'Awkes, when we was not so much as invited to the funeral. Us as 'ad looked after yer since you was only six weeks old! Loved yer like our own, we did, seein' as 'ow I only 'ad dead

babies of me own. Female troubles," she said to Dev delicately, who nodded
sympathetically. "Not so much as an 'int," Mrs. Hawkes went on, bosom
heaving in outrage. " 'Private,' says Miss Keller. On account of yer ma's
family. 'Inting as 'ow me and 'Awkes wouldn't fit in, more like. But yer ma
wasn't like *that!* She was a *real* lady, and straight as a die. Never owed so
much as a penny's rent all the time she was with us. And every penny she 'ad
spent on you. Always dressed like a princess you was, and yer long yeller 'air
brushed till it shone . . . And always the best stuff, oh, yes. 'Arrods, she
went to, or Liberty's. Many's the time she'd bring a bit o' stuff from the shop
and make it into a dress she coulda sold for a mint o'money but, no, always
fer you, they was. She made me a lovely dress one Christmas, real velvet, it
was. A bit of material left over from a dress made for a lady as 'ow she said
cost a 'undred pounds! That's what she did, yer see. Sewed 'andmade dresses
for a shop in Bond Street somewhere."

"Which shop was that?" Dev asked casually.

"Some place with a foreign name, French I think it was. I never could say
it proper. Somethin' like Maisong Reboo. Yer ma did all the special embroidery and fine sewin'. Nothin' she couldn't make up, there wasn't. Even the
little bits o' fur she brought 'ome sometimes she made into muffs for yer little
'ands, and put bits of velvet on collars. A real princess you was, and no
mistake."

Once again Mrs. Hawkes had to dab at her eyes.

"You must have been very distressed when you heard of her accident,"
Dev prodded sympathetically.

"I was that! Gorn out of 'ere a quarter to eight that mornin', she 'ad, like
always. And when it got to a quarter past six I knew somethin' was up. She
wasn't on 'er usual bus, yer see. We always met it," she went on to explain.
"Me and Elizabeth. 'Awkes was always 'ome just after five and yer ma on the
bus that arrived at the corner about five minutes past six. So I used to give
'im 'is dinner first and then I'd take you down to the bus stop. Well, we
waited for the next one but she wasn't on that one neither . . . That was
when I began to get worried. I didn't know what to think when it got to
seven o'clock, I was that worried. Then Miss Keller came." Mrs. Hawkes's
bosom heaved again. "But to take yer orf to a Home! Now that weren't right!
That weren't right at all! If I'd 'a known that!"

"She was a good friend?" Dev asked interestedly.

"Well, it was Miss Keller as brought the two of them to me in the first
place. 'Awkes 'ad an accident at work, yer see—'e was in the buildin'—and
we needed a bit of extra cash, so I took in boarders. We had a spare bedroom,
so I put a card in the newsagent's winder and next thing I know Miss Keller

calls and asks if I'd object to a young widder and 'er baby. Not if they can pay
the rent, says I. Three quid a week and all found. So she brought 'em round
next day and that was 'ow it was for five years."

"That would be until 1952?" Dev asked.

"That's right. The year the old King was took . . . the very same month,
in fact. February, it was." Mrs. Hawkes sighed heavily. "All seemed to 'appen
at once, it did." She shook herself briskly. " 'Oo wants more tea?"

"Thank you," said Dev. "Reminds me of home."

"None for me, thanks," Cass said hastily, but Elizabeth passed her cup
over.

" 'Ave some cake," Mrs. Hawkes urged Elizabeth. "It's yer favorite. Always loved pink icin' when you was little. Remember 'ow I always let yer lick
the bowl afterwards?"

Elizabeth, with the air of someone mesmerized, took a piece of the pink-
iced cake.

"So you knew 'er ma, then," Mrs. Hawkes observed affably to Cass. "She
was a lady, wasn't she? A *real* lady, I mean?"

"Yes," Cass answered. "A real lady."

"There, didn't I say so!" Then, delicately again: "Cast orf from 'er family,
was she?"

"Yes."

Mrs. Hawkes's tongue clicked like a turnstile. "I thought as much. Used to
cry at night, she did, when she first come. I'd 'ear 'er when I went up to bed.
Never let me see 'er, mind you. Always proud, she was." She drank deeply
and thirstily. "Was 'er 'usband not quite 'er class, then?" she asked.

"Yes. Her—family—did not approve."

"Downright wicked, I calls it! I thought 'as 'ow she was 'idin' . . . kept
'erself to 'erself all the time; never went nowhere except to take the mite out,
o' course. Every night she always come straight 'ome from work and spent all
'er time with you . . . like you was very, very precious to 'er . . . you'd 'a
thought nobody'd ever 'ad a baby afore." Mrs. Hawkes chuckled. "And no
friends except that Miss Keller."

"She came often?" Dev asked.

"Regular as clockwork, every Thursday night, and always with somethin'
for the baby. I'll say that for 'er, she was a doer, that one was. It was 'er as got
yer ma 'er job . . . I daresay she was very fond of yer ma in her own way—
many's the time she said to me, 'I don't know what I would 'ave done
without Marion'—so I didn't really 'ave a leg to stand on when you was took
orf . . . You was only lodgers after all, even if we thought you was family

. . . But if I'd known you was goin' to be took off to some orphanage I'd 'a been down the Council and no mistake!"

Cass set her cup down with a clatter.

"More tea?" asked Mrs. Hawkes. But as Cass refused, she demanded belligerently, "And where was you in all 'er trouble, then?"

"In—in America," Cass answered. "I had no idea where she was, you see."

Mrs. Hawkes sniffed.

"She—disappeared," Cass said.

"You could of looked!"

"If I had known where . . ."

"Well . . ." Mrs. Hawkes was slightly mollified. "I don't suppose 'er 'igh-and-mighty family would 'ave thought to look in Camden Town, would they? Which is why I don't doubt Miss Keller brung her to us in the first place!"

"And no one else ever came to see her?" Dev asked.

"Not a soul!"

She picked up the plate of cake again. "Eat up!" she encouraged. "I like to see a clean plate!"

"I don't suppose you have any old photographs?" Dev asked with a deeply interested smile.

"Oh, but I 'ave! I was lookin' at them not long afore I 'eard yer knock."

She heaved herself up from the table and went to the sideboard where she opened one of its cupboards to take out an old-fashioned chocolate box, the type with a raised lid and a tray inside. "Just snapshots, mind you, except for this one 'ere. Yer ma 'ad it took on yer first birthday . . . Took you to Jerome's in the 'Igh Street, special, you and 'er together. She 'ad this one took orf fer me."

She held out a faded eight-inch-square photograph, mounted on beige-colored board. Elizabeth took it gingerly, and Cass and Dev craned forward to look over her shoulder. Against a background of dark-velvet curtains, on a high chair with a carved back, Helen Tempest sat with a child in her lap, an enchanting child with wide, bewildered eyes and a corona of candy-floss blond hair, plump and dimpled and gazing into the camera, wearing an exquisite embroidered dress, frilled at neck and sleeves.

Struck by their intense silence, Mrs. Hawkes said aggressively, "It's a lovely photo."

Cass was gazing at Helen's radiant face, as she looked down at her child with the expression of a Memling Madonna. "Yes," she said, her voice thick, "it is a beautiful photograph."

Picking it from Elizabeth's trembling hands, Dev turned it over. On the back was written in Helen's handwriting: *"Elizabeth's first birthday. January 1st 1948."*

"That's why it was took special," Mrs. Hawkes explained. "She made the dress 'erself. Pure silk, it was, every bit of tuckin' done by 'and . . . You looked a proper picture and no mistake."

Cass in turn took the picture from Dev. She gazed at it with a sad, some-how guilty look. "How happy she looks," she said in a stifled voice.

"She *was* 'appy!" Mrs. Hawkes said indignantly. She was sorting out some other, smaller snapshots. "These is just odd ones taken 'ere and there . . . This one was in the backyard . . . That's 'Awkes."

He was a big, bald-headed man in striped shirt and leather braces, laughing up at Elizabeth, who was perched on his shoulders and obviously squealing with delight.

"You was always askin' 'Awkes ter put you up on 'is shoulders. 'Up!' yer used ter say, 'Up!' and 'e'd swing you up on his shoulders and carry you round, you laughin' yer pretty little 'ead orf." She handed over another one. "This was took at the Festival of Britain . . . one of them street photogra-phers come up and says, ' 'Ow about a picture? For a souvenir?' "

Mrs. Hawkes, younger, dark-haired, but still buxom, wearing a cotton dress and a cardigan, white plastic bag over one arm, stood with the other through that of her husband, he holding his bowler in the crook of his arm, one thumb through his braces under his open coat. Next to him, Helen Tempest, also in a summer dress, stood with her four-year-old daughter in front of her, she holding a plastic windmill in one hand, a miniature Union Jack in the other, her long blond hair tied in bunches with ribbon bows, her dress an-other exquisite confection of lace and ruffles, below which were knee-length white socks and bar-strapped patent leather shoes.

"Lovely day that was." Mrs. Hawkes smiled in fond remembrance. "You went on all the swings and roundabouts; Battersea Park was opened special for the Festival . . . *and* we saw both the Queens." She sighed. "That was the last time we was all out together."

"I wonder"—Dev smiled dazzlingly at Mrs. Hawkes, who patted her hair and simpered—"would it be possible to borrow these, do you think? Only for a very short while. I promise I would bring them back to you myself."

"Well . . . I don't know as 'ow I'd want to part with them."

"I would take the very greatest care, I promise."

The blue eyes were warm, the smile special. Mrs. Hawkes went red and looked flustered.

"Well . . . seein' as 'ow it's you." She giggled. "I can't see no one sayin' no to you . . . leastways, not a female."

"You are very kind," Dev said, and she flushed a deeper shade of scarlet and hid herself behind the teapot.

"These are all you have?"

"Yes. She wasn't one for photographs. It was me as persuaded 'er to 'ave that big one took. Funny thing was, it was such a lovely one they put it in the window, like they used to do with all the best ones—and she was that upset! Made them take it out, she did . . ." Mrs. Hawkes's lips thinned. "I think she was frightened in case she was found out!"

"Yes," Dev said simply. "She was afraid her family would discover her whereabouts and want to take her back."

"Never!" Mrs. Hawkes was scandalized. "Toffee-nosed lot, I'll be bound!" Then she cheered up. "But they must 'ave made it all up? Took you in, seein' as 'ow you were family, like?"

"Yes," answered Elizabeth, sounding like a ghost. "They—made it up."

"Well, and glad I am to 'ear it . . . And Miss Keller? What 'appened to 'er?"

"She ran the orphanage," Elizabeth answered colorlessly. "She died some years ago."

"Ran the orphanage! Well! I suppose that does make a difference," Mrs. Hawkes allowed grudgingly. "But it was the least she could do! Still, I'm glad you 'ad someone you knew . . . you was that upset when yer ma didn't come 'ome. I was fair upset meself, cried all the time I was packin' your things . . . and Miss Keller in such a tear . . . went round like a whirlwind, she did, picking every stick and stitch up and packin' it away. 'Are you sure this is everythin'?' she kept askin' me, like she didn't want to leave no trace. And when she'd taken you orf, it was like you'd never been 'ere. All we was left with was memories and them photographs—and I wasn't goin' to let 'er 'ave them, so I never mentioned them. They was mine, after all."

"And very glad we are that you didn't," Dev said with another smile.

"Not 'alf as glad as I am to see my little Elizabeth again! And lookin' so smart and elegant! It's only right yer ma's family should do you proud. The Council man said as 'ow you'd come into money."

Elizabeth seemed to start. "What? Oh, yes . . ." Then again: "Yes! The money." She turned round distractedly. "My handbag . . ."

"Here." Dev picked it up from the chair, handed it to her. Elizabeth took out her checkbook.

"Now 'ang on," Mrs. Hawkes protested, bridling proudly. "I ain't 'avin' you thinking as 'ow I was 'intin'."

"Please." Elizabeth looked up at her in such a way as to make her subside, red-faced. "This is something I want to do very much. You have no idea what this means to me; finding you again . . . hearing what it was like. You did so much for us, my mother and me. Let me do this for you." She was writing rapidly. "And money is the least of my worries, I can assure you." She tore off the check, held it out.

Mrs. Hawkes accepted it gingerly, peered at it, then fell back in her chair as if poleaxed. "Gawd almighty! This is for a thousand pounds!" She went from red to white, then red again. "I can't take this! It ain't right! You don't owe me nothin'! Yer ma always paid her rent, she did, right on the dot! Never owed a penny."

"I know that. But *I* owe you. So much . . . Please . . . for my mother's sake."

Elizabeth's face was as Cass had never seen it. It made her look away quickly.

"Well . . . I'm sure . . . I don't know what to say . . . I never expected . . ." Mrs. Hawkes burst into tears.

Instantly Elizabeth was out of her chair and round the table, going down on her knees.

Cass's jaw dropped as she watched her put her arms around the shaking bulk.

"You were so kind to us . . . It was the only home I have ever had."

Mrs. Hawkes's sobbing rose to a frantic wail. "You was part of the family . . . like my own," she sobbed.

"I know . . . I know . . ."

"And to think you remembered me . . . came back when you was rich and mighty to see yer old Ma 'Awkes . . . In all my seventy-six years I never thought to see the day."

The massive arms enveloped Elizabeth, who disappeared inside them and was rocked back and forth. Cass sniffed, peered through blurred eyes for her own handbag, felt Dev shove a handkerchief into her hand. She blew her nose like a trumpet. She was dying for a cigarette but there were no ashtrays.

Mrs. Hawkes finally released Elizabeth, sat back, mopped her own eyes, blew her own nose. "Whatever must you think of me! But I was always one for the waterworks. 'Awkes used ter say as 'ow I was always runnin' like a tap!" She chuckled waterily. Then she touched Elizabeth's face with a reverent hand, which Elizabeth caught and pressed to her own. "Just like your pore ma . . . spittin' image . . . She was just about your age when she come to us." She nodded approvingly. "But you ain't like she was altogether. I can see you can fend for yourself." Her eyes were wet again when she said shakily, "Yer ma would'a been proud of yer." She sniffed, smiled round. "I think this calls for a pot o' tea—no, I think it calls for somethin' stronger.

'Ow about a nice drop o' port . . . I always likes a drop of nice port . . .
first time you ever 'ad it was right in my 'ouse," she said fondly to Elizabeth.
"One Christmas, it was. Wanted to taste it, you did, so I put a tiny drop in a
lot o' lemon and didn't you just drink it down and ask for more!"

This time the sideboard disgorged a bottle of port and four tiny gold-
rimmed glasses. When each had a brimming glass, she raised her own.
"Gawd bless yer!" she exclaimed to Elizabeth in an emotional voice, "and
Gawd rest yer pore dead ma!"

They drank. Cass gagged on hers; it was sticky sweet. She just had to have
a cigarette. "Would you mind if I smoked?"

"You do as yer like, dear. I've got an ashtray somewhere . . ." It was pink,
pearlized, bearing the legend "A Present from Southend."

Cass proffered her pack.

"No, thanks very much. Never took it up . . . But I do like a nice drop o'
port. More?"

"No—no, thank you." Lying manfully: "That was delicious."

Dev held out his glass. Elizabeth had hardly touched hers.

"This 'as been a day and no mistake," Mrs. Hawkes exclaimed happily,
pouring liberally.

"It is nice to have visitors—especially unexpected ones," Dev agreed with
a warm smile.

"When you don't get none, it is. Me sisters is both dead and 'Awkes's
brother and 'is wife moved to one o' them new towns. I do miss the old
street. We was friends as well as neighbors there."

"I think you must be the proverbial good neighbor," Dev said truthfully.

Mrs. Hawkes fired up again. "Go along with yer . . ." She winked at
Elizabeth. " 'E yer feller, then? I often used ter wonder if you was married
with young 'uns of yer own."

"No. I am not married."

"A lovely girl like you! I daresay you've got them runnin' after you, though
. . . I remember as 'ow yer ma had one or two castin' sheep's eyes, but she
wouldn't 'ave none of 'em . . . not over your pa, she wasn't."

In a voice that raised the hair on Cass's neck, Elizabeth asked, "What
happened to his photograph?"

"Miss Keller took that when she took everythin' else . . . left nothin' of
yer ma's . . . nothin' at all, even though she was in a tearin' 'urry."

She poured herself another glass of port, settled her bulk more comfortably. The port widened the trickle into a flood. She needed no prompting.
She was lonely, and delighted to talk over a happy time in her life. And talk
she did. It was only when Cass had smoked her last cigarette that she looked

at her watch, saw to her astonishment it was four o'clock. They had been
sitting there more than four hours.

Mrs. Hawkes saw her glance. "No need to rush off," she protested, flushed
with port and good company.

"We have taken up a lot of your day . . ." Dev had been aware of
Elizabeth's glazed look for some time as she sat and listened to her life's
story. She looked as if she could not absorb any more.

"But you'll come again?" The eagerness was pathetically touching.

"That's a promise," Dev said.

"Any time you like! I don't go out much. It's me legs, yer see . . . and I
do enjoy a nice natter."

"We will be back," Dev promised again.

Mrs. Hawkes sighed heavily. "Then I suppose you'll be orf back to foreign
parts?"

"Not before we come and see you," Dev told her.

At the door she embraced Elizabeth tearfully. "It's been lovely ter see yer
again."

She shook hands with Cass, but Dev kissed her. She blushed fiercely. "Go
on with yer!"

She stood in front of the lift until the doors closed on them.

Heedless of the dirt, Cass slumped against the wall. "Jesus! What a
woman! I feel I've been drowned in words. And that port!" Piteously: "Lead
me to a dry martini . . ."

Elizabeth too was leaning against the wall, eyes closed. She looked drained.
Dev put an arm round her. "You drive," he said to Cass.

"Where to?" asked Cass, when they were in the car, Dev in the back with
Elizabeth.

"Elizabeth's flat."

"Okay."

Through the mirror she could see Dev holding Elizabeth protectively in
the curve of his arm, her face against his shoulder. Something about her
troubled Cass, left her feeling helpless and unaccountably guilty, until she
realized what it was. Dev had told her, when she had demanded to know why
he was coming along, that Elizabeth was in need of care and protection. And
when Cass, outraged, had demanded huffily, "Protection from whom?" he
had answered, "Herself." The truth of his words tasted bitter, but Cass
swallowed them. Strong as Elizabeth was, capable as she was, she had been
subjected to an exhumation of her past which had obviously left her feeling
shaken. Mrs. Hawkes had shone a bright, white light and it was no doubt

that which made Elizabeth close her eyes. Until she got used to the glare, all she would see, imprinted on her retinas, was that same bright light.

Cass was conscious of a reluctant admiration for Dev's ability to see, like the great chess players, six moves ahead. She even admitted to herself that she was glad he was along. Had she been on her own, she would not have known how to handle this new Elizabeth, one she felt needed the kid gloves she had left behind. Cass had always favored the straight-from-the-shoulder attitude, but she had never bothered herself about the consequences of the blows delivered. And there was about Elizabeth a sense of having been hammered.

Yes, she thought, stopping at the lights, resent Dev as she might, be jealous of him as she was, he obviously gave Elizabeth something she needed. And we won't go into the whys and wherefores of *that.* Just be grateful he is giving it.

When they arrived at Waverley Court, Elizabeth leaned on Dev's arm in a way Cass could not have supported. So she trotted ahead, carrying Elizabeth's handbag and opening doors.

"She's out on her feet," Dev said, when they entered the flat. "I'm going to get her to bed."

Cass did not argue. She turned it down, switched on the electric blanket. Her feeling for Elizabeth was one of anxious solicitude. As Dev helped Elizabeth to undress, she swaying drunkenly, Cass folded the clothes away tidily, drew the curtains once Dev had got her into the big double bed, then stood looking down at her, feeling worried and distressed.

"Will she be all right?"

"She's been shown a lot of things long forgotten. Told things about herself she did not know. Were you watching her as Mrs. Hawkes was speaking?"

"I was too busy watching Mrs. Hawkes."

"I was. I think her memory was stirred. She had such a strange look on her face . . . fascination, and something like surprise at something recognized from long ago. I think that is what has overwhelmed her."

"That old lady would overwhelm *anybody!*"

"And you are only a bystander. Try to imagine how *Elizabeth* must feel."

Cass shivered. "And that is something she is not used to, either." Sadly she gazed down at her, face pale and slack, lashes lying like scratches on the colorless face. "Poor bitch," she said miserably. "She must feel like everything is falling apart—and she can't *stand* that!"

"That's why I came along."

He went to the door. Reluctantly, Cass followed. Then as her eyes hit the trolley: "I need a drink. You?"

"No, thanks."

"I need one after that yucky port."

Dev had brought out the photographs. Going over to sit by him, Cass said, as they gazed at the studio portrait, "Do you notice Helen's smile?"

"Yes. No sadness."

"No . . ." Cass sighed. "That came afterward." She tossed off her drink. "Christ, what a bastard!" she said.

But Dev was looking at Elizabeth. "She was a beautiful child."

"She's a beautiful woman." Cass shook her head. *"Helen's* daughter! It's all so fantastic."

"Now you begin to understand how Elizabeth feels."

Another sigh. "Yes . . . Today dispelled all doubts. That old lady is *twice* as large as life."

Dev was concentrating his thoughts. "Mrs. Hawkes said that Marion Keller told her Helen had run under a bus. If that is true, she must not have been looking where she was going . . ."

"Running from something?"

"Or someone." Dev looked up. "Mrs. Hawkes said it was the twenty-third of February, 1952. Can you remember where Richard was then?"

"Jesus." Cass sat back and thought hard. "Fifty-two . . . that was the year Eisenhower got elected, which was also the year we bought into the French combine. That took a lot of to-ing and fro-ing, as I remember . . . We were back and forth to Paris like a yo-yo." She sat up. "But one time, Ferrault came to London." Her eyes rounded. "February . . . I remember because the weather was lousy and Richard caught flu . . . That was why Ferrault came over here."

They stared at each other.

"Think back," Dev said. "What else comes to mind?"

Cass put a hand to her forehead, rubbed it as though her fingers were electrodes.

"It's all so long ago." She scowled ferociously as though inwardly flogging her slow memory. Then she shook her head. "I can't remember. We were so busy on the French takeover . . . That monopolized all his time . . . Wait a minute!" She sat up as if the electrode had jabbed her spine. "He sent me to Paris on my own, on a holding mission. He said he couldn't make it because there was something else he had to do . . . I remember he called me." Cass's voice was rising with excitement. "He said I knew everything and I was to stall, give him twenty-four hours, forty-eight at the latest; then he would come over to finish it—them—off."

"And did he?"

"Yes . . . I remember now. I went on a Friday night but he didn't arrive till the Monday morning. I thought it was a woman."

"I think it was. Helen."

"Yes, but wait a minute. That's what Marion Keller *said*. How do we know it is the truth? Accidents mean police, ambulances . . . witnesses, statements . . ."

"Which Richard could easily deal with, you know that. Even so . . . Here's where you use your clout, Cass. Find out what you can. Friday, the twenty-third of February. Helen worked somewhere around Bond Street. Restructuring Mrs. Hawkes's fractured French, it must have been for a shop named Maison Reboux. Get onto it, Cass. If she was on her way home, concentrate on around five to seven p.m."

Cass looked doubtful. "It's an awful long way back . . . I don't know if they keep records that long."

"Try, anyway. And start now."

"Well, I have the contacts but—and it is a big but—it does all hang on what, if anything, is still in the files."

"That's your job. It is what you do best."

Cass reached for her coat again. "On my way . . ." She paused. "You'll be here?"

"Yes. Elizabeth shouldn't be left alone."

Dev was being practical, but it still rubbed Cass's sore spot. On the one hand she was raring to go; be able to *do* something—and something vital at that . . . but: "Wait a minute," she said. "What's the purpose of all this? We *know* Helen is Elizabeth's mother. Does it matter, now, how Richard got her back into his clutches?"

"It does to Elizabeth."

Cass could have kicked herself. "Shit! The explanation of why she was abandoned."

"The all-important explanation."

Cass nodded. But again chagrin choked her. Why did he *always* have to hit the nail? He made her feel ham-fisted. Well, she would show him what *she* could do. Her little black book was in her desk at the office on the Embankment. Just let her get to that and a telephone . . . "Leave it to me," she said crisply. "If there is anything to know, I'll find it out." She checked her watch. Four-thirty. A couple of hours should do it. "See you!" she said, and was out the door.

When Elizabeth woke it took her a moment or two to orient herself; to realize she was in her own bed in her own bedroom, but in London, not at

Marlborough. Reaching for the clock, she saw it was almost midnight. She had slept deeply and had dreamed the wildest things . . . Then she sat bolt upright. What she had dreamed had happened. The incredible afternoon, the lightning-bolt revelations of Mrs. Amelia Hawkes; her own, mind-bending reactions and feelings. It had all been so weird. And that was how she felt. Not herself. Someone who had been presented with a missing piece of herself and was having difficulty making it fit into what she already was.

As she lay back on her pillows, a whole series of pictures flashed through her mind and she felt, once again, the physical recall which had accompanied them and been the strangest thing of all.

Like when, on raising her cup of tea to her lips, the fragrance that drifted with its smoke into her nostrils had swept her back in time. She was a small girl, sitting on Mr. Hawkes's ample lap while he drank his own tea, occasionally blowing on it to cool it, then allowing her a sip of the strong, hot, heavily sweetened liquid. Now, once more she *felt* the hardness of that knee, the brawniness of the chest against which she leaned, the solid support of his arm, the smell of the thick woolen shirt; Lifebuoy soap and pipe tobacco and strong, male sweat. It had made her dizzy, all but knocked her off balance.

And it had happened again when she bit into the pink-iced cake, not wanting it but wanting to please Mrs. Hawkes. The sickly, mock-strawberry scent had once again whirled her back in time and she was standing on tiptoe at the big, wooden, scrubbed kitchen table, watching Mrs. Hawkes sweep pale pink icing over a sponge cake and waiting to be given the bowl to lick clean . . .

She had had to hang on to the table, but the memories had stood firm. Inside her closed lids she now saw, once again, the pictures those smells had illuminated. She *remembered*. She could see the small house; the little hall, the short flight of stairs, the square window on the landing depicting a galleon in full sail; the worn red carpet, the faded blue wallpaper. In her mind, she went up those stairs and into the bedroom where she had slept with her mother. There was the big brass double bed, the well-worn but clean faded pink-silk counterpane, the washstand with its marble top, the satin-mahogany dressing table with its triple mirror, spotted and stained, the lace curtains at the window, the picture above the tiny iron fireplace: a reproduction of Holman Hunt's *The Light of the World* . . . She could see herself, standing on tiptoe to reach for the small bottle of perfume which stood on a crocheted mat.

Once again she sat bolt upright. Perfume . . . remembered smells . . . She scrambled out of bed and ran to her own dressing table, snatched up a box standing there, took from it an atomizer which she sprayed into the air before sniffing interrogatively. So that was why she had always liked *Diorissimo* . . . lily of the valley; the perfume her mother had always worn. As the smell penetrated her brain, another series of jagged pictures flashed through it. Her mother, dabbing the perfume behind her ears and at the base of her throat; herself drinking in its sweetness as her mother bent over her to tuck her in the big brass bed . . . the way she had kissed her good night. First the forehead, then in the hollow of each eye, then on her mouth, this last sweetly lingering, and the softly breathed words, laden with tenderness and love: "Good night, my precious."

A sob broke from her; rising from her depths, jolting the sound from her lips. She leaned forward as if in pain, her arms hugging herself. "Oh, God . . ." Like a bubble, something inside her burst, and once again memories overwhelmed her. Her own voice, the voice she had heard on the tape, proffering her mother a gingerbread man she had made under Mrs. Hawkes's supervision, and Helen—yes, Helen Tempest, *her mother*—down on her knees exclaiming in wide-eyed delight: "For me! But how clever of you, my precious!" and eating it all, down to the last currant eye. And running, running, freeing herself from Mrs. Hawkes's restraining hand, to where the figure of her mother was alighting from a red London bus . . . her mother turning, opening wide her arms . . ."

"Oh, God!" Another wild sob burst from her.

Of standing, ever so still, while her mother, her mouth full of pins, fitted a dress; all starched white organdy and green-velvet ribbons. "To match your eyes, my darling."

"Oh, God. Oh, God . . ." Her voice burst from her in gasps and she bent over, struggling for breath between sobs.

The door burst open and Dev stood on the threshold for a second before swooping forward to enfold her in his arms, saying, "It's all right, my darling . . ."

"I re-mem-ber." Her voice was jolted from her in spasms. "So—many mem-or-ies . . . She is my mother . . . *She is* . . . I can remember her . . . It was the sm-ells . . . I rem-em-ber-ed the smells."

She was wild, distraught, laughing and crying at the same time. "She *is* my mother . . . She is . . . she is . . . Oh, I do remember her, I do . . . Oh, my poor mother, my poor, lovely mother!"

It was as if the words had a special taste. She kept repeating them, laughing and crying and clutching at him fiercely, as if to communicate to him, too, all she was feeling and remembering.

Suddenly she was shoving herself free of his arms. "The phone . . . I have to telephone her . . . tell her . . ."

"All right." Dev let her go but not completely, letting her draw him out of the bedroom. "We will telephone."

But her hands were shaking so badly she could not dial, kept missing the holes.

"Let me do it."

Still keeping one arm round her, he used the other to lay the receiver down while he dialed the international operator.

"I want to place a call to the Bahamas . . . to an island called Tempest Cay . . . It's a private line . . . The number is Tempest Cay 54321 . . . A person-to-person call to Mr. Hervey Grahame . . . Yes, I'll hold on."

Elizabeth was agonized, all of a tremble. "My mother," she hissed frantically, "I want to speak to my mother . . ."

"She will be asleep . . . Better to talk to Hervey first," Dev lied soothingly, knowing that Elizabeth had completely forgotten Helen was in the hospital and this was not the time to say so. But Hervey, being Helen's shadow, would be better than nothing. And if it would help calm her . . .

"Hervey? Dev. I—"

But Elizabeth had torn the receiver from her hands, and in a voice that shook with sobs, pitched between laughing and crying, gasped, "Hervey . . . please . . . tell me . . . how is my mother?"

"You are *what?*" demanded Cass.

"I am taking Mrs. Hawkes back to Marlborough."

Cass flashed a look at Dev. On completing her inquiries, which, using every bit of pull she could muster, had not taken long, she had gone back to the flat triumphantly with her findings, only to find that after giving them to Dev she was herself once more dismissed, Elizabeth still sleeping and Dev firmly and implacably in charge. She went furiously back to the Eaton Square penthouse, where she made herself a great pile of cold roast beef sandwiches which she washed down with a tumbler of Glenlivet before going furiously to her bed, where she lay awake all night in frustrated torment, mental and physical, because she had bolted the sandwiches and given herself acute indigestion.

She was mixing herself an Alka-Seltzer when the phone shrilled, and she leapt for it, convinced it would be Dev. But it was an excited and hectic Hervey, demanding to know what was going on, having had the oddest phone call from Elizabeth, who had sounded so unlike herself as to alarm him. She had demanded to know, he stuttered, "how her mother was!" He complained bitterly of lack of information from Dev, who had merely told him, calm as you like, that he would be in touch again next day. "After all but putting the frighteners on me," Hervey said irritably. "Why aren't you there, Cass? As co-executor you should be privy to whatever is going on . . . What on earth is happening over there?"

Without mincing words, she told him. She could imagine him gagging on the unpalatable facts. He did sound rather sick. "So it is all true, then." He sounded as if he would like to cry.

"Absolutely, undoubtedly, positively true . . . and with photographic evidence! For five whole years Helen lived with her daughter in a small terraced house in Camden Town."

"I see." He sounded desolate. "Oh, well, then, I suppose you had better come home—bringing your evidence."

"Not until I've investigated this latest bit," Cass said grimly. "I'll call you back . . . Yes, yes, as soon as I know . . . You're wasting time, Hervey! Good-bye!"

She slammed down the receiver. That bastard! she seethed, throwing on clothes any old how. Now what have you engineered? A hysterical Elizabeth! What the hell *was* going on?

As soon as she walked into Elizabeth's living room, she knew it was everything. An Elizabeth she had never seen before was lighting the room with a multiwatt radiance.

Cass blinked. "What happened to you?"

"I remembered! Suddenly it was coming at me from all sides . . . I remembered, Cass! It was the smells that did it . . . plus Mrs. Hawkes. I knew she was vital, I knew it!"

Cass was speechless. It was like seeing the spring burgeon; verdant, green, fresh and young—yes—*young*, after a long, hard winter. Elizabeth had blossomed. For the first time in her life Cass realized what was meant when they spoke of a bloom on a woman. The icy aura had melted to a warmth and radiance which, after appearing briefly as a result of the hypnotherapy, had faded once she was back in her old familiar world. Now, positive proof had swept away every doubt. She remembered. Everything.

". . . and that's why Mrs. Hawkes *must* come back with us to Marlborough. My mother must see her, as I did . . . to be helped to remember. Who could *ever* forget Mrs. Amelia Hawkes?"

No doubts, thought Cass. Like St. Paul, she's been struck by lightning, undergone the same life-giving transformation. Maybe I should go to church more often.

"What *has* happened to her?" she whispered to Dev when Elizabeth had left the room for a moment. "I don't recognize her."

"Well, she discovered the old, original self . . . and the exhilaration has got her right on the crest of the wave. What we have to watch for is the moment when it breaks. That's when there could be danger of her being swept under."

"I'm being swept along myself! God help Mrs. Hawkes when she sees Marlborough!" Cass clapped a hand over her mouth to repress her sudden, almost hysterical laughter. When she could: "Can you just imagine Hervey's face when he sees *her?*"

Dev grinned. "It will be worth her trip just to see it!"

"I want to leave tomorrow," Elizabeth announced, sweeping back in. "We have to get organized . . . I don't suppose Mrs. Hawkes has a passport, so you'll have to use your influence again, Cass. All it needs is the relevant forms and photographs—I'll see to them. After that, it is up to you to get her passport issued on the spot." She smiled very confidently. "I'll go and see Mrs. Hawkes first thing, collecting the forms on the way. She can fill them in. I'll take her to have her photograph done, and then you can take the forms down to Petty France and throw your weight about . . ."

She looked at Cass's dumpy figure and giggled. Cass was so dumbfounded at the giggle that she forgot to be incensed. "Can I have some brandy?" she asked feebly. "You may not, but I rather think I am going to need it . . ."

Mrs. Hawkes was collected at four o'clock the next afternoon. She was pale with fright and clutching a battered fiber suitcase, as though afraid that she would be swept up by the whirlwind which had engulfed her at half-past nine that morning when Elizabeth—such a different Elizabeth—had appeared on her doorstep waving ominous-looking forms which she filled in with Mrs. Hawkes's panic-stricken answers and got her to sign, before whisking her off to Chalk Farm Tube to sit her down in the instant photography booth and have four snapshots—at which Mrs. Hawkes winced—taken, after which they went back to Heathview to be met by Cass, who promptly left again for Petty France. Whereupon, after a reviving cup of tea, Dev and Elizabeth helped Mrs. Hawkes to pack.

"But what about me rent? And the milkman? And then there's me insurance."

"You tell me what and where and I'll see to it," Dev said, and Mrs. Hawkes, with trembling hands, handed over her rent book and her insurance book and Dev went off to pay both.

"However long will I be gorn?" she asked anxiously, when he returned.

"Indefinitely," Dev answered with an encouraging smile. "You are going to have the holiday of your life!"

"I don't know as I'm on me 'ead or me 'eels!" Mrs. Hawkes quavered.

"First you tell me yer pore ma ain't dead . . . then you tells me you lorst yer memory which is all of a sudden come back . . . now yer takin' me orf to the other side of the world . . . Me pore 'ead's fair spinnin'.'"

"Once we are on the plane we will have a nice long talk," Elizabeth promised, rapidly packing camisoles and Directoire knickers.

Mrs. Hawkes blanched and sat down suddenly. "Aeroplane . . . oh, my Gawd. I ain't never been up in one of them."

"Nothing to it," Elizabeth assured her. "It's just like being in a car—except it's in the air."

"But it ain't safe!"

"Of course it's safe! I flew here, didn't I?"

"I don't know as 'ow I should . . ."

Elizabeth paused in her packing to kneel by Mrs. Hawkes's chair as she had done the afternoon before.

"Dear Mrs. Hawkes . . . I know it is all sudden and shocking and—well, breathtaking. It is for me, too . . . But this is all so important to me, and to my mother . . . What you did for me was so wonderful. Now I want you to do it for her."

"But—what did I do? I never did nothink!"

"Yes, you did . . . You gave back to me something infinitely precious."

"I'm sure I don't know what you're on about," Mrs. Hawkes protested fretfully. "All this is too much for me."

Which Dev, knowing very well, smoothed down by coming back with a bottle of Mrs. Hawkes's favorite port. Several glasses of that and her shock-blanched cheeks were flushed and she was as excited as Elizabeth. She let Dev help her into her best coat, with its imitation Persian lamb collar, and settled her best hat—mauve satin embellished with a shocking pink rose—on her head.

"Well," she pronounced, turning from the mirror, "I don't know as I ought, but I'm goin' to anyway!"

"I knew you would!" Dev said promptly, giving her a smacking kiss, under which she bridled and swelled an even brighter pink.

When she saw the Rolls, the chauffeur, she gasped. "Whatever will the neighbors think!"

"Why, that at least you're off to Buckingham Palace," Dev said, at which she chuckled, gave him a shove that moved him backward, and with a "Go on with yer!" clambered into the back and settled herself like the Queen Mother, bestowing waves and bows on the curious neighbors and assorted neighborhood children who stood in little knots, heads together and tongues working overtime.

"That'll give 'em somethin' to talk about!" she chortled.

They drove right out to where the Lear jet was parked in the private plane lot at Heathrow, and when she saw it, gleaming white but for the giant, stylized *TO* on its tail, she clutched nervously at Dev's arm and quavered: "It don't look very big."

"Big enough for all of us and more. Come along, let me help you up the steps."

Dev, heaving her on one side, and Elizabeth and Cass, pushing her on the other, got her into the plane and settled in one of the big, pale-blue suede chairs, a small table in front of her. "Why, it's like the pictures . . ." she breathed, eyes like saucers.

"That's what you'll see if you want to," promised Dev. "What's the movie, Cass?"

"Pictures! Up 'ere?"

"And a good dinner with as much port as you want."

"Well, I never!"

Dev strapped her in, then himself in the seat across the aisle, where he took her hand. She gripped his tightly, eyes squeezed shut, as the plane's engines wheezed into life and the cabin vibrated with their thrust. She kept them shut as they taxied, and when they took off, and the gravity forced her back in her seat, let out an alarmed squawk. But when a cup of tea was placed in her hands by a smiling steward, she said, "Now that's more like it . . ." But she was careful not to look out of the window until Dev said, "If you look down, that's London below us." She peered out, drew back again at once, and then gingerly inched forward again. "Well, I never . . . so it is . . . I can see the river!" And from then on, until they had nothing below them but first the sea and then, as they climbed, cloud, she leaned back in her chair, looked round, and pronounced it as being "Not so bad after all . . ."

She took off her hat, enjoining Dev to place it carefully on the rack above her head, and let him undo her seat belt and take her coat. " 'Ow long did yer say?" she asked him.

"Eight hours—more or less. You can have a little sleep, if you like—or look at these magazines, listen to the radio, or watch the movie . . . Then in a little while we'll have dinner."

"Gawd almighty! What next?"

But by the time dinner was served she had recovered enough to do hearty justice to what she liked best: good English roast beef and trimmings, followed by apple pie and cream, finished off with another cup of tea. Afterward she announced she would have a nap. "Wake me up when I get there"—she

nodded at Dev, who had assumed the status of the All Powerful in her eyes—
"I don't want to miss nothin' . . ." She closed her eyes.

"How about you?" Dev asked Elizabeth.

She shook her head. "I couldn't sleep."

"All right then. Want to talk?"

She shook her head again. "No. I just want to . . . sit."

"Okay."

So he and Cass played gin rummy for a while, then, while she read, he napped, until the steward announced Tempest Cay was ten minutes away.

Mrs. Hawkes woke to his touch, yawned, and when he said, "If you look down you'll see the Island . . ." she leaned forward to peer out of the window at the curving S-shape, lushly green; one of many now not so many thousands of feet below.

"It's ever so small!" she protested. " 'Owever will we 'it it . . ."

"Watch and you will see it gradually get bigger and bigger."

But as they banked in a great, graceful curve, and the undercarriage went down with a thump, she clutched his hand and shut her eyes, uttering another squawk as the wheels hit, bit, and raced along the runway. Only when they slowed, stopped, taxied, then came to rest did she open her eyes, hearing Dev say, "Welcome to Tempest Cay!"

Reassuring herself that they were well and truly once more on solid ground, she visibly relaxed enough to say condescendingly, "Well, that was very nice I'm sure . . . Don't seem like five minutes."

"Seven hours and fifty minutes," Dev said. "We had a tailwind."

She chuckled. "Go on," she said, "I could 'ear the engines."

"You must change your watch," Dev said, nodding at the Timex embedded in the rolls of fat at her wrist. "We are five hours behind London time." When he saw she did not understand: "Here, let me . . ." He took it from her, reset the hands to five minutes to six, and gave it back.

"But it was three o'clock when we left my 'ouse!" And when she heavily and carefully descended the steps, felt the sun, saw it shining, she shook her head and marveled: "So it is." She fanned her face. "It's ever so warm . . ."

"It always is, out here."

The air-conditioned cool of the Rolls was more to her liking, and this time she climbed in grandly, as though it was the least they could do. But when, as they drove up the hill road, the House began to appear from behind its trees and shrubs, she gasped audibly and in a faltering voice said, "You never said nothin' about no palace . . ."

"It's a house," Elizabeth said, leaning forward pacifically. "Just a big house."

Cass glanced at her sharply. Elizabeth's voice had sounded defiant, and the radiance, so apparent in London, seemed to have lost power. Probably the competition, Cass assured herself. Over there we had no sun . . .

As they helped Mrs. Hawkes from the car, Dev said softly, "Damn . . . they've formed a welcoming committee."

Cass glanced up to the top of the steps: Hervey, Mattie, David, Nieves, Dan, were all standing there, waiting expectantly.

"Oh, shit!"

Unable to contain her excitement, Nieves flew down the steps to hurl herself at Dev. "I've missed you!" she exclaimed joyfully, her eyes lighting on Mrs. Hawkes and widening as she gasped audibly.

"Hello, love . . . we've brought an old friend to stay . . . Mrs. Hawkes. This is Nieves, Mrs. Hawkes."

Nieves said politely but shyly, "How do you do?"

"Pleased to meetcher," Mrs. Hawkes said nervously.

"Why don't you take Mrs. Hawkes's other arm?" Dev asked Nieves easily.

"There's a good girl," Mrs. Hawkes said gratefully. "It's me legs, yer see . . . and all these steps."

"Take your time," Dev soothed. "There's no hurry."

The group at the top fell back as he and Nieves propelled Mrs. Hawkes to a big chair in the hall, into which she fell heavily, panting like a grampus.

"Get your breath back," Elizabeth said solicitously. "Here . . . let me take your coat."

Hervey stepped forward, obviously appointed spokesman. "Mrs. Hawkes," he said politely, offering a hand, "I am very grateful to you for coming all this way to help us."

"My pleasure, I'm sure," Mrs. Hawkes said feebly, taking it.

"It has been a strenuous day for Mrs. Hawkes," Elizabeth said protectively. "I think it would be best if she went to her room."

"I could do with a cup of tea," Mrs. Hawkes volunteered.

"You shall have a whole pot," Elizabeth promised. "Let me take you to the lift." It was obvious she would never make the stairs. "You can meet everyone later."

Nieves stepped forward again. "May I help?"

"Bless yer pretty face," Mrs. Hawkes wheezed gratefully, "but I think Mr. Loughlin 'ere is more my size."

Between them, Dev and Elizabeth heaved her to her feet and she tottered across to the gilt cage of the lift, concealed behind Sir Richard's portrait. It rose, taking them out of sight.

"What a magnificent old dame!" exulted Mattie. "Where on earth did you find her? I'm absolutely *dying* to hear *everything!*" She put an arm through that of Cass. "Now come along and tell us *all.*"

Hervey was staring upward. "Helen actually *lived* with *her?*" he asked faintly.

"For five whole years—it would probably have been Happily Ever After if Richard hadn't happened along . . ."

Dan laughed. "The Princess actually lived with the Pea . . . the purebred with that common, vulgar old woman." His eyes on Hervey were alight with malice.

"Gold can be vulgar," Cass said cuttingly. "But that 'common and vulgar old woman' happens to have a heart that is one hundred percent pure!"

"Did you see that hat!" marveled David. "Purple satin!"

He shut his mouth under Cass's icy gaze. "Purple is the color of royalty, and that old lady is a queen, let me tell you!"

"That's what we are all waiting for!" Mattie urged impatiently. "To be told. I've been hanging by a thread ever since Elizabeth called."

"Yes, come on . . . out with it," Dan said greedily. "Particularly that photographic proof you've brought back."

"All right, all right." Conscious that she had an audience, Cass prepared to give the performance of her life.

They all went into the drawing room. Only Nieves, hanging back, sped up the stairs.

"I don't suppose you need a tongue-loosener, but I prepared one just in case . . ." Dan went to pour Cass a martini.

She tasted, sighed, gulped. "It's about all you *can* do but you make a perfect martini." David had the cigarettes and a lighter. Thus fortified, Cass decided to let them out of their misery.

"Well . . . we all turned up on Tuesday afternoon at Mrs. Hawkes's door . . ."

They all listened without interrupting once. Only when Cass had described, even down to the ripe accent, Mrs. Hawkes's reactions during the flight, at which Mattie laughed so much she cried, did David, still grinning, say, "What a story! If it was fiction, you'd condemn it as preposterous! I mean—Helen Tempest of Marlborough living in a two-up, two-down in Camden Town and working in a sweatshop!"

"It's true," Cass said, nodding, "and that old lady upstairs is not the only proof. I did some checking, and it was all confirmed. Helen worked for a small, classy establishment called Maison Reboux, no longer in existence now. It had a shop in Upper Brook Street . . . with the workrooms above. She did all the special embroidery. As a matter of fact, she worked on some of the special embroidery used for the coronation dress of Queen Elizabeth II!" With triumphant pride she nodded again at their open mouths. "I got that from a lady who worked with her . . . retired now, but not so old she did not remember Helen *and* her work. She said they all knew there was some mystery about her; that she had more class than most of her customers . . . They all thought she was perhaps the by-blow of some noble family, educated beyond her station but not so that she didn't still need to work for a living. But she never talked about herself . . . passed herself off as a war widow."

"Mrs. who?" asked Dan sardonically.

"Mrs. Helen Sheridan."

"Why Sheridan?"

"You'll have to ask Helen that—how is she, by the way?"

"Louis Bastedo has her under wraps. No visitors. He says she's—and I quote—'doing nicely,' " Hervey said gloomily.

"To get back to the main event," prompted Dan impatiently.

"Yes, well . . . the last the workshop staff saw of her was on a Friday night. They all used to walk to the bus stop together. This particular Friday they had just reached Bond Street and were waiting on the traffic when this big black car rolled to a stop in front of them and a man wound down the window and said just one word: 'Helen.' " Cass paused dramatically, but her audience was hooked. "Helen stopped dead, went the proverbial snow-white, took one look at him and ran! Right out into Bond Street and under the wheels of a number 25 bus!"

Eyes were round, faces rapt. "Well . . . you can imagine the chaos. People, police, an ambulance . . . But according to my eyewitness the man in the car took charge. The last they ever saw of Helen was an ambulance taking her away toward Piccadilly. The following Monday somebody called the shop —they could not tell me who—and said Helen would not be returning to her job. They never heard from or saw her again."

"Where was she?" asked Dan.

"No idea. I could not turn up any hospital records. Evidently they don't hang on to them for more than twenty years. Obviously Richard removed her somewhere . . . I even tried the London Clinic and various other places but no trace. Your guess is as good as mine."

"Was she badly hurt?" Mattie asked subduedly.

"Well, we know she had a fractured skull." Cass shrugged. "As for the rest . . ."

"It must have been pretty bad for Marion Keller to go straight for the child and whisk her away," David pointed out. "For all she knew, Helen might die."

"All strictly academic at this late date and doesn't matter a damn," Dan said impatiently. "What matters here is that it is proved, beyond even an *unreasonable* doubt, that Elizabeth Sheridan is not—repeat *not*—Richard Tempest's daughter. She is his niece. Ergo . . . his will is a lie, which means it is also invalid."

Everybody looked at Hervey. "My specialty is not probate," he allowed, "but I have taken advice. Whether or not Elizabeth is Richard's daughter is not the issue; whatever or whoever she is, she is still the named beneficiary. And we do not know that Richard did not believe, at the time he made his will, that Elizabeth *was* his daughter."

"Oh, come on!" Dan was not having that.

"I assure you—"

"Hervey, don't waste your time assuring anything," Cass interrupted, fixing Dan with a hard smile. "He's not going to contest that will publicly. All this has been for the benefit of a nice *private* little settlement. He is trusting to our *honor*, isn't that right? Especially yours, Hervey."

"You malign me, Cass," Dan protested, looking hurt. "Of course I have no desire to see the Tempest name laid in the mud for a greedy public to trample on . . ."

"Or your own, come to that!"

"Anyone's!" he protested virtuously. "All I want is my share and no hard feelings."

"That," Hervey pronounced distastefully, "will be up to Elizabeth."

"Oh no it won't . . . She doesn't get a dime until the will is probated. This has to be signed, sealed—and delivered up to me—*before* you put your signature to any application. I only want my share."

"And how much is *that?*"

"Well, we—that is, David, Margery, and myself—expected to share what there was between us; a four-way split."

"Never! No way will I countenance the Organization being carved up!" Cass flared instantly.

"Oh, you can keep your Organization . . . it's the proceeds I am interested in. And if you don't keep it running there won't be any, will there? But for starters, we can do a deal on the money."

"Now wait a minute . . ."

Once more the old wrangle got under way until Hervey, holding up a quelling hand, said in his best Justice Holmes manner, "Allow me a word as co-executor. Nothing will be done, *nothing*, do you hear me, until we know what is going to happen with Helen. Until she is well enough, sane enough, and fully able to take part in any arrangement, I do not propose to enter into any. And that," he went on, rising to his feet and fixing Dan with a baleful stare, "is my last word on the subject!"

FOURTEEN

Elizabeth had always intended to take up Louis Bastedo's invitation to visit the hospital. It was her island and she ought to know about everything on it, but she had not expected it would be this way: to discuss a patient who happened to be her mother . . .

It was all white and acres of glass, set in landscaped grounds with sprinklers swirling sprays of gauzy water over lush lawns, neat paved paths cutting through scrupulously tidy beds of flowers.

As she drew up under the portico, a young boy ran up to park her car, flashing her a cheerful grin.

The entrance hall was square and filled with light. A parquet floor on which she could have skated, and comfortable leather couches set against white-painted walls. A nurse sat behind a small enclosure, a girl behind her at a switchboard. It held the usual hospital smell, antiseptic and sterile, but overlaid with the scent of great bowls of flowers.

"Good afternoon, ma'am," the nurse said, smiling recognition and respect.

"Good afternoon. Dr. Bastedo is expecting me. Miss Sheridan."

"Yes, ma'am. If you'll just take a seat, I'll tell him you are here." She reached for a telephone.

Elizabeth went over to the couches, but paused to examine the portrait hanging above them. A beautiful woman in full evening dress, wearing a tiara and matching parure of diamonds, rubies, and pearls and a sweet smile. Lady Eleanor Tempest, the brass plate said. Benefactress and founder of the first free clinic on the Island in 1926, after whom the hospital was named. Her grandmother. The face was familiar, but Elizabeth felt as strange as her surroundings.

She sat down, ankles crossed, hands folded. It was very quiet. Only the buzz of the switchboard, the soft murmur of the voice of the operator.

Everything calm and peaceful. Like Louis Bastedo, she thought. As was the man, so was his hospital. She felt comforted, knew her mother was safe here.

She heard the sound of lift doors opening, looked down the corridor to see Louis emerge from them and walk briskly toward her, white coat flapping, stethoscope bouncing in his pocket, and in spite of herself she found herself rising, going to meet him, anxious and not a little afraid.

But his smile was the usual, sleepy-eyed one, his voice placid when he said, "Hello, there. Welcome back." His hand was as warm as his smile, and he slipped it into the crook of her elbow, held it as he went on: "Your trip was a success, then?"

"Yes . . . in every way."

"Good. Come along and tell me all about it."

He turned to the nurse at the reception desk. "No calls," he said, "except dire emergencies."

"Yes, sir."

"Not that we get many of them," Louis said as he walked her along to the lifts.

"Is the hospital full?"

"No; right now I'm playing to a half-empty house." His grin was cheeky. "But this is one show that will run forever, so I'm not worried . . ." He was making small talk, knew she was nervous. The arm under his fingers was tense, the muscles taut.

"I'll show you round afterward, if you like. Give you an idea of what you're spending your money on."

"I've seen the appropriation. Hervey explained it all to me."

"Yes, he's one of the Trustees. Your mother is the other . . ." Another grin. "That's why she gets the extra special deluxe treatment."

The lift took them to the second floor. His office was at the end, overlooking the gardens at the rear.

It was filled with sunlight, yet cool. His big desk was under the window. On one wall was a range of filing cabinets; on the other, a row of small glass boxes, the kind used for viewing X rays. The desk was scrupulously neat; few papers, but a large bowl of flowers. He sat her down in the chair in front of the desk before going round it to his big leather rocker.

"Right," he said. "I'm dying to know . . . what happened?"

She told him. He roared with laughter when she came to Mrs. Hawkes, his spaniel-brown eyes alight with delighted appreciation.

"That's one lady I've just got to meet," he said.

"I hope so. That's why I brought her back with me. She performed some kind of miracle for me. She was there, you see . . . She knows—and she remembers. Since her I have remembered so much more on my own. All the time things keep coming back to me . . . things totally forgotten, yet— once I remember them—incredibly familiar."

"I told you," Louis reminded, "the mind never truly forgets anything."

He saw her hesitate: "That's why—I want Mrs. Hawkes to see my mother. She is so—natural, so spontaneous . . . If she did it for me, why should she not do it for my mother?"

Louis noted the absolutely natural inflection of the last word. No strain. It was said as though it had been said a hundred thousand times. And recently.

"Well, now, it's early yet to confront your mother with Mrs. Hawkes. She is not ready for that, I'm afraid, which is why I asked you to come and see me. I thought that as your own picture is now so much clearer, and that you are obviously coping so well with all that has happened, you would like to know what exactly it is that happened to your mother—and why."

"Yes. Yes, I would."

"Physically she is fine. I have done a thorough checkup. She is under-weight"—a quick smile—"but what fashionable woman isn't? What ails your mother is not physical. It was shock that did for her. But let me start from the beginning."

He took out his pipe, began to fill it from the stone jar on his desk. "I have been your mother's physician for the last seventeen years, since taking over from Dr. Walters, who had looked after her before then. He was an old man, a good doctor but a product of his time and training. He qualified in 1920. What he was—and remained—was an old-fashioned country doctor, at the horse-and-buggy stage. And he was isolated here. Not part of the enormous leaps medicine has made these past forty years. All he had was a small clinic and all he had to cope with was births, deaths, minor ailments, the occasional accident. The Islanders are a healthy lot. Perfect climate, no stress, no smog, no artificially flavored food. Old Doc Walters was never called on to cope with anything he did not understand or could not cope with. Until your mother."

Louis had his pipe well alight. "But the old doc was a scrupulous notetaker. Your mother's medical history is well documented, which is how I come to know he was so hopelessly out of his depth. She was subject to periods of unstable behavior—quite out of character. She was also epileptic. He put the two together and diagnosed mental insufficiency. It was on his advice that she was kept out of the world. He thought people excited her, so he advised seclusion. He connected her fits of unstable behavior to the moon, you see. But he totally overlooked another and much more likely connection . . . It was for this reason your mother was overprotected, wrapped in cotton wool,

made to think she was not only kept apart but was, in truth, a being apart
. . . not normal, in fact. That was why she was given a nurse-companion.
Seraphine was of the Island. And from his notes I think old Doc Walters was
scared of her. He was of the opinion that she had far too much influence on
Helen. Seraphine's family had been the medicine men of the island until he
came." Louis grinned. "I think he daily expected she would put the juju on
him for doing her out of a job . . . Anyway, it was on his advice that Helen
was put in the care of a trained nurse-companion, not only because of the
periodic rampages but because of the *petit mal.* Do you know what that is?"

"A form of epilepsy . . ."

"Yes, but the mild kind. Not like *grand mal,* where you go into violent
convulsions. *Petit mal* is where sufferers tend to—slip out of time. A sort of
trance . . . They do not hear, see—feel, sometimes. Come back to find
themselves in a different place, having lost that time completely. That is
what your mother suffered from. I say suffered because it has been under
control for years now with the right drug. However, at that time, it was
accompanied by her hysterical outbursts. And this—reading old Doc
Walters's notes—was what convinced him she was mad."

Eyeing Elizabeth's face professionally, he saw it was stiff but composed,
only the eyes showing her inner anguish. Such different eyes, he thought, as
if they had been washed of years of debris and were now seeing, really seeing,
for the first time.

"Her parents were terribly distressed. The thought of institutionalizing her
was not to be borne, especially by her father. Your mother was her father's
girl. So Dr. Walters suggested instead that they make their own, private
asylum. Part of the House was shut off from the rest. It was there that your
mother lived, with only her nurse-companion—and Seraphine."

Louis paused. "I do not know how or why it was her brother took her to
Europe. I know the old doc had put her on morphine, which had probably
reduced her to a docile 'thing.' Be that as it may, I think that it was Marion
Keller who saw a chance to get her out from under her brother's influence."
Pause. "And that was total . . . Anyway, by the time I took over in 1957
your mother was a ghost. Years of being shut away had all but atrophied every
response. But her brother was adamant she be kept apart. He told me she had
inherited—through her mother—that streak of madness which every now
and then plagues the English branch. I believe the present Earl is nutty as a
fruitcake . . . but I was not convinced. And when he left the Island on a
six-week trip, I brought your mother to the hospital and subjected her to
every test I could think of. Her ECG showed the *petit mal,* all right, and I

also discovered that she had once fractured her skull, dangerously near to the brain stem, which accounted for her amnesia."

Louis paused to puff at his pipe. "I also discovered she had had a child. So I consulted Seraphine." Louis mused silently for a while. "Strange, powerful woman, Seraphine . . . comes on like a cretinous old crone when she doesn't trust you, but when she does . . . I'd rather have her as a friend than an enemy. Fortunately, I do. Anyway, with what she told me added to old Doc Walters's notes I was able to deduce what was really wrong with your mother. So I put her on the Pill. It was being tested at that time, and some very odd things had come to light in the way of side effects. One of which was the miraculous relief of menstrual cramps, which according to Seraphine had left your mother in a bad way every month. More than that . . . her unstable and uncharacteristic behavior had always manifested itself around the same time."

Once again Louis puffed in silence before resuming. "At that time we were still studying endocrine disorders, so I contacted a man whose specialty it was. He suggested the Pill, thank God. The change was miraculous. A dead flower bloomed. You see"—Louis leaned forward urgently—"your mother had never been even remotely mad. What she had suffered from was a classic case of premenstrual tension caused by a hormonal imbalance." Louis sighed. "God knows how many women have been locked away as mad because of that!"

Elizabeth was frowning, so he hastened to explain further.

"The endocrine is a vital series of glands—the thyroid, the adrenals, and such—which are linked to the ovaries—that all-important part of the female reproductive system. Now these secrete a hormone to the bloodstream at particular times of the month, and if for any reasons those secretions should be unbalanced . . . well, a woman can turn into a Mrs. Hyde, which is what your mother did." Another sigh. "Old Doc Walters didn't have a clue . . . It was Seraphine, thank God, who put two and two together and left me to make it into four. Oh, I did all the tests, I consulted every specialist in the field. There was no doubt. And the change in your mother once she started having regular doses of progesterone proved it. All she needed, you see, was the right diagnosis."

Elizabeth was silent, suffering.

"She was locked away all those years for nothing," Louis said with angry frustration. "Condemned as mentally faulty when what was wrong with her was purely physical." His manner calmed. "But I mustn't blame old Doc Walters. He did what he thought was best."

Elizabeth put her face in her hands. Her tears trickled through them to fall on her cream linen dress, making dark splotches. She wept silently, grievingly. Louis let her. Tears washed the soul, he always thought.

"My poor mother, my poor, helpless, unhappy mother!"

Louis opened his drawer, found a box of tissues and leaned over to press them into Elizabeth's hands. She took them, wiped her eyes.

"There was no need for any of it," she said. "All her torment . . . all those years of terrible silence . . . no need, no need at all."

Louis sighed. "Old Doc Walters was out of his depth. He was good for what he knew." A shake of the head. "However, I have to tell you this: in my opinion, your mother's amnesia was deliberately aggravated. It is my belief that she was brainwashed, if you like, into believing her dreams were the fantasies of a hopelessly disturbed mind, that during the five years she could not remember, she had been made to believe that she had been quite mad."

He was monitoring the white face, the glazed eyes, but she was taking it well . . . especially the realization that it was in no way going to be as simple as she had thought. Which was why he had to tell her in the first place.

"I have no means of proving this, of course," Louis went on, "it is merely the picture I have formed since acting in the capacity of your mother's physician."

From between stiff lips: "How?"

"Because of the permanently planted fear—which is what has your mother in its grip at the moment—that she is inherently, congenitally mad. I think that if your mother had received the right kind of care and therapy, her memory impairment could have been overcome with time and patience. Instead, while she was suffering from recurring memories which terrified her, that fear was aggravated and she was deliberately led to believe that those memories stemmed from madness, constantly fed by lies which she came to accept as incontrovertible truth. She has told me what she was told . . . things which led to an intolerable mental strain, which in turn led to the sleepwalking. I had to work long and hard to undo all that. I had managed to bring your mother forward, right out of her fears, in fact. What Dan Godfrey did the other night was shove her right back. She is once again a terrified, distraught woman who believes herself to be incurably insane."

He saw Elizabeth close her eyes, clench her hands into fists.

"She is not, of course, and it is my job to get her to believe it. That will take time. Fortunately, I have Seraphine to help. Her influence on your mother is profound. Between us, I think we can bring your mother through."

Elizabeth nodded.

"But I am also concerned about you . . . because you are going to have to wait."

Another nod.

"I know that you must have hoped that Mrs. Hawkes would right things here as they were righted in London . . . but you see now, don't you, how much more complicated it is where your mother is concerned, how intricate and complex it all is."

"Yes . . ." Her voice was constricted, so she cleared it to say again: "Yes."

He saw her hesitate slightly as if framing and reframing the question he could see in her eyes before she said: "You have consulted a psychiatrist?"

"I brought an analyst in, yes. He spent quite some time with her and it is under his guidance that I am treating your mother. I know her, you see; her history and what she is so afraid of. He wanted to take her into his care, but that would really terrify your mother. Her fear of doctors and hospitals is deep-seated because of what she was subjected to once before—things you need not distress yourself about. And she needs the security of this island— and me. She trusts me."

"As I do," Elizabeth said.

"And trust is very important . . ."

He came round the desk to her, drew her to her feet, holding her hands in his. "You *can* trust me, you know that?"

"Yes."

"And you must trust in yourself to wait."

"I'll try."

He smiled. "Courage . . . you have already shown you possess no small store of that. Be assured that I will do my very best."

"I know you will."

"As soon as I think she is up to it to be brought into full knowledge of everything—then I will do so. She, too, has tremendous courage. Just think of what she did for you."

He saw the eyes well again. "I do—all the time."

"And remember I am here to help." Pause. "So is Dev."

Her lashes fell. "I know."

"He truly wants to help you—did so even before all this."

Silence.

"Let him," Louis said. "He wants to. Very much."

A nod. Then, lashes lifting, eyes urgent: "Could I see her—just to look at, no more?"

It was a plea.

"I don't see why not."

He took her along the hall to the lifts and up to the third floor, where he ushered her into a small room lined with glass-fronted cabinets containing supplies. One wall was hung with a curtain. Pulling it aside he motioned Elizabeth forward. Behind the curtain was a window, and beyond it, in a room filled with flowers and the late evening sun, Helen Tempest lay asleep on a high, white hospital bed, her face turned to the light, a look of tranquility on her face.

"She is sedated," Louis said. "Rest is important."

He let Elizabeth look her fill. When he heard her faint sigh he dropped the curtain.

"Better?"

She nodded. "Yes."

"I will do my best," Louis repeated.

"I know."

"Use these days to come to terms with yourself, with all that has happened. Get your own life to rights. That will stand you in good stead when it comes to the concerted effort needed to get your mother back on the rails."

Again she nodded. "And remember I am always here."

"Yes. Thank you."

He saw her down to the entrance, stood until she was in her car, waved as she drove away. Only when she was through the gates and out of sight did he go back into his hospital. She'll do, he thought. She's tough. Tougher than her mother. She can fend for herself. That her mother never really could is where all the trouble started . . . He went back into his office, sat down at his desk, and was still sitting there, far gone in thought, when a nurse came to remind him that it was time for Helen's medication.

Elizabeth drove automatically, one part of her mind given to driving, the rest preoccupied with what she had been told. Nearing the golf course, on an impulse, she turned off onto the track that skirted it. It brought her to where the dunes dropped away to the sea. There she stopped the car and sat, looking out to sea, thinking, thinking . . .

Dusk was deepening. The sun was low over the sea, turning it to molten glass, the surf reduced to a single frill decorating the water's edge. It was serenely peaceful. There was no one around. Only the palms stirring lazily before the last gasp of the dying wind and the faint click of pebbles as the sea dragged them down the shore disturbed the silence.

Her mood matched her surroundings. She felt sad, deeply, achingly sad. Not for herself but for her mother. Her own life might have gone off the rails, but that of her mother had been deliberately all but destroyed. What Louis had told her, when she put it together with everything else she had painfully learned, made an ugly, depressing picture. And yet she was conscious of a strange lift of a certain part of her spirits, a warmth where for so long she had been cold. She had *not* been deserted. Her mother *had* loved her. Oh, yes, how her mother had *loved* her. She knew it; she could feel it, remember it. The doors of her mind had been opened not only to memory but to understanding.

Unseeingly she stared out at the flaming ball of the sun, about to drop into the bronzed blackness of the sea, thinking how they had both been manipulated, used . . . forced into positions that were both unnatural and painful, abused emotionally, thwarted in their desires, deprived of love and the reassurance it gave.

Into her mind came the words Dev had said to her: "He who would love must first love himself." How true. She had not loved herself. Not even liked herself. Unerringly he had placed one of those long, strong fingers of his right on the deep crack at her center and it had all crumbled. She *had* been flawed. Self-invented. Self-everything . . . In no way had she been what she had believed. The plate glass had shattered and she felt all pink and new and tingling. Alive. She saw, felt, understood so much, now. Louis had completed the picture Dev had begun. A picture she was part of, because it was her life.

It was strange. She was now more vulnerable than she had ever been, yet never had she felt stronger. Knowledge *was* power. Who had she said that to? Dan Godfrey. Yes, that first night. Once again she was swept by a conviction that all this had been meant. That from the first time she heard the bell tolling for Richard Tempest, fate had been pushing her inexorably to this point, not allowing her to stop and pick up the pieces of self she dropped along the way. All along she had been conscious of a web, but even as she had carefully picked her way through the strands, others had already been winding themselves about her, sticky but strong. Now, sitting here, she was aware that the clinging miasma had gone. The soft breeze was everywhere about her and she felt clean and whole and renewed.

She felt herself opening up—dipped then immersed herself fully in the waters of memory, no longer afraid that they would scald and hurt, knowing, instead, that they could soothe and heal.

Yes, she would wait. She could wait, now. It was all she could do, but she wanted to do it. To give something, anything, everything . . . And not only to her mother. It was time, now, to tell Dev. All this time he had waited, been patient, understanding. Never once had he complained, pressed himself on her. When he had come to her, asked her if there was anything he could do, once Mrs. Hawkes was settled and the London business all squared away, she said, "Yes. Just leave me alone."

And he had done so. On the flight back, when she had wanted to be by herself to think, ponder over all that had happened, he had left her alone to find her way. Yet she had been conscious, always, that he was there. Even as she sat alone with her thoughts, she had been aware of him, his presence, his strength.

He had taught her so much, she reflected. About her own body, for a start. Brought that to clamoring, greedy life. Even sitting here, thinking about him, that clamor began again. But not only that. He had taught her how to love physically *and* emotionally. That to give *was* to receive. And had waited, patiently (and knowledgeably, she reminded herself), for her to give to him. Well, now was the time. In the long weeks of waiting ahead she would need his comfort, his strength, his unshakable confidence.

Suddenly she longed for the sound of that warm, vibrant voice, the look of those blue eyes that bathed her in bottomless security, the feel of those strong, hard arms. She had already kept him waiting far too long. And there was so much she wanted to tell him . . . She started the car.

It was dark now. The sky was strewn with stars. The lights of the car swept over trees and bushes, brought clumps of flowers to brilliant life as she swept by them. Then suddenly, as she rounded a bend, her foot hit the brake. Directly in front, shining wetly in the headlamps, was a pair of elaborately carved and gilded double gates: the Old Burial Ground.

She shut off the engine. For a few moments she sat there, then with a decisive air got out of the car, walked a few paces before turning to retrace her steps and switch on the lights. This time she put her hands on the lion's head that formed the handles and pushed the gates open. They swung silently, on oiled hinges. In front of her, gray and ghostly in the starlight, a path stretched away before her, disappearing into shadowy trees. She stood for another few moments, then with long, determined strides began to walk down it.

There was no noise but her own footsteps. The path dipped, ran through a hollow, came out from under a lush growth of trees, and there it was in front of her. A beautiful garden, marble monuments, tombs, effigies. As her eyes grew accustomed to the dimness she could make out angels, carved draperies, and soulful expressions. But what she was looking for had none of these. A plain, marble slab set into the ground but raised slightly, the words incised deeply, so as to withstand the erosion of time: RICHARD TEMPEST 1910–1974.

She stood in front of it for a long time. At first, she found she was waiting, tensed against something. But there was nothing. Her breathing was normal, her heart steady, her legs firm. No distress now, no panic. She could gaze her fill.

Well, she thought. It took me some time, but I've done it. I'm here. And
so are you. Because your power is gone, whereas mine . . . She smiled down
at the polished slab. "Mine is just beginning," she said out loud. Her voice
disturbed birds, who squeaked in fright, rustled for a moment, then subsided.

"I don't know what it was you were after," she continued thoughtfully,
quietly, "but whatever it was, you won't get it . . . not now. I know, you
see. And you—this—doesn't frighten me anymore . . . Miss Keller was
right. Knowledge *is* power." She stretched her arms out wide, as if beckoning
it to her.

Then she laughed. It rang exultantly in the silence. The last pieces of a
dead self had dropped away and she was free. Free . . . The man who lay
here was the dead past. Turning her back on the grave, she strode unhesi-
tantly toward her future.

Nieves had watched Elizabeth drive off, the car taking the curve of the road
with a sweep as arrogant as the woman driving it.

"Horrible, *horrible* woman!" Nieves had shaken with fury. "How I loathe
her . . . She won't find me fawning about her, hanging on her every word
. . . I'm glad she's not Gramp's daughter. I'm glad! I wish she'd take that
car and drive it into the sea and sink, then she'd never come back."

She sank down on the window seat, where she had been curled up with
one of her romances. It wasn't fair . . . nothing was fair anymore. *She* had
taken everything, and now she had Dev.

Her glance fell on the cover of her book. It depicted a demure young girl,
all wide-eyed innocence and misty white dress, shyly avoiding the impassioned gaze of a tall, dark, handsome man. Dev . . . Closing her eyes, she
let herself drift away into her favorite daydream.

She was the girl in the white dress, and the man was Dev, but he was not
standing looking at her, he was on his knees, his hand on his heart, the blue
eyes pleading and abject. "It is you I want, my dearest, darling Nieves . . .
not *her*—never *her*—why did I not see it before . . . You are the one, the
only one . . . All these years I have loved you and not realized it until I saw
you just now, looking so beautiful . . . My beloved, my own, sweet Nieves."
And Elizabeth, seizing his arm, trying to pull him away, and he shaking her
off, so violently she fell on the floor, but he did not see, did not hear her
crying, having no eyes for anyone but his own, darling, his sweet Nieves . . .

And another scene: she and Dev at this very window, arms about each
other, watching that same car drive away, but this time piled with luggage,
driving away forever, never to return, and Dev saying, "Good riddance," and
turning to her, Nieves, and saying, "Forgive me, my darling . . . for not

knowing, not seeing it was you all the time," and taking her in his arms, and there was music playing and he was kissing her . . .

She sighed, opened her eyes dreamily. That was how it should be. Why wasn't it like that? Why didn't Dev *see!*

She sat up, lips parting in an O of comprehension. "Because he doesn't know!" she said out loud. "Of course! He doesn't *know* I love him. How can he do anything if he doesn't know?"

That was how it was in all the romances she read by the dozen. The hero and the heroine always loved each other but neither *knew* . . . well, not until the last few pages, anyway. Always the hero said to the heroine, held fast in his arms, "Why didn't you tell me, my darling?" And it was always because the heroine was so young . . . her own age . . . and shy.

"I only have to tell him!" Nieves was astounded by the simplicity of it all. He just did not know! Well, she would soon change all that. But first of all she had to set the scene.

She flew upstairs to her room. Quickly she went into the shower. When she was dry she dredged herself in talc, put on clean underwear and then her prettiest dress. She brushed her hair until it shone, pinched her cheeks, bit her lips to make them red and tempting. If only Aunt Helen would allow her to use makeup . . . It was part of the course at school but not until the last term. But Aunt Margery had piles and piles of it . . .

And there it was: jars and tubes and boxes and sticks and little brushes and jells and everything she could possibly want.

Her hands were shaking so much she got mascara in her eyes, which stung and made them water, so she had to go and wash them, but the second attempt was better. In the magnifying mirror her lashes really were long . . . perhaps a little more shadow. And some blusher on her cheeks . . . She hesitated over the dozens of lipsticks, finally chose a pale-pink one that felt sticky but gave her full lips a tantalizing gleam. There! She *was* pretty. Everyone said so anyway.

Finally, after sniffing and testing, she drenched herself from a bottle named L'Air du Temps. Then she pirouetted in front of the big mirrors, delighted with herself. What did Elizabeth Sheridan have that she did not have—apart from eight extra inches and at least forty pounds? She could not wait to show herself to Dev. Oh, he would be so surprised!

She knew he was at the beach house because he had said he was going there to work. She would surprise him. She would open the door and stand there and he would look up and see her and—

She came out of her daydream with a start as she heard a car door slam, and darted to the window. It was him! He disappeared from view as he entered the House. With a last frantic glance in the mirror she ran downstairs. Even as she skimmed down them he came out of the drawing room, looked up and saw her. She stopped her headlong pelt and, trailing one hand on the banister, after an effective pause, came down the rest of them with a satisfied little smile, waiting for his surprise.

"Hello, love," he said. "Seen anything of Elizabeth?"

Nieves stopped dead. "No."

At her voice he stopped, turned. Then he really saw her. "What have you done to yourself?" he asked, and there *was* surprise in his voice.

Saucily: "Do I look different?"

"A gilded lily always does."

She was not sure what that meant, but she took it as a good sign. "Do you think I'm pretty?"

"Haven't I always said so?"

"Yes, but—"

"But what?"

"Well . . . really pretty."

"*Very* pretty." The smile was in his voice as well as his eyes. She glowed. It was all coming right . . . But then he was turning away.

"Where are you going?" She could not keep the panic from her voice.

"I want to find Elizabeth." He was checking all the rooms, opening doors and peering in.

"Why?"

"She went to see Louis Bastedo."

So what? Nieves thought sulkily. What about me? Don't I matter? Her face set into lines Dev took note of.

"What's the matter, love?" he asked lightly. "Nobody to play with?"

"Will you stop treating me as a child!" Her face blazed, so hot, so angry, he was taken aback. "I am not a little girl to be patted on the head and told to run away and play—I'm sick and tired of being treated as one!"

So that was why she was got up like a dog's dinner—all that stuff on her face. And that dress. Far too young for her, he realized, along with the truth of her words. It was more suited to a fifteen-year-old. Sweetheart neckline and puffed sleeves, yet . . . His experienced eyes registered a sense of desperation, and his nostrils confirmed it.

"Nobody takes any notice of me," Nieves went on bitterly. "Everybody is far too busy being concerned with *her* . . ."

"Poor love . . . But I thought you were keeping Mrs. Hawkes company . . ."

"Seraphine is with her. They are always together now. Even they don't

need me." He saw the chocolate-drop eyes well. "Nobody needs me around
here . . ."

Oh, dear, thought Dev on a sigh. Jealousy *and* hurt pride . . . Damn you
David, he thought.

"You can help me look for Elizabeth if you like."

No, I don't like! Nieves thought mutinously. I want you to look for *me*—at
me! Oh, why won't you look at me, see *me*. She would just have to disabuse
his mind of the idea that she was still a child. Show him she was a woman
now . . .

Dev was aware of every shade of feeling shifting across the expressive,
highly emotional face wearing far too much makeup, and that ill-applied. But
the body in the subteens dress was that of a woman. The trouble was, her
emotional development had not kept pace; had not been allowed to. She was
at a dangerous age, one where she needed support and reassurance. And
whose else had she to turn to but his?

"All right," Nieves said, but sulkily. "I'll come."

His smile mollified; so did the way he took her hand in his.

"Why do you want to find her?" she asked aggrievedly.

"She went to see Louis Bastedo. He had to explain some—unpleasant
facts."

"About Aunt Helen?" Nieves asked shrewdly.

"About everything." He glanced down at her. "I know you feel neglected,
love, but things around here are not exactly—normal—these days."

"I know *that!*"

They halted for a moment at the edge of the terrace and Dev looked down
over the gardens to where the white ribbon of the road stretched. Empty.

"Nothing has been normal since *she* came," Nieves went on resentfully.
"She changed it all . . ."

And was changed, Dev thought. I hope. But no use trying to explain that
to Nieves. All she saw—and felt—was the ground shaking underneath her.
She was not concerned as to its reasons, only its cause.

"Let's go down to the bench," he suggested. "We'll be able to see the car
coming from there."

Silently, Nieves walked beside him, her mind hunting feverishly for ways
and means to turn his attention her way. There was not much time: she had
to turn it before that car came into sight. But how? How? Her mind went
back to the romances, her guide to the world of adult emotions. There was
always a scene in them where the hero managed to get the heroine in his
arms, and it always ended in a passionate kiss . . . Sometimes the heroine
fell and sprained an ankle or sometimes they were in danger and had to be

326 THE RICH AND THE MIGHTY

rescued. Well, she was in no danger, but if she could somehow manage to fall
. . . That was it! If she could somehow engineer a situation where he had to
hold her, feel her, become *aware* of her. She knew if she could do that it
would all go on from there. He would hold her in his arms and she would look
up at him and he would kiss her and then . . .

Her mind was made up. That was what she would do. But how? How?

At the bottom of the terrace steps Dev struck out across the lawns, making
for the shortcut via the rose garden. Beyond that the road ran, and set on the
curve was a marble bench, where you could sit and smell the roses as you
admired the view. But, Nieves remembered, the rose garden was sunken, to
protect the heavily laden bushes from the constant depredations of the
winds. If she could manage to stumble, perhaps slip on the short flight of red
brick steps? The light was going, the dusk all purple and mysterious. So easy,
then, to misjudge her footing, clutch at him, be supported in his arms, lifted
up into them . . .

And even as they reached the steps, as if her obsessive and excited will
enforced the deed, she did slip on the worn smooth edge of the very top step,
feeling her foot slide and her body fall forward, arms outstretched, with a
startled squawk.

Dev's fast reflexes had his arms out instinctively as he half-turned to break
her fall. The impetus of it carried him backward down the steps, her arms
grabbing for him in instinctive fright and clinging round his neck so he had
to put his arms around her. He regained his balance on the next-to-last step,
shifting her in his arms to give him greater purchase.

It was then, her face on a level with his, her arms about his neck, with a
quick lick of the lips to make them shine more excitingly, that she husked, in
a voice meant to sound sexy but giving the impression she had a sore throat,
"Kiss me, Dev. Kiss me!" and before he could open his astonished mouth to
laugh, her own was pressed against it, lips firmly closed, so hard his teeth
protested. She had a grapple on him, her arms so tight about his neck he
could not move. When she had to come up for air, she looked at him with a
breathless smile—and there, on the other side of the road, stood Elizabeth.
She must have topped the slope even as Nieves had kissed him. Oh, it was all
too perfect!

"You don't have to hold back anymore," Nieves said, wide-eyed and
clearly. "I know you love me and you can tell me now . . . There is no need
to suffer in silence any longer, really, there isn't!" As Dev opened his mouth
to speak, she covered it with her fingers. "Let me tell you first . . . I love
you," she said in a ringing voice. "There . . . now you know . . . I want
you to know . . . I love you! You don't have to pretend anymore, honestly. I

understand now . . . you don't have to protect me anymore, really . . . You can tell me you love me now . . . I know you do but you can really tell me now." She pressed her mouth against his again with such force that he teetered once more.

This time he had to swing her up in his arms and retreat down the last step to the safety of the grass at its foot, she clinging to him all the while. When Nieves came up for breath Elizabeth had gone.

When Dev spoke his voice was smothered as he set her down on her feet. "Now, then, what was all that about?" he asked in a voice that sounded as if he was choking.

"I told you!" She all but stamped her feet. "I love you!"

"I know you do. As I love you."

"No, not *that* way!" He had said it in the old, pat-on-the-head way; not passionately and like a declaration, as he was meant to do.

"Oh? Which way, then?"

"You know . . ." Nieves said frantically, "*real* love! Like this!"

Once again she reached up, pulled his head down and pressed her tightly closed mouth against his.

"Oh," Dev said, when she had released him, that strange quiver still in his voice, "*that* love."

She recognized that quiver. He was laughing at her and trying not to show it! "Don't laugh at me!" she said, in a voice which made him stop. "You are not supposed to laugh at me!"

Quietly: "Then what *am* I supposed to do?"

"You are supposed to tell me you love me too!"

"I have just told you!"

"Not that way!" She was all but hopping from foot to foot. "I mean *really* tell me . . . because you know I love you now, so you can, but you were not sure before because you thought I was too young, but I'm not and—"

Dev put back his head and this time his laugh was uncontrollable. "Oh, love, you've been at those novels again . . . I *told* Helen it was time you moved beyond them."

"Don't laugh!" Nieves exclaimed passionately. "You are not supposed to laugh at me! I am not a child, I am *not!*" She burst into the kind of tears which disproved her every word.

"I'm sorry, love." Dev's voice was different, so grave she lowered her knuckles and stared at him, sniffing. "My fault. I should have realized."

Her face lit up. "You do love me! You do! Oh, I knew you did!"

She made to hurl herself into his arms again, but he took her wrists, held her off.

"I am grown up, I am," Nieves chattered feverishly. "Can't you see I am?"

Dev sighed. This was the last thing he wanted. And at this time . . . He raised his head to scan the road. No sign.

"Don't look for her!" blazed Nieves. "Look at me! It's me you love, not her!"

"Since when?" asked Dev.

His voice made her stare at him in dismay. She knew that tone of voice. It made her take fright. She hung her head.

"Since your grandfather died?" Dev asked. "Since Elizabeth came?"

He was right, but in her terror she attacked. "What difference does it make when? I found out—and that's all that matters."

Dev shook his head. "No," he said. "It is not."

He took her hand, walked her across to the bench they had been making for. She saw him once more rake the road with a glance. Then he sat her down beside him, firmly.

"I do love you," Nieves's voice was forlorn. "Lots of girls my age love men older than they are . . . I shall be eighteen soon! Lots of girls get married at that age!"

"You are still seventeen, and not old enough either to know what you are saying or what you want."

"I am, I am! I want you! I do, I do!"

"No." Dev's voice brooked no argument. "What you want is to be loved, I know that—but like this." He put his arm around her, and it was the old, comfortable way. He did not seize her with arms like iron as he was supposed to do. His hold was reassuring rather than passionate.

"I know you love me," he said gently, "which is not the same thing as being 'in love' with me . . . I love you, but I am not 'in love' with you either."

"I am, I am!"

The blue eyes held hers. She stared back like a trapped rabbit. "All right—show me."

Falteringly: "Sh-show you?"

"Yes. Kiss me properly—the way lovers do."

"P-properly?" She was confused. What did he mean—properly? There was only one way to kiss. You put your lips against someone else's lips and pressed.

In all her carefully guarded and overly protected life, Nieves had never been privy to kisses given and received in passion. Romances were all she had been allowed to read, and had provided her with no working knowledge. Even the films she saw were carefully selected. She had never gone out with a boy. She had been led, blindfold, through the highways and byways of

Margery's sexuality; Mattie Arden was a Friend of the Family. The nuns had been vigilant; Madame Laurent equally so—her girls left her care virginal in thought and word and totally mystified as to deed. There was always a high price on virginity and were not her charges up for sale? Their parents expected their daughters to go to their husbands' beds untouched; to be taught, not teach. Once the heir had been born—preferably several—then they could turn their attention to lovers. But until that time, sex not only never reared its ugly head, Madame Laurent ensured that none of her girls would recognize it if it did.

Now, Nieves was totally at a loss, had not the slightest idea of what Dev was saying.

"I thought you loved me."

"I do . . . I do!"

"Then prove it!"

Nieves was panic-stricken. How? In the romances, kisses were described as sweet, passionate, rapturous, but never more explicitly.

Dev read her face with his expert eye, met her eyes when she hinted: "You could show me . . ."

"But if you love me you should know."

Nieves was almost in tears again. "Oh, please, please show me . . . it's just that"—her blush was a furnace—"I've never *kissed* anyone before."

"I know that." Dev's voice this time really made her eyes prick.

"I shall never learn," she sobbed desolately.

"Oh, yes, you will, but not from me, love."

"But I want to learn from you . . . please, Dev . . . please!"

Dev's face was suddenly that of a stranger. The eyes did not seem to see her in the same way. They held a look which made her heart flutter.

"You are sure?" he asked.

"Positive! Please, please, Dev, show me how lovers kiss."

She heard Dev sigh. "I'm sorry, love . . . but it is time you grew up." And then he had her in a strong grip and with horror she felt his tongue invade her mouth—and his hand was on her breast! She was horrified! She struggled, squirmed, wrenched her face away before shoving him away and retreating to the other end of the bench, the back of her hand scrubbing furiously at her lips. "That was horrible! That's not how people kiss!"

"That is how lovers kiss," Dev answered, and with a shuddering comprehension she recognized the truth in his voice. "People who are old enough to know what love—and being a lover—means. Offering yourself to a man means your body as well as your heart."

Nieves gasped.

"If I asked you to, would you let me make love to you? Take off all your clothes, lie naked in my arms?"

Nieves squawked in fright and scuttled off the bench. This was not Dev! Not her familiar, lovely, comfortable, reassuring Dev, saying these awful things!

"Love is not romance, sweetheart. It is very many things—and one of them is sex!"

Nieves gasped again.

Gently: "Love is what we call it—but sex is what we do when we love and are loved . . . men and women. Is that how you love me? Enough to have sex with me?"

Nieves had her hands over her ears. "You are being horrible! You must not say such awful things!"

"But you said you loved me." Dev was gently remorseless. *"Really* loved me."

Nieves burst into tears. Then she felt herself sitting on the old familiar knee, the old familiar, comforting arms around her in the way that was so different from that other, *awful* way. She felt his handkerchief thrust into her hands.

"I do love you," she sobbed, "but not *that* way . . ."

"I know, love. That is what I had to show you."

She raised drowned eyes. "Is that why you did it?"

"Yes. Because when you are ready for it—when you meet the man you will fall 'in love' with, then it will all be different . . . the most wonderful thing you have ever known."

Wide-eyed and hopeful yet still doubtful: "Will it?"

She could not think so. The romances had never said anything about how *physical* it all was. How frightening. But the eyes that were smiling at her were not frightening anymore; his arms did not hold her trapped, his lap was comfortable and he smelled of that fresh, deliciously Spanish cologne he used. She heaved a sigh of relief. He was still lovely, familiar, reassuring, comfortable Dev. "You were teasing me," she said with a relieved smile.

But his voice was grave when he said, "No. If you loved me, as you say, you would want to do those things . . . and expect me to."

Uneasy, disturbed, she stared into the steady blue gaze. "I would?"

"Yes. You would."

Too late, she saw that she had ventured into a strange country. Too late, she saw, with sudden, shocking clarity, that romance was one thing, love was another.

"But you don't want me to do that, do you? This is not what you want from me, is it?"

Silently she shook her head.

"What you want from me is this." He settled her more comfortably on his lap, his arms about her in the old familiar way. "You wanted to be reassured, love, because suddenly you feel nobody has time for you anymore. And for that I am truly sorry, because you are loved, sweetheart. By me, by Aunt Helen, by Cass, by everyone—including your father."

"No, not him!" Nieves said bitterly.

"Yes, by him too."

But Nieves tightened her hold. "Just so long as *you* do."

"I do—and I always will. Nothing will change that—ever." The smile came back. "Friends?"

Nieves hugged him hard. "Oh, yes, yes . . . the very best of loving friends."

"Yes, that is what we are, you and I. Loving friends." He smoothed her hair back from her face with gentle, tender hands, but his face had a brooding look. "There never has been much love in this place, has there? And you felt you were losing what little you had." Once again the smile bathed her in its warmth. "Well, you haven't. Nothing has changed, sweetheart."

Nieves sighed. "That was all I wanted to know," she said shyly. "That"— very carefully—"that she hasn't changed *everything.*"

"Most of all herself," Dev said quietly. "That's why I want to find her. You say you felt alone. Have you thought how alone she must be feeling right now? Suppose it was you who learned that you were not what you had either thought or been told you were . . . that your father was not really your father and you did not know who your mother really was."

Nieves shivered. She had never thought about that.

"You needed comfort; don't you think she does too? That's what I want to do, love. Help her."

Nieves nodded slowly, her tender heart swelling with sympathy and an ever-deepening realization of how *kind* Dev was.

"So let's go and see if we can find her, shall we? Maybe walk down the road a way."

Nieves opened her mouth to say, "Oh, but I just saw her," and closed it again, swallowing dismay. If she told Dev what she had just done he would be so angry. Her heart leapt in fright. Oh, she could not bear that, not now, when they had only just reached this new understanding. Oh, dear . . . she thought, awash with fright. Now what have I done? She should tell him, but the very thought made her squirm. Later, when they could not find her, perhaps . . . or when they did find her. Yes, that was it . . . she would explain to Elizabeth it had all been a stupid prank. But the thought of making confession to those cold green eyes frightened her even more. There had been no expression on the face that had looked across the road at them. It had been set, stony. She had just—walked away. Surely, if she loved Dev, she would not have done that. She would have stormed across, demanded to know what was going on. But then Nieves remembered her romances. So often the heroine saw the hero kissing another woman and got totally the wrong idea . . . But had not Dev just said real love was not like that? Oh, dear, she thought, all frightened confusion. She just did not know what to think, what to do . . .

Nervously she slid a glance at Dev's face; it was frowning. Oh, she wailed inwardly. He will be so angry . . .

Then they saw the lights of a car far down the road.

"That will be her," Dev said, and suddenly there was a light in his face she had not seen before. Why, she thought, unable to control the pang which pierced her, he does love her.

Dev stepped into the middle of the road, held up his arms. But it was not Elizabeth. It was Dan Godfrey at the wheel of his Aston Martin.

"Good God!" he said amusedly. "What is this? My money or my life?"

"I thought it was Elizabeth. You didn't see her on the road?"

"Didn't see her anywhere. Why? She gone missing or something?" He sounded hopeful.

"No. But she went to see Louis Bastedo. About Helen."

"Ah . . ." Dan smiled. "Come now," he chided, "you don't think she has decided it is all too much and decided to end it all?."

Listening, Nieves felt worse than ever. But she could not say anything in front of Dan Godfrey.

"Perhaps she decided to walk back," Dan was saying. "You know what a walker she is. Hop in, I'll drive you back and we'll probably find she is waiting for you. You'll have to sit on a lap," he said to Nieves as he leaned across to open the door. "But you won't mind that, will you?" Nieves refused to meet his eyes, and when she got into the car, on Dev's lap, held herself stiffly. She felt traitorous, stupid, and—worst of all—guilty. What have I done? was all she could think, sick at heart. What have I done?

FIFTEEN

Margery felt as if she was struggling to escape from smothering layers of black velvet. She struggled against them, clawing and moaning, finally burst through them and through her closed lids saw the pinkness of light, opened her eyes then closed them again as the dazzle from the chandelier above her head sent splinters of light into her eyeballs. She moaned and the sound was like a dull blow to the temples. She felt sick and she hurt. Cautiously she opened her eyes to slits, turned her head slowly and carefully. There was a big mirror on the opposite wall, one she did not recognize, but it was large enough to reflect a rumpled bed under a mirrored ceiling, clothes strewn over the white carpet, empty bottles and glasses strewn around, roaches of joints, squashed cigarette stubs. In the air was the sickly sweet smell of hash.

There must have been a party, but where . . . Where was this? Carefully she raised herself up on one elbow. There was a digital clock carved from a piece of rock crystal on the table by the bed. It read two thirty-five and the date was the fifth of May. She had lost three days. How? Where? That meant she had been on a constant high of drink and drugs ever since—Then she remembered and with a moan flopped back onto the bed, her face buried in the pillow. Her mind was a whirl of bodies and hands and tongues and penises of various colors and sizes. She could vaguely remember being passed from hands to hands, bodies to bodies, being part of a writhing, moaning, frenzied group, men squeezing her between their bodies, men who gave way to women . . . A violent kaleidoscope of sensations and memories whirled her round and round. She ached all over and was still dizzy from all the champagne—yes, there had been champagne—and all the coke she had sniffed, the Colombian red she had smoked. But where? Feeling sick, she tried to remember. And then it hit her: her own bedroom in the house in Venice; seeing through the half-open door, which she had approached silently, intending to surprise Andrea, but receiving the surprise . . . the shock . . .

It all came back to her. The big, mirrored room, dim from only one small lamp, but light enough to reflect the two naked bodies on the bed, plunging together in writhing ecstasy punctuated by harsh breathing, stifled moans, and gritted cries. Andrea. And—she knew that red hair—Barbara Dillon, the rich-bitch cosmetics queen who had been trailing her lures in front of him for months now. She had stood there, rigid, muscles clamped and aching from the effort not to move, not to make a sound as she listened, watched . . . feeling a sickening sense of loss and dizziness and anguished terror as the scene imprinted itself on her brain, sending her blood rushing to her head so that she saw them, heard them, the steady slap of flesh on flesh until, as she saw the bodies strain, surge, heard the rasping gasps which preceded the final harsh cries, she had burst in on them, screaming obscenities, leaping at Andrea, long nails curved to rend and tear, sinking them into his flesh . . .

Nausea rose and she knew she was going to be sick, but when she leapt from the bed she staggered as the accumulation of booze and hash hit her, and she fell to her knees, managed to crawl across acres of carpet toward a half-open door and saw with relief that it was a bathroom and just made it to the toilet, where she heaved and gasped and retched, feeling the sweat break out on her clammy body, until she was weak and empty. Collapsing onto the tiled floor she lay there for a long time. Finally, hauling herself up hand over hand she stood swaying, saw her body reflected in a multiplicity of images from the mirrored walls, and moaned as she saw the welts, the livid bruises, the striping of purple weals across her breasts, her stomach, her thighs. Her face was puffy, her eyes slit, her mouth bloated and foul-tasting, her hair a tangled mess. Weakly she made for the shower, turned on the water, and when it was as hot as she could stand she stood under it, leaning with propped arms, while the water beat down on her, soothing, cleansing, washing away the debris of dirt inside and out, so that memory, exposed, sharpened and brightened, made her moan and shiver.

There had been a terrible scene. She could see behind her squeezed-shut lids the mirrored walls of her bedroom, cracked and shattered where she had thrown anything to hand against them. She could smell the sickly smell of mingled perfumes . . . Arpège, Joy, L'Air du Temps. She remembered sinking her teeth into Barbara Dillon's breast, heard again her anguished scream of pain. Then Andrea's brutal blows . . . Turning on him, kicking with her wickedly pointed high heels, aiming for his groin and all the while screaming the foulest of obscenities, out of control and demented with rage and pain and loss and betrayal, knowing she had lost . . . lost . . . Andrea, the money . . . everything . . . had nothing left to lose.

She remembered Andrea forcing her fingers back from Barbara's body, then slapping her across the face, shouting at her, "Bitch! Foul-mouthed whore! I don't want you anymore! We are finished!" And hitting, slapping, beating her into sobbing, cringing hopelessness. Then she must have passed out, because when she came to they were gone and only the destruction was left. She had lain there a long time.

What then? After that it was blurred. She remembered panic, the feeling that she must not lie there . . . that she had to keep moving, because if she did not she would never move again. She had to show them; and there was only one way. Faces . . . men . . . she vaguely remembered a bar . . . then a car . . . a man, or was it two men? Being groped by many hands . . . After that it all went into a spinning kaleidoscope of sensations and impressions.

Feeling sick, she tottered to where towels hung, wrapped one of them around her body, another round her hair. Her head was splitting, her body sore. Using the wall for support, she managed to get back into the bedroom. As she stepped into it, a door at the other end opened and a man came in. Naked, powerfully built, and with a thick mat of black hair at chest and groin, which, as he saw her, produced the fastest erection she had ever seen in her life.

"Well, baby." His accent was guttural but his English was clear. "Out from under?" He took a swig from a bottle. "And ready for more?"

Margery remembered who she was if not what she was. The sight of this—animal—warned her how far she had already traveled from her usual circles. For the first time she felt fear like a stab in the guts. She drew herself up. "Who are you?" she demanded imperiously.

"You mean you've forgotten me? After all we have been—and done—to each other?" He sauntered across to her. "Never mind . . . I have something that'll make you remember." Pawing among the debris on the night-stand he came up with a small metal inhaler.

"Oh, no you don't," Margery began angrily.

"Oh, yes I do." Before she could move, he had grabbed her with one of his sledgehammer hands, twisting her arm behind her in a grip that made her howl with pain and stiffen. But he only increased pressure, so that to move was agony, before jamming the inhaler up her nostril. Pinching the other closed, his thick fingers smothered her mouth so she had no other recourse than to breathe the inhaler. Like lightning, as she jerked reflexively, he did the same to her other nostril. The popper exploded in her brain like a fire-work, making colored lights soar and her blood roar in her ears.

"Better?" His grin was evil as he ripped the towel from her body, threw it aside, drew her toward him.

"No . . . no . . . don't. I don't want any more . . . I can't."

"Yes you can." His hands were all over her body, probing and gripping, hurting her. "You liked it before . . . couldn't get enough of it."

"No, please." Margery was moaning, feeling sick and dizzy. "I'm sick, please . . . can't you see I'm sick?"

"Not of me, you aren't. Nobody gets sick of me."

The smell of him, sickly and musky, added to the popper, increased her feeling of nausea and dizziness. He laughed brutally, indifferent to her protests. "The party's not over yet, baby!" Raising his voice: "Giorgio," he shouted. "Reina . . ."

The door opened again and two more people stood there. One was a negro; tall, slim, sinuous, his body painted in wild swirls of psychedelic color; the other was a woman, naked but for a spangled G-string. She had small, perfect breasts and long, smoke-black hair. She wore a half mask, and beneath it a full red mouth smiled, showing small, white, very sharp teeth. Beneath the mask her eyes were crazy.

"Ah . . . ready for more of the same, are we, love?" She had a mocking voice, a cut-glass English accent. Her smile was vicious, cruel.

"No . . . no . . . please." Margery's voice rose pleadingly. "I'm sick, can't you see . . . I'm sick." She felt terrible. In spite of the popper her head was pounding and there was a point of bursting pressure low in the pit of her stomach which went all the way through to her back; it was heavy, grinding, unbearable. She felt that even the slightest pressure there would burst her like a grape.

"We've got just the thing for that," the negro said in a dreamy, singsong voice. Reaching into the small suede bag tied around his neck with a thong, he brought out a small plastic packet filled with white powder. "This will make you feel all spaced out, baby . . ."

Advancing toward Margery he tore at the plastic with his own sharp teeth, shook some of the powder onto a thumbnail and held it out to Margery. "Here's your passport to paradise, baby!"

Again Margery tried to avert her head but the big man had her pinned and once again she had no choice. She inhaled the coke, which exploded in her brain like a great white light. Unconsciously she reached forward to flick the empty nail with her tongue.

The negro laughed. "That's right, baby . . . I can see you ain't no stranger to this paradise." He repeated the performance with Margery's other nostril. She felt herself disintegrate, clung to all three of them as they moved in on her, lifted her, carried her, laid her down on the bed . . .

The telephone woke Harry from a sound sleep. Groping for it he said a blurred: *"Pronto!"*

He listened, then sat bolt upright, clutching the phone with both hands.

"What? Where? When? How?" His voice was rapid, rising. He listened again and his face paled, his hands shaking. "Oh . . . Oh, yes . . . I see. Yes, of course. I will come at once . . . Where? Yes, yes, all right. Yes . . . Thank you."

He had trouble cradling the receiver, then just sat, numb, white and shaking. When he tried to get up, he fell back; his legs were useless. He closed his eyes, put shaking hands up to his face, took deep, calming breaths. Finally, when he could manage it, he got up and went for his clothes.

They were having lunch when Moses entered and said, "Telephone for you, Miss Cass. The Count calling from Italy."

"Harry!" Cass frowned as she shoved her chair back. "Now what?" But her voice was cheerful when she said, "Harry? What's up?" She could hear breathing and what sounded like someone crying. "Harry! Harry, are you there?"

"Cass." His voice was muffled, choked. "Cass . . ."

"Harry, what is it?" Suddenly she felt afraid.

"Margery." His voice went. "Margery is dead."

"Oh, my God . . ." Cass fell into the chair by the desk.

He was weeping openly. "The police called me from Rome . . . they found her body in a car in a back street . . . she had bled to death."

"Jesus Christ!" Cass's voice was a screech. "Bled to death! In God's name, how?"

"She had . . . there was . . . she was all torn and lacerated . . . they said . . . they said there was evidence of sexual perversion . . ."

"Oh, God!" Cass felt sick.

"She was all bruised and . . ." His voice went completely.

Cass pulled herself together forcibly, pinched off everything but what must be done.

"Where are you? Are you in Rome?"

"Yes, yes . . ."

"Then stay there. What's the address?"

She heard his voice fade as he talked to someone, then his voice came back, stumblingly repeated an address.

"Right . . . You stay there, do you hear? Don't leave the station, Harry. I'll have someone there with you as soon as I can. Do you hear me, Harry?"

"Yes . . . yes . . ."

"Who is in charge there? Let me speak to them."

She waited, biting her lip, drumming her fingers, dying for a cigarette.

"Hello? Do you speak English? Oh, God. *Momento per favore.* Dan!" she raised her voice to its hog-calling bawl. He came to the door of the dining room, napkin in hand. "Here, quick . . . I need your Italian."

He took in the face, the voice. "What's the matter?"

She told him. He was stunned. But he took the phone, relayed Cass's questions in Italian to the man on the other end, translating them back to Cass. Finally: "Let me speak to Harry again," she said. "Harry? Now listen carefully . . ."

She finished the conversation by putting a finger on the cut-off button, looked at Dan.

"Jesus!" he muttered. "What the hell had she got herself into?" He was pale, sweating, guilty.

"A one-way street," Cass said grimly. "All right, go on—you'll have to tell them. I've got work to do. Go on!"

She began to dial the Rome number of the Organization.

When she went back into the dining room they were all sitting in shattered silence.

"I've just talked with Vito Arabinieri," she said flatly. "He's a good man and he's got all the right contacts. I want this kept out of the papers as far as possible. Fortunately it was the police who found her. That was at three o'clock this morning. She was wearing an evening gown and sandals—that's all. And she was drenched in blood, the car too."

"Whose car?" Dan asked.

"Her own, thank God . . ." She turned to Dan. "I thought you said she had gone to Venice."

"That's what she told me. That's where Andrea Farese was."

"So what was she doing in Rome?" Hervey asked.

"It's not that far," Dan sulked.

"No—but Margery never drove. She always flew everywhere."

"Maybe—someone else drove it," Dan said.

"Bled to death!" David sounded on the verge of tears.

Hervey pulled himself together. "You are sure Vito Arabinieri can handle everything?"

"That's why I told him to," Cass said shortly.

"Who is he?" Elizabeth asked.

"He . . . troubleshoots for us in Italy," Cass said neutrally. "He knows the system and he knows everybody. I've told him to play it down as far as it will go."

"But—" Hervey moistened his lips.

"Yes, I know. Murder." Cass said the word they were all thinking.

"Can he do that?" Elizabeth asked, sounding surprised.

"He'll have a damned good try," Cass answered succinctly.

Silence fell.

"I've given him a free hand," Cass said after a while. "If"—she lit a cigarette with an unsteady hand—"if Margery had been indulging in her own peculiar kind of fun and games we don't want that on any front pages. As for the rest . . ." She drew deeply on the cigarette.

"Poor Harry," Mattie said, shaking her head.

"He's all but in pieces," Cass said. "He had to identify her."

"How did they know who she was?" Elizabeth asked.

Carefully tapping ash: "Margery was very well known in Italy," Cass answered expressionlessly.

Another silence fell, until Hervey cleared his throat. "Do the police have any clues?"

"No. It was her car and only she was in it. She was dumped, evidently. And she must have been bleeding badly when she was—which is no doubt why they dumped her."

"Have they been in touch with Andrea Farese?"

"I don't know. I didn't mention him and I told Harry not to either. But . . ." Cass shrugged. "As I say, Margery was well known."

David shuddered. "What a mess," he said. "Jesus Christ, what a mess."

The news cast a black pall. The already explosively fragile mood of the house underwent another change. Nobody had cared much for Margery, and they had all known the fine line she trod between indulgence and excess, but the manner of her death was horrible. They waited for the telephone to ring— which it did regularly and always for Cass, to whom Vito Arabinieri reported at regular intervals. And when the papers came, everybody pounced on them. But Vito Arabinieri had done his work well. The death was reported and there were headlines, but it was because of the circumstances in which she was found. Murder, they said, in the course of robbery, because the Contessa's maid had reported her as leaving her house in Venice three days before wearing a fortune in jewels. Which were missing. There was no mention of Andrea Farese but for a brief statement saying that the Contessa had been "a great and good friend" and that he was deeply shocked. There was no mention, either, of the shattered room in the house in Venice.

In the final report Cass received from Vito Arabinieri, he told her the necessary repairs had been made and that the cost would be included among the "disbursements" when he presented his bill. Cass made the necessary arrangements through Organization channels.

Where Margery had been and what she had been doing during the three

days in which she had "vanished" was never revealed. But the postmortem—
a copy of which Cass also received but which she showed only to Hervey—
revealed, among other things, that Margery had been far gone in cancer of
the womb. That was what had caused her to bleed to death. Certain objects
had been used on her in the most brutal of ways and there were bruises,
burns, lacerations, and deep scratches on her body. She had also been riddled
with drugs. Cocaine, marijuana, and various other stimulants. She was probably unconscious when she was dumped, which led to a deep coma, in which
she had bled to death. Investigations, the papers said, were proceeding, but at
the inquest the cause of death was given as exsanguination.

Her body was brought back to the Island by Harry three days later. It was
taken straight to the church, and the next morning, very early, she was buried
quietly and quickly with only the Family present. The coffin was never
opened. Margery had been prepared for burial in Italy. Vito Arabinieri had
seen to everything.

It was only afterward, when they got back to the house, that Harry, still in
a state of shock, told them how it had been.

The car had been found in a back street in the poorest part of the city. A
patrolling policeman had spotted the expensive car—a Ferrari Dino—and
gone to investigate because cars as costly as that one stood out in such
surroundings. Margery had been in the driver's seat, wearing a dress that had
originally been silver lamé but was now stiff and soaked with blood. Even her
sandals were filled with it, and the car seats; it had even dripped from the
door and formed a puddle in the gutter. There was nothing else. No evening
purse, no coat, no jewels. The owner of the car was traced through its license
number.

The Contessa's maid said she had left the house at about ten o'clock on
the Wednesday night alone, in her own private vaporetto. Her driver said he
had taken her to Harry's Bar. They said she had left with two men. They
were traced and said they had taken her to a private party. No one remembered seeing her leave that. Or with whom she had left. That had been at
about four o'clock the following morning. Between that time and the time
she was found, three days later, no one knew where she had been or how she
had got to Rome. None of her friends had seen her; they had not even known
she was in the city. No one had come forward to say they had seen her. All
inquiries drew a blank.

"They only know it must have been an orgy," Harry said, white still, and
bleaky subdued. "That she had—she had had many men . . . and—and
other things." He was still suffering. "I had to see her, Cass . . . to look at

her . . . so white . . . the most hideous white . . . and all bruised and scratched and burned . . . on her breasts and her thighs and—" He shuddered, gulped at his stiff drink. "Never have I seen such sadistic, sexual abuse. What sort of monsters were they? What kind of depravity did she take part in? Who would do such terrible things? How could—that—be thought of as pleasure?" He sounded sickened. "I knew of her—appetites—but this . . ." He took another swig at his drink. "Never had I dreamed of anything like this. Did you know of such things? I did not."

Cass did not answer. She could have told him much, but he had enough to contend with.

"And she was riddled with drugs." In a very controlled voice: "They told me it would only have been a matter of months for her, anyway; that the drugs she had been taking—for a long time, they said—would have dulled the pain, because there would have been great pain." Once more his voice struggled for clarity. "So they dumped her . . . left her to bleed to death . . . but they said—they said she was probably unconscious . . . I hope so." His eyes welled and he sobbed. "I hope so . . ."

Poor bitch, Cass thought heavily. Poor, doomed, helpless bitch. In spite of everything, a natural-born victim.

The funeral had been almost furtive, as though the sooner Margery was under the ground the better. Above it she was a silent reproach to those who had shrugged their shoulders, said indifferently and with raised eyebrows: "Oh, *Margery* . . ."

Only Harry had cried, all through the services, all through the committal. And it was the women he clung to. Cass had held an arm on one side and—surprisingly, because Cass had not even expected her to attend—Elizabeth on the other.

"Are you coming?" she had asked when Elizabeth had joined them as they waited for Father Xavier to finish giving communion to Nieves and her father, who had, for a change, remembered he was a Catholic. As had been Margery. Once.

"Yes. I'm coming."

And she had stood, dry-eyed, next to Harry, not stiff and embarrassed as Cass had expected; towering over the little man, yes, but like a tall pillar to hang on to. In a plain black dress—for Margery's was not an Island funeral—she had never looked more beautiful or, thought Cass with another *frisson* of shock, more sad.

And afterward, in the drawing room, where they sat around stiffly and awkwardly, she had sat by the sad little man. Cass had heard them talking in low voices but could not hear what was being said. As it was, Cass was glad to leave her to it. Harry's grief was something which weighed heavily. It made her feel guilty. As they all felt, she thought, looking round at the shuttered faces, conscious of the way eyes did not meet, voices were strained.

Poor bitch, she thought again. Bought and sold by the pound from the time she had any value. Oh, Margery had been murdered, all right. But not only by the years of booze and drugs, the legions of lovers, the self-destroying indulgence in unbridled sex. Nor the unknown people who had dumped her and fled. None of them. One man had done it. One man . . .

Harry left next morning. He was composed, but his sadness had become bitterness.

"I'm sorry, Harry," Cass said miserably. "This has been such a terrible thing."

"What is not, in this house."

Cass was taken aback. The brown eyes were still red-rimmed and he looked exhausted to the point of failure, but his voice was strong. "Thank God I shall never have to see it again."

"But—" Cass began.

"I shall never return to this island. I would not have wished to be set free in such a way, but I am free."

He turned to Elizabeth, standing silently by. "Be glad you are not *his* daughter," he said violently. "Be glad instead that your mother is that good, kind, gentle woman who showed me the only kindness I ever had here . . ." He bowed over her hand. "I wish you luck," he said.

And he was gone.

When Elizabeth awoke, the sun had traveled right across the sky. She had slept for hours for the first time in weeks. It was three weeks since Margery's hurried, almost furtive, funeral. Since then, time had become a long, seamless length of misery and despair. Had done, ever since *that* night; when she had seen and strickenly accepted what she had always uneasily suspected though never willingly faced. She had known of the special relationship between Dev Loughlin and Nieves. Everyone had spoken of it lightly, even teasingly. But with respect. It had tenure, standing, had long been accepted as something "special." And left her on the outside again, looking in.

It had devastated her. That one, long, disbelieving glance had seared her with such force it had melted her wings, sent her plummeting to the ground, which she had hit with such force she had been wandering around in a daze ever since.

Nothing in her solitary life had prepared her for this kind of lonely desolation, so that the only thing she could do—knew how to do—was retreat into herself as of old, which was what made her realize that her metamorphosis was far from complete. It had not been a miraculous change overnight. Bits of her old self still clung to her, like rags. Only in one respect had she changed irrevocably. She could now feel.

Why else should she be so hurt, so betrayed, so envious, so sullenly jealous? For the first time in her life she was at the mercy of the emotions he had released in her, and she spent her days going right through their spectrum, only to end up at the beginning, ready to start all over again. Her mood was morosely heavy and she wanted only to be alone, to brood. She knew it was wrong, that she was acting like the child who had been so badly hurt all those years ago, but she could not help herself. She still lacked confidence, she realized. Was still not possessed of that necessary sense of her own importance. She needed him to give her that. And she had lost him.

She had avoided Dev as if he was contagious. Which, she thought despairingly, he was. She was still infected with a raging fever for him which the sight of him only sent soaring. So she kept out of his way. In any case, she did not think she could have spoken to him with composure. If and when she had to, it was coldly. Her pride would not allow of his knowing how she felt. No, she was not so changed. She was still evolving, still in the painful process.

Now she laid her head on her knees, closed her eyes. How long, she thought. How long . . .

It was not fair, she thought for the thousandth time. Nieves is only a child. It was the woman he saw in me he said he wanted . . . But had not Nieves said, "You don't have to hold back anymore. I know you love me and you can tell me now . . ."? Putting into words what she must have known he felt—what perhaps even he, so experienced with women, had not known, perhaps not dared to admit.

She had known there was some special feeling between them. That Nieves worshiped him. Everyone had regarded it as a crush, which had also been wrong. Nieves loved. It had been in her face, her voice, the radiant joy of her face.

And me, Elizabeth thought. What about me? That makes every word he said to me a lie. Laden with hypocrisy. He was a liar and a thief and a profligate sensual man . . . and how she longed for him. That was what was worst. This ceaseless, constant longing for him. The touch of those strong, sure hands, the sound of the loin-caressing voice, the vivid blue of the eyes and the warmth in them.

Lies, she wept inwardly. All lies . . .

She could not—she would not—think of it anymore. That way lay madness. She must concentrate on her mother; gather what strength she had to go on waiting. Hoping. Perhaps something had happened today . . . Rising to her feet, she walked slowly down to the water. The long swim lay ahead. She had been prepared to go to him, say, "Help me." Now, there was no one to help her but herself.

She came out of the water a good hundred yards down the beach from where she had left her clothes, which was well away from the beach house. She could not bear the sight of that. But as she trudged along the edge of the shore, head down, she heard her name being called. It was a shout, carried on the wind. Shading her eyes, she looked up the beach. No one. But there it was again . . . yes, *her* name. A man's voice—shouting. Her heart plunged. Something had happened. Without stopping she snatched up her dress, her sandals, and continued on her way, at a run now. It was only when she rounded the curve by the outcropping rocks that she saw David, above her, on the path, in the act of raising his hands to his mouth to bellow once more: "E-LIZ-A-BETH."

"I'm here," she called, and he looked down.

"Where the hell have you been? I've all but shouted myself hoarse!"

Swiftly she ran up the path toward him. "I swam across to Sand Cay. What's the matter? Why are you shouting for me?"

"It's Helen . . ."

Her nails sank into his arm. "Why? What's the matter? What happened?"

"All hell let loose, that's what! Old lady Hawkes and Seraphine cooked up a little plot between them with Nieves aiding and abetting . . . smuggled the old lady into the hospital." He nodded vigorously at her blanched face. "True . . . without telling anybody. They must have been planning it for days . . . Louis is fit to explode."

"Is she all right? My mother—is she all right?" Her face was blazing with urgency and her grip on his arm threatened to cut off his blood supply.

"Yes, she's all right." He prized her fingers loose. "I've been bellowing my head off for God knows how long! We've had the whole place upside down searching for you."

But she was already off at a run. "See Louis first!" he bawled after her.

Once again she took the short cut through the gardens, leaping across flower beds, crashing past bushes. Her dress and sandals she dropped somewhere along the way; nor did her bare feet feel the change from grass to gravel, or the hot stone of the terrace steps as she took them two at a time. Voices told her where everyone was.

They all jumped as she burst into the white drawing room. At the sight of her face, the swimsuit, the bare feet, the sound of hard breathing, Mrs.

Hawkes, standing clutching Seraphine's hand, burst into terrified tears. "I didn't mean no 'arm . . . honest I didn't . . . we was only thinkin' to 'elp."

"It was my idea," Seraphine overrode that. She was quite calm, almost subjugatingly so, no sign of guilt or fear. Only certainty.

"And mine . . ." Standing in the shelter of Dev's arms, Nieves looked up, face tear-stained. "I wanted to make it up to you . . . I wanted to tell you, but you looked so fierce and I was afraid you would be angry with me."

Blankly, Elizabeth stared at her, not comprehending, then she turned as Louis came forward.

"It's all right," he soothed. "We've had quite an afternoon but it is all under control now."

"But my mother . . ."

"Resting. Seraphine made her one of her tisanes. She was excited, somewhat—overwrought, but she is all right. Better than I could have hoped for."

He grabbed her when she swayed, as reaction took over. "A chair!" he said quickly, lowering her gently into the one Cass hastily pushed forward. Gently he pushed her head down between her knees. "Take it easy . . . deep breaths."

Her pulse was racing, but it was strong.

"I'll kill David," he heard Cass mutter. She hovered distractedly. "God knows what he told her."

Elizabeth raised her head. "He said—all hell had been let loose." Her eyes were filled with dread. "Has it? What happened?"

Louis nodded toward the bulk of Mrs. Hawkes which was crowding into the spare, erect figure of Seraphine, calm as an idol. "These two took it into their heads to—accelerate—matters. Seraphine went to the hospital as usual while Nieves"—another nod which made her shrink even closer to Dev— "ostensibly took Mrs. Hawkes for a drive. What she really did was smuggle her into the gardens, where I have been allowing your mother to sit every afternoon."

"And?"

"Surprise, surprise," Louis answered dryly.

"She—she took it well?" Elizabeth's face shone with hope.

"Marvelously, superbly well. I think Mrs. Hawkes got the worst of it."

"I was that overcome," sobbed Mrs. Hawkes. "Ter see yer pore ma again after all these years . . . and she was that glad to see me."

"She *knew* you!"

Mrs. Hawkes wiped her eyes. "Thanks to Seraphine, she did."

Elizabeth's eyes went to her. Seraphine nodded. "I had been—preparing her." Nothing disturbed her impenetrable calm.

Elizabeth's eyes went back to Louis. "What we in the medical profession call "sleep learning." It has been found that the unconscious mind is capable of retaining information fed into it while the conscious is taking a rest. That is what Seraphine—I *now* learn—has been doing every day these past few weeks. Giving your mother one of her witch's brews and then diligently planting information, bit by bit . . ."

As Elizabeth's eyes once more turned her way, Seraphine inclined her head in gracious yet quite unruffled admission.

Mrs. Hawkes nodded vigorously. "True as I'm sittin' 'ere . . . When I went in and she sees me, well, you should 'ave seen 'er face . . . Then she gets up and opens 'er arms ter me and says, 'Mrs. 'Awkes . . . my dear, kind Mrs. 'Awkes . . .' Well, I bawled me 'ead orf, didn't I, and she pattin' and soothin' me . . . Then when I got meself together, why, we sat down and 'ad a fair old crack . . . Told 'er all about you, I did, and 'ow yer come ter see me and everythin' . . . and Miss Keller and 'ow you was took orf and where . . . Then she asked me ever such a lot of questions with such a queer look on 'er face . . . We was there a fair old time, we was . . . she 'oldin' me 'ands that tight and smilin' and noddin' and the tears running down 'er face."

Mrs. Hawkes wiped her own. "I never seen a body so 'appy, never . . . Then she puts 'er arms round me and kisses me and says, 'Ow can I ever thank you . . .' and I says, 'You don't owe me nothin' . . .' And she says, 'Oh, but I do . . . I do.' Then she stands up and says, 'And now I must go home to my baby.' Wouldn't be put orf no 'ow . . . 'I 'ave to go to my baby,' she keeps sayin', 'my Elizabeth.' So we 'ad to send for the doctor 'ere." She stole a guilty look at Louis's impassive face. "And 'e—well, 'e eventually says it's all right . . . So we all come back 'ere but you was nowhere to be found . . . We've 'ad this island gorn over from top to bottom. That's what worried yer ma, yer see . . . made 'er upset, like . . . But Seraphine 'ere, she calmed 'er down, made 'er another o' them drinks of 'ers and then puts 'er to bed . . . And then you was found—and that's all," she finished nervously.

"All!" said Elizabeth, laughing and crying. "All! Oh, my dear, marvelous Mrs. Hawkes . . ." Her embrace was heartfelt. Then she turned to Seraphine. "And you . . . how can I thank you?"

"My lady's happiness is my thanks," Seraphine answered with great dignity.

"It could have gone *very* wrong," Louis said emphatically, "but Seraphine had done her groundwork. It was less of a shock than I had feared."

"When can I see her?" Elizabeth sounded eager yet nervous.

"When she wakes she will want to see *you* . . ."

"Where were you, anyway?" Cass asked curiously.

"I swam over to Sand Cay."

"Sand Cay! Jesus! No wonder we couldn't find you."

"So that's where you've been hiding yourself," Louis said softly.

She avoided the all-knowing eyes, was conscious that ever since she had entered the room those of Dev had never moved from her, but she resolutely refused to meet them also.

"Well, we've found yer now," Mrs. Hawkes said happily. "And I didn't mean ter do nothin' wrong, honest . . ."

"What you did was right," Elizabeth said, with another hug of the trembling bulk. "That was why I brought you back, wasn't it? So that you could do for her what you did for me."

"That's what Seraphine said—and she knows yer ma better than anybody in this world . . . I know that now . . . so when she said it was all right, I never for a minute doubted 'er."

"Neither do I," Elizabeth replied simply. She turned to Seraphine. "I might have known you would know what to do."

"It was only a matter of knowing the right time," Seraphine answered composedly.

"Thank you," Elizabeth said, offering a hand, which Seraphine took.

"And pretty Miss Nieves too," beamed Mrs. Hawkes. "It was 'er that took me to the 'ospital."

Very slowly Elizabeth turned to face Nieves, who looked as though she would like to crawl inside Dev, swallowed hard and faltered in her breathy whisper: "I only wanted to help . . . to make it up, like I said." Another swallow, then, in a rush to get it over and done with: "It wasn't what you thought, you see . . . I was all mixed up and didn't understand, but Dev put me right and—and he didn't see you . . . Only I saw you and—and that's why I did it!" She burst into tears again.

"Did what?" Cass demanded, thoroughly mystified and not liking it one bit, staring suspiciously from one to the other.

But Elizabeth was finally looking at Dev, full into the blue eyes, her own filled with a mixture of emotions that had the body in the navy-blue swimsuit taut as a bowstring. As Cass stared, she saw the face, the eyes, change, and suddenly it was as though the broad shoulders had laid down a heavy burden. The smile Elizabeth released was dazzling. "Nothing important," she said clearly, and it was as though she sang the words. "A misunderstanding, that's all . . . a silly misunderstanding."

Nobody spoke. Only watched. David, lumbering in through the door, stopped dead in his tracks. He saw Elizabeth nod at Dev, once, as though communicating some silent acknowledgment, then turn away, saying, "Now I must go and put some clothes on."

It broke the silence. Everybody began to babble at once.

"I think you have something to tell me," Dev said softly to Nieves, taking her aside, away from the general welter of conversation.

Taking a deep breath, Nieves told all. "You are not—angry—with me?"

"Not now, I'm not. But I wish you'd told me before, love."

Nieves squirmed. "I felt so—so stupid . . . and—well, I just couldn't get up the nerve . . . I was afraid you would be angry and we wouldn't be friends anymore."

"I thought I had explained all that."

Now she looked guilty. "I know, but—I'm sorry," she pleaded. "And Elizabeth understands, doesn't she? . . . I saw the way she looked at you."

"Yes," said Dev. "A lot has been made clear this afternoon."

Elizabeth floated up to her room feeling a strange, excited calm. It had all been taken out of her hands, somehow. She would not fight anymore. The was no need to now.

She was standing by the window when he came. For a long moment they only looked at each other. Then Elizabeth said softly, "Forgive me?"

He opened his arms. As they closed round her she let everything go.

"So that was why you kept me away . . . I knew something had gone very wrong, but for the life of me I could not find out what. I've gone over every word, every look . . ."

"I doubted you," she said, her voice muffled against his neck. "I'm sorry."

He put her away slightly so that he could look deep into her eyes. "No; it was not me you doubted. It was yourself. In spite of all I have told you, you still lacked that final, absolute confidence in yourself . . ."

"I know that—now."

"Otherwise you would have come to me, demanded to know what the hell was going on . . . But it was the same old story, wasn't it? You felt you had been rejected."

A silent nod.

"What you saw was a frightened child seeking reassurance . . . But you believed the lie." She heard him sigh. "My fault . . . I pushed you too hard, rushed you along too fast, expected far too much. I was so impatient, you see

. . . and I wanted you so much. That's what I was doing . . . coming to look for you. I thought you might need me. I hoped you would."

"I did—I do! I was coming to you . . . that's why it was such a shock."

Unflinchingly: "You see, I know that you love Nieves," Elizabeth said.

"Yes. I do. But I am *in love* with you . . . you are the one I want."

"I'm sorry, I'm sorry . . ."

Once again he looked deep into her eyes. "You believe me now?"

"Yes. I believe you now."

Her eyes were clear, openly honest. He searched them, deeply, probingly, then he smiled. "Then that's all right." Soberly: "You have no need to be jealous of Nieves. It was because she was jealous of you that she did what she did. She was desperate. And I was all she had. I have always protected her, you see, all her life. I stood in for David—which was wrong of me, but there was no one else. You are, and always will be, the one I want."

He was serious, and she saw, suddenly, that he looked tired, strained. It was then she understood that he had been with her every step of the way these last weeks—only treading a different path. She had taken everything he had to give—his patience, his understanding, his help, his love—while she . . . she had not been willing to give him so much as the benefit of the doubt. It was her turn to give now, to show him. She put her mouth to his.

For a long time they stood locked together, kissing deeply and passionately, and this time she gave of herself in a way that was deliberate, wholehearted, unrestrained, letting him know, through her mouth, her hands, her whole straining body, what he meant to her. All she was, all she hoped she would be, she now gave up to him.

"I love you," she said, for the first time in her life. "I've always loved you, even when I did not know what love was."

"But now you do."

"Yes, I do now . . . and I want to show you."

It was she who locked the bedroom door, came back to him, her hands going to the belt of her robe, pulling the knot so that the thin silk fell away from the naked body beneath. It fell to the floor and she stepped out of it, gloriously flushed with desire. His breath caught in his throat. And then they were together, she aiding and abetting his own stripping until he lifted her, carried her to the bed, laid her down. Under his hands, her skin vibrated with electricity and her open mouth was avid, passionate. Her need of him was plain, and he was flooded with compassion. She had yet to face what was perhaps the greatest test of her life, and it was from him she was seeking the strength, the reassurance . . . Tenderly, achingly, adoringly, he gave it to her.

There was no frantic greed, no tearing haste this time. It was slow and deliberately prolonged. His hands, his mouth, were gentle, left a trail of fire. Whereas before his ruthlessness had driven her wild, now his absorbed tenderness left her weak and helpless. The waves this time were gentle but their surge powerful, left her gasping and fluttering for breath. She felt he was absorbing her inch by inch, and for the first time in her life understood what was meant by the act of reciprocal possession. Never had she felt so completely possessed; never had she possessed so completely, even before the long, delicious slide of his entry. For a moment he did not move, allowed her to feel not only that part of his body but all of *him* inside her. She looked up at him with shining eyes. Words were unnecessary. Then instinct took over and their bodies began to move in perfect synchronization, but still no haste or greed, just a long, slow climb to total fulfillment, the waves rising higher and higher and sweeping them forward so that she moaned deep in her throat and felt him trembling and bit his tongue and drove herself up and against him, opening not only her body but her entire self to his taking. *Giving,* for the first time, and yet conscious of receiving everything, and as the wave gathered them in, lifted them up, held them for a moment at a dizzy height before casting them down, flinging them far up the shore of physical felicity, she cried out once, "Yes!" and they both knew she had finally found herself.

Then they just lay and gazed at each other, until Elizabeth said softly, "Oh, my love, what a marvelous, marvelous man you are . . . I love you so much I could die."

"We just did," Dev said, in that laconic, sheathed voice he used at times of deeply felt emotion. "The French call it *la petite mort.*"

Still softly: "It was worth the wait, wasn't it?" she murmured.

The blue eyes glowed. "Now you begin to understand."

"Because of you. You have showed me so much . . . torn down the wall I hid behind."

"Yes," Dev said. "You had built yourself a king-sized wall of Jericho,"—the eyes laughed at her, lovingly—"only I happened to be the boy with the trumpet."

They talked then, as they had never talked before. Able to say everything. Elizabeth felt gloriously free; his physical penetration of her had been a key which had opened her up to life. She was brimming, now, with the confidence she had lacked. She felt, now, as if she could do anything. Not only was she filled with a singing, physical peace, her mind was at rest too. He had given her—as she had known he would—the respite she needed. Because she now knew she had him, in all the ways there were, she would be able to accept her mother, wanted to accept her mother, because she had no doubt, now, that the woman lying asleep along the corridor *was* her mother.

"It's all one, great big wheel, isn't it?" she mused drowsily. "And it has come full circle."

She told him, then, of how she had heard the bell tolling for Richard Tempest; of how it had filled her with dread, sent her headfirst into the pool of memory.

"I think I knew subconsciously that it was tolling for me . . . I don't know why, but looking back, I think that was why I was so afraid."

"Perhaps you are psychic. You are perceptive . . ."

"Oh, but *you* are the one who is perceptive! Look how you read me!"

"That was recognition," Dev answered. "We—collided because we were irresistibly drawn to each other."

"That's why I fought so hard—"

"And I pursued so relentlessly!"

"I'm glad you did." She shivered, tightened her arms around him. "If you had not, I would still be living in that sterile vacuum." Her face, her voice were somber.

"And now you have a lover *and* a mother."

But she did not smile. "How do you think it will go?" she asked.

"The way you want it—and she leads."

"You saw her—how was she, really?"

"Excited, radiant, nervous—and happy as I have never seen her. She gave off light . . ."

He heard her sigh once, heavily. "I hope I don't put it out . . ."

He shook his head. "Never. Not now."

He felt her relax in his arms, but there was a tiny vibrato in her voice when she said, "It will be very strange."

Very gently: "You are somewhat strangers to each other, but only because of all the years between. You lived with her for the first five years of your life, and you loved each other very much—that we know. Losing her all but did for you; losing you was something she never got over. You remember, now, what it was like . . . hang on to that. Nothing has changed. The only difference is that you are both older. She loves you; I saw it this afternoon. And you love her. I saw that too. She wants you back as much as you want her. You *need* each other. What she can give you is entirely different from what you need and want from me . . . We are all made up of layers, each with their different responses. But it is from our mothers that we learn to love. It was because you learned from her to love so deeply, so completely, that you dared not, having lost that love, seek to love again. Miraculously, it has been returned to you. Go with it, show it to her, give it to her . . . I do not begrudge it. You have more than enough to give."

She flung her arms around him, tight. "Oh, I do love you . . . You make me feel so—human!"

He laughed. "You are, my love, you are . . . at last."

They talked on until the darkness fell and Dev switched on the lamp. "I want to look at you," he said, running his hand down her body. "I shall never tire of looking at you."

And then they made love again, once more with sweet, passionate tenderness, and it was as they were lying, bodies still joined, that Seraphine's voice, following her knock announced, "My lady is waiting for you."

Elizabeth sat up, flung the covers back, her body under the lamp all rosy and golden.

"Five minutes!" she called breathlessly.

"I will come for you."

Dev chose her dress. "This one," he said, coming out of the dressing room with the pale-green silk chiffon. And he did her hair, brushing strongly, leaving it loose. Finally, under his eyes, she stood proudly. "Will I do?" In spite of herself there was a catch in her voice.

Dev's eyes kindled, bathing her in their light, imbuing her with confidence and strength. "Oh, yes. You will do . . . my love."

Seraphine knocked once more.

"A kiss for good luck," Elizabeth said quickly. She clung to him, hard, for a moment and he could feel the tautness of her body, but her smile was confident, proud. "I will come to you," she promised. "Wait for me?"

"I'll be at the beach house."

She nodded, her smile flaring. "Yes, there."

Then she was gone.

Seraphine looked Elizabeth up and down, then smiled. "Her favorite color," she approved.

"And mine."

Seraphine turned. "Come. She is waiting."

But Elizabeth caught at her arm. "She is—all right?"

Seraphine's smile was broad. "Never better."

The door to Helen's bedroom was wide open, every lamp lit. In spite of the love, the confidence with which Dev had filled her, Elizabeth felt a sudden plunging in her stomach; could feel her pulse racing. As Seraphine stepped aside to allow her to enter the bedroom, she instinctively adopted the old attitude: head up, shoulders back. Then she stepped through.

Helen was reclining on a chaise longue upholstered in turquoise velvet, her eyes on the door. As Elizabeth appeared, she swung her legs down, stood up. The movement released a cloud of fragrance which drifted over to Elizabeth, who recognized and remembered. Lily of the valley. Suddenly the exquisite room was gone; she was in the small back bedroom at 23 Mackintosh Street looking up at her mother, who was holding out her arms, as she was holding them now—wide open. Her mother's eyes were suffused, the gentle face expectant yet tremulous. A face she remembered. And that smile. Suddenly she *knew*. They both did.

"My baby," Helen breathed, a catch in her voice, "my Elizabeth."

Neither was conscious of moving toward the other. They only knew that they met, that their arms went round each other and they stood, holding tight, not able to speak, only to feel. And then Elizabeth was weeping. It was wholly natural, quite uncontrollable.

"You are my mother, *you are* . . . I remember you . . . I do, I do . . ."

She could feel her mother's body trembling, did not know if the tears that wet her cheeks were hers or her own.

"Thank God," Helen kept repeating, over and over again like a litany, "Thank God. Thank God . . ." And then: "My Elizabeth, my own, sweet precious Elizabeth . . . dear, precious heart."

The remembered words totally did for the last shreds of Elizabeth's composure. "You used to call me that," she wept. "I remember."

"Because that is what you were to me . . . are to me . . ."

Helen held her daughter's face between her two hands, her eyes blurred and streaming. "I did not dream you . . . you are real . . . you did and do exist . . . I was not mad."

She pressed her lips to the wet eyes, to the trembling mouth.

"Do you remember? That was how I used to kiss you each night, before you went to sleep."

"I remember. I remember . . ."

Weeping, trembling, they clung to each other. Not for some time were they able to let go, and even then their hands clung, even when Helen drew her daughter down to the chaise longue, under the light of the lamp, so as to be able to look her fill.

"It is a miracle," she whispered, "a God-given miracle . . . to find each other after so many years."

She gathered Elizabeth to her once again, rocking her back and forth against her breast. "So many wasted years . . . so much time lost . . . My poor, lost, lonely baby."

Only when they were finally able to did they begin to talk, when they could not stop from just smiling at each other; fatuously, foolishly. It was disjointed at first, interrupted by exclamations and excited promptings. They found they could laugh and share things—all they remembered about the little house in Camden Town. It was when they came to the years apart that Helen became distressed, her hands fluttering and patting and caressing, making soft sounds of distress, her eyes welling once more. "How you must have suffered!"

"I! No, it was you."

She had listened with mounting horror to what Helen was able to tell her about her years of "madness."

"It was not you who were mad," Elizabeth exclaimed passionately and protectively. "It was *him!*"

Helen stared, quavered: "Richard?"

"Yes. Your loving brother!"

"Oh, no," Helen said, with a scandalized headshake, "Richard was never mad! Why, he was the cleverest man I ever knew."

"And the cruelest! Who else but a sadistic and vindictive man would claim his sister's child as his own and attempt to destroy that sister's mind in order to do so!"

Helen paled, a hand to her throat. "Oh, no . . . do not say that!"

"I must say it! It's the truth! He was prepared to tell the world I was *his* daughter when all the time he knew I was yours! Is that not madness?"

Helen shook her head, still pale. "No . . . no, he was not mad . . . but he was deeply unhappy." Helen's lashes fluttered. "He—he was flawed, you see. He was not able to have children of his own. I know that now, but when you came, I thought . . . they can do such wonderful things nowadays and it was all so long ago . . . medicine has made such strides so I thought it must have been put right, and God knows he tried hard enough . . ." Her disjointed voice trailed off before the force and brilliance of her daughter's eyes.

"Put what right?" she asked, in an almost fearful voice.

"Why his sterility, of course." Helen's eyes welled again. "My mother told me. She didn't mean to . . . She was ill and delirious at the time. He caught mumps from me. He blamed me."

Elizabeth shook her head, as though trying to clear it. "Sterile!" she repeated. "Richard Tempest sterile!" She seemed dazed, having difficulty in believing.

"He never knew I knew, of course, but I knew he was angry. It meant so much to him, to be part of a continuing and unbroken line . . . He was so proud of his lineage, and he wanted his own flesh and blood to carry it on."

"So he took yours." Elizabeth's mouth was open, eyes wide to match. "Of course . . . that's why he did it! A twofold purpose: the continuation of the family—even through a female line—and revenge on you!"

"Revenge?" Helen recoiled again.

"Oh, yes—revenge! He hated you for what he thought *you* had done to him! That was why he had to destroy your mind . . . destroy *you!*" Her arms went about her mother with fierce protection. "And he almost did."

Her face over Helen's shoulder was acrid in its hate. "He *was* mad . . . He could not—would not—accept his sterility. The fact that *you* had a child must have been unbearable. That was why he would not hear of your marrying, because you would have the children denied him . . . so he made it his business to deny you. And that's why he married widows with children, mature women who would raise no eyebrows if they did not conceive. It was too risky to marry a young, fertile woman . . . the nonappearance of children would have raised doubt, perhaps meant tests. And being the man he was, he would not be able to *stand* anyone knowing he was sterile, not Richard Tempest, so virile, so powerful! Never! He would rather have died." A livid smile appeared. "And he did . . ."

But Helen was appalled, white-faced and shaken, not willing to believe. "Not Richard," she moaned, "he would not be so cruel."

"Oh, yes, he would!" Elizabeth contradicted. Then she remembered that Helen had always shut her eyes to what her brother did. Created a new world for herself—even as her daughter had done—into which she had retreated. When she had not wanted to know, or see, she had merely taken off her glasses. And with every cause, Elizabeth thought protectively, once more putting her arms around the sobbing, trembling body of her mother; she was probably, in spite of what she told herself, afraid of him . . . remembering always what her own mother had said.

She was appalled at the final picture: a real Dorian Gray, hideous, monstrous, deformed and twisted, warped and malevolent, so bitter that he had laid waste whatever he could in his rage and despair. What a monstrous irony! Of all men, the golden, leonine, unbelievably rich and mighty Richard Tempest—"King" Tempest—sterile. Unable to do the one thing that ninety-nine percent of all other, ordinary men could do: impregnate a woman. He, with his renowned virility, his wives and his women, in his own eyes not a man at all . . . With a sudden, shattering insight she knew that was why he had hated Dev Loughlin so much. Somehow, somewhere, Dev had proved his own virility. She knew it. And perhaps—no, probably—with a woman Richard had wanted. Who? she thought vengefully. Something else she would find out. And suddenly, gloriously, did not care to because all that mattered was that she knew. Oh, Dev, Dev, she thought, cradling her

mother in her arms, I owe you so much . . . I don't care if you have a
thousand bastards, just so long as you give *me* a child of yours . . .

Then it was that she understood how her mother had felt about her father.
Gently, she wiped her mother's eyes.

"It is all behind us now," she said tenderly. "He has lost. We have found
each other . . . We have won, in the end." And in her newfound confidence and the buoyancy of Dev's love, felt, underneath the revulsion, the
anger, a flicker of pity for the man who had been unable to come to terms
with his own flaw.

"Tell me about my father," she asked simply. "There is so much I want to
know . . ."

Cass glanced at the clock for the umpteenth time. "Jesus . . . what *are* they
doing up there? It's been two hours now."

"And twenty-odd years to catch up on," Mattie reminded.

"I expect they are goin' at it nineteen to the dozen," Mrs. Hawkes allowed
happily. "Like we did this afternoon."

"But my nails are down to the elbow!" wailed Cass.

Oh, she thought, to be a fly on any of those walls . . .

"It'll all come right in the end." Mrs. Hawkes nodded wisely. "I've a
feelin' in me bones."

Cass squirmed. "It's the end I'm waiting for."

"You never could stand not knowing anything, could you?" David grinned,
but it was not malicious. Not this time. The whole house was alive with
excitement. Even the servants went around grinning. "Have a drink," he
said.

Cass glanced over at a huge silver cooler containing half a dozen bottles of
Krug '68. "I'm waiting for the actual launch," she fretted, "but if it doesn't
happen soon *I'll* sink!"

When Seraphine silently materialized in the doorway, no one noticed her
at first. Only when Cass saw David stumble to his feet did she turn, lunge to
her own feet, and take a step forward, to find suddenly she was feeling all of a
tremble, had to reach out for a chair.

There was a triumphant glitter to Seraphine's smile when she announced,
deceptively blandly, "My ladies will see you now."

Cass beat everyone. She fell in through the door of Helen's bedroom only
to stop short at the sight of Helen and Elizabeth, as alike as if mass-produced,
sitting side by side on the chaise longue, holding hands. Then her grin split
her face as she threw both arms in the air in a boxer's salute. "Hallelujah!"

It was Mrs. Hawkes, lumbering into the room last of all on the arm of a fondly solicitous Nieves, who summed it all up once the welter of voices and congratulatory confusion had abated somewhat: "I don't know as when I've been so 'appy . . . Thank Gawd I lived ter see this day!"

"Amen!" Hervey added, wax melted to a puddle.

"But do *tell!*" moaned Cass. "We've been hanging on hooks . . . How did it go? What did you *do?* What do you *know?*"

Elizabeth laughed. "Oh, Cass . . . Cass. I think you had better sit down because you aren't going to believe it."

"Listen!" Cass retorted, "after what's been happening around here, I'll believe anything! What is it?" she asked suspiciously.

And as Elizabeth had predicted, she did not believe it.

"STERILE! *Richard Tempest sterile!* Jesus H. Christ!" Then, for once in her life, words failed her. She could only sit and stare. Until it hit her.

"Oh, my God!" she said in a screech. "That's why he sank so much money into that clinic!"

All conversation stopped.

"Which clinic?" asked Elizabeth.

"The one in Zürich." Cass almost wept. "He subsidized the damn thing . . . God knows how many millions of dollars. He said if the Organization patented some new drug that was a sure cure for sterility, it would be like holding the patent on penicillin, a license to print money . . . But it wasn't for money . . . all the time it was for him . . . years and years of research."

"It did not happen, then—the new drug?"

Cass shook her head. "No, nothing worked." She slapped her forehead hard. "God, what a dum-dum! *Why* didn't I realize?"

Dan's laugh was hugely enjoyable. "Come on, Cass. Richard Tempest looking to be cured of sterility?" He bent over double, slapped his knee. "Oh, what a marvelous turnup for the books! Of all men . . . oh, how absolutely beautiful!"

"That was the last thing it was!" Elizabeth said in a voice that cracked a whip. "It was why he did everything he did."

It cut Dan's laugh dead in mid-cackle.

"That's the explanation we were looking for," Elizabeth went on quietly. "His reason for everything."

Nobody spoke. Mrs. Hawkes, quite bewildered by it all, went from one stunned or bitter or tightly clamped face to another. Every one of them looked as if they had lost a thousand pounds and found a penny.

Hervey cleared his throat. "There is no doubt, I suppose?"

Helen shook her head sadly. "No . . . My mother told me, you see."

"She also told me," Seraphine announced calmly. She had taken up station behind the chaise like some lady-in-waiting. Helen turned round in surprise. "She told *you!*"

"When she was dying . . . And she asked me to look after you. To protect you from him." The totem-pole face seemed to crack. "I failed . . . for which I now, in the presence of others, ask your pardon."

Helen shook her head, her hand reaching up and out, which Seraphine took with her own.

"No one could have won out against him, Seraphine. I see that now. He was obsessed."

"Nevertheless, it was a trust which I failed to keep."

"No, no," Helen denied. "You saved me, Seraphine, time and time again."

"Why did you not say anything when Miss Elizabeth came?" Hervey asked reprovingly.

"Because I had sworn not to tell anyone. Which I never did until I told Mr. Dev. Because of what had happened, I felt released from my vow."

Elizabeth jerked. "You told Dev?"

Seraphine met her startled eyes. "Yes. He came to me the night my lady had her shock. He explained to me all that had happened and said he wanted me to help him to help you. He took me into his confidence, so I repaid him by giving him mine." Her eyes swept over Dan like a brand. "He is a man who can be trusted."

Dan's normally pale face flushed. "Now just a minute . . . if it hadn't been for me, not so much as a hint of all this would ever have come out."

"Yes it would," Seraphine contradicted flatly, "but in a very different way."

Dan's face tightened and his eyes slid away from Seraphine's. "Well, it's out now." He shrugged sullenly, defensively. "But naturally I know better than to expect gratitude."

"I have no doubt you will present us with your bill," Hervey sneered.

"You are damned right I will! And I expect payment in full! Come to that, I think I deserve a bonus." He began to laugh again.

The laughter echoed like a ricochet round and round Mattie's vacant mind. Sterile! *Richard sterile!* Then the child Richard had made her kill had not been his . . . that was why. And he had not told her. Let her think . . . Oh, God . . . She felt sick. It had been Franco de Giusti's child. After she had flounced away from Richard following that monumental row in Salzburg she and Franco had gone to Paris and spent the entire weekend in bed. It was not until she got back to New York ten days later that she and Richard had made it up, in the most passionate of ways. That was why she had not doubted, not for one moment, that it was Richard's child, had been unable to comprehend why he insisted she have it aborted. But he had. It was the child—or him. And when she had asked him why, he had said: "The Tempest heir must be legitimate."

"Then divorce Angela! Marry *me!*"

"The Tempests never divorce, you know that."

"But it is *our* child, Richard!"

"Is it?" he had asked, and she had known then he knew about Franco, thought that was his reason, that he was not sure. But he had been sure . . . Oh, God, how he had been sure . . . That was why he would not let her have it, accept it as his own. It had to be a Tempest—and that damned webbed foot would have been missing.

God, he had had it all worked out . . . known all the time. Everything. She felt he was using a knife to scrape flesh from her bones. How he must have laughed! Knowing . . . *knowing* all the time . . .

She wanted to howl, scream, rend her clothes, tear her hair. She sat with her body clenched, in silence.

David was just as stiff in his chair, but for an entirely different reason. He felt if he released his clamps he would float up to the ceiling. A great weight had been lifted. The terrible engines of his mind, the ones he had tried to rust with liquor, had been turned off. One short word had thrown the switch: sterile.

He had the sensation of having had a ceaselessly throbbing abscess drained. He felt empty and, for the first time in many years, at peace. He had to hang on to the arms of his Louis XVI armchair, he felt so light-headed. It had all been just another finely woven tissue of lies, so thin you could see through it, but it had shrouded him like a blanket and bent him double under its weight, sent him staggering through life. And all for nothing. Inés had not lied. All she had sworn to him, over and over again, had been true. Nieves was not Richard's daughter. She was the daughter of Inés de Barranca by David Anson Boscombe!

You stupid, self-deceiving bastard! he lashed at himself. You blind, bloody fool! Why did you believe him? Why did you let him use you? Because you wanted to believe him, he told himself, holding up the mirror of truth and for once facing his own, true reflection. You wanted to suffer. You enjoyed it . . . Poor, stuttering, shambling, shuffling David Boscombe. Who preferred to be thought of that way rather than accept any kind of responsibility. You couldn't stand even the thought of that—which Richard knew. Oh, he knew all right. He knew you would accept what he told you because it relieved you of that responsibility . . . and he also could not stand the thought that you, that same, stumblebum failure called David Boscombe, could do what he couldn't—father a child. With all his glittering bravura, his looks, his charm, his wealth, his power, he could not impregnate a woman.

Oh, God, he thought, feeling his upward soar check, stop, send him plunging back to earth, what have I done?

He looked across at his daughter—*his daughter*—sitting with a look of sadly forlorn envy as she gazed at Helen and Elizabeth, mother and daughter. It was all his fault that she had lost her own mother. It was his fault that Inés, unable to take any more, had fled to her family in Cuba; his fault it should unfortunately have been on the brink of that country's revolution, which had taken her and her family. Had it not been for Dev, at that time filming in Cuba, and Richard's power and influence . . . "She is my daughter, David," he had said, with such convincing sadness, "and I accept the responsibility."

David wanted to curl up and die, he felt so ashamed. Lies! he wanted to bellow to the world. All lies!

But he could not. Nieves would never be able to stand that . . . or would she? Perhaps—perhaps that was what she needed from him. He could start by being honest with her, make confession, beg for forgiveness, for understanding. God knows, she had heard enough tonight to see how easy that would be. If he told her all, bared his soul to her . . .

As if she felt his burning gaze, she turned her head, met it. He saw her expression, sad, doleful, change to one of surprise, then question, then—yes, it was—hope. Edging his chair sideways like a crab, he put his mouth to her ear and, under the other voices, said, "Not to worry, sweetheart." He felt her shock at the endearment. "I *know* he was not what he seemed . . . and if you'll let me, I'd like to tell you why."

Again she turned her face. This time it *was* hopeful, all of it.

"It was all done with mirrors," David went on steadily, "and in the sure and certain knowledge that people are their own worst enemies." Gazing firmly into the doubtful brown eyes: "God knows I was mine." He forced himself to hold her gaze, to stop his mouth from trembling. "Not anymore," he said firmly. "Not if I can help it . . . and *you* will help me."

Her lips parted. She seemed even more breathless than usual when she said, very, very carefully, "If you *really* want me to . . ."

"I want you to." Then, wide open and unashamedly, nakedly desperate: "I need you to . . ."

He felt her hand taking hold of his. He laid his other one on top. "All right," she said and she was smiling at him. It was radiant, made his eyes fill with tears. "I will. I'll help you, Daddy."

"All very nice, I'm sure," Dan was saying snidely. "I'm very happy for you both," he added, in a voice that held the patent on insincerity, "but may we now return to the nub of it all?"

"How much?" Cass asked scornfully.

"How much is there?"

"Nothing, until the will is probated," Hervey said from the bench. His upraised hand stilled Dan's objections. "What we have heard tonight in no way alters that will. Elizabeth is the named beneficiary." He looked round them all. "And that is how it must be."

"Why?" asked Dan.

Hervey's nostrils flared. "You know very well why."

"All those nasty little skeletons?"

"What we now know must remain known only to us. Only us," he repeated. "Let us have no scandal added to that which will be created anyway."

"I am proud to acknowledge my daughter!" Helen said with fierce pride. "And will do so to the world!"

Hervey's glance was tender. "Of course you would—but it would not do, I am afraid. It would call into question a great many things and leave us with nothing but trouble. It would mean, you see, that Richard died intestate." He threw up his hands. "I dare not contemplate the resultant confusion."

"Speak for yourself," Dan said with a grin.

"I am," Hervey said, the black eyes buttoning firmly. "The will must stand." Pause. "And you must stand for it. Once probate is obtained, arrangements can then be made . . ."

"Like what?"

Hervey steepled his fingers. "I have been giving consideration"—Cass coughed—"*we* have been giving consideration to setting aside certain—funds —from which you may draw an income commensurate with what you would have had in the event of things being different."

"Like what?"

"Two million dollars a year free of tax."

Dan's eyes sparkled.

"The same for David, of course . . ." Hervey cocked an eye, expecting a refusal.

"Which I will take," David nodded, "thanks." This with another nod in Elizabeth's direction.

"What do you need money for?" Dan was amused.

"I have plans," David said confidently, his daughter's hand warm in his, feeling an answering squeeze.

Nobody mentioned Margery.

"When?" Dan asked next.

"I anticipate probate by the end of the year," Hervey answered.

"The end of the year!" Dan's chair came down with a thump, and Helen for once did not care. She had eyes and ears for no one but her daughter. "I'm not hanging about for the next six and a bit months!" Dan was definite. "I want it now."

"But I must draw up the necessary papers."

"So draw them—here, use my pencil."

"Signed in blood, more like!" snorted Cass.

"Whatever—but *now!*"

"Do it, Hervey," Elizabeth said curtly. "I want this all squared away too."

"Sensible girl," Dan approved warmly. He rose to his feet. "That concludes our business, then, I think? In which case, I have no further interest in these—er—proceedings. I shall be leaving in the morning, by the way. When the document is ready for signature, all you have to do is whistle."

He sauntered over to Helen, bowing with a sardonic flourish before bending to kiss her cheek.

"You will let me come to Marlborough now and then, won't you? After all, if it wasn't for me—it wouldn't be yours, would it?" He smiled sunnily.

When he'd gone: "Somebody open a window!" sniffed Cass. But she too rose, albeit with reluctance. "Come on, then, Hervey. Let's get this thing worked out and typed up. I want his tongue tied as well as his hands."

Helen smiled up at him. "We will talk later, you and I," she promised. He went pink with pleasure.

"Dear Hervey," she murmured fondly. "Such a good friend."

But Mattie had now come to stand before her. Helen looked up into the set face and her smile faded. "Dear Mattie . . ." Her voice was sad. "I wish . . ."

"Don't," Mattie cut in flatly. "They never come true—well, for you maybe." She turned to Elizabeth. "And for you."

"I'm sorry," Elizabeth said.

Mattie studied her. "Do you know, I believe you mean that."

"I do."

"You have changed," Mattie murmured sardonically.

"I hope so."

"Not too much," Mattie warned, with sweet venom, "I might not recognize you . . ."

That she herself showed all the change she felt was evident in the anguished eyes, the flippant and fragile quality of her voice.

"I am sorry, Mattie." Helen was deeply troubled. "I know you loved him."

Mattie's heart-shaped face lit fiercely. "I still do," she confirmed vibrantly. "In spite of all he did"—her voice faltered—"and what he was." The full mouth trembled. "But *what* was he?"

"A deeply unhappy man," Helen said gently, her magnificent eyes unbearably sad. "I know that now. I wish I could have helped him."

"You can say that—now?" Mattie was incredulous. "After what he did to you?"

"He was desperate," Helen answered sadly.

"But he lied!" Mattie said fiercely. "He cheated and—" Her teeth sank into her lip. She flung her head up, blinked furiously. "God, I feel so *used.*"

"We all were," Elizabeth said gently. Then, gazing full into the pansy-purple eyes, soaked and tragic: "But nobody else knows."

Mattie's face changed and a faint, comprehending smile appeared. She nodded. "No," she agreed softly, "they don't, do they."

"And never will," added Elizabeth.

Mattie's deep breath squared her shoulders, inflated her ego. "Too true," she said strongly.

"Then we go on . . ." Elizabeth said. They exchanged a smile of total complicity.

"Yes," Mattie said, teeth baring in a wolfish grin, "we go on."

"Don't worry about Mattie," David advised, when she had gone. He had been watching and listening. "She'll survive. Just let her get that ego reflated and she'll bob to the surface."

"Dear David . . ." Helen's embrace was a smother of fragrance.

"I'm glad for you both," he said gruffly.

"Thank you," Elizabeth said, and he knew she meant it. How are the mighty fallen, he thought, in all directions. He had never seen anyone change so much so fast. She was still confident but its quality had changed. Whereas before it had been cold, cutting, an offensive weapon, now it was the sureness of security. Love, he thought, will do it every time . . . It had absorbed her mystery. The enigmatic visitor from Olympus had gone; in her place was living, breathing flesh and blood—*warm* flesh and blood. She had been empty before, he realized with a sense of shock, and he had filled her with his own imaginings. Someone else had filled that vacuum—Dev, of course—but with her own, belatedly realized self.

For a moment he felt a sense of loss which wrenched at him, but at the stirring of his daughter's hand in his own it vanished. He had his own flesh and blood, as warm as he could wish for. No more yearning after the unattainable, he admonished himself. In any case, Dev had already attained it. But there was still a way.

"About that portrait," he said confidently. "When you are ready just let me know."

"You still want to do it?"

"More than ever now."

"All right. But give me a few days, will you?"

"As long as you like. I'll be here." He put an arm around Nieves's shoulders. "We'll be here."

"You are not going back to school, then?" Elizabeth asked Nieves.

Nieves shook her head. "No . . . I don't need school anymore, but Daddy needs me."

For the first time, she met eyes that were no longer coldly green but as warm as the Island sea. Then Elizabeth smiled. "Friends?" she asked.

Nieves's answering smile was shy but certain. "Friends . . ."

Downstairs, in the library, Cass finished taking Hervey's measured dictation and sat back, pushing her glasses onto her forehead and rubbing at the crease in her nose.

"That's that, then. I'll get it typed up, two copies, and we get him to sign it in his own blood."

"It would burn the paper!" Hervey snorted.

"It could have been worse," Cass reminded. "That will *is* invalid, in that Elizabeth Sheridan is not Richard's daughter . . . He could have taken it to court, as we both know."

"Maybe, but he doesn't—and don't tell him!"

"Me!" Cass was outraged.

"Not that he will," Hervey went on with a conspiratorial smile. "I still have that dossier of his."

Cass sighed. "Richard certainly went to an awful lot of trouble . . . and all for nothing."

"He was not to know that."

"I wonder. He was never under any illusions as to the size of Dan Godfrey's greed. He must have known Dan would not lie down for one second under any of it."

Hervey made a dismissive gesture. "No more suppositions, please, Cass. I am up to here with incontrovertible proofs as it is."

Their eyes met.

"Who would have thought it?" Cass asked yet again. "Richard Tempest sterile! It's like saying God is impotent."

"But explains everything."

"Elizabeth always believed they lay somewhere."

"That's because she never quite—believed—in him. Persisted in trying to reduce him to size."

"Only it was Helen who did that . . . and, God knows, he has shrunk in my eyes. No giant after all; just a little man who could not come to terms with a physical flaw."

Hervey snorted once again. "Flaw! I can see you are not a man, my dear Cass!"

"I know, I know . . . ego can go no further than a reproduction of self."

"We were both well acquainted with the size of his!"

Cass glanced down at her shorthand notes. "And this should cut the other one down to manageable size, too." Her voice was creamy, her smile bland: "And we get our million dollars . . . for fraud and conspiracy yet."

"Fraud! Conspiracy!" Hervey met blandness with blandness. "There is nothing in the will which makes it conditional upon relationship, besides which Elizabeth Sheridan is the named beneficiary."

Their eyes met and they both began to smile, which turned into a laugh.

Dan read every word twice, weighing them carefully.

"It is a solemn covenant," Hervey reminded him. "Break it—and I will break you!"

Dan raised silky eyebrows. "No chance of that," he murmured, and affixed his signature with a flourish: *Danvers A. Godfrey.*

"You have no questions, no . . . observations as to validity?"

Dan looked hurt.

"You made it, my dear Hervey."

He folded his own copy carefully, tucked it away. "And that other little document of mine . . ."

"Remains with the bank until probate is granted."

"But after that . . . surely I can have it?"

"That," Hervey said, looking down his nose, "remains to be seen."

Not if I can help it, thought Dan.

Elizabeth put a head round the door minutes after he'd oozed through it.

"Your presence is requested," she said to Hervey. He turned from the safe, where he had locked away his copy of the all-important document. "But not too long, will you? She is on the edge of exhaustion." Her smile took away the sting of the warning. Hervey pressed the button that sent the paneling sliding, concealed the drum of the electronically guarded safe.

"You must be tired yourself," he returned warmly.

"No . . . not in the least. Only content."

Hervey stopped by her on his way out. "Do you remember what I said to you, the first time we met?"

"You said a lot of things."

"But one in particular. I said to you, 'You'll do.' "

Elizabeth smiled. "I remember . . . And I said, 'Yes, but what?' "

"Well, now we know, don't we?" Hervey said simply. "And I, for one, will always be grateful."

Then he went up to his love.

"How about a drink?" Cass asked.

"I thought you'd never ask."

They went into the white drawing room, where Elizabeth collapsed fluidly down into a chair with a sigh and Cass exclaimed disgustedly, "For God's sake—we forgot the champagne!"

"Never mind. I'm drunk on euphoria anyway."

"Even so, we must drink a toast."

Cass prized off the cork with expertise and had the foam in the glass before it could spatter its way around. She handed a sparkling crystal flute-ful to Elizabeth, before raising her own in salute.

"Here's lookin' at you, kid!" she growled. "As old lady Hawkes would have it." She drew up her own chair, reached for the cigarettes. "Where is she, by the way?"

"Gone to bed, tired but happy."

"Aren't we all—and as she would have it, I don't know as I'm on me 'ead or me 'eels."

"Likewise," Elizabeth agreed.

Cass licked her lips over the dry, stingingly chilled wine. "Who would have thought, when you came here ten weeks ago, that it would all end like this!"

"Ten weeks! Is that all it is?"

"To the very day, believe it or not—are you listening, Ripley?—and by God, it *is* the day."

"I'll drink to that," Elizabeth said.

They did.

Drawing another chair to her with her feet, Cass shucked off her shoes and hoisted her legs. "So," she asked airily, "what else is new?"

Elizabeth's face broke only a microsecond before Cass's own, and for several minutes the two of them howled, wheezed, gasped with laughter. Each time they caught each other's eyes it broke out again, causing them to hold their sides and rendering them helpless. Cass had a painful stitch when she finally groaned, "God, but I needed that . . . I mean, the whole damned thing is funny, isn't it? Ha-ha *and* peculiar."

"Very peculiar," Elizabeth agreed, which set them off again.

"I feel better for it, anyway," Cass avowed, sniffing as she wiped her eyes.

"Me too . . ."

"Thank God, we can laugh at it," Cass went on, sobering, "because, when you get down to it, it's not a laughing matter."

"That is why we *are* laughing," Elizabeth said, pinpointing it as usual.

On a sigh: "Yeah . . ."

For a moment Cass watched Elizabeth, who had leaned back and closed her eyes.

"How was it—up there, I mean?" she asked finally.

"Much easier than I expected. Like . . . coming home."

"Well, you have, haven't you?"

Elizabeth smiled. "Yes. I have."

There was a secret quality to her smile which gave Cass a pang, because she knew it had to do with more than Helen.

"I really am glad for you, you know," she said, hiding behind her glass.

"I know you are."

The way it was said made Cass's throat hurt, making it difficult to empty her glass, which she promptly refilled, topping up Elizabeth's at the same time.

"Let's get stoned," she said recklessly. "We have every excuse."

"Since when did you need one?"

Cass giggled. The vintage was getting to her.

"You have changed," she marveled.

"I know . . . I feel changed. It's like—like I'd recovered from a long illness. I feel my center of gravity has shifted. Before, it was here." She touched her brow. "Now, it is here." She laid a hand on her heart.

The lump in her throat rendered Cass incapable of anything but a brimming smile.

"Did you ever think it would end like this?" Elizabeth asked after a while.

"Baby—I thought it had all ended, period!"

"But what we have is a beginning . . ."

"And *I'll* drink to *that!*"

Which meant another refill, which emptied the bottle.

Rehoisting her feet to the chair—"Don't tell your mother"—Cass winked conspiratorially before yelping with delight. "See! Even I can say it." Drunkenly: "Everyone should have a mother," she pronounced. "Even *I* have a mother."

"Whom you don't see very often."

"This is my family." Cass waved an expansive hand. "I declared my allegiance long ago . . . You might say I was adopted."

"And no regrets?"

"Don't try handing me back! You are stuck with me."

"I hope so. I shall be counting on you more than ever in the future, Cass. To run things while I spend time with my mother. You will have to cope with the Organization on your own."

Cass licked her lips. "Just give me the chance."

"I am." Elizabeth's grin was teasing. "But only because I know you'll leap at it."

"Hell, I *am* running it!" Cass said confidently. "Have been ever since Richard died."

"I know . . ." It was dry but said in a way that added a full twelve inches to Cass's height. Staring blearily at her glass, she wondered why she felt it was running over.

"That is why I am going to rely on you more than ever. It always was ninety percent, now it will have to be the whole one hundred. You don't mind?"

Cass looked indulgent. "What foolish questions you do ask."

"I thought perhaps you might take a look-see . . . show the flag, so to speak."

"You mean a PR job?" Eyes gleaming: "John the Baptist to your Messiah?"

Elizabeth's laugh was free and full. "Exactly."

Cass added another twelve inches. In spite of the momentous events of the present, here was Elizabeth still giving thought to the future. Not changed altogether, then, Cass thought, comforted. "When?" she asked.

"As soon as it can be planned, I think."

"Done!" agreed Cass promptly.

They lapsed into a companionable silence. The strangeness of the day, its shock waves, were fading, becoming distant echoes. Yet they both knew that nothing would ever be the same again.

"We got Dan Godfrey all tied up, anyway," she said comfortably after a while. "If he so much as tries to undo a knot, he'll strangle!"

"And that would not worry me, either," Elizabeth said dryly. Their eyes met.

"Poor Margery . . ." Elizabeth added.

"A born victim." Cass nodded sanguinely. "Nothing but a small-town girl at heart, delivered up to high society and the lowest of morals at an early age." She sighed. Then: "What's all this about a portrait?" she asked breezily. "David says he is going to paint you . . . Oh, my God!" Her feet hit the floor with a thud.

"Now what?"

"That crate, the one that came this afternoon. I forgot all about it!"

"What crate?"

"Richard's portrait. It's come down from New York; to be hung alongside his ancestors . . . There was so much else going on I didn't have time to deal with it. I'm afraid I just told Moses to dump it somewhere." Cass heaved herself up and reached for the bell.

It was in the garden room, where Helen did her flowers. A burlap-wrapped bulk inside a crating of wooden slats.

It was Elizabeth who reached for a pair of secateurs.

Together they prized away nails and laid aside wood, finally cutting the thick twine that held the wrapping secure and peeling away first the burlap and then a thick layer of wadding, making a pile at the foot of the portrait like kindling for a fire. Straightening, Elizabeth ran her eyes over it, then drew in her breath, took an involuntary step backward, as though she had collided with someone.

"I know," Cass said dryly. "Doesn't he, though."

He stood with his feet slightly apart, hands thrust into the pockets of his trousers, head up and back, smiling slightly as though at his own effect. The colors were mostly greens and yellows, with little flecks of brown in the tweed of the suit, and it had been applied thickly, almost frenetically, as though the artist had been in the grip of some powerful emotion. You expected Richard to step from the frame and thrust out a hand.

"I had no idea David could paint like this," Elizabeth said, sounding shocked.

"Neither did he. That's why he never did it again."

Elizabeth could not take her eyes away. "Is it—him?"

"As he was. There he is."

Cass stared into the eyes, green as a somnolent lion's. They followed you wherever you moved. Just like he did, she thought. Once he had you in his sights, he never let you go, and the reason you swore allegiance was not from choice but out of necessity.

Even though, now, she knew this, it still did not quench the boiling rancor, the feeling of helpless futility. What else could I do? she thought. Let it get back to my parents, to Proper Boston and all that entails? "Prominent Bostonian Family's Daughter Arrested for Illegal Sex Act." No way! My mother would have died and my father quietly resigned from the Athenaeum before taking the gentlemanly way out. And all because I didn't lock a door, she thought. Too much greed, too much haste, too much need . . .

And afterward, all those agonizing hours spent with the psychiatrist Richard insisted she go to. God, that had been awful! And done no good. Just driven her desires underground or sublimated them into a single-minded competition with men, to prove she was as good—if not better—than they were; to become the right hand of God. Only nobody knew he was Mephistopheles.

Take a good look, she thought, glancing at Elizabeth's intent, intense face, and be glad he was *not* your father.

"It's marvelous," Elizabeth said at last, sounding defeated.

"You hadn't expected it to be?"

"No. I'd always expected David to be a failure as an artist, as he was with everything else."

"This is why. He was far too young and far too—besotted. Oh, yes," she nodded, "he worshiped Richard too . . . Why else do you think he hates him so much now?"

Elizabeth's sigh was a breath. "Of course."

"He *believed*, you see . . . passionately and devotedly. This one was done with love. The rest were done for money."

"Why? *Why?*"

"Once this was shown, everybody wanted to sit for David Boscombe. If he'd painted twenty-four hours a day for the rest of his life, he still couldn't have done them all. It went to his head, and when Richard went for his heart . . ."

"His dossier?"

"Yes." She forced herself to meet Elizabeth's eyes, to read there what she knew she would see: the inevitable question.

"Yes, he had me by the short hairs too . . ."

Elizabeth made a gesture, as though cutting with a sharp knife. "It is your business, Cass. I have no wish to exhume other people's skeletons. I still have to rebury mine." Her voice was as sharp as her gesture.

"You mean"—Cass had to moisten a fear-dried throat—"It doesn't matter?"

"I don't give a damn about your past, Cass. As from today we are all looking to the future."

Cass's burning eyes blurred. Her voice had gone for a moment, but she nodded, said when she could, "Fair enough."

She knew the subject was buried forever when Elizabeth turned back to the portrait. "So we hang it at the top of the stairs."

"You want to?"

"He must go there." For a moment, the old, steel-tipped smile came back. "Where my mother and I will see it."

Oh, beautiful, thought Cass. Are you listening, Richard?

"But for now . . ." Elizabeth bent to the pile of burlap, lifted it with both hands and threw it over the portrait, shrouding its brilliance. "Cover him," she quoted with an inimical smile, "mine eyes dazzle . . ."

Then she went over to one of the zinc troughs which lined one wall and ran the tap.

"Pontius Pilate?" Cass asked innocently. "Or is it Lady Macbeth?"

Elizabeth turned, reaching for the towel. "Washing my hands of him is easy," she said finally. "It won't be so easy to erase the rest."

"You will be known as his daughter, you mean?"

"Exactly."

"Not to worry," Cass consoled. "We know you are not."

As they headed for the door: "Another drink?"

"No, thank you. I have one last thing to do."

"Dev?"

Elizabeth smiled. Cass had never seen her look like that before. "Dev."

"So that's why he went to the beach house . . ."

"Yes," Elizabeth answered simply. "To wait for me."

Cass's smile was wry. "He's waited a long time for you."

Elizabeth was regarding her contemplatively. "The Great Schism that occurred between Richard and Dev . . . was it a woman?"

Cass stared. "How did you know?"

"I didn't. It was a—guess, if you like." Pause. "Who was she?"

When Cass said the name Elizabeth exclaimed, "Never!"

Cass nodded. "Richard took the big fall for her . . . like a lot of men."

"She was very beautiful . . ."

"But she fell for Dev. Richard had offered her carte blanche—how she loved spending money—but in spite of his taking her up to a high place and saying, "All this is yours if you will be mine," she said, 'Too late . . . I'm going to have Dev Loughlin's child.' "

She saw Elizabeth wince.

"It killed her, of course. The doctors had warned her she would never carry a child to full term, but she wanted to because it was Dev's. Richard never forgave him . . . Dev didn't know, you see, that she had been warned about pregnancy . . . nobody did until she died and it all came out . . . and it hit him hard."

"He—loved—her?"

Cass knew no less than the truth would do. "Yes." Then, rushing on: "But it was all a long time ago . . . He loves you now. I don't know what happened between you"—Cass's voice was walking on eggs—"but he's been in flat despair these past few weeks."

"I know," Elizabeth said. "He told me."

"Believe him. Dev does not lie." A twisted smile. "He never needs to."

True, thought Elizabeth. He has not lied to me about this. Just not told me. And I only have to ask him . . .

But she knew she wouldn't. It was not important. It was in the past. And had he not taken her—all she was not as well as all he knew she could be? Had he not trusted her, implicitly, wholeheartedly? Had she not realized it was now her turn to give? Even if it was only confidence. Except she knew it was much, much more. They still had so much to learn of each other, and all the time in the world in which to do it. But what he was, at this moment, she was prepared to take—and be grateful for the chance. No conditions. No terms. Life dictated them. And it was *her* he was waiting for. Even now. In the beach house. Waiting patiently. *For her.*

"I'm going," she said, turning eagerly for the door.

"Give him my love," Cass said.

Hand on the knob, Elizabeth turned. Cass had never seen a smile like that.

"After I have given him mine," she said.

CHECKS LIST SINGLY	DOLLARS	CENTS
1		
2		
3		
4		
5		
6		
7		
8		
9		
10		
11		
12		
13		
14		
15		
16		
17		
18		
19		
TOTAL